I0582931

PURGATORY OF THE ANCIENTS

WILD GREEN FLAME
BOOK ONE

STEW ADAMS

PROLOGUE

Prologue - Zadkiel's Return

* * *

The Archangel Michael stood in the centre of a small stone chamber, his eyes fixed on the stand that bore his armour. Light coming from the golden breastplate illuminated the room. The soft glow of power was inviting, yet the armour brought memories of his last battle and monumental failure.

Michael stretched his wings, the long white feathers pressing against the walls of the chamber. He tried to shake the feeling that maybe today was the day. If the heralds proclaimed war, he would don the golden armour and wield his broadsword once more. The standards of the Light would fly, the sound of battle horns would fill the air and they would march on Hell and Darkness. Heaven waited on word from Eden. Zadkiel was the last Archangel, and if he fell....

'My Lord Michael,' a voice interrupted from outside the chamber.

'Come.'

Michael glanced back to see Metatron opening the door. His grey wings brushed the archway as he passed through.

'What is it?' Michael asked, his attention back on his armour.

'Zadkiel has returned.'

Michael whirled on the angel. 'He's here? Where? What happened?'

'We did not speak. I saw him enter the library. You ordered me to let you know when—'

Whatever else the angel had to say was lost. Michael was already moving, pushing past Metatron, barely registering him in his haste to leave. Bursting out into the open air, he leapt off the edge. Michael tucked in his wings as he dove through the air. The wind howled in his ears as thoughts raced through his head. Why had Zadkiel not reported to him directly? Was the Archangel shamed in defeat?

The library appeared through the clouds, made of old stone and curved archways. Michael banked towards one of the landing pads. He spread his wings at the last possible moment, catching the wind, allowing him to swoop and land at a run. The need to know outweighed everything else. In a breath, he was past the marble statues and through the silver-laden doors. He searched through the rooms of scrolls, past the walls of books, unable to find the Archangel in the main hall, the lecture rooms, the auditorium, or the room of Light.

Had he acted in haste? Should he have had Metatron show him where Zadkiel was?

Before his misgivings could completely fuel his doubt, Michael found the Archangel in a small hidden writing room. He was bent over a desk, a quill scratching the parchment. He looked up and gave Michael a weary smile.

'What news? Is the Light victorious?' Michael asked, his breath ragged.

'No.'

Michael's heart sank. Their eternal war would continue. The price of holding the line would be more angel blood. He would need to assemble the Legions of Light.

'But neither was the Darkness,' Zadkiel said.

That didn't make any sense.

'What of Astaroth?' Michael demanded.

'No longer a threat,' Zadkiel said. 'But not because of me.'

'Did Naberius kill her?'

Zadkiel shook his head.

'I thought all the Ancients were dead.'

'They were.'

'Then, how?'

Zadkiel took his time in answering. He cleaned the nub of his quill before straightening. His movements were slow, like one of the elderly humans, their joints stiff with age. He stood in front of one of the stained-glass windows, light illuminating him and his white wings.

'It was the humans.'

Michael growled in frustration. Zadkiel was being deliberately obtuse. Before he could lose his temper, he caught Zadkiel watching him with a wry smile.

'Do you remember the forest around Barleron?'

'What does that have to do with—' Michael said, but stopped and took a deep breath. 'Why do you always do this? Why can't you just tell me plainly?'

Zadkiel watched him, grey eyes still holding the same intensity Michael remembered from aeons past. 'Because some things require patience.' Then the angel smiled, his features lighting for the first time. 'And it amuses me.'

A huff of laughter escaped Michael. He seated himself on a nearby stool. Assembling the legions could wait until Zadkiel had said his piece. Barleron was where they had held their peace talks. The city had grown up around it, yet still, neither Hell nor Heaven held sway. The surrounding forest was one of the last strongholds of the Ancients.

'Is that the forest where you almost died?'

'The same,' Zadkiel said, stretching his wings, inspecting them with clouded eyes, before he continued: 'It began a few decades after your demise.'

Michael suppressed a shiver. His death and resurrection had not been pleasant.

'The humans harnessed the power of the forest, and that changed everything.'

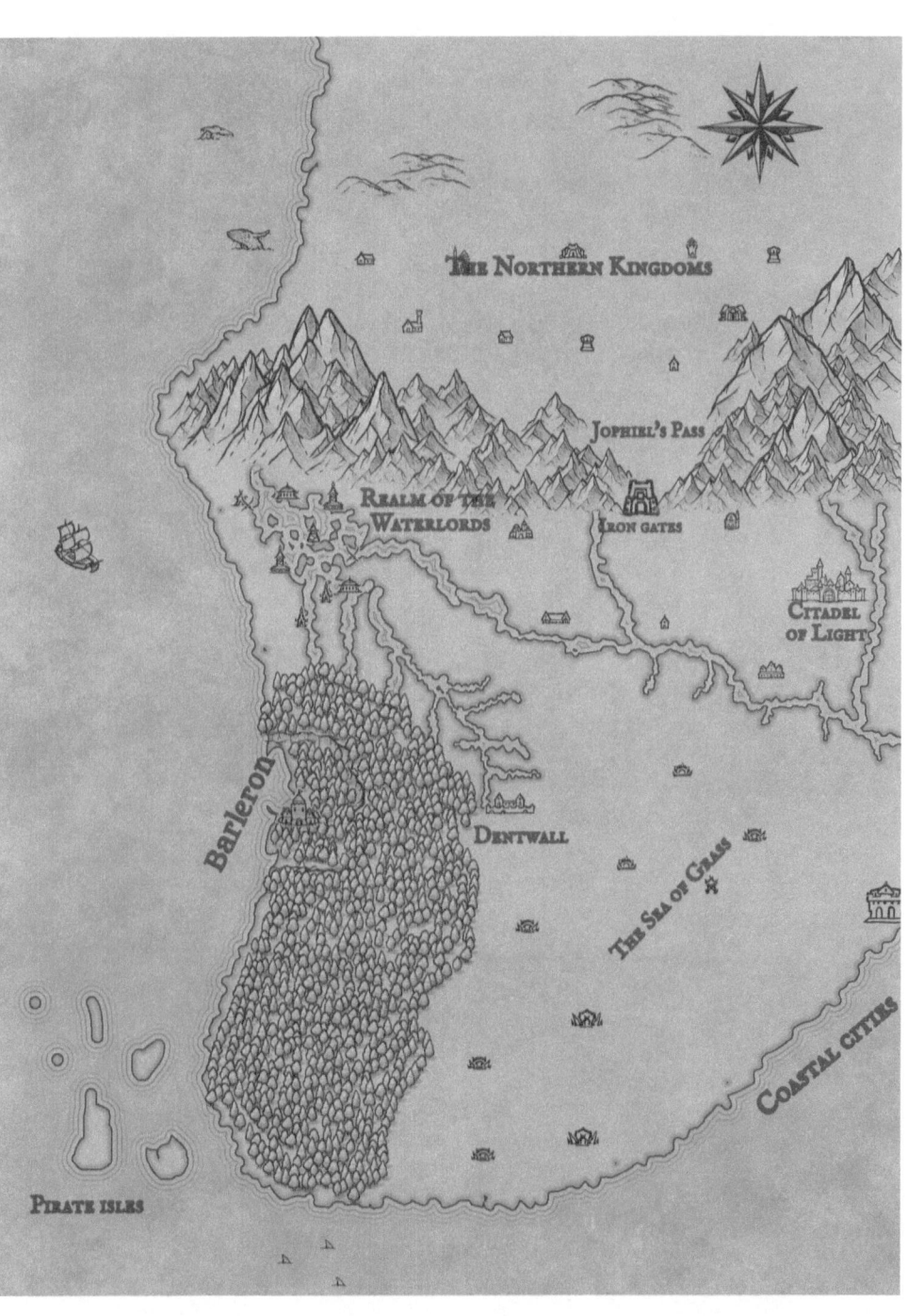

PART I

CHAPTER ONE: THE VENOM OF THE FROGS

***

he war between Heaven and Hell waged for aeons, but we were unprepared for the power that awaited us on the world of Eden. When the battle for control began in earnest, it was a slaughter.
— Zadkiel, *Chronicles of Eden.*

***

ARDAN PUSHED THE BRANCH ASIDE, wary of allowing the green leaves to brush against him. His feet stepped lightly around the thin sticks and dry fronds. As light as his feet were, they still stirred the forest floor, filling the air with a woodland fragrance. He looked up and could see his father, Tristan the woodman, against the trees, his bow slung across his chest. The man moved silently through the forest with practised ease; he slipped behind some brush and was gone. Ardan cursed and moved forward, keeping his footing measured, eventually getting to where his father had vanished. He got a quick glimpse of the leather bag on Tristan's back before he again disappeared behind the trees. Frustrated, Ardan sped up, sacrificing caution for speed.

He rapidly arrived at the next small clearing. His father's face, beneath his tangled hair and beard, looked shocked. Ardan smiled triumphantly and stepped down, his foot landing heavily on a stick that couldn't hold his weight. It snapped with a resounding crack. His father's eyes widened.

'Don't move,' Tristan hissed.

Ardan froze, his eyes searching for the danger. He could feel his pulse quicken while his father's warning rang through his head. *'Treat the forest with the same respect as you would fire. It is far more dangerous, mind you, but once you understand it, once you know it, you can predict it just a little. But the moment you stop treating it with respect, well, that's the moment you get burned.'*

His eyes darted around until he spotted what his father had seen: perched on one of the nearby trunks was a blue tree frog, camouflaged against the foliage. Ardan felt his stomach drop, and he desperately fought the urge to run. He's seen a frog spit faster than an arrow flew, and its venom burnt through blood and bone. He drew a ragged breath and forced his trembling legs to stay still. At this range, he wouldn't be able to dodge it.

From the corner of his eye, he could see his father moving slowly and deliberately as he took the bow off his chest and silently pulled an arrow from his belt quiver. The frog sat on the tree, its stance innocent, eyes watchful. How long it would stay quiescent, Ardan had no idea. His heart was thundering in his chest, and he feared the sound would startle the frog into striking.

The sound of his father taking a quiet, deep breath made Ardan steal a glance. He saw his father draw the arrow up against his cheek, aim, exhale and release. The arrow flew true, but by trick or chance, the frog sensed danger and spat its venom before it found its target. Ardan instinctively leapt backwards, but felt a spatter on his tunic as he tumbled. He scrambled to his feet as the heat of the venom ate through his clothing. His father appeared at his side, his hunting knife out as he calmly cut the garment, using the blade to throw the infected cloth and most of the venom into the brush. There was a drop left on his skin. The warmth of the venom quickly transformed into a burning pain. Instinctually, he tried to brush it off, but his father locked his arm back with a vice-like grip. He could smell his flesh burning. Ardan squirmed, trying to break away, but his father used one hand to hold him firmly, the other working quickly to sheath his knife and pull out his waterskin. Using his teeth, Tristan pulled the stopper and then poured water over the injury.

'Hold,' his father said, releasing the arm. Ardan immediately pulled away. 'Hold, damn you.'

Ardan gave a terse nod and held his shoulder under the steady stream of water. His father's hands were already in action: he pulled out some old cloth and dabbed at the venom, alternating with water and the cloth to mop it all up. The pain dulled to a hot throbbing. Ardan took a deep breath before he mustered the courage to look at it. The spot was red, puffy, and surrounded by clusters of white fledgling blisters.

'Your mother's going to kill me.'

'It was my fault.'

'She won't see it that way,' Tristan smiled. 'She's right; I shouldn't have expected you to move that quickly. Those things are hard to spot at the best of times, but you should be proud. You reacted calmly when you needed to.'

'Falling over myself trying to get away?'

'When I needed to fix the burn,' Tristan amended. 'You remained calm despite your fear, that was true bravery. Someone who doesn't feel fear can never be brave. And they're a fool,' he said, all the while bringing out more cloth from his pack and bandaging up Ardan's wound. His hands flashed, and the cloth was bound onto the injury with the bare minimum of firmness.

'Flex it.'

Ardan gingerly moved his arm, feeling the skin tug at the motion. 'It doesn't feel too bad.'

'It'll get worse, but we got it in time. There shouldn't be any permanent damage. Just a scar that will help you impress the ladies, eh?' he said, his eyes glinting.

'So should I rip my shirt off whenever I see a woman?'

Tristan gave him a wry smile as he stood. 'What about Alice? She seems nice.'

'She's more interested in Davan. Besides, she's eighteen.'

'So?'

'She's old.'

Tristan nodded sagely, though a smile tugged at his lips. 'Alright, young one, let's check out this blue frog and see if it's got any venom left. It wasn't what we were looking for, but the rich always pay a good sum for it,' Tristan said, walking over to the tree. The arrow protruded from the rear of the frog. Its head and the upper part of its body were untouched.

'Did you mean to shoot it like that?'

'I got lucky,' he replied with a wink. He reached into his pack and retrieved a glass vial. Tristan unstoppered it, took a calming breath, and stepped closer to the tree. Quick as a snake, he snapped forward, one hand holding the vial at the frog's mouth, the other squeezing its body against the tree. The drops were slow in coming, but the stench that accompanied it smelt like oily, rotten fruit.

'Fragrant, eh? Hard to notice when it's burning through your skin, I guess. Even though it's worth more than gold,' Tristan said, putting the stopper in the vial. The glass vessel contained half a dozen drops. His father stepped back and yanked the arrow out of the tree. The arrowhead had turned brown. 'Leave this half a day and the metal would probably melt away. It's like what I always say—' His father looked at Ardan expectantly.

'*The forest is a place that must be respected.*'

'That's right. We're only on the outskirts here. When you're older, I'll take you to parts of the interior.'

'What about the heart of the forest?'

His father's expression darkened. 'No. I will never take you there, and nor will any sane man. The outskirts are usually enough for most people.'

With the ache ever present in Ardan's shoulder, he couldn't help but agree.

'Alright, now, what is the most important thing to remember when moving through the forest?'

'Be aware of your surroundings.'

'And?'

'Make yourself unnoticed or, if you can't, unthreatening.'

'Good. Always remember that.' His father stood, dusting himself off, his eyes searching round about. He locked on something nearby. 'Cut some of that wildflower for your mother, will you? Next to the walking palm.'

Ardan found what his father was looking at: small, bright-yellow flowers sheltered by the many protruding roots of the walking palm. He knelt down, careful of his injured shoulder as he used his knife to cut them gently at the stem. Despite it being after midday, cold dew drops still clung to their petals. He then got his own cloth out of his bag and wrapped them together. The sweet crisp smell of the flowers wafted through the air.

'What are these for?'

'Your mother is fond of the smell. Got to bribe her with something after today. Come on, let's go.'

'We're leaving already?'

'With the venom from this little bastard, we can cut our trip short. Plus, there are a few stops I'd like to make. I need to get some things done before your mother murders me for putting you in danger. Well, with these flowers, she might only maim me,' his father said. He turned and led them back the way they had come. He was much slower this time, making sure Ardan could keep up with his injury. But like before, Ardan felt clumsy compared to his father's stealthy movements as they continued through the forest.

CHAPTER TWO: BARLERON

* * *

hen we first encountered the Ancients, they were as alien to us as we were to them. They sheltered us, while their generosity held no ulterior motives. We could not say the same.
— Zadkiel, *Chronicles of Eden.*

* * *

ARDAN FOLLOWED in his father's wake as they moved through the forest, weaving around tangles of vines, over fallen trees, and across small streams. Their general direction was largely to the south. Thankfully it was mostly downhill, but their progress was always slow and cautious. His father would barely pause in his movements as he stole a glance at the sun, assessed their surroundings, and made a minute adjustment in their course. Ardan knew woodcraft, but he wasn't sure he could ever determine their position with such ease and alacrity. The concentration required for every step had taken its toll, and weariness was seeping in. At one point, his father pointed out a creeping vine and easily stepped past it. Ardan tried to imitate him, but the tendrils moved with surprising deftness, reaching out and tripping him. The vine wrapped around his leg.

Ardan yelped as he fell. Before he could recover, he felt himself sliding across the fallen leaves as the vine dragged him. He fumbled for his knife, at last wrenching it free. 'Get off me, you nasty hell spawn!' he yelled, hacking at it. The vine released him and retreated into the brush.

Tristan's brown eyes danced with amusement, belying the knife held ready in his hand. The man sheathed his weapon and flicked his head, indicating they should keep going. Yet they'd barely made it a hundred yards when Ardan tripped again, this time over the root of a kapok tree. It was something that didn't move or hinder him, which was nice.

'I might need a breather,' Ardan said.

'There's a nice place near here, come.'

He followed his father's trail for close to ten minutes before they emerged onto a rock protruding from the hill. It was blessedly free of foliage. From this high up, the green spread out for miles as the tall trees fought to reach the light, while the bushes and vines beneath them squabbled for the scraps. Further to the west, the green met the blue of the ocean, expanding as far as he could see.

On the coast, he could just make out the city of Barleron, their home. It was an oasis of civilisation in a tangle of green. From this distance, he could only make out the three most significant aspects of the city: the white stone of the Cathedral of Light, the black jutting pyramid of the Temple of Darkness, and the luscious green of the Tree of the Ancients. The size of those three dwarfed anything else inside the city's walls. Ardan took a sip from his waterskin and sat on the rock, his feet dangling over the edge.

'Father,' Ardan said, breaking the silence.

'Yes?'

'Where did the Tree of the Ancients come from? I mean, I know the Temple of Darkness and Cathedral of Light were built by men, but where did the Tree come from?'

'Were they built by men?'

Ardan thought for a moment. 'Who else would do it?'

'Who indeed?'

'Alright, but I'd still like to know where the Tree came from.'

'I think the better question is, what's older, the Tree or Barleron?'

'But that would mean....' Ardan began.

'If you've got energy for questions, you've got energy to move. Let's go. I'd like to hit the markets before they close.'

Serves me right, he thought as he followed his father down the escarpment. Their direction constantly veered this way and that, according to the whims of the forest. They came across a waterfall near an outcrop of rock that fed a small creek. The two of them followed the stream, the jungle giving way to the water. The dirt was softer here, but Ardan kept his feet out of the creek and relatively dry.

It was hard to tell time in the jungle, but eventually, the chaotic tangle of the forest gave way to the orderly fields of crops that surrounded the city of Barleron. As Ardan and Tristan emerged from the trees, two field workers jumped up together, holding their scythe and pitchfork in front of them. Their eyes were wide like startled deer. After a moment, they laughed in embarrassed relief before returning to their work.

'How's the shoulder?'

Ardan gave it a quick turn, feeling the small tug of the burn, before shrugging.

'Happy to jog the rest of the way back?'

In answer, Ardan started off at a light run towards the city. It felt good to be out in the open for a change, not having to jump over logs or duck under branches. They ran past continuous fields, as almost every piece of arable land between the city and the forest was being worked. The sun was just creeping towards horizon as the moss-covered walls of Barleron rose before them. By the time they'd reached the gate, Ardan was breathing heavily while his father looked almost as fresh as he had at the start of the day.

There were two Merchant Guards watching the gate. His father waved, and one of the guard's faces lighted with recognition. The man wore a blue tunic beneath a breastplate that was polished to an almost mirror shine. He moved to intercept them but left his spear leaning against the wall.

'Tristan,' he called.

'Issac,' Ardan's father said. The two clasped hands.

'Good run?'

'We did well enough. Here,' Tristan said and pulled some of the hard green stalks out of his pack. 'They're not as good as the Empiric salve, but they should help your son's skin.'

Issac took the stalks and tried to speak but stopped, settling for nodding his head in thanks.

'Wish we could stay and talk, but much to do.'

'Verrick was looking for you,' Issac said.

'What about?'

'Didn't say,' Issac said, then paused. 'Look, I know it's not my place, but be careful around him, alright?'

'Did he cheat you at cards too?'

Issac gave a half-hearted smile.

'It's alright, I can handle him,' Tristan assured him.

The guard looked unconvinced, but nodded shrugged.

They continued on, Ardan following his father as they moved under the gate's arches and into the city. Buildings made from grey, chipped and weathered stone dominated the landscape, intersected by cobblestone streets. Despite the late hour, people filled the byways. Tristan moved through the throng with the same ease he'd had in the forest. Ardan did his best to keep up, but his father would often have to pause and wait for him to catch up. They had been moving for almost a quarter of an hour before Ardan recognised the archaic stone style of the buildings that made up the Ancient Quarter.

They stopped at one of the market squares. Stalls crisscrossed an area almost as chaotic as the jungle. People moved and milled around in the different avenues, while the stall vendors yelled at anyone close enough about their wares. Ardan followed Tristan as he stopped at a perfume stall, passing over some of his plant cuttings. At the next stall, he exchanged a hare pelt for some coins. They kept this up, visiting over a dozen stalls inside an hour.

'Just two more stops—next one's at the Docks, so a bit of a way,' Tristan said.

'Alright,' Ardan said as he tried to stifle a yawn.

'Trust me, you're going to love our last stop. Let's go.'

The two of them left the markets, heading down a major thoroughfare from the Ancient Quarter to the Docks. The sea breeze carried the salt air, while the streets had emptied in the failing light. Warehouses and inns replaced stone houses the closer they got to the Docks. The night fishermen were making their way down towards the sea, carrying nets and unlit lanterns.

They could hear the chaos of the Docks before they saw them: men and women yelling at each other, their voices carrying a cacophony of curses and insults. When the half-moon bay came into view, the sun was dipping behind the horizon. The Docks stretched out like fingers into the harbour while the sailors and fishermen moved in a melee of activity. The ocean-going vessels were still unloading their cargo, while the fishermen were trying to load their own boats up for the night. Curses were as common as breathing. A fistfight had even broken out on one Dock, where a man ended up throwing another into the water.

In the centre of this storm stood a tall, broad-shouldered man, his black hair streaked with grey, dressed in what Ardan guessed were old sails held together by a rope at his waist.

As they got closer, the man glanced at them before turning back to one of the smaller fishing boats. 'No, you blood-cursed hellfish, tie your line back up. Can't you see Lucky casting off? She'll crush your little rowboat.'

'Sod off, Quillen.'

Quillen stepped forward towards the edge of the Dock. The man who'd made the comment shrank back into his vessel.

'You will tie off your boat. Wait your turn, or I'll gut you here and now for trying to mess up my harbour.'

The venom that accompanied Quillen's words implied he'd make it happen, despite not seeming to have a weapon. The man in the offending boat nodded shakily and picked his mooring rope back up.

It took him several tries before he caught the bollard at the edge of the Dock to pull the boat back in.

By the time Quillen was finished, Tristan had pulled out a bundle of reeds. He handed them to the Dockmaster.

'What are these?'

'River reeds. Chew on them, they'll help with seasickness.'

'Boys without sea legs,' Quillen said, nodding. 'How much?'

'Buy me a drink later and we'll call it even.'

'Get those sails up, you're holding up the bloody line,' Quillen snapped at the nearest boat, then turned back to them. 'Got any more of those blue mushrooms? They're good with yellowfin.'

'You'll have to talk to Verrick. I don't go near the Southside anymore.'

'He didn't have any either. Speaking of, he was looking for you earlier. Didn't seem too friendly, either.'

'He's always like that.'

'Even so, watch yourself,' he said, before yelling at another boat.

They left the man to his work, but as soon as they were out of earshot Ardan asked, 'We came all that way just to give him something for free?'

'He did me a good turn when I needed it. I try to give him something back when I can.'

Ardan mulled over that answer, thinking that he just wanted to go home. He'd had enough of sleeping on the forest floor. Still, he followed his father as they headed towards their last stop in the Ancient Quarter. The previous crowds had dispersed, with only the returning fieldworkers left on the streets. Most of those were seeking a tavern, and Ardan figured it wouldn't be long before the streets were completely deserted.

CHAPTER THREE: DEALING WITH DEMONS

* * *

In all the worlds I have seen, none deserved their namesake as much as Eden did. It was lush and breathtakingly beautiful. The custodians of the world worked as one with nature. We named them the Ancients because their age may exceed even our own.
— Zadkiel, *Chronicles of Eden.*

* * *

SURELY THEY HAD to be near the end, Ardan thought, trying to stifle another yawn. At least they were heading back towards the Ancient Quarter and home.

'Our last stop is Raigel's shop,' his father said as he turned down one of the side alleys.

'It is?' Ardan said, his weariness vanishing.

'When we go in, treat him as you would anyone else. He's got wings and horns but don't make a big deal about them. We're friendly as far as these things go, but he'd rob me blind given the chance.'

The lack of lanterns in the alley made Ardan step more carefully. 'Then why do you deal with him?' he asked.

'He can buy, sell and make things that most people can't. Plus, once you pin him to his word, he has to abide by it.'

'He does?'

'It's an unbreakable rule for their kind. I don't fully understand it.'

Ahead of them, a woman had opened her front door to shake a rug. She eyed them as they passed, not pausing as she shook out the piece of carpet.

'Then how do you know they can't break their word?' Ardan asked.

'I don't, but like the sun rising in the morning, I trust it.'

That made Ardan think. Eventually, he asked, 'Do I need to do anything?'

Tristan's steps slowed, and he glanced at Ardan out of the corner of his eye. 'Mind your tongue. I mean it.'

'But I'm always charming,' Ardan said.

Tristan grunted. They continued down the street until they came to a shop with dried herbs hanging down the front of some opaque windows.

Rusty hinges creaked as Tristan pushed open the door. Ardan could smell sulphur in the air as he followed his father in. A horned demon stood behind the counter, dressed in a simple brown robe. Red and black scales covered the rest of his body, glowing like coals. The demon observed them as they entered with one red eye and one green.

'Good evening Tristan. You have the smell of the forest on you. And someone new, your spawn?' His voice was rough, like wheels over gravel.

'My youngest son—been teaching him the ways of the forest.'

'What of the elder one?' Raigel asked, the scales on his face creasing together in a frown.

'Taught him what I could, but I don't think his heart is really in it.'

Raigel nodded in understanding. 'I assume you've brought something for me?' he asked, clasping his long spindly fingers together.

'Fresh blue frog venom,' Tristan said, pulling the vial out.

The demon took the vial carefully. Ardan watched the demon hold it up to his red eye, shaking it a bit, causing some bubbles to form. 'There's not a lot here,' he said, taking the vial stopper off and giving it a cautious sniff. 'How old?'

'Half a day, give or take.'

If Ardan hadn't been watching him so closely, he would have missed the slight widening of the demon's eyes.

'Unfortunately, demand for this has dropped,' he said, putting the vial down.

Tristan smiled.

'What's in demand now?' Ardan asked, unable to help himself.

The demon studied him. The two coloured eyes were appraising. 'Oh, nothing has taken their fancy just yet. The wealthy are fickle. Last week it was the spice of blue frog venom. Next month people will season their food with ground-up whalebone.'

'So how much for this?' Tristan asked.

'You've got to understand, I'm getting overstocked. It's just not selling like it used to.'

'How much?'

'Two copper temples.'

Tristan laughed.

The demon smiled in return, revealing pointed fangs.

'Normally I'd ask for a silver temple for each drop, but as we're old friends, I'll let you have the whole vial for five.'

The demon leaned over the counter, his horned head brushing the herbs he had hung from the ceiling. 'Do you plan on insulting me in front of your ilk? It might teach him bad habits.'

'I'm teaching my son about all the elements of forest stalking. Can't have him miss out on the important parts.'

Ardan watched as the two continued to dicker back and forth before settling on two silver temples and four silver pennies. They exchanged the money and a handshake before the two humans left the shop. Once they were out the door, his father handed him the four pennies and a whole silver temple. Ardan looked up in surprise at his father's smiling face.

'You earned it. I think we should probably buy something on our way home so your mother isn't too angry with us, eh?'

'Do people really sprinkle venom on their food?'

'They have to dilute it some. Make it safe to eat without hurting them.'

'But,' Ardan said slowly, 'why?'

Tristan laughed and went to pat him on the shoulder, but one look at the bandage made him think better of it. 'Maybe they like the taste, maybe it's the prestige, maybe it's something only known to them. Maybe you will figure it out and then you can—' Tristan's voice trailed off, his entire posture stiffening.

Ardan looked up to see what had drawn his father's attention. There were four men coming down the alley towards them. No, not all of them were men. One of them was a boy around Ardan's age, but he was tall, with light brown hair and an awkwardness that came with recent growth. The man that trailed him was shorter and slightly wider of frame, though their shared sharp nose marked them as father and son. The dark-haired man in front was weasel-faced and led the others with the same effortless grace his father showed, although his leather armour struggled to contain his bulk. Silver and gold rings adorned his hands. The last man's gigantic frame dwarfed the others. Yet his bulk was muscle rather than fat. He wore a heavy axe on his belt.

Ardan felt his father's arm push him up against the wall of the alley. He felt something scrape against his chest. There was a slight jingle as a weight pressed inside his tunic. His father had slipped him the money purse.

'Verrick,' Tristan said easily, but he was gripping his knife so hard, the whites of his knuckles were showing.

'I guess I shouldn't be surprised to see you here,' Verrick said casually. As he spoke, the others fanned out in front of them, effectively blocking them in. 'Just got back from stealing from our runs again, have you?'

'You know I don't go near the south side,' Tristan said.

'And yet our traps are always empty, our trails always barren.'

'I warned you about over-using your runs. The forest will change its habits once it knows yours,' Tristan said.

'Convenient,' Verrick said, almost idly. 'The day we got your warning was the same time that pickings on our runs became slim. Not yours, though. You seem to bring in more than the rest of us combined.'

The anger radiating off the other two men was almost tangible. The lanky youth was looking to his father. Ardan went to step forward and provide support, but his father stepped in front of him.

'So, you found it easier to lay the blame rather than doing your job. Angels above, Verrick, if you're not comfortable about picking new trails, I'll show you how to do it. The place has pitfalls and dangers and I can show you how to avoid them.'

'It's too late for that,' Verrick said, although he didn't seem to notice the other men exchanging glances.

'And your plan is to beat me bloody in the middle of the Ancient Quarter? How long do you think it'll be before you go before the Magistrate and he extracts his price?'

'Plenty long. He thinks that you've been stingy in your tributes, now that I explained to him what you've been doing. Well, your mark was very affordable,' Verrick said.

'You ... you're lying.'

Verrick pulled a coin from his purse and flicked it towards them. It spun head over head before clanging on the cobblestones; the sound filling the otherwise deathly silent alley. The bronze coin had a round hole in its centre. Ardan's father stared at it for a long moment before he looked up.

'You don't have to do this.'

'No? You've stolen our livelihood, starved my family. With you gone, I can put food back on the table. Seeing my little ones stare at me while I have to muster the courage to tell them there's no dinner— it's heart-breaking, you know?'

'Oh please,' Ardan burst out, unable to contain himself. 'Like you've ever missed a meal,' he said, pointing at Verrick's midsection and strained leather armour.

A silence settled over the group. All eyes shifted to Ardan, as though they hadn't fully appreciated his presence. The lanky boy chuckled. Verrick shot him a glare. Ardan felt his father's hand on his shoulder. He shut his mouth.

'What will you do when your runs continue to be dry?' Tristan asked, breaking the silence.

'Pass my condolences to your family,' Verrick said.

'And miss the opportunity for me to show you how to farm the forest properly? Make your men richer than you've ever been before?'

Silence settled over them like a heavy blanket.

'You'd really teach us?' the sharp nosed man asked dubiously.

'He'd never teach you,' Verrick snapped.

'I would,' Tristan said. 'There's enough for all of our families to grow fat.'

'What about food for my family now?' The big man said, his hand resting on the axe in his belt.

Tristan turned towards him, careful not to present his back to Verrick. 'Liam, you're welcome to our table anytime, you and your family. All of you are. Forest stalkers need to stick together.'

The man's eyebrows rose as he searched Tristan's face. After a moment, he nodded. The others looked at Ardan's father, their expressions unreadable.

'Cillian, and your son Regan, is it?' Tristan asked of the sharp nosed man and lanky youth. 'You and your families are welcome too.'

'We don't have enough food to feed all of them,' Ardan said.

The hand on his shoulder was much firmer this time. The men's anger, that had been as pungent as frog venom, was now draining like water from a leaky bucket.

'You'd really do that?' Verrick asked.

Tristan nodded.

'Will you shake on it?' Verrick said, trying to search Tristan's face, but he didn't meet the man's eyes.

Ardan's suspicion was growing. The man's anger had suspiciously vanished.

'Of course,' Tristan said as he took a step forward, offering his hand.

Verrick took a hesitant step forward. There, among the rings, Ardan saw a glint of sharpened steel.

'Father, no!' Ardan shouted. It caused his father to look back in confusion. Verrick took advantage of the distraction. He grabbed Tristan's arm, yanked him forward and used the momentum to thrust the concealed dagger under the ribcage, towards the heart.

'For your lies,' Verrick said, pulling out the long and bloody dagger.

Ardan stared in shock. The other three were equally stunned. His father slumped down to his knees. He looked up at Verrick as the blood quickly pooled out over his tunic.

'You damned fool,' Tristan said and folded backwards.

Ardan dropped to his knees and caught his father before he fell. The hot red liquid flowed over Ardan's hands and onto his own tunic. He cradled his father's weakening body.

'Father,' Ardan said, looking down at him. He wanted to say something. His father was dying. He knew he should say something. The words wouldn't come. *Flaming hells, think, say something, anything,* Ardan thought desperately.

His father's pale face looked up at him, his eyes wide and searching. He tried to lift one of his arms as though to touch Ardan's face one last time, but his strength failed him and it fell back to his side. 'I'm ... cold.' The surprise lingered on his face while his head drooped. His chest gave one last shallow rise and fall. It didn't rise again. His father's eyes glazed over and his muscles went slack. Ardan knew what had happened, but he pushed it out of his mind. His father had been so strong, he'd been invincible. He just couldn't be—

CHAPTER FOUR: THE CATALYST

* * *

They tried to show us their power, how to commune with Eden, but none of the angels held any aptitude. In our arrogance, we blamed the Ancients, not realising that they held no concept of deceit. Half the world was aflame before we fully understood that fact.
— Zadkiel, *Chronicles of Eden.*

* * *

'He brought this on himself, you know.'

Ardan was still staring at the still form of his father. The words broke the stupor that had surrounded him. He was surprised to see the four of them still there. The reality of what had happened crashed down like a hammer. Tears formed, blurring his vision. Grief tore a void in his soul. These men had stolen his father from him. His mind grappled with it, corrupting his thoughts with fury. Anger buried his grief, leaving only rage.

'You hell-begotten bastard,' Ardan said, his voice raw and choked. Before he knew it, he was up, his hunting knife in hand as he pelted towards Verrick. They stood stock still, stunned at the sudden change. Ardan wanted blood. He gripped the hunting knife tightly and swung it high above his head and plunged it towards Verrick's chest. It almost worked, but at the last second, Verrick leapt back. The knife missed his chest by inches, but the momentum kept him thrusting downwards before he sank it hilt deep into the man's thigh.

Verrick roared in pain, and backhanded Ardan so viciously that he instinctively let go of the dagger, spinning as he fell to the ground. He tasted his own salty blood. Shaken, he pushed himself up and looked for a new weapon. His father's hunting knife was sticking out from his belt. He reached for it, but his hands fumbled with it several times before he could wrench it free. This time, the others stood between him and his target.

Verrick was hopping backwards, putting some space between himself and Ardan, the knife still protruding from his leg. Ardan darted forward, trying to manoeuvre around the others to get at his father's murderer. They reached for him, but his coat of blood made him slippery. He dodged past one, slipped through the hands of the second, but the third, Cillian, stood in front of him with a short sword. A cold madness gripped him and Ardan slashed wildly. A red gash appeared on the man's forearm, and he dropped his sword. Ardan was already past him.

Verrick stood there, leaning against the wall as a crutch for his injured leg. Both his hands were empty. Ardan's need for vengeance pushing him forward. Verrick was ready for him. The man pivoted on his uninjured leg and brought his fists up in a fighter's pose. Ardan wasn't even thinking to defend himself, so as soon as he was close enough, Verrick's fists lashed out with three lightning strikes. Ardan stumbled back, his vision hazy. It was then that Verrick delivered a heavy body shot to his midsection. Pain exploded in Ardan's stomach, causing him to double over, coughing and winded. His feet couldn't find purchase and he fell against the cobblestones. Ardan's vision was slow to clear. He pushed himself to his hands and knees.

There was a flash, and he flopped hard back onto the cobblestones. It took him a moment to realise Verrick had struck him across his face. His limbs collapsed of their own accord. He shook his head to try and clear it. Though dazed, his anger lent him strength. He tried to get up.

'He's a tough bastard.'

'Stay down, son, you don't have to die.'

'Hit him in the legs,' Verrick said. 'That'll keep him down.'

Liam pulled the hatchet from his belt with practiced ease, his large shoulders and short neck making him look like a bull. He held the axe so he would strike with the blunt end, like a club.

Ardan had to use the wall to steady himself. Each breath caused a sharp pain in his ribs. His knife was only a needle against this monster of a man. He lunged, but Liam already had his hatchet moving. The back of the axe struck Ardan's leg with such force that it snapped his legs together. His thigh exploded with pain and he went down in a tangle. As he hit the cobblestones, he lost his grip on the knife and it bounced away with a dull clank of steel against stone. His whole body felt as if it were on fire. His mind could not comprehend the full extent of the damage done to his body. He coughed, trying to catch his breath, which only made it worse.

'He's as bad as a forest viper,' Verrick said.

'Look what that son of a bitch did to my arm.'

Ardan was on all fours and trying to force himself up when Cillian's blood-soaked arm was thrust in front of his face.

'Look what you did,' he bellowed.

A boot slammed into Ardan's side. He collapsed to the ground, coughing saliva and blood. Another blow connected with his arm that was hard enough to force him to roll him onto his side. He curled up into a ball. His vision became a swathe of indistinct colours as he repeatedly felt boots on different parts of his body.

'Cillian, he's already down,' Liam said.

'So what?' came the petulant reply.

'I think he's had enough,' Regan said.

'We should probably kill him anyway,' Verrick said.

A heavy silence fell over them, broken only by Ardan's ragged breathing.

'What of the Magistrate?' Liam asked at last.

'The little bastard attacked us.'

'That's not what I asked.'

'It'll be pricy to smooth things over, but I think he'll be under-standing.'

Ardan tried to peer up at them, but one eye had swollen shut. The four men stood over him. His vision swam with the effort he could do nothing else but close his eyes with a groan.

'I don't want to kill him,' Regan said.

'Neither do I,' Liam argued in a low grumble.

'I'll kill the little bastard for what he did to my arm,' Cillian said.

'What do we have here?' a feminine voice rose over them.

'Marion,' Verrick said gruffly.

'Help,' Ardan gasped. Could she even hear him?

'By the Light, that poor boy. What happened to him?' she asked. Only silence met her question. 'I see.'

'Leave it with us, Marion,' Verrick said.

'You already have one body to take care of. I think that should be enough for tonight,' she said, her voice challenging. 'You—Liam, isn't it? You're big enough. Pick him up, gently mind you. I know of a decent healer nearby.'

Ardan lay there, not trusting himself to open his eyes to the spin-ning world.

'We have the mark,' Verrick said.

'I just spent the day with the Magistrate and he told me he sold only one mark. I must have misunderstood, because you know how he feels about unendorsed killings.'

'Are you here to police us?'

'Just a fortunate coincidence, I'd say. I have another appointment with him tomorrow. Maybe I can help him sort out this little misun-derstanding. I'll even take the boy to a healer for you.'

'Stay out of this,' Cillian said.

'You're not untouchable, you know,' Verrick said at the same time.

'But I am,' she said. 'To the likes of you, at least. We've already wasted enough time. Liam, pick him up and follow me.'

There was some grumbling between the others, but Ardan felt two gigantic arms pick him up. He felt pain flare in every inch of his body. Ardan tried to fight the man, but all he did was shift his arm slightly before the pain overwhelmed him. Each step sent a jolt of agony through him, keeping him awake.

The journey felt like an endless stream of pain. It ended as Marion's hand rapped on wood. After a minute, Marion knocked again. The door eventually opened to reveal a man with thinning brown hair and a ragged beard.

'Marion?' he asked blearily.

'Hello Eoin. It's good to see you. I know it's late, but this boy has been beaten badly.'

Ardan felt more than saw the healer approach him. He could smell the waft of cheap wine on the man's breath.

'He's not in good shape. Bring him in.'

Liam carried him inside to a large room. There were six cots spaced out along the walls. Five had been neatly made, while the sixth was occupied. Off to one wall was a workbench and shelves lined with carefully labelled jars of dried herbs. Head spinning with the effort, Ardan closed his eyes for some respite.

'Put him next to Riordan. I'll be over in a moment.'

Liam carried him over and placed him in the bed as softly as though he were handling a newborn.

'Keep him awake. I can't let him nod off just yet.'

Liam propped him up so he was sitting on the bed.

Eoin made his way over. He poked and prodded every sore spot Ardan knew about, and a few he didn't. The physician spoke the whole time: 'Heavy bruising on the chest and back, possibly broken ribs, swollen eye, but that should be fine. Swollen jaw. Leg is possibly fractured.' Liam shifted uncomfortably. 'The blood isn't his. Oh wait, some of it is,' Eoin continued and by the time he had finished, Ardan was gasping and covered in sweat.

'He'll survive,' Eoin said standing up, 'He'll be sore and recovery will be a right pain in Lucifer's backside, but he'll be fit as a fiddle in no time.'

'You do work wonders, Eoin.'

'How do you plan on paying?' Eoin said, with a peculiar lilt in his voice.

'Not like that,' she said gently.

Eoin harrumphed. 'Fine, three silver temples should do it.'

'Eoin,' she said, patting his arm fondly, 'I'll give you one silver temple for the healing and lodging.'

He grunted.

Marion pulled out a purse that looked strangely familiar. He moved as quickly as his injuries would allow, reaching for his tunic. The purse was gone. He used his one good eye to stare at Marion accusingly. Her eyes were a startling green as they stared back. She gave an unapologetic shrug and put the purse inside her blouse.

'Take better care of yourself next time.'

Liam laid him back in his bed. Ardan felt sick to his stomach with that man handling him. He watched the two of them go with a sense of relief.

It didn't take long for the healer to pour some foul-tasting concoction down his throat. His eyes started to droop, and his mind became fuzzy. *Maybe this has been some horrible dream*, he thought as unnatural sleep crept up on him. He shut his eyes with a desperate hope that it was true.

CHAPTER FIVE: FOUL TASTE OF RECOVERY

*** * ***

*W*hen the power of Eden appeared unobtainable, we blamed the Ancients. Those gentle creatures fled before the forces of Heaven and Hell alike. They always opted to flee, but eventually there was nowhere to flee to. When they turned to fight, countless angels and demons fell before them, including Gabriel, Sariel and Beelzebub. It was then that we realised how much we had underestimated them. It was our turn to run.

— Zadkiel, *Chronicles of Eden.*

*** * ***

ARDAN SLOWLY RETURNED TO CONSCIOUSNESS; he opened his eyes and immediately felt dizzy. Whatever the healer had given him was still affecting him. Either that or he'd taken more blows to the head that he didn't know about. He shifted his weight slightly and felt something flare in his ribs. He tried to compensate by putting pressure on his hand. Pain like liquid fire shot through his fingers. He saw two of them had splints. He added them to his list of injuries.

As though on cue, the healer reappeared. The man had combed his hair and trimmed his beard. Yet when he got closer, his eyes were bloodshot and the familiar scent of wine was already on his breath.

'You're awake. Good. Means you're not dead,' Eoin said.

Ardan canned his neck to look at the person in the next bed.

Eoin followed his gaze. 'Our friend is recovering from the bite of a forest viper. He is also not dead.'

'Where?' Ardan asked, then regretted it, his injuries blazing.

'Caravan guard, somewhere on their run. He knew enough to wrap it. Even so, he's lucky to be alive. I expect it'll be another week at least before he can stay awake more than a couple of hours at a time.'

The man in the cot next to Ardan gave a soft snort, rolled over and settled, his chest rising and falling in the steady rhythm of sleep.

'For someone who turned up in the state you did, you're pretty lucky too,' Eoin said as he placed his hands at certain points on Ardan's ribs, applying pressure and shifting. Ardan sucked in a breath between his teeth, but Eoin was relentless. 'The ribs will cause you pain for some time, but they should heal up fine. How old are you?' he said, stepping back.

'I dunno,' Ardan said, 'Sixteen?'

'Body of a man, mind of a child,' Eoin said, stepping forward to examine Ardan's swollen eye. 'The swelling will go down. Can you see out of it?'

Ardan was feeling like a pound of bread from the man's constant kneading.

'A scowl is as good as a yes, now follow my finger.'

Ardan's eyes followed the man's finger as it moved back and forth.

'Good. It'll be tender and you'll look a fright for a while, but your eye will heal up fine. Now, can you move your fingers? Touch each of them to your thumb. Good. I'll keep them splinted for now, but you should eventually return to full function. Your leg, though—it's not broken, but you'll have trouble walking on it for the next few days at the very least. If you overexert it, you'll mess it up, maybe for good. Then there's that,' Eoin said, pointing towards Ardan's shoulder. 'It's a burn, to be sure, and recent. It'll leave a scar but should heal without problems. The question is, though, how in the hells did that happen in an alley brawl?'

'It was a blue tree frog.'

'What?'

'A blue tree frog spat at me.'

'Who's stupid enough to keep one of those as a pet?'

'It was in the forest.'

'In the *forest*,' Eoin repeated slowly.

'My father was teaching me how to be a stalker.'

'He and I might need to have words,' Eoin said. The lines of his face pressed together with stern disapproval.

'He's dead,' Ardan said. It felt surreal to say it. His father had died in his arms only yesterday, yet all he felt was cold grief. The only things he knew about it were from theatre plays; they had taught him that he should be crying or cursing at the world, yet his mouth continued as though he was talking about something as simple as the weather. 'Killed by the same people who gave me this,' Ardan said, indicating his injuries calmly while suspecting something was seriously wrong with him. In the place of anger, sadness, or anything else, there was nothing but an emotionless void.

Eoin looked down and opened his mouth a couple of times as though to say something before eventually mumbling, 'I'm sorry.' He busied himself with his work, avoiding Ardan's eye, putting a kettle over the fire and going to his worktable. He pulled down different jars of dried herbs. Ardan watched the man's movements closely; if he focused on what the man was doing, then he could avoid reality, keep it suppressed. Eoin crushed the herbs in his mortar and pestle. After he was done, he pulled the kettle out of the fire and poured the hot water into the teapot before dropping all the herbs into it. The smell that came out of it made Ardan visibly recoil. It was as though the man had mixed week-old rodent entrails with the sludge that seeped out of Ragtown's refuse. Before he knew it, Eoin was before him with a mug of the foul-smelling concoction.

'It will help with the pain and the swelling, drink it,' Eoin said in a no-nonsense tone.

'Uh no, thank you.'

Before he knew it, Eoin's other hand had reached out and pushed Ardan's head back into the cot, pinching his nose. Ardan opened his mouth in surprise. Eoin took advantage of this to pour the liquid down his throat. He coughed and spluttered, losing some of it down his shirt, but he swallowed the rest of it. The pouring stopped.

Eoin promptly stepped back. If he had stayed close, Ardan would have struck the man.

The taste was just as the smell had promised: foul and gut wrenching. Ardan tried to cough and spit the foul taste out of his mouth.

'Next time, just drink it.'

The herbs acted fast and Ardan could feel his eyelids drooping. He lay back on his cot and didn't fight the oncoming darkness.

What felt like only a second later, the door to the house burst open.

'Ardan! Are you here?' He heard his mother's voice from the next room. He was blearily trying to wake up when she appeared. Her usually immaculate clothing was creased and there were some stains on her blouse. Her black hair was a mess and her eyes were red and puffy. She paused briefly in the doorway as she stared at him, then she rushed forward.

Ardan still hadn't quite worked himself up into a sitting position before she'd closed the distance. She saw his bandages and stopped herself from embracing him. Instead, she settled for clasping at his arm between her hands as though to affirm he was real.

'I was so worried about you,' she whispered, her hands tightening their grip.

Behind her came Ardan's two siblings. His brother, Davan, came in first, the handle of his giant axe poking up over his shoulder. He had to duck his head so he didn't bump it on the frame. He wore the tunic of the Red Wolf mercenaries, with a blue training band on his arm.

Their sister Liá came next, practically flying around Davan as she leapt onto the bed. She was a few years younger, her looks a reflection of their mother's in her youth. Her black hair was bound into a braid, and it whipped him across the face. She gave him a fierce hug that caused him to cry out in pain. Davan pulled her off him by the collar of her dress, almost tearing it with the force he was applying.

'Can't you see he's hurt?'

Her dark eyes took in the bandages for the first time. She danced backwards. 'Oh Ardan, I'm so sorry. Does it hurt?'

'What's all this then?' Eoin interrupted, reappearing from the back room, 'Family?'

'Is he going to be okay?' Ardan's mother asked.

'He'll recover just fine. There's nothing immediate, Lady…?'

'Alaine.'

'Lady Alaine. I can fill you in when you're done.'

'Thank you.'

Eoin mumbled something before retreating to his back room.

'Who's that?' Liá asked, looking at the sleeping form in the cot next to him.

Ardan shrugged. 'He hasn't been awake since I got here.'

'We found Father's body,' Davan said.

A chill fell over the room. The three faces of his family turned towards him, waiting.

'I was there,' Ardan said.

'What happened?' Davan asked.

It took some time, but Ardan relayed the events of the day in the forest, and how they'd encountered the four men outside Raigel's shop.

'Did you hurt them?' Davan asked, his hands clenching.

'Davan,' Alaine admonished.

Davan ignored her, 'Did you?'

Ardan told them about the wound he gave Cillian and how he drove the knife into Verrick's leg.

Davan gave a grunt of satisfaction.

He continued the story of Marion's intervention and how he'd ended up in the healer's rooms, his voice cold and emotionless.

'We're lucky she intervened, even if she robbed you.'

'I guess,' Ardan said.

His mother nodded and rose from her kneeling position in one smooth motion. She went to the back room and knocked politely. Eoin reappeared.

'What else is needed for him?'

Eoin relayed the extent of Ardan's injuries, and the care needed. 'I would like him to remain here for the next few days, though.'

'What? Why?' Ardan demanded.

'Your recovery is proceeding nicely, but it's best to be sure.'

'It's okay, Ardan. I'll be back as often as I can.'

'There is one minor problem though,' Eoin said.

'What?'

'Not all of his medical accounts have been settled.'

'How much?' Alaine said, reaching for her purse.

'For all the effort and herbs I've used and will use, two silver temples.'

Alaine stopped fiddling the purse, instead laying a steady gaze on the healer.

Eoin quickly wilted, 'Alright, alright, four silver pennies.'

She reached inside her purse and handed it to the man. He took the money and retreated into the back room. After he was gone, Alaine looked at each of her three children for a long time, new tears welling in her eyes. She grabbed onto the cot for support. Her facade broke, and her shoulders began to wrack with silent sobs. Liá went forward to comfort her. After a moment, their mother pulled Ardan and Davan into a rough embrace.

Ardan ignored the pain it caused and patted her arm awkwardly. Eventually her crying subsided, and she looked at him, her eyes red rimmed.

'I have been so focused on finding you, and now that I have...' Alaine said. She stopped speaking, as though she might lose control again. She collected herself and finished in a whisper: 'Your father really is dead.' Ardan didn't know how to respond. None of them did. The four of them sat in silence on his small cot. Ardan tried to say something a few times, but just as when his father had died, he couldn't think of a damn word to say.

'What is going to be done about father?' Davan asked.

'What do you mean?' she said, her brow frowning and her eyes going hard.

'His funeral.'

Her face softened immediately. 'The forest was always his home. I'll ask some of his friends; we'll need some escorts.'

'Some of the Red Wolves would do it,' Davan said.

'Where will you bury him?' Ardan asked softly.

'His secret glade,' Alaine said.

There was a long silence as Ardan thought about his father's spot. It was Liá who spoke first. 'It's a good place.'

'It is,' Ardan said, looking down.

'It is going to be done tomorrow,' Alaine said and saw Ardan's face. 'When you're well enough, I'll take you, but you won't be well enough tomorrow.'

Ardan wanted to go now, but he had trouble turning over in his cot. He knew he'd be nothing but a liability to everyone if he tried to go.

His mother seemed to read his thoughts. 'I'll be back tomorrow night and we will hold our vigil for him together.'

Ardan grunted.

They continued to speak of small things until it was time for them to go. When they left, Eoin returned with his foul tonic. After he'd swallowed it and finished cursing Eoin, Ardan lay down in a position that didn't ache too much. Sleep felt slow in coming, with the taste of the tonic on his tongue and dark thoughts of the four murderers on his mind.

CHAPTER SIX: THE MERCENARY

* * *

The wrath of the Ancients was like nothing we had seen. Their power materialised into beings that could not only challenge a High Demon or Archangel but soundly beat them. I nearly met my end at the hands of one of these creatures.

— Zadkiel, *Chronicles of Eden.*

* * *

ARDAN STARED at the thatch-roofed ceiling as the morning light crept through the window and illuminated the untidy mess of his cot. His injuries made sleep difficult, causing him to continuously shift throughout the night as he tried to find the least painful position. Now he faced the dilemma of his full bladder and the distance between himself and the chamber pot. He eyed the walking stick with reluctance before reaching for it. Careful of his two broken fingers, he got shakily to his feet. His injured leg cramped as he stood. He shook it out at an awkward angle until the cramping stopped. He took his first step, wobbled, and steadied himself before taking another step.

The journey was slow, but the relief and triumph he felt at the end was intoxicating. At least until he had to make the return trip. He kept the same slow, exhausting rhythm. By the time he lay down, sweat had soaked his shirt and each ragged breath brought a flare of pain to his ribs.

Ardan closed his eyes and concentrated on taking smaller breaths. The agony slowly subsided, which presented him with a fresh problem: the wounds beneath his bandages itched. He sighed and pulled himself up, trying to scratch them.

'Don't touch them,' Eoin called from the backroom.

'But they itch.'

'So?'

Ardan ignored him and kept scratching. He looked up to see Eoin's head poking around the corner, watching him. Ardan raked his fingers across the bandages one more time before he settled back down into his cot. Eoin eyed him for a moment longer before his head disappeared again.

He thought of his father's funeral; he imagined the group going through the forest. His father's body would have been cleaned and dressed in the burial wraps of the Ancients, their runes etched all over it. The Red Wolf mercenaries that had come to say their farewells would have dug the grave. Their family and friends would say some kind and thoughtful words. They would lament, cry and mourn together while Ardan was here, alone.

Ardan shifted around until he was on his side, his fingers, ribs and leg all protesting throughout, so he could look out the small window onto the street. He could see people walking past and he felt irrationally angry at their apparent carefree attitude. He knew he was being unreasonable, but it didn't help. His anger remained.

'Rough few days, lad?'

The words had come from his bunk mate. Ardan glanced at the man in his cot. He was looking at Ardan with soft green eyes that were framed by curly red hair and at least a week of ginger stubble.

'I heard what happened,' he said. 'I'm sorry.'

Ardan shifted, causing some discomfort, not sure how to respond.

'I'll be an ear to listen if you need it. I know what it's like to lose a father.'

'Did you hold your father while he died in your arms?' Ardan shot at him.

'Near enough.'

Ardan's mouth hung open, his anger draining.

'We were mercenaries together, fought all over. Wherever the fighting was thickest was where we'd go. The pay was best there, you see. Anyway, we got caught in the Dog War; it was too much for us to handle. My father died defending the Iron Gates.'

'You were there?' Ardan asked, curiosity beating his resentment. 'Did you see Naberius?'

Riordan pushed himself up into a sitting position. 'Aye, at a distance.'

'What was it like?'

'Three-headed black dog, bigger than a draft horse, moving like quicksilver, tearing soldiers apart with its teeth and breathing the demon fire. Terrifying, lad. Absolutely, soul-crushingly terrifying. Anyone who tells you otherwise is a liar. Thankfully, I only had to deal with his legions. It felt like years while we fought them on the wall. They almost had us, too. If Naberius hadn't fallen and broken their spirits, we would have lost.'

'Did you see him die?' Ardan said. He'd heard the stories at school, passing tap rooms, in the markets, of the Dog War and the fall of Naberius. Plenty of the people he'd seen had claimed to be there, but there was something about the way Riordan spoke that made him believe.

'No. Too busy fighting, trying not to get myself killed.'

'Did you get to see the body?'

'No lad. Nor did anyone else. I'm not sure it works like that when angels and demons fall, either.'

'So, he could still be alive?'

Riordan let out a heavy sigh and a shrug. 'No one saw the body, and only one Templar survived. He hopes the demon's dead.'

Ardan saw the man hunch his shoulders, draw in on himself. 'Was it bad?'

'Aye. We saved whoever we could. My Pa had taken a gut wound. By the time the healers made it to him…. Well, it was too late. He pulled me aside and said, 'Riordan, you're my son and you've grown into a hell of a man. I'm proud of you. You need to settle down and enjoy things besides fighting, drinking and whoring. Find a woman, have some brats. I've been selfish not letting you do it sooner', Riordan said, looking down, his green eyes glistening. 'He was great with a spear, but not with words. Still, those words have stuck with me ever since.'

The two of them fell into silence. Ardan thought through the injustice of his own father's death.

'My father's last words were 'I'm cold'.'

Riordan smiled grimly. 'Despite what the bards sing, no last words ever hold much wisdom.'

'Except your father's.'

'He'd be happy to think so. I expect he didn't die for another few days, but he didn't want me around to see it.' The man sighed. 'By the Light, how I miss him. I noticed his absence during the aftermath of the battle, when we had to drag all those bodies into the huge funeral pyres. That's when I felt it; he just wasn't there anymore. Each day would be one without him, and it was new to me. It got easier, but the beginning was the hardest.'

The silence stretched for a long time; the void inside Ardan stopped him from breaking the silence. He almost turned away just as Riordan started speaking again.

'Afterwards, I wandered around for a bit, not really sure where to go. All I knew was fighting. I eventually ended up here, taking the job of guarding a caravan through the forest. I've done it before, knew it was risky, but didn't expect to get bitten by a forest viper the first day in.'

Ardan felt a weak smile tugging at the corners of his mouth.

'Just thought I'd let you know I understand what you're going through, lad. If you need to talk about it,' Riordan said, his voice trailing off, letting the silence stretch.

Do I want to talk about it? Ardan thought, staring down at his bandaged leg and side. His mouth spoke before he was ready, but the story came out, disjointed and, at times, incoherent. But eventually, the ambush in the alley and his father's murder was all told. Riordan didn't speak until he was sure Ardan had finished.

'Aye lad, that is a grim tale.'

'How could they blame him?'

'The world rarely seems fair. The best we can do is try to make it better.'

That advice was not helpful, Ardan thought. He thought of Verrick's weaselly face and rage blossomed in him, overflowing to the other three. 'I will make them pay for what they did.'

Riordan gave a wry smile. 'Ambitious lad, but what about after? What's your goal if you get all that?'

'I don't know. I don't care.'

'You should have a goal beyond just killing.'

'Fine, then to stop it from happening to anybody else.'

'Like one of those heroes from the stories?' Riordan asked, a small smile playing on his lips.

'If I have to,' Ardan said, remembering the helplessness he had felt. He didn't want to feel that way ever again.

'I'd like to see that.'

The red-haired mercenary was smiling. Ardan glared at him. 'You're making fun of me.'

'Only a little,' Riordan said. 'It's a good idea to have, noble and ambitious.'

'I'll still do it.'

Riordan smiled again, and after that, their conversation moved on to lighter things. However, the lingering effect of Riordan's recovery took its toll. Soon the man was yawning. He made his apologies and lay down.

It left Ardan without little to do but consider the man's words as he watched the world through the small window.

CHAPTER SEVEN: BARONS AND ARCHBISHOPS

* * *

We were being hammered between the Ancients and the forces of Hell. In our desperation, Michael introduced humans to Eden. Their numbers bolstered our ranks and at last we could hold the line.
— Zadkiel, *Chronicles of Eden.*

* * *

THE REST of the day passed slowly. The only breaks were customers coming into the healing house. They were all women, most of them young. Some looked nervous, others tried an air of nonchalance, but none looked comfortable when Eoin handed them a pouch of seeds in exchange for a few coins. They would leave, and Eoin would use the opportunity to check on Ardan and Riordan. The further the day progressed, the more unsteady Eoin became, and the stronger the smell of wine on his breath.

It wasn't until mid-afternoon that the door opened and Ardan's mother entered. He wanted to feel angry, to vent his frustration. But the sight of her tear-streaked face, accompanied by the grass stains on her black dress, quickly dispelled any lingering resentment.

'How was it?' Ardan asked, forcing his tone to be gentle.

Alaine almost spoke, but hesitated, trying to collect herself. 'As good as can be expected. There were a lot of people that turned out, but only a dozen made the journey to his glade. I think he will be happy there. The ceremony was simple. No priests, just old friends and family there to say their farewells,' she said, a tremor haunting her voice. Ardan was worried that her facade would break, but she took a deep breath, blinked back tears, and gave him a forced smiled. 'I'll take you there when you're well again.'

His heart welled up and threatened to fill the void he had felt since his father passed. Then it deflated again. The glade was half a day's journey into the forest, and they weren't skilled enough to get there alone. When he looked up, his mother had pulled out a familiar lacquered box.

'For now, though, I think we had best spend our time continuing your education.'

Ardan frowned, wondering what his mother was getting at.

'In part, it's to keep us both busy, but it is a good way to train your mind,' she said, opening the box and pulling out a deck of playing cards.

'But you've never played Kings with me before. I didn't even think you knew how,' Ardan said.

Alaine smiled. 'Your father wanted to teach you, despite not being terribly good at it, and I was to take over when you were older. To teach you the subtleties required to play. The skills learnt in this game are transferable. It will help you to read people; the shifting of their eyes, the nervous twitch, their unsteady breathing can all be indications of what is coming,' she said, placing the six playing pieces on the board.

'It's just a game.'

'I think we'll start the first lesson on how to govern your emotions,' Alaine said, continuing as though he hadn't spoken. 'At least when possible. There is a time and place to expose your feelings, but when the cards are on the table, that is the time to guard your thoughts and fears,' she said, as her hands moved of their own accord, cutting and shuffling the cards.

'You didn't do that yesterday,' Ardan said.

'No, I didn't,' she said with an edge in her voice. 'But I governed my emotions long enough to do what I needed to get done,' she went on, placing the deck down on the board of the many twisting and turning paths that led to a throne in the centre.

Alaine held out the dice shaker for him.

Ardan took it and rolled a seven, and then picked up the Baron. His mother rolled a three and took the Archbishop. He watched as she dealt the cards, confident that he could beat her to the centre of the board and win the throne. The first to the throne was the winner, but it wasn't the only way to win. The cards, dice and playing style dictated who survived, often making the winner the last man standing. Ardan rolled first and made use of his character's superior mobility. As his piece moved, he kept trying to get a gauge on his mother's cards. He avoided her attacks and built up his defences nicely. He outpaced her on the board, but the closer his character got to the throne, the more uneasy he felt. She laid down an Excommunication card, something that he couldn't block, but he doubted it would matter. His next roll brought up a nine, and he realised he was potentially only one roll away from winning. He had his armies in play; he had a band of nobles to protect him. It should be enough to counter anything his mother threw his way.

'Now your lesson begins,' Alaine said, and started laying down cards. The first card was a Holy Crusade. It was a devastating card when wielded by the Archbishop. He grimaced, but he would survive. However, she wasn't done. She then laid down three more cards in rapid succession: the Peasant Revolt, the Seductress, and finally the Assassin.

Ardan rolled the dice in his defence. He rolled high enough to block the Crusade, but the Peasant Revolt annihilated his army. He rolled again, much more poorly this time, and the Seductress removed his entourage of nobles. That left him completely exposed to the Assassin. Her Excommunication blocked his holy cards, and he had nothing else with which to stop her. He rolled the dice, and it pulled up an eleven. His mother's knowing smile cut deep.

'You played well, if a little too straightforwardly. Few people win a one-on-one game by getting to the throne. You were easy to read, both through your actions and your unguarded moments.'

'If I blocked the assassination attempt, I might have won by blind luck,' Ardan said.

'It's true; sometimes no matter what you do, luck prevails.'

'Not this time, though.'

'No,' Alaine said, smiling. 'There are different styles depending on who is playing. I think this game was enough for today. Before our next game, go through the deck and read each card. Try to figure out their value before you continue.'

Ardan sighed. It sounded tedious. He already knew all the cards.

'Once you realise every card has value, then you can improve,' she said, rising. She kissed him on the forehead. 'I will see you in the morning.'

Long after his mother had left, Ardan continued to stare at the board. His mother had been barely halfway to the throne, yet she had won. Grumbling, he began to go through the cards. Despite what his mother had said, some cards seemed completely worthless, like the Vagrant Daughter. He couldn't see how he could pick this card and not be disappointed.

Eventually Eoin came out and checked his dressings one last time before blowing out the candles. Ardan put the cards down and lay in bed, thinking about the game.

Over the next few days, the game of Kings kept him sane. Riordan would keep him company until the odd times during the day when his mother would turn up. Before each game, his mother made sure Ardan got up and did his exercises. She had a knack for knowing when he was nearing the end of his patience, and then they would begin. Sometimes Riordan would play with them. His style was always high risk, and that rarely paid off. Though as often as not, he'd be sleeping off the viper's venom. Every game, Ardan would try something new, certain this time he would get her. Yet her winning streak continued, rarely by more than a single turn of the dice. After four straight days of losses, he suspected how much of a master she truly was. At the end of each game, she would give him advice. Afterwards, he'd pore over the cards, thinking of ideas and strategies. Whenever grief threatened to overwhelm him, he focused on the cards. They helped. After a few more days, Eoin gave him the okay to head home.

'Already?'

'You're healed up well enough; it's unnecessary to stay any longer. Your mother knows what to do. You've been a good patient, too,' he said, nodding his farewell before retreating into his back room. Despite the early hour, he thought he detected the familiar smell of wine on the man's breath.

He just needed to wait until his mother arrived.

'Off at last, lad?' Riordan asked.

'Seems like it.'

'I have one last bit of advice for you.'

'Mmmm?'

'I just want you to be on your guard for when it happens,' Riordan said. He hesitated, as though searching for the right words.

Ardan's thoughts immediately went to his father's four killers. *Is Riordan going to give me advice about that?*

'Your mother is rather attractive.'

Ardan stared. Then the statement found roots, and he felt like gagging.

'I mean, you should know. Despite being recently widowed, men will try to take advantage of her vulnerable state. She's intelligent and enjoyable company.'

Ardan opened his mouth, ready for it to run away from him.

'I don't have any designs on her, lad,' Riordan said quickly. 'I just want you to be aware. She hides her grief, but she is hurting. Sometimes people make poor decisions in their grief. I just want you aware and to watch over her.'

Ardan chewed the advice like cold, hard gristle. His father was barely in his grave and now he was being told his mother would be the source of unwanted male attention.

'Thanks,' he grumbled.

Riordan waved it off. It took the last energy out of him and he lay down. Ardan knew the man was fighting the venom, but it was getting the better of him.

It was only another hour before his mother arrived, and Ardan gave his farewell to a sleepy Riordan. The man mumbled something but didn't open his eyes.

Ardan and his mother set off at a slow pace towards home. She stood on his weak side in case he stumbled. The streets were bustling, but the two of them stuck to the edges as people circled around them. They had barely gone a few blocks along the stone houses and cobblestone streets before Ardan felt exhausted. His legs were aching and sweat covered his body. He knew he must smell bad, but his mother made no comment. It was lucky that their home and the healing house were both in the Ancient Quarter. After a few more blocks, Ardan had to rest against a building. He regained his breath and started off again. His mother fell in beside him. It took another fifteen minutes before he could see their house, a quaint thatch dwelling built into the side of the hill. The sight of it gave him renewed strength, and he pushed on.

When he entered through the front door, he thought he'd feel relief. Instead, it felt surreal. Their dining table and dual benches remained clean and bare. The small fire pit and stone chimney gave off the smell of burning wood. The cooking pot sat just above their fire, filled near to the brim and slowly bubbling. Material hung from the roof to create the illusion of privacy between each of their cots. His father's workshop was at one end with his replacement bowstrings, arrows, vials, and traps. It was there that Ardan realised the difference. His father would never be back to claim them. He would never pull any of his tools down to his workbench again. They were little more than dust collectors now. The cold, heavy reality weighed him down like a stone.

'You're home!' his sister squealed as she flew at him. She stopped before crashing into him, careful of his injuries as she hugged him. 'I'm so glad you're home.'

'Me too,' Ardan said, but the void felt worse now, despite his sister's attempts to fill it. It had now contaminated his home.

CHAPTER EIGHT: THE LADY ALAINE

* * *

The humans, as they often do, upset our expectations. Many succumbed to the temptations of the Darkness, but those that defected towards the Ancients gave us pause. They were given shelter, and before long they too had access to Eden's power and fought alongside the Ancients, against us.

— Zadkiel, *Chronicles of Eden.*

* * *

ARDAN LAY on his bed and stared at his walking cane. He was debating whether he should spend the morning in his bed or at the table. The rest of his family was already up and moving. It had been almost a week since he had left the healing house; his bruises had changed to an ugly yellow and were finally fading. He was still stiff in many places, but each day brought improvement.

'Lying about all day again?' Davan said.

'Get up and do what, exactly? Hobble around the house?' Ardan snapped.

Davan had been irritable all week. His trials were coming up and his nerves were getting the better of him. Ardan, not able to leave the house, was getting a little stir crazy. They were interrupted from really getting into it by their mother.

'I need some things from the market, are you up for it?' Alaine asked.

Ardan stared at her, not immediately realising she was speaking to him. He swung his legs over the edge of the pallet and snatched up his cane. She had insisted he needed to stay inside and heal. Now was his chance. He stood so quickly that spots appeared in his vision and his head spun like a whirlwind. He covered the mishap by trying to stretch his injured leg. His mother hadn't looked up. He smiled, thinking he got away with it.

'Maybe you should stay home,' Alaine said, glancing at him sideways.

'No, no, I can do it,' Ardan said quickly.

'Let him be useful for once,' Davan said.

Ardan silently thanked his brother, the arsehole.

'Take the purse and head down to the market. We need more food for the pot. I want the bag full of mostly vegetables, then you can get some meat. Only after you've got the vegetables, mind you,' Alaine said, her eyes narrowing until he nodded. 'Keep some on the fire, I may not get back until late.'

'Wait, why are you not coming home?' Liá asked. After a recent growth spurt, she was rapidly outgrowing her clothes. Her brown dress was bordering on scandalous. Since Riordan's comment about how attractive his mother was, Ardan had become acutely aware of how much everyone likened Liá's looks to their mother's. Though she had the grace of a new born colt, her long legs and figure showed a promise that Ardan didn't like.

'I'm coming home, dear, just a bit late.'

'Why? What are you doing?' Davan asked.

'Just a few things here and there. I wish I could come with you today. There are whispers that the senior Red Wolves are arguing over who gets to mentor you. I'll be sure to be home in time to celebrate with you,'

Alaine said, giving Davan a warm smile. He didn't return it, but his face looked less grim. Their mother continued, 'Liá, you should be ready to go. Ardan, can you take her to class and pick her up afterwards?'

Ardan had been playing Kings with her often enough to know she was trying to distract them, but he said nothing. He wanted out of the house.

It wasn't long before the three siblings left together. Davan immediately strode towards Mercenary Square.

'Learn anything interesting yesterday?' Ardan asked as he and Liá made their way through the crowded streets towards the schoolhouse. It wasn't far, but with his limp, the going was slow.

'Ooh, yes. Raigel came up in conversation.'

'Really? How?'

'Delaney began discussing the importance of trade through Barleron. If people didn't have such a high distrust of the Waterlords—'

Ardan interrupted with an exaggerated yawn.

She ignored him. 'Anyway, someone asked how a demon became a merchant. Because, you know, we only ever hear about them being the bad guys in stories. Delaney said it wasn't unusual; angels and demons used to rove the land in droves and they took up all sorts of roles. Merchants, bakers, butchers, you know, normal stuff.'

'They did?' Ardan said, surprised. He had only heard of their exploits in battle.

She nodded. 'There were so many of them that some didn't fight, so they did what we all do.'

'But if there were so many, where did they all go?'

'That's what I asked! Delaney just shrugged and said he didn't know but guessed the breaking and the endless wars killed them off and now there are only a few demons and angels left.'

'That's a shame. It would have been something to see. Imagine eating some angel-made bread,' Ardan said, imagining eating warm, soft, freshly baked bread that was somehow better than the usual fare.

'I hadn't thought of that.'

After the daydream had faded, Ardan asked, 'So how does Raigel fit in?'

'Delaney wasn't sure. He said the demon had probably found something he liked, and he keeps to himself, mostly. No fighting with the Light or anyone else.'

'Nothing?' Ardan asked incredulously.

'It's what he said. Apparently, the demon has shunned any outright confrontation.'

'What about when those soldiers from....' Ardan trailed off, thinking.

'The Citadel of Light,' Liá interjected. 'He defended himself. A few were injured, but he didn't kill anyone.'

'Interesting,' Ardan said, thinking about the demon. The murderers had killed his father just outside the demon's shop. Could Raigel have helped him? He didn't seem dangerous; more of an over-grown vulture with scales, but then again, Ardan had nothing to compare him to.

They arrived at the old two-story house that served as the school. Delaney owned the house, had turned the ground floor into class-rooms, and the second floor into small study spaces for those who wished to learn alone. Ardan had spent countless hours, both upstairs and down, scratching away on small pieces of slate.

Delaney was out the front in his brown tunic, covered in chalk dust.

'Ardan, I haven't seen you in an age,' he exclaimed, motioning with his hands. The last few vestiges of his greying hair swung valiantly with him. Ardan felt like the man had missed his calling as a stage performer. 'Have you been keeping up with your studies?'

Ardan shrugged.

'Ah yes, I can imagine that it has been difficult of late. I'm sorry that I couldn't make it to your father's funeral. Terrible business, yes indeed. How are you handling it?'

'Well enough, I guess.'

'You're welcome to come back to my class. Might take your mind off it. It won't cost anything, at least until your family is back on their feet.'

'Thank you,' Ardan said, feeling a budding glow of inner warmth. 'I'm just dropping little Liá off for class.'

'I am not little.'

'She's not,' Delaney said, looking fondly at Liá. 'She's one of the most advanced in the school. Some of the boys are frustrated at how she focuses on her work rather than on them.'

'Boys are stupid.'

'When you're around, they certainly appear that way,' Delaney said with a laugh.

'Who are they?' Ardan asked.

'Oh, no need to take it like that, there's no harm in it,' Delaney said, holding up his hands in a placating gesture. 'I stop it before it goes anywhere and they grow out of it before too long.' He paused for a moment before adding, 'Usually.'

'I should get inside,' Liá said, her cheeks red.

'I should too. I was just waiting for the latecomers. Are you sure you don't want to join?'

'Not this time.'

The squat man smiled and waved farewell before heading inside. Ardan stared at the building, remembering how much he'd hated the grey walls and being forced to sit for hours on end not doing anything. Grateful he didn't have to put up with it anymore, he started heading towards the markets. He paused and quickly felt the pocket on the inside of his tunic and cursed. The money purse was still at home. With a sigh, he headed back towards the house.

Eventually, he made it home and pushed open the front door. He paused mid-stride, staring at the stranger sitting in front of the wash-basin. She had painted red and black patterns around her eyes. Her dress was dark blue, white laced and cinched at the waist.

'Mother?' Ardan asked incredulously. She wore the clothes easily. He had seen the merchant wives that had married into wealth and wore it awkwardly, or tried to overcompensate by being gaudy, but she ... she looked comfortable, natural even.

'Close your mouth, dear. It's unseemly,' Alaine said, the brush at her eyes.

'You look like a noble.'

'That's the idea. I'm trying to enter their society and find a means of supporting us. This is the best way I know how to do it, without doing things that are—undesirable.'

'Doing what?'

'This and that,' she said, leaning back from the mirror, inspecting herself. She turned to face him as though to say, *how do I look?*

'You look great.'

She gave a small smile, one that suited her new persona.

'I know you have questions and I'll answer them later. I'm already running late. Remember to get the food ready,' she said, giving his arm a quick squeeze as she left.

Left standing alone in the house, Ardan's mind was a whirl. He'd known that there was something hidden about his mother's past from how she played Kings to her insistence on table manners, but this was something else. He collected the purse, trying to figure out what she was up to.

CHAPTER NINE: DABBLING WITH DARKNESS

* * *

*D*espite the centuries I spent on Eden, there were things that were destined to remain a mystery. How did the humans access the power of the Light or Dark without celestial aid or intervention? In all the worlds I have seen or heard of, this aspect was unique to Eden.

— Zadkiel, *Chronicles of Eden.*

* * *

HE ANGLED his path so he would pass the Park of the Ancients on his way to the market. After not having seen the place for almost two weeks, he missed it.

Vine-covered walls separated the park from the rest of Barleron. As he passed through the portal, he could see the green grass blanketing the ground inside the park. There was a small hill in the centre that supported the massive Tree of the Ancients. People wandered around under the massive branches, or sat in the soft grass, yet despite their numbers the place didn't feel crowded.

Ardan walked up to the tree. Its trunk only went up a short way before its branches burst forth and sprawled out across the park, blanketing the sky in green leaves. Ardan placed his hand familiarly on the trunk.

A powerful surge flowed up his arm.

Ardan recoiled in shock. He shook his hand, staring at the tree. *That's never happened before.*

He reached forward and tentatively touched the tree's rough bark again. No surge greeted him this time. He wanted to shrug off the incident, but his hand still tingled. He rested his full palm against the trunk, looking to feel the relaxing sensation that the tree normally brought. It never came. Instead, he felt a thread within him, leading toward the tree. Curious, he followed it. An ominous dread filled him, as though something horrible was coming. It welled up and terror flooded him. He pulled his hand back, but the terror didn't subside. Reacting to something primal, he ran.

He only made it a few short bounds before his injured leg spasmed, and he stumbled. He threw his hands in front of him as he fell. The jolt of the ground shocked him into reality, his thoughts returning. Standing above him was a man watching him with piercing dark eyes. His black hair was closely cropped, while his black robes seemed out of place on the bright, cloudless day.

'You look like you've been through it,' he said and offered a hand to Ardan. A silver necklace slipped out from his collar and at the end was the silver symbol of Lucifer. A priest of the Dark. Ardan felt the fear from the tree grip him again.

'None of that,' the man said, grabbing Ardan's arm and yanking him to his feet. 'No damage,' he said, looking over him. 'Well, your pride might have taken a hit, but everything else seems to be fine.'

'Thanks,' Ardan managed but looked at the priest as though he might turn into a deadly forest viper.

'Don't mention it.'

The hand felt creepy as the priest clutched his arm.

'Worried I'm going to kill you and eat your bones?' The priest asked, suddenly pulling him close. For a moment Ardan wondered if he just might. The man released him with a laugh. 'The ignorance in this part of the world is astounding. Priests are just people like everyone else.'

Sure they are, Ardan thought. 'What brings you here?' Ardan asked, trying to hide his apprehension.

'There's something about this place, is there not?' The priest said, his eyes on the tree. 'A remnant of the Ancients' power. It's something I don't recognise and I quite like it. There's nothing like this back home.' The priest suddenly raised one of his arms. Shadow and darkness congealed into a ball, despite the bright sun beating down on them, absorbing the surrounding light. He shot it at the tree like an arrow. Before it struck, the Tree of the Ancients flared up in a green flame, absorbing the darkness and breaking it apart. Once the darkness was gone, the flame around the tree died down, leaving not a single burnt leaf or scorch mark anywhere. The people in the park saw the exchange and immediately made for the exit.

'Definitely nothing like this back home.'

'Why would you attack the tree?' Ardan demanded, his fear forgotten.

The priest turned, his dark eyes searching Ardan and smiled. Ardan didn't like it.

'I have to go,' Ardan said, somewhat lamely.

'May the Darkness embrace you,' The priest replied, waving him off, his attention returning to the tree. Ardan walked faster, ignoring the strain it put on his injuries. He wanted to put as much distance between himself and the priest as possible. As he got further away from the tree, his fear subsided. Though the encounter with the priest troubled him all the way to the market near Barleron's main gate.

The stalls lined the entire space, with haphazard aisles that didn't seem to follow any particular order. Ardan almost jumped the first time a stallkeeper yelled out at him to examine their wares. The loud cacophony of noise and organized chaos helped push thoughts about the priest to the farthest corner of his mind, as he wandered past stalls covered with northern kingdom pottery, exotic fruits from across the sea, and leathers and furs from the horsemen of the plains. Guards stood next to jewellery stores, while smiths worked on weapons. The bedlam of the place helped Ardan forget about the priest and the tree. It took him almost fifteen minutes to locate the food store that his mother frequented. The store owner, a matronly old woman, barely even glanced at him.

'You're Alaine's boy?' she said, then clucked her tongue and turned before he could answer, loading a leather bag with bread, vegetables, fruits, cheese, some meat, and a small satchel. She handed over the bag and held out her hand. 'A silver half penny.'

Ardan gave her the coin without thinking.

'Return the bag next time,' she said in dismissal.

Holding the carryall and feeling out of place, he slung the single strap over his shoulder and started walking. The exertion of the day was taking its toll. His leg and fingers ached, while sweat beaded his forehead. He frowned. *Two weeks ago, I could run the length of Barleron twice over, now I get tired on a leisurely walk.*

By the time he stood outside the front door of his home, he was panting and drenched in sweat. He didn't dare lift his arms in case some horrid stench escaped. Pushing open the door, he put down the bag and immediately filled the washbasin. He washed himself and soaked his shirt before wringing it dry and hanging it up.

Now clean, he opened the bag and placed the dark loaf of barley bread and the half round of cheese on the table. He pulled out the vegetables, cutting the onions, parsnips, carrots, and mushrooms before putting them in the pot. The pouch of saffron and pepper was added, along with a few pork bones. He kept the fire hot enough to bring the pot to a nice simmer.

He stirred until the pot bubbled, then sat down, with nothing left to do besides watching the food. His mind wandered, thinking about the priest and the tree, then his mother. *If every day is like this, maybe I should stay home.*

He pottered around until it was time to pick up Liá.

When he met her at the schoolhouse, she picked up on his mood and their conversation was subdued. They got back to the house and Ardan returned his attention to the stew. He gave it a stir, making sure that nothing had stuck to the bottom.

'Did you do your exercises today?' Liá asked.

'I got sidetracked.'

'Ardan,' she said reproachfully.

'You sound like Mother.'

'Someone needs to make sure you don't do anything stupid,' she said, glaring at him, daring him to defend himself. A ghost of a smile appeared on his lips and he continued to stir.

'You've got your work cut out for you.'

'Oh, we know,' Liá said, coming over to have a look inside the bubbling stew, now giving off the pleasant aroma of slowly-cooking meat and vegetables. 'Should we wait for the others?'

'We should,' Ardan said.

Together they waited, long past when they'd expected someone else to come home, but neither their brother nor mother appeared. The tantalising aroma of the stew was difficult to ignore.

Liá yawned.

'Well, we can't wait around forever,' Ardan said, getting up.

He served them both generous portions. The thick, warm stew kept their conversation to a minimum. The pork had permeated the entire stew, and he tried to savour each bite. Before he was ready, the meal was gone. He used a slice of barley bread to mop the bowl clean.

Night slowly descended and neither their mother nor Davan had come home. It was getting later and later. Liá announced she was going to bed. At the same moment, the door slammed open and Davan burst through into the room.

'Guess who's drunk?' he exclaimed, spreading his arms wide.

'You?' Ardan asked.

'Damn right.'

'Went well today?'

'It did,' he said with a big, stupid grin on his face.

'Well?' Ardan asked.

Davan looked between the two of them. 'Well, what?'

'What happened?' Liá asked, exasperated.

'I won all my duels,' he said, holding a fist in the air triumphantly, but then he suddenly held up a finger and pointed at them, 'but that wasn't the real test.'

'It wasn't?' Liá asked.

'Noooo,' he said, stumbling over and barely making it onto the seat. 'Between the duels, I was getting asked all sorts of questions. Like what do we do in the forest? How do you treat a gut wound? Make sure water is safe to drink? That sort of thing.'

'And you said the right things?'

'I did,' he said, that big grin back on his face. 'I'm an official Red Wolf, and Lachlan is now my mentor.'

'Lachlan,' Ardan said, making sure he'd heard right. 'I didn't think the captain could take on protégés.'

'Neither did I, but he is anyway.'

'That's amazing,' Liá said.

Lachlan and their father had been friends, but even counting that, it seemed unusual.

'Thanks, little sis,' Davan said as he struggled to get to his feet. It was painful to watch. 'I think I may have had a little too much to drink so I'll be going to bed. Good night!' He stumbled over to his pallet, falling onto his cot with a loud crash. At first, Ardan was worried he'd hurt himself, but before they could check on him, Davan was already snoring.

Ardan exchanged a glance with Liá and burst out laughing. Once their mirth died down, Liá sought her own cot. Ardan set out the game of Kings. His mother had made a habit out of playing with him when she got home. He killed time by reading through the cards, but after a while, he just started randomly rolling the dice out of boredom.

CHAPTER TEN: MYSTERY AND MURDER

* * *

I have faced many of the High Demons in the past. My victory or defeat was always fleeting, as we would be resurrected when the time came. It is a power not shared by the Ancients. As our war continued through the decades, I wondered if we were marching towards genocide.
— Zadkiel, *Chronicles of Eden.*

* * *

HOURS LATER, Ardan woke with a start. It took him a moment to recognise where he was. He'd fallen asleep on the table, and the playing cards were stuck to his face. He rubbed his eyes and looked for his mother, guessing she hadn't wanted to wake him, but her bed was undisturbed. His weariness vanished as he realised, she hadn't come home.

Outside he could see a procession of flickering lights and heard a muffled curse. It was probably the night fishermen coming back to shore. Their appearance meant dawn was only an hour or two away. He tried to get up quietly but banged his leg on the table. He tried to stifle a yelp of pain. It wasn't enough. Liá pulled back the hangings from around her cot.

'What's wrong? Why are you up?' Liá asked as she glanced at him and then at their mother's undisturbed bed. 'Where is she?'

'I'm ... I'm not sure. She never came home.'

'You don't think something has happened to her, do you?'

Ardan shook his head. 'She's tougher than—' They could hear their brother grumble behind them as he shifted in his cot. Ardan shifted to a whisper: 'No, she's tougher than she looks. I'm sure she'll be fine.'

'But what if something did happen?'

'You know how, whenever we went to the markets, it would always take *forever* because she had friends at every stall?'

'Mm-hmm.'

'If something were to happen to her, there would always be someone there to keep her safe.'

'I guess,' she said.

'Plus, she's pretty tough herself,' Ardan said. 'She'll be home soon.'

'But what if she isn't?'

'Then I'll go out and bring her home,' Ardan said. He worried the words sounded hollow, but his sister seemed to accept it.

'Will you two shut up?' Davan said, pushing open the curtains, his bloodshot eyes glaring at them. He grumbled, and let the curtain fall back as he lay down.

Liá looked at Ardan, who shrugged.

An infant's cry came from outside, quickly hushed. Ardan went to the shutters, opening them to look out. A group of people, illuminated by torches, were moving down the street. There were woman and children there, their arms loaded with belongings. These weren't fishermen, but families, hurrying through the city.

'Where are they going?' Ardan asked, as he observed a second and third group walking down the street in a tight huddle.

'What?'

Ardan motioned for her to come join him.

Liá came to the window, her head craning up and down the street. 'What ... what is happening?'

'They look like they're running from something.'

'Running from what?'

'I'm not sure, but I don't think it can be good. I'm going to head out, look for mother and find out more about what is going on.'

'So, I'm just supposed to stay here?'

'Yes, in case mother comes back,' Ardan said. *Or I don't,* he thought.

Liá didn't look happy, but she nodded anyway.

He took his cane and headed outside. He passed scores of people, each group going quiet as he did so, only speaking once he was out of earshot.

Ardan's sense of unease grew each time.

'Out of the way!' a man yelled.

Ardan's head snapped around to see two riders racing towards him, leading a group of laden packhorses. He tried to do an awkward dive backwards, but he stumbled on his injured leg, hopping back a couple of steps before falling to the cobblestones. He covered his head as they thundered past. The ground shook as the hooves narrowly missed him. Ardan peered out through one eye, but the riders didn't look back. He ran a hand over himself, surprised he wasn't hurt. Ardan didn't need to curse them. The laden packhorse train meant they were heading for the forest. Riding that recklessly would get them killed in that place. He got up and dusted himself off. The charging horses had broken the cane.

'Hellspawn,' Ardan spat.

Without the cane, he continued towards the market square at a more sedate pace. Ardan's eyes kept glancing behind him to make sure there were no more wayward horses galloping in his direction.

The market was different today. Less than a quarter of the stores were open. At first, he attributed it to the early hour, but as he moved deeper into the market, several vacant spaces lined the aisles, while other stalls were completely cleared out. There were queues at the weapon and food stalls.

The smell of seafood wafted from the fishmonger's stall. A large man with a thick black beard was gutting and cleaning a fish on a bench in front of him. Despite the mess, his brown clothing was clean. He looked up and his black eyes met Ardan's.

'Fresh fish. What are you after?'

'My mother,' Ardan said plainly.

He laughed. 'Not sure I can help you. My wife's been dead for years and I doubt you're one of hers,' the shop owner said and took a closer look. 'You're one of Alaine's boys?'

Ardan nodded.

He paused in his work, staring at the fish in concentration. 'I haven't seen her for a couple of days. She normally visits my shop at least once a week. Good woman. What's she done?'

'She didn't come home last night.'

'Not like her?'

Ardan shook his head.

'Hey Martha,' the shop owner yelled at a woman several stores across.

'What?' she yelled back.

'You seen Alaine recently?'

'Who?'

'Pretty woman, dark hair. You know her, pays fair, comes around once a week.'

'Oh yes, yes. Umm. No, not seen her for two days, hang on. Connor!' she yelled at another stall.

'May as well make yourself comfortable,' the fishmonger said, indicating a stool next to his stall. Ardan gratefully sat down, his healing muscles grateful for the respite. People continued to walk past him. Some bought fish, but most just cast furtive glances, as though expecting something dangerous to burst out of the shadows.

'Harrod,' Martha yelled.

'What?' the fishmonger yelled back.

'Peter the weaver saw her in Ragtown last night. Said she was with a group of well-dressed people.'

'What was she doing there?'

'No idea,' she shouted.

'Well, there you have it, boy. Can't be too many well-dressed people in Ragtown. Does it make you think of anyone?'

Ardan didn't think she'd know anyone well dressed, let alone people in Ragtown.

'She wasn't involved in it, was she?' Harrod asked.

'Involved in what?'

'I suppose the news is still fresh. Still, I thought everyone would know by now. The Magistrate was murdered.'

'What!'

'They found him in Ragtown, dead. Not sure how he died; his guard were dead or missing.'

'What?' Ardan stammered again. 'But how?'

'Not really sure. I thought he was untouchable, too. Been running this city for what, fifteen years?'

Ardan gave him a blank stare before Harrod eventually shrugged and continued, 'I hope she wasn't involved, lad. She's a nice woman, your mother, but if other people know she was there, they might want to ask her some questions. Be good for her to lie low—some people's questions don't come softly.'

'She wasn't involved,' Ardan said.

'You know her best,' he said, returning his attention to the fish and using his knife to start on another one. 'You're probably too young to remember when the Butcher died, but if it's anything like that, well, this city is likely to become a battlefield. I think it will be a few more days before it gets into full swing, but this place will be a bloodbath, and they will destroy half the city before the end. Hells, the forest might be safer. You best find a good place to hole up until a new boss emerges from the pile of bones.' The entire time he spoke he continued to clean the fish of scales, removing its guts and then putting some string through the mouth and handing it to Ardan. 'Keep yourself safe.'

'What about you?' Ardan said, taking the fish.

'I've secured my passage out of here already. I leave later today, but thought I'd try to sell some things before I left.'

Nodding numbly, Ardan thanked him and left. After moving past his stall, he picked up some vegetables to go into the pot before he started home. What had his mother been doing in Ragtown? *She couldn't be involved in it, surely*, he thought, desperately wanting to believe it.

As he walked, Ardan felt the eyes of the derelicts and street urchins following him. After limping the first few blocks, he was wary of any passers-by. He could feel their stares as the hairs on his neck rose. Ardan watched everyone suspiciously. He had little to tempt thieves, but he wondered if that would stop them. One of the street beggars gave him a toothless grin.

A group of people came out from a side street. They were armed well enough to belong to a mercenary group, although none wore identifying markers. They didn't look directly at Ardan, but they were striding purposefully in his direction. It was enough for him to move as quickly as his limp would allow. His house wasn't far away. He hobbled faster and faster, just keeping ahead of the group. He wished he had his knife on him in case they attacked him. His home was so close.

Their footsteps fell like the beat of a death bell. Breathing heavily, Ardan kept up the pace. His house got closer until he could make out his front door. Breaking into a shambling run, he burst into the house, slamming the door behind him and bolting it. He leaned against it, hearing the group tramp past.

It took a few moments for Ardan's heart to stop beating so rapidly. So, they weren't after him.

Davan was sitting on the corner of his pallet, his head in his hands and a bucket beneath him. From the smell coming from it, Ardan guessed he'd recently been sick. Liá was there, rubbing his back sympathetically. She watched him with raised eyebrows.

'The Magistrate is dead,' Ardan said.

Davan's head snapped up, but he then dove for the bucket, dry heaving. He looked up, bleary-eyed, once he'd finished. 'Say that again.'

'The Magistrate was killed late last night in Ragtown,' Ardan said. He went over to the washbasin to clean himself up.

'That's what I thought you said.'

A fist battered against the door, causing Ardan to jump, and the wash water to splash on the ground.

'Open up,' the voice commanded.

Ardan glanced at the others, unsure of what to do.

'It's Lachlan. I need to see Davan.'

Breathing easier, Ardan unlatched the door, letting Lachlan in. The man's long blond hair was tied in a single braid, going well past his shoulders. He wore chainmail that only emphasised his warrior's build and he was armed with a long sword and shield.

'The Magistrate is dead,' he said without preamble. 'I'm here to collect you. The Wolves are gathering everyone and fortifying Mercenary Square.'

Davan nodded, forcing himself to his feet. He staggered to the washbasin and plunged his face into it. His long dark hair was dripping water on his face and shirt when he'd finished. He shook his head like a dog and did it again. After settling, his eyes shifted between Lachlan and Ardan, before going over to his discarded armour on the floor. He picked it up and began buckling it on himself. He put the straps across his chest and slid the axe across his back.

'Where's Alaine?' Lachlan asked

'She didn't come home last night,' Ardan said.

Lachlan gave a thin press of his lips before replying, 'Have you got any savings? We want to get all the families to Mercenary Square until the aftermath settles, but it's five silver temples per person.'

'Five silver temples?' Ardan exclaimed.

'There are no exceptions,' Lachlan said. 'By tomorrow we're going to start allowing the other mercenary groups and their families to quarter with us. By that point, we will fill up quickly. Once we're full, that's it.'

'We don't have that sort of money,' Davan said.

Ardan was about to agree.

'You don't?' Lachlan asked, surprised. 'But Tristan was the best forest stalker in the city. He should have a fortune.'

Instead of answering, Davan walked over to their wardrobe and reached up and pulled a sword from the top. It was a slightly curved, medium-length blade wrapped in a brown sheath. He walked over to Ardan and handed it to him.

'This was to be your next name-day present. Much like mine,' Davan said.

Ardan felt the soft leather of the hilt in his hand. The cross guard of polished metal gleamed as he drew the sword from the sheath. It was a single-edged, flawless blade. He hefted it, slashing the air a few times. Its weight and balance felt perfect.

'It's made from Ancient steel,' Davan said.

Lachlan whistled. 'An Ancient steel falchion.'

'They spent everything on that?' Ardan asked.

'Father likely found the materials himself, but working Ancient steel is difficult and expensive,' Davan said. 'With father's passing and Ardan's healing, I don't think we have anything left.'

'The sword is worth a fortune. It would be enough,' Lachlan said.

'No,' Ardan said, clutching the sword tight, his father's face flashing in his mind.

'It's his sword,' Davan said.

'Alright then,' Lachlan said matter-of-factly, 'We'll tear this place apart. Find if there's any money they've hidden under the floorboards or in hidey holes. Don't be shy about it. This place will be ransacked before the end.'

Methodically, they searched through their home. Ardan took the fireplace, his hand running over the brick and stone. His hand ran over one that was loose, sending small rivulets of dust floating to the floor. He grabbed it; the stone slid out smoothly to reveal a small pouch behind it.

'Ahah,' Ardan said triumphantly and pulled it out. He could feel a few coins in there. He poured them into his hands. Two silver temples and several coppers. 'Hell's fire,' he said, cursing.

'That it?' Lachlan asked, disappointed. 'I can't cover you either. My wife and four children have already drained my reserve. Do know anyone you can borrow money from?'

'Not that sort of money,' Davan said.

'You might find refuge at the Cathedral of the Light. They take people in, but it's rough. It can become a bit lawless in there, but safer than in the city.'

'You could play the tables,' Liá said.

'What?' Davan said.

'The tables at the Establishment. Gamble the money.'

'Who?' Lachlan said. 'And how do you know about the Establishment?'

Liá shrugged. 'Ardan's been playing Kings incessantly. He could win.'

'I've never beaten Mother.'

'Time's wasting. Davan, I'll need you with me,' Lachlan said.

'Sir,' Davan said, not moving.

Lachlan looked back at him. 'We need all hands at the Square for the next few hours. I'll make sure you can come back tonight, good enough?'

'Good enough,' Davan said.

'Keep the doors and windows barred until your brother's back,' Lachlan said.

After they'd left, Ardan did as instructed. The first time the door rattled, Ardan barricaded it for good measure. The second time, Ardan said in as low a voice as he could muster, 'I'm armed.'

There weren't any more attempts after that, but it didn't stop Ardan and Liá from feeling as if they were trapped in a henhouse with a fox outside.

CHAPTER ELEVEN: KINGLY STAKES

* * *

t one point, the Ancients did the impossible. They used their power to deny entry into Eden. They could not expel those already on their world, but no reinforcements would be forthcoming from Heaven or Hell. From then on, it became a war of attrition.
— Zadkiel, *The Chronicles of Eden*

* * *

ARDAN AND LIÁ stood at an intersection near the edge of the Docks. He adjusted the sword at his hip; his father's last gift comforted him. Davan had gone inside the nearby Inn to get some directions to the Establishment. In the taproom, a fiery redhead was dancing on the bar in an outfit that exposed her flat stomach and slender shoulders. Despite her evocative dancing, most of the patrons were huddled away from her at their tables, drinking sombrely and talking in hushed whispers.

'Stop ogling the women,' Davan said, loud enough to cause Ardan to jump.

Ardan felt his face flush. He hadn't been staring at the dancer, at least not just at her. Davan started walking without a word. Ardan followed behind, struggling to keep up with his injured leg. After a few blocks, they reached the waterside. A cool sea breeze washed over them, as the sound of water gently lapping in the bay filled the atmosphere. They walked past the harbour warehouses until the smaller, more well-presented stores of the Merchant Quarter replaced them: shoe shops, sweet vendors, dressmakers and tailors, places that catered to the wealthy. The stores eventually gave way to the Establishment. It was an old nobleman's manor, converted into a gambling den. If a clientele had a game they wanted to play, the Establishment hosted it. Every window shone with light as an awkward symphony of shouts, laughter, and drunken revelry erupted from the place. Out front were several men in stark black uniforms. They all had wooden batons on their belts.

The three of them made their way to the door. From behind, Ardan could see the tenseness in Davan's shoulders. His brother wasn't enthusiastic about the idea, but he couldn't think of anything better. One bouncer moved forward to greet them. He had a shaved head and an ugly black eye that gave him a sinister look.

'We don't do charity.'

'We're here for the tables,' Davan said.

'We've had a few children in here tonight already. People that couldn't hold their drink or handle their losses. Be sure you don't cause any trouble while you're in there,' the bouncer said as he stood aside.

'Or what?'

The bouncer stopped moving and eyed Davan. 'Or you'll find trouble you're not ready for, boy.' Another bouncer walked over, his long, braided hair threaded with jewellery that jingled as he walked.

Davan's hand twitched as though he were going to reach for his axe. The bald bouncer's hand moved too. He was shorter and thinner than Davan, but he had scars on his face and arms, both fresh and faded. The tension bristled in the air as the two of them stood almost chest to chest, neither breaking eye contact.

'It's okay,' Liá said, trying to push herself between the two. She gave up when neither budged. 'With all this trouble going on, my brother is just being extra protective. He meant nothing by it.'

The bald bouncer's eyes never left Davan as though his stare could bore a hole into his skull. The braided-haired man put a hand on the other bouncer's shoulder. 'Hey, I'd feel the same if my daughter were out in the streets at a time like this.'

They waited there for what seemed like an eternity before the bald bouncer nodded and stepped to the side. Ardan let out a breath he didn't know he'd been holding. They entered the place quietly.

'Stop thinking with that giant axe of yours,' Ardan said.

'What? I won't be pushed around.'

'Let's get to the tables,' Liá said.

Ardan bit back a reply to his idiot brother. Angrily, he stomped into the place and had gone a dozen steps before fully taking in the faded opulence of his surroundings. *Probably an old ballroom or something equally useless,* he thought. Now it had been converted into a gambling den, with dozens of tables filled with different games of cards and dice. There were serving men and women weaving between the patrons, carrying trays of drinks. Ardan felt like a wide-eyed puppy as he stared at the different card tables. They walked past a room where a ring of people were shouting and yelling. He stopped and stared. In the centre was a forest viper, hissing at a badger. The badger snarled as it lunged at the snake.

'Ardan, come on,' Davan said.

Tearing himself away, he moved with them through the place until they found what they were looking for: a small room devoted to the game of Kings. They'd lined the circular walls with chairs, all facing towards the single table in the centre that had six chairs around it.

The table had a time glass with sand trickling through it. Ardan guessed the game would start once the timer ran out, regardless of whether the table was full or not.

'Five copper temple buy-in,' the usher said as he walked over. His brown doublet bespoke the uniform of the employees.

Ardan exhaled. *Five coppers just to play?* Hesitating, he looked at his siblings for support, but they were still finding their seats. The usher smiled at him, and Ardan sighed. He reached inside the purse and handed the man the money. The coins quickly disappeared and Ardan was urged forward.

He moved up to the table and picked an empty chair beside a rotund man in a rich burgundy tunic. The silver signet ring of the Merchant Guild stood out amongst all his other gold rings. To his right was a lithe, tanned woman who wore a sleeveless shirt common amongst sailors. There was an empty chair across from him, while a young couple occupied the last two. They were leaning towards each other, and the man's tone was hushed. While Ardan couldn't make out what he was saying, he could deduce the intent from her smile. There was cheap perfume coming from the two of them—an overabundance of it. Ardan wrinkled his nose at the offending odour.

The sand in the upper half of the glass was disappearing fast. He glanced back at his brother and sister; both were sitting there quietly. His brother had put his axe across his lap. He wasn't the only one there that was armed. A man sitting back from the merchant had two large daggers in his belt.

The entire table watched as the final grains of sand drained to the bottom.

'I am not too late; excellent,' a deep voice said.

A man had appeared, in black robes adorned by a single silver chain with the emblem of Lucifer at the end, and with familiar dark hair and piercing black eyes. It was the dark priest from the park. He dropped some coins in the usher's hand and took measured strides to the unoccupied seat. The couple tried to shrink away from him.

'I apologise that you all had to wait so long,' he said. As he spoke, they all realised they'd been staring. The merchant played with his rings. The courting couple glanced guiltily at each other. Ardan's hand went to the hilt of his sword.

'We have been waiting here for some time,' the merchant admitted.

'Finally, we can get started,' the sailor said.

'Of course. I wouldn't want to keep you. Shall we set the stakes?' the priest asked.

'A few silver pennies?' Ardan suggested.

'I didn't come here for penny games,' the sailor said with a flick of her hair.

'Then what would you suggest?' the merchant asked.

'Two silver temples. Winner takes all.'

The merchant baulked at that price, and so did Ardan. It was all he had.

The priest of Lucifer smiled and laid two coins down on the table. A clink of coins followed as the Sailor laid her coins down. The man laid four coins for the over-perfumed couple.

'Oh, are you sure?' the woman asked.

'Of course, it's no problem,' he said, a little wide-eyed.

Ardan looked behind him but could find no help from his sister. His brother shrugged and nodded. He took out the two silver temples, leaving only a couple of coppers. He let out a long breath. It was all on the line now.

The five of them looked at the merchant expectantly. The man eyed the coins in the centre of the table.

'Go on, even the kid put in money,' the sailor said.

The merchant eyed the woman before he eventually opened his purse and pulled out two silvers. He fingered them before he put them down with a clink of finality.

The sailor snatched up the dice and rolled. She drew the Baron. Then it was Ardan's turn, and he drew the Archbishop. The priest was the last, picking up the Waterlord. The merchant shuffled the deck and Ardan cut it. They all drew their cards.

Ardan kept his face blank as he looked over his cards. They were okay, but nothing brilliant. He hoped it would be enough. The only time he had played in a game like this was with his family and those had been all-out free for all. This was different. The sailor was the first to roll, advancing her piece far on the board. Ardan used some of his turn to lay down some cards.

So the game went, and each player moved, careful not to attract much attention. This kept up until they were entering the midrange of the board. Ardan was careful to keep his piece near the centre of the pack, with the priest. Out front was the over-perfumed man. The sailor was close behind. The cards on the table surrounding each player were becoming exorbitant, and none would make the first move lest they attract retribution. As they drifted through the middle of the board, Ardan kept drawing new cards, first the Excommunication card, then the Peasant Revolt, and lastly the Holy Crusade. His breath caught. He already had the Assassin and the Seductress in play. They were the same cards his mother had used to beat him in their first game. He realised his breath had caught and tried to act normal. Everyone seemed absorbed in their own cards, except for the priest, who smiled at him. Ardan didn't like it.

The perfumed man was the first to make a move for the throne. He used all his rolls for movement instead of defence or attack. He advanced wildly, making himself quite the target. The priest was the first to attack, and then the sailor. It went around the table with everyone, except his date, taking a sizeable chunk out of him. The next turn he tried to recover, but everyone kept up their attack, with the merchant knocking him off the board.

The overly perfumed man looked down, hoping something in his cards might magically save him before he eventually folded. 'I'll just sit here until the end of the game,' he said with a forced smile.

'I'm afraid that won't be possible, sir. If you wish to stay you can, but it will have to be in the spectator area,' the usher said, indicating the circle around the table.

'Of course,' he replied, trying to laugh it off as he rose stiffly out of his chair.

The next round, the players returned to their cautious advance until it got to the well-dressed woman. She glared at the merchant as she rolled her dice. She used every card at her disposal to attack him while the merchant desperately rallied his defence.

Ardan, the sailor and the priest quickly left them behind. They were getting closer to the end of the board, but none of them broke ranks. It was the sailor who broke the stalemate when she rolled high. She used it all for movement.

It was Ardan's turn. He tried to read the priest, but the man seemed almost bored by the game. Ardan rolled the dice. A decently high number lay out in front of him. He could chase the sailor but she would still likely reach the throne first. Pursing his lips in thought, he knew he had to go on the offensive. *How much do I need to throw at her but still keep myself in the game?* Ardan wondered. He kept his mother's cards in reserve and threw everything else he had against the sailor.

'Little shit,' she swore at him as many of her defences went down.

The well-dressed woman and the merchant continued their own private war until it got around to the priest. He continued the assault on the sailor. He wiped out all but one of her cards.

'Hah!' she yelled in triumph.

Ardan felt deflated. She would likely make it to the throne on the next roll. He should have attacked harder. The priest laid down one last card. The Tidal Wave. It stopped her from moving unless she rolled high.

The sailor looked at the dice and smiled, showing a wide set of teeth. If she rolled right, she would be the winner. The rattle of the dice reverberated around the room as everyone watched with bated breath. She threw the dice. They rolled and bounced across the table, eventually coming to show their faces.

'Fuck that and fuck you. Dirt eaters and demonspawn!' she yelled, standing up so abruptly that her chair was knocked backwards. She picked up her ale and stared at it for a moment before she threw its contents over the priest. She had a satisfied smirk on her face before she walked towards the exit.

'Ma'am, if you leave then that will forfei—ah,' the usher's speech was interrupted as she shoved him on her way out.

They all stared at her retreating form in silence, with furtive glances cast at the priest. They had all heard stories about the Black Clergy.

'I thought she took her loss rather well, don't you?' the priest said, still dripping with ale.

Nervous laughter broke the tension. The usher came over with some clean napkins to help mop up the priest. Ardan studied the board; the others were too far removed to matter. It was just him and the priest now. Ardan looked at his five cards: the Excommunication, Peasant Revolt, Holy Crusade, Seductress and Assassin. They were his mother's cards. Ardan tried not to ignore the money piled off to the side of the table. He returned his focus to his cards.

After what seemed like an age, they were ready to resume. Ardan took the dice and rolled. His shoulders slumped. The numbers were low. He advanced a few spaces and passed the dice. The merchant and the woman kept up their own internal war and then it came to the priest. He rolled a high number and moved his piece forward. The priest was now closer to the throne than the sailor had been. Ardan's turn came, and he rolled high enough to use his cards. He put down the same order his mother had used against him, urging her luck to help him.

The priest smiled and laid down his defence: Waterways, River Guardians, Shapers and Ships. Used by the Waterlord, they were powerful. Ardan's cards were better, but if the priest rolled high, then he'd save himself. The priest picked up the dice, looking completely at ease. Ardan could feel beads of sweat forming on his spine. The priest rattled the dice in his hands and threw. They bounced and spun across the table, coming to rest face up. A perfect twelve. Ardan looked at the dice as though he had been punched in the gut.

'Lucifer's luck,' the priest said, smiling.

The people surrounding the table burst into applause. It was only then that Ardan realised how many people had watched the last moments. He avoided looking behind him, willing this not to be real.

The dice were passed around the table one last time. The priest rolled the dice; it was enough. He moved his piece to sit on the throne.

The game was over.

'The day is mine,' the priest said and picked up the coins. Ardan sat there in mute silence. The priest kissed the symbol of Lucifer before letting it fall. He spread his hand in an odd farewell before he left the room.

Ardan watched the priest leave, with their hopes of staying in the sanctity of Mercenary Square with him. He felt an anger rise up in him. He hated feeling helpless. Before he knew what he was doing, he was hobbling out the door, leaving Davan and Liá behind, as he pursued the priest.

CHAPTER TWELVE: AN EXPENSIVE COIN

* * *

As our numbers dwindled, the humans grew more plentiful. Their power grew, and they became harder to control. The endless war shaped them into something barbaric. The atrocities they committed in our name will haunt me for millennia.
— Zadkiel, *The Chronicles of Eden*

* * *

ARDAN KEPT JOSTLING people as he chased after his quarry. People naturally made a path around the priest, but as soon as he passed, they closed ranks again. Ardan tried to push through, but he bumped into a burly man with the tattoo of a ship on his arm.

'Watch it,' the man said in a thick accent. He gave Ardan a cuff across the head that made him stumble. By the time he'd recovered, the priest was gone. Ardan assumed he was making for the main exit and pushed his way through the crowd as quickly as he could. He received more than a few curses before he broke free into the brisk night air.

He caught one glimpse of the dark robes before they disappeared around the corner.

'Ardan!' he heard his brother shout from inside.

He ignored the call and sped up, his injured leg aching. He gripped his sword and rounded the corner. The priest was a dozen paces away. Doubt suddenly plagued him, and he kept some distance. What would he do to a priest of the Dark? Every street presented a new excuse; there were too many people on this street, too few on the next. What would he do if there was no one to intervene? How would he deal with someone if they did? These thoughts continued until the Black Temple loomed up in front of them. The ominous pyramid blocked out the evening sky. Whatever he was going to do needed to happen before they reached the Temple. Ardan steeled his resolve, banishing the thoughts that this was suicidal, and quickened his pace. The priest turned to greet him.

'I was wondering if you were ever going to build up the courage to confront me.'

'I want that money,' Ardan said.

'So?'

Ardan hesitated. 'Give it to me.'

'Or else?' The priest said, a small smile playing on his lips.

Ardan felt distinctly unsettled by it. Bedtime stories about the powers of the Black Clergy rose in his mind. He pushed those thoughts down and drew his sword. 'I mean it.'

'First time using that sword?' the priest asked.

'No.' Ardan suddenly felt self-conscious. He stepped forward and held the sword at what he hoped was a menacing angle. 'I don't want to ask again.'

The priest raised an eyebrow in response. 'Alright, I'll give you the winnings, provided you give me a good reason why I should.'

Ardan stared, unsure he heard him right. The priest folded his arms and looked at him expectantly. He lowered the point of his sword while he thought about it. 'It is for the safety of my sister and me.'

'That's it? How disappointing. Try again.'.

It felt like the priest was toying with him. Ardan raised the sword again; it came up much more naturally this time. 'How about I stick you with this thing if you don't?'

The priest gave a broad smile. 'Better, but still no.' He raised his left arm, palm outstretched. Ardan thought it was a trick of the light, but the Priest's hand was getting darker. The same liquid darkness he'd thrown at the tree congealed and pooled. It broke into steams, dancing across his fingers and around his hand. 'I am Esalon, of the Black Clergy. I have enough power to give pause to anyone, angel or Ancient. Who are you to me?'

Something inside Ardan stirred in response to the Darkness. The strange sensation banished the fear he should have felt.

'Priests are just people, like anyone else,' Ardan quoted, 'Which means you'll bleed just as much as anyone when I cut you with this.'

Esalon gave a huff of laughter and lowered his hand. 'You've got fire, boy. I like that. Not enough to give you the money, but there's something about you,' he paused, musing. He reached for a small pouch at his belt and pulled out a single silver coin. 'Take this,' he said and flicked it towards Ardan. The coin spun in the air before landing on the cobblestones with a definitive clink. The image of Lucifer was clearly visible on its surface.

'What in the nine hells am I supposed to do with this?' Ardan said.

'It will spend with those who follow Lucifer.'

Ardan glanced at the coin and then stared hard at Esalon.

'Just give me the silver.'

'The audacity, my boy, is wearing thin. Take the coin with good grace and go.'

When Ardan didn't move, Esalon raised his left arm in response.

Ardan hesitated only a moment before he said, 'To the hells with it.'

The dancing, spinning black liquid reappeared around Esalon's hand. It pooled together and shot forward, striking Ardan's chest like a hammer. He cartwheeled and landed on the cobblestones, his sword skittering away. All the air was driven from his lungs. He tried to draw in breath but couldn't. Deep in his mind, he knew he was winded, but that didn't stop him from trying to suck in more air. It took a few panicked seconds, or minutes, he wasn't sure, before his lungs started working again and he could breathe enough to sate the burning sensation in his chest.

'I look forward to seeing you again,' Esalon said at some point during the ordeal.

Ardan didn't try to get up until he could breathe without concentrating. He rose unsteadily to his feet and shakily retrieved his sword and sheathed it, before hobbling over to the coin. Lucifer was imprinted on the surface, the angular face framed by his wings, a small smile playing on the devil's lip. He picked it up. The metallic surface felt as cold as the winter sea. Ardan tested the weight, thinking the coin felt unusually heavy for its size. No matter which way he angled the coin, Lucifer stared straight at him.

'There you are,' a voice roared at him.

Ardan looked up to see Davan striding towards him, fists clenched, his face a furious thundercloud. Before he could say anything, Davan's fist lashed out. Pain exploded across Ardan's cheek, and he tumbled, landing in a sprawl on the ground again.

'Davan!' Liá cried.

'What do you think you were doing, running off like that? You chased a flaming priest of the Dark! Are you insane?' Davan said as he paced back and forth in front of Ardan. His hands kept clenching and unclenching. Ardan got to his knees, tense, in case Davan hit him again. But Liá came to stand between them, staring directly at Davan.

'Thanks,' Ardan said.

Lia turned and glared at him. 'He's right, you know. We don't want to lose you, too. It was foolish, and I expect better of you.'

Ardan looked down at the ground, feeling further deflated. Both his siblings had left their mark.

'I'm sorry, I wasn't thinking.'

'I flaming know!' Davan shouted.

'I just, I don't know, I thought I had won and that we could all go to the Square. I wanted to fix it and it was the only thing I could think of.'

Silence fell over them.

'You deserve to be dead. It's Lucifer's luck you're not.'

'He said that if I could provide him with a good reason, he'd give me the coins. I tried, but he said no. So I attacked him, or tried to anyway.'

'You ... attacked him?'

'He struck me down with some black shadow or something. It took the wind out of me, but I'm okay.'

'You really are as dumb as horse dung,' Davan said.

'He gave me this coin,' Ardan said, showing them the silver coin. 'It's better than nothing.'

'It doesn't matter. It's not enough. We'll check home one last time, but after that we're going to the Cathedral,' Davan said. Liá wanted to say something, but Davan interrupted, 'We're nearly out of time. If you want my help, then this is it.'

Liá closed her mouth.

Davan led the way while Liá and Ardan followed in silence. They left behind the sleek wood buildings of the Dark Quarter to walk amongst the old stone buildings of the Ancient Quarter as they moved onto more familiar roads.

When they neared home, Ardan could see that the shutters of their house were open. They all stopped. There were more shadows moving through their home.

'Mother's back,' Liá exclaimed.

'No, wait,' Davan called, but he was too late. She was already running towards the house. Ardan and Davan ran after her, but she was too quick, pulling the door open.

Davan and Ardan arrived a moment later.

Inside were four men wearing chainmail, each with a sword strapped to his belt. They had all stopped in the act of looting the home. One was looking beneath the pallets, another was shifting through their father's workbench, while the third held the spoon at the pot. A fourth drew his sword when he saw them in the doorway.

'That's them,' the fourth man called.

Davan had already pulled his axe. Its size would be a disadvantage in such small quarters.

'Don't let them leave!' one of them yelled.

The man with the drawn sword advanced, but Davan reacted first. He stepped forward and jabbed out with the top of the axe, hitting the man in the chest with enough force to send him flailing backwards. He then turned, grabbed Liá, and launched her outside.

'Run!' he yelled.

Despite the fear in her eyes, Liá took off.

Ardan looked back at Davan, who stood in the doorway.

'Get her out of here,' he ordered without turning. He had stepped back from the entrance, giving him room to swing his axe but still bottlenecking the men inside. Ardan drew his sword too. 'I can outrun them, just go!' Davan screamed, as he swung his axe at the first man, who threw himself backwards to avoid it and crashed into the others.

'Work as a team, always.' He could hear his father's voice. 'Even bad orders are better than no orders.'

Ardan turned and ran after Liá, quietly hating himself for how quickly he did so. She was a shadow in the distance. He glanced back at Davan, who was swinging his axe wildly. He awkwardly sheathed his sword while running, trying to keep Liá in sight. There was a shout behind him. Two men had gotten past Davan and were now running in their direction.

Ahead, Liá darted down another alley. Ardan followed. He had no idea how she could run so fast in that brown dress of hers, but he wasn't complaining. His fear lent him strength, and he hobbled as fast as he could, following her as she wound herself down the maze of streets, twisting and turning. She slowed, so that they ran together. His injuries were flaring painfully, and he knew he couldn't keep this up for long. He smelt something awful coming from one alley. An idea struck him, and he reached out, just managing to get a hold of his sister. Without a word, he pulled Liá into it. She understood. They hid behind the refuse that had piled up alongside the walls.

They were both breathing heavily, trying to catch their breath, when they heard footfalls slapping hard on the cobblestones. Liá looked at Ardan and he could see the whites of her eyes.

The footfalls slowed and then stopped.

Ardan tried desperately to quiet his breathing, his chest burning, but it sounded like a howling wind. Fear gripped him—they would surely hear him.

'Where in the name of the angels did they go?' a gruff voice said.

'Hells if I know, but we got to find them.'

'Where then?'

'You head to the Docks, and I'll head to the Light Quarter.'

'You don't think they'll head back home?'

'Quinn will be there if they do.'

'Right,' the gruff voice replied.

Ardan and Liá stayed still until the sound of their footsteps disappeared.

'You don't think they got Davan, do you?' Liá asked quietly.

'With that ridiculous axe of his?' Ardan whispered back, trying to make light of it. 'No, he gave us enough time to run, and then he would have, too.'

'But what if they caught him?'

'No way. He'd have kept ahead of them. They are wearing mail and he didn't have any armour. He would have been able to outrun them for sure.'

Liá mulled over that, chewing her lip, before she nodded. 'Good.'

'We will wait here until morning when people are moving again, then we'll head for the Cathedral.'

'Here?' she said, looking around them, her nose wrinkling from the stench of the refuse in the alley.

Ardan nodded. They tried to make themselves as comfortable as possible in the alley. They sat against the wall, using each other to keep warm. Despite what he'd said about Davan, doubt gnawed at him. Had the men got him? Who were they and what were they after? Why had the priest given him the silver coin? Would the Cathedral accept them in the morning? What in the nine hells had happened to his mother? As the thoughts weighed him down, he realised how much he had taken his old life for granted. He tried to recall the comfort of it as he sidled up against the cold stone walls, while the stink of the alley suffocated him.

CHAPTER THIRTEEN: SANCTUARY

hen rivers of fire flowed from the mountains and killed a battalion of human warriors, I thought it was the Ancients. Then the tidal waves came, walls of water smashing over the lowlands. The mountains erupted, shaking Eden for days on end while they filled the sky with ash and soot. I thought it was the end times. Eden itself had risen in response to our war. It destroyed entire civilisations while angels, demons and Ancients all fell to its retribution.

— Zadkiel, *Chronicles of Eden*

ARDAN WATCHED the morning light slowly illuminate the grey clouds blanketing the sky. He hadn't dared fall asleep in case the people hunting them returned. It was finally light enough to move through the streets. With some difficulty, he got up, his muscles stiff from sitting against the stone. He cracked his back, trying to get the kinks out before gently waking Liá. She blinked a few times, her mouth opening into a wide yawn. Ardan cautiously looked out from the end of the alley. Enough people were moving through the streets for them to blend in.

As soon as they left the alley, Ardan took a deep breath. It felt as fresh as the highest hill in the forest. Breathing in that reeking alley had been like inhaling through a blanket of garbage.

He could see the Cathedral from the distance, the immense structure jutting out into the skyline. Without a word, they both started walking towards it. Davan knew to find them there; he would come for them. It was an idea that Ardan kept telling himself, desperately quashing the thought that his brother might be injured. He was so lost in his thoughts that he didn't notice the people in the streets carved a path around them, wrinkling their noses as they passed.

Small churches appeared on street corners. They passed a candle shop with living quarters above. An image of Zadkiel was rendered in plaster above the shop entrance.

The sound of synchronised marching drew Ardan's attention. There was a contingent of guards coming towards them, their feet beating on the ground like a drum. In orderly lines, their eyes trained forward, the men marched with spears and shields. They wore matching leather armour and uniform tabards emblazoned with silvery holy fire.

Ardan and Liá continued their journey deep into the Light Quarter. The stone buildings were free of the moss commonly seen in the Ancient Quarter. The major streets were cleaner, but there were considerably more refuse-filled alleys. People looked down their noses at them as they passed, taking in their dirty appearance.

From this distance, they could make out the stained-glass windows of the Cathedral. Yet despite how close it appeared, it took them another thirty minutes before they made it to Heaven's Way, the wide street that led directly to the Cathedral. By the time they reached the doors, they were both flushed from exercise. Above the large oak doors were the carved figures of the seven archangels. They stood there looking down at them, their expressions grim. Ardan was so caught up in them that he didn't notice one of the church guards was shouting at him.

'Oi, you deaf?' he said.

'What?' Ardan said, looking around. The church guard had gotten closer to them, the man's expression difficult to read beneath his helm's metal nose guard. The other guard was sitting on the steps, not bothering to get up.

'I said, are you seeking sanctuary?'

'Oh yeah. Yes, we are.'

'It'll be a while yet before they open the doors. The Bishop's the one that decides who can come in,' he said, his voice suddenly breaking into a high-pitched squeak. Ardan realised the guard was much younger than he'd originally thought. The guard looked at them closely. 'Has it started already?'

'Has what started?'

'You know, the war. The succession.'

'I have no idea. I just know that it's dangerous out there.'

'Oh,' he said, disappointed.

'There'll be more than enough blood by the end. Enjoy the peace while it lasts,' the other church guard said. 'If the Bishop grants you entry, mind yourselves in there. The place will become a mite crowded.'

'You lot smell something awful,' the younger guard said.

Ardan shrugged. There was nothing to say to that. Eventually, the young guard went to lounge against the walls of the Cathedral.

The four of them waited in mutual silence as the morning matured, the grey clouds above them darkening. The warmth from their exercise had long since faded, and Ardan pulled his cloak tighter.

A splash of rain hit his cheek, then another. The four of them stood under the limited shelter of the archway as the rain started in earnest, a new chill accompanying it. Any movement of his cloak stole any meagre warmth he had.

'Can you make out the city?' Ardan asked Liá, wanting to take his mind off the cold.

'What?' Liá said.

'Out there. Can you see Ragtown?'

'Yes,' she said tartly.

'Show me.'

She pointed at the crumbling Keep in the centre of the city. Worn and splitting sails, spotty thatch and other makeshift cloths were strung between the ruined walls, earning the place its nickname.

'The Countess's palace?'

It took her longer to find it. The centre of the Merchant Quarter was located there. It wasn't a tall building, but she eventually pointed it out.

'The Dark Temple?'

She pointed at the looming Temple of the Dark on the complete opposite side of the city. A sudden arc of lightning struck behind it, sending a flash of light over the city.

'Shouldn't point at the Darkness like that,' the older guard said.

'You scared of the Dark?' the younger said.

'Aye, and you should be too. Best not to draw attention to yourself.'

The cranking of the lock on the cathedral door interrupted the younger guard's reply. The wood creaked as the doors opened. A tall man with iron-grey hair walked out, dressed for battle. His chainmail clinked as he walked. He carried a long spear with a shield strapped across his back. He adjusted the bags draped over his shoulder and revealed Zadkiel's symbol on his tabard.

Ardan noticed that a second man was following the warrior. He wore the brown habit common for the Clergy of the Light, but he had the faded purple sash of a Bishop. He had rapidly thinning hair that contrasted with his young features. The man was already a Bishop at mid-twenty.

The Bishop looked at the younger guard. 'Corey, can you go to the stables and help Auley bring out the black charger? You know, the young spirited one?' Corey paled at the request. 'He's good with the beast, but I think he might need help.'

Corey nodded, moved, then paused and brought his fist to his chest in a salute before setting off at a run to one of the side gates.

'Are you sure you can't stay?' The Bishop asked, ignoring all but the warrior. 'Your leaving couldn't come at a worse time.'

'It can't wait.'

'They could be nothing more than rumours. You may be risking yourself for nothing when you are needed here.'

The warrior's grey eyebrows furrowed before he replied, 'What you say may be true, and for that, I am sorry. But I must know for certain if Naberius is indeed south of the mountains. The havoc he could cause if left unchecked…. Well, I must learn more.'

The Bishop gave a defeated nod.

The warrior's expression softened. 'You're a good man, Frederick, and more than capable. You do the Light's will.'

'Let's hope it helps me keep this place standing in the coming storm.'

'Blaspheming is beneath you.'

Frederick sighed.

There was a loud neighing and a crack, and the sound of splintering wood. Corey appeared out of the side gate, holding a long leather strap. He was straining hard against it. Then another man appeared, and they slowly dragged a black horse into view. The beast was fighting them every step of the way. Corey gave a tremendous tug. The horse reared up, slashing with its front legs. The two men pulled on the straps while trying to avoid its hooves.

Ardan instinctively stepped in front of Liá.

The warrior walked forward, not pausing as the stallion landed hard on the ground. It tried to bite him, but his hand moved deftly, and he got one hand on the bridle and another on the horse's nose. Something inside of Ardan stirred and his chest fluttered like a bird caught in a windstorm. The feeling fled but left Ardan feeling unsteady. By the time he looked up, the warrior was stroking the horse's nose. The charger's eyes were closing in pleasure at the man's attention.

'Corey, is it?' the warrior asked.

'Uh, yes, your worship.'

'Just call me Phillip.'

'Yes, your Phillip worship.'

Phillip sighed. 'What's his name?' he said, indicating the horse.

Corey looked at Auley.

'Hellion,' Auley said. It earned him a reproachful look from Phillip, and he shrugged defensively. 'I didn't name him. He just is.'

Phillip gave the horse one final scratch before he put his saddle-bags over the back of the horse, adjusting them until they sat comfortably. Once they were set, he swung himself up into the saddle. He nudged his mount over to the Bishop.

'Give me your hand.'

Frederick tentatively reached out a hand, and Phillip grasped it. A glow of light appeared in the warrior and flowed down his arm and into the Bishop. The same sensation surged in Ardan's chest in response to the Light. When they stopped, the sensation vanished.

'You should have kept it for yourself. You'll need it for the forest,' Frederick said.

'I have some to spare. Plus, if you already have more refugees turning up,' he said, with a nod towards Ardan and Liá, 'then you might need it more.'

Frederick nodded. 'May the Light grant you speed.'

'Keep the faith,' Phillip said, adjusting himself for a moment. He looked at the church soldiers and then at Ardan and Liá. He clasped his left fist in the palm of his right, making the sign of Zadkiel, and nudged his heels into the horse's side. It moved forward without hesitation. They watched the warrior disappear down the hill and into the city.

'We can't afford to lose the protection of a Templar at a time like this,' Frederick said.

'No, Bishop,' Corey replied.

Frederick was silent as he gazed at the city. It took some time before he broke his reverie and turned to the others. 'There is much to be done. You two come with me,' he said to Ardan and Liá.

They followed him into the Cathedral.

Stone pillars lined the nave, arching gracefully up across the ceiling. Stained glass murals decorated the walls and wooden benches were uniformly spaced out, focused toward the white marble altar. Hundreds could sit in the room. At the back wall, there were marble statues of the seven Archangels, each standing in their separate alcoves. Ardan had seen the place before, but it never failed to bring awe.

Liá nudged him.

Ardan looked around and realised Frederick was already at the rear doors, waiting for them. He hurried along the stone floor to catch up, imagining his father's instruction to stay aware of his surroundings.

'You're one of the first to arrive. There are some empty cells in the traveller's lodge. We'll put you there for the moment. Though it may not be too long before I have to move you elsewhere,' he said as he walked.

The ringing of hammer on steel greeted them as they left the Cathedral. The stone courtyard expanded out from the rear of the great building. It was its own walled community and was as large as any city block. A well for drinking water stood in the centre, with a variety of buildings spread out around it. They all shared a similar stone construction, with thatched roofs. A blacksmith was hammering on a horseshoe at the smithy, while a glow emanated from the kitchen ovens. The place felt as stark as the darkening storm clouds overhead.

Bishop Frederick was already moving, leading the two of them to one of the larger buildings. It was comprised of a long hallway with doors lining the walls.

'Take the third room on the left—there are two unoccupied pallets in there. I expect the two of you to work while you're here; there's always plenty to do. Not today, though. Take today to ease yourself in. Followers of the Light are always welcome,' Frederick said, his nose wrinkling slightly. 'There's also a small bathhouse near the kitchen where you can wash. I'll find someone to show you around.'

Frederick went to a different room, knocked, and entered a moment later. They could hear him murmuring to someone in there.

Ardan went into their new room. It contained two straw-covered pallets and a small table with an oil lantern beneath a shuttered window. The room was unadorned, save for a small replica of Zadkiel's shield, Red Cross and all, on one wall. Ardan sat on the bed, grateful to be off his feet. His weariness flooded him all at once and he tried to stifle a yawn.

Liá went to their tiny window and opened the shutters, letting light fill the room.

The Bishop reappeared at the doorway, giving a polite knock to get their attention. Next to him was a lanky boy just entering manhood. He had sleek brown hair and a sharp nose that defined his face. It was Regan.

It transported Ardan back in time, to when his father had died. He remembered looking down at his father's form, his lifeblood flowing over his hands. One of the four murderers now stood before him. Ardan felt a rage unlike anything he'd felt before. It surged and rose in him like a tempest. Conscious thought fled him, just like it had in that alley. With a barely human cry, he charged Regan. He wanted to choke him, pummel him, tear him apart. Regan stepped back, eyes wide in sudden terror.

Ardan lunged, trying to rake his fingers across Regan's eyes, but he couldn't quite close the distance. He struggled and clawed, trying as he was to get at one of his father's killers, barely registering that something was holding him back.

'You will calm down,' Frederick's voice thundered through him.

The power inside of Ardan blasted apart, the primal energy emptying out of him. The change was so sudden, it was as though he had woken from a trance. Dizziness overcame him so that he worried he might faint. Then a weariness plagued his entire body, worse than before. He looked up to see Frederick glowing with white light, a single outstretched arm holding him suspended in mid-air.

Regan had his back against the wall, his eyes wide and arms raised defensively. He cautiously lowered them, though he looked like a rabbit ready to bolt.

Frederick lowered Ardan to the ground, the glow around him fading. 'I want an explanation.'

'He killed my father.'

Frederick looked sharply at Regan.

'I didn't.'

'Why do you say he killed your father?' Frederick said, looking back at Ardan.

'Because he did.'

The Bishop pursed his lips, with a barely restrained sigh. 'Tell me what happened, every detail, from the beginning.'

Ardan took a deep breath, his mind still a jumble of rage and confusion. He started slowly, the words tumbling out until he got the story across.

'Now your side,' Frederick said to Regan.

'My father, Cillian, was teaching me how to stalk in the forest. The traps had strange things happen to them. They'd be broken or empty. We couldn't find any of the valuable herbs or plants. Verrick came to us, and said Tristan was stealing from our runs. Said he wanted some backup when we confronted him.'

'Did you know about the Magistrate's coin?'

'No.'

You lying, murderous bastard, Ardan thought. The wild energy in him was back. He recognised it, just barely stopping it from over-whelming him.

'What were you expecting to happen?' Frederick said as he clasped his hands before him.

Regan fidgeted, looking uncomfortable. 'We would demand the things he'd stolen from us back or the money to pay for them. Stop him from doing it in the future.'

Frederick appraised him for a long time. 'Can you tell me truth-fully, under the protection of the Light, that you didn't go there expecting to murder him?'

Regan swallowed before he nodded.

Ardan inwardly seethed, but he held on to his emotions.

'Of *course*, my first refugees have a blood feud going on,' Frederick said to no one in particular. 'Both of you have something to be angry about. One is accused of robbery, the other of murder. Regardless of the past and the expectation of justice, the two of you have claimed sanctuary at this place. I will not tolerate violence in the house of the Light. Is that understood?' Frederick said, rising to his full height, glowing with white light again. He stared both of them down, his grey eyes unrelenting.

They both acquiesced.

The Bishop's glow faded, and he looked normal again. 'Good. We of the Light have to weather these crises together. But I am not naïve enough to believe it will happen without help. The two of you will have duties, but rest assured they won't be together.'

CHAPTER FOURTEEN: STONE AND LIGHT

* * *

I lost track of time during those years. It could have been decades while we were shepherding ourselves and our followers from one place to the next, trying to survive. Disease and starvation were as deadly as Eden's wrath, or our wars with the Darkness and the Ancients.
— Zadkiel, *Chronicles of Eden.*

* * *

ARDAN'S BREATH misted in the late autumn air. *It is cold enough for an angel to freeze their wings off,* he thought, pulling his cloak tighter. The glow from the kitchen ovens was the only illumination in the grey stone courtyard. Liá bumped into him, shivering slightly as they made their way towards the glow. The kitchen had a high slate roof but was otherwise open to the elements. They'd been working under Donnacha, the Cathedral's cook, since shortly after their arrival here.

The man was already moving. His muscular forearms hefted the large pot around his round belly. He flashed them his usual smile. He rubbed his hands on his apron, leaving smudge marks on the otherwise clean cloth, then spread his hands, indicating they could take whatever duty they felt like performing.

The warm fire and the pleasant aroma of the baking bread greeted Ardan like old friends. Liá moved to the large pot, now sitting on the fire. The three of them fell into the routine of making and kneading the dough, baking the bread, tending the fires and stirring the porridge. None of them strayed far from the warmth of the oven while they worked. The food cooked as dawn gave way to day.

When the sun was peeking above the valley hills, the refugees appeared. Men and women like Ardan began emerging from the Cathedral and the travellers' lodge. They fanned out, going to the half-constructed buildings being built along the courtyard walls. The Bishop came out in his plain brown habit to confer with the master builder, a squat, balding man who liked to wring his hands.

Ardan returned his focus to the ovens, using the long wooden paddles to pull out the baked bread. He put the quickly growing rows of bread onto the serving line.

Soldiers walked out of the barracks. Two scores of armed men and women took their rations, devouring them with quiet efficiency, before forming up. Their lines were crisp, with sound shields and rust-free spears. White tunics emblazoned with the holy fire insignia covered their leather armour.

The sergeant shouted and the troops turned, marching in sync out of the main gate. The sound of their footsteps echoed off the cobble-stones long after they were out of sight.

About ten minutes after the morning patrol had left, the night patrol returned. Their steps were still in sync despite tired eyes and hunkered forms. They were dirty, but this morning their spears and tunics were free of blood, though several sported fresh bandages.

Donnacha was filling bowls with thick porridge. Without a word, Ardan took the bowls and lined them up on the counter. The soldiers would walk past, barely saying a word as they took their food.

They had no respite, as the refugees glanced towards them with envious eyes. Ardan fell into his routine, using the long paddle to switch out the baked loaves with the uncooked ones, and kneading the dough as soon as Donnacha made more. Liá started a new pot of porridge. The queue of refugees kept getting longer as more arrived every day.

'That should be enough bread for now, Ardan my boy,' Donnacha said, clapping a hand on his shoulder. 'But there's more work to do, even though our stores are full to bursting, the Bishop wants more. So, you know what we're going to do?'

'Get more?'

'Exactly right, my boy. Exactly right,' Donnacha said. The Bishop was out in the courtyard, helping hoist some thatch to the roof weavers. 'He struck a deal with the Dock Master, so we're getting more fish delivered than we can rightly eat. So we're going to cure them. Do you know how to cure fish?'

Ardan shook his head.

'Easy to do. Clean them, chuck them in a barrel of salt.'

Ardan ignored the obvious oversimplification. 'What are we doing first, curing the fish or making beer?'

'No beer today. Can't get the grain, farmers won't harvest until next week. They're gambling, they are, with everything going on, but not my problem. Ah, here we are,' Donnacha said, brushing his hands on his now-dirty apron.

A man leading a donkey cart came through the main gate. He wore the thin clothing common among Dock workers. His skin was as dry and weathered as old leather. He whipped and cursed at his donkey, despite the animal neither slowing nor stopping.

'Unload it over at the tables,' Donnacha called.

The cart driver spat on the ground and complied.

'Help him out, would you?' Donnacha said to Ardan.

Ardan had barely made it to the cutting tables before the first fish was thrown at him. He deposited it on the table, barely turning before another was flying at him. The slick scales slid through his hands, but he caught it by the tail, flinging it neatly next to the first. He spun, catching the next one just in time.

So that's how it's going to be, Ardan thought. Fish after fish, Ardan caught them and kept up, never making a mistake. The dockworker scowled.

'If a fish hits the ground, I won't pay a bent copper for it,' Donnacha said from the kitchen door, brandishing the wooden spoon like a sword.

'Ain't my fault if he can't keep up.'

'Not one bent copper.'

The fisherman grumbled, his expression turning sullen, but he slowed. Ardan didn't bother to hide his smirk. When they'd finished, the driver spat on the ground, collected his coins and led the donkey and cart out the gate.

'Clean the fish, I'll get the barrels and the salt,' Donnacha called.

Ardan took a knife from the kitchen and returned to the cutting tables. Memories flooded into him of the forest and the first time he'd cleaned a fish. The crystal-clear flowing waters, deep in the forest, his father standing waist deep in the middle of the river, arms submerged and perfectly still. With a sudden movement, he had caught a fish, and thrown it to shore, before repeating the process again a few minutes later. He'd shown Ardan the trick of it, although, like most things, his father had made it look easy. It had taken hours before Ardan had gotten lucky. He'd grasped the fish and barely got it to shore before dropping it. Yet he could see the pride in his father's eyes.

Grief flowed through him, and he suppressed it, focusing on the fish as he gutted it and threw the offal in the bucket for the pigs. He took the fish and hung it on the racks to dry. He found a certain monotony in the work.

'That's enough for now,' Donnacha said from the kitchen doorway. Ardan blinked, realising the sun was high in the sky. 'Nip straight into the kitchen and get your food. Come back this afternoon—we've got more work to do.'

'We've got classes,' Liá said.

Donnacha held up some fingers, counting them off until realisation dawned on his face. 'I lost track of the days. Of course, you do. Hmmm, I'll manage, but come back right after you're done.'

Ardan and Liá assented, waving farewell while they took their bowls to eat in the stone courtyard. The porridge was so thick Ardan had to force his spoon through it. He took a bite, and the warmth moved through him, combined with a hint of cinnamon.

They ate as they walked. They went past the queue of refugees lining up for the kitchen, men and women bundled up in older clothes, while children clung to their mothers' skirts, or ran and played together in the courtyard.

Regan's head stood above those around him. His once sleek brown hair had become increasingly greasy. 'How did you skip the line?' he asked.

A few people looked curiously towards Liá and Ardan.

'We helped cook it,' Liá said.

'We all do work around here. Doesn't mean we get to skip the line.'

'You think you're better than us?' Turlach said. He was a recent addition to the refugees who had immediately taken to Regan. In his early twenties, he was stocky and had a perpetually grubby face, even if had just left the baths.

'No,' Ardan said, but he could see the other refugees glancing at each other.

'Hey Donnacha, why do they get served without waiting in line?' Regan called out. 'Even before some of the soldiers?'

Several refugees began muttering to each other.

Donnacha looked up from serving more bowls of porridge. His voice boomed across the courtyard. 'They've been working with me hours before any of you have gotten up. Anyone got a problem with me rewarding people for working?'

Silence stretched over the waiting refugees. No one spoke.

'And you, both of you,' Donnacha said, holding his spoon towards Regan and Turlach. The surrounding people took a step back, as though the cook was aiming a crossbow. 'Next time you want to accuse others, make sure you're not slacking yourself. I've seen the work you put in. You should leave the line and wait at the back. If there're any scraps left, I might let you have them.'

Ardan watched Regan and Turlach grumble, shuffling their feet as they went to the rear. He took a large bite of porridge while holding eye contact. Regan glared back. Ardan knew it didn't help, but he didn't care.

'I'm glad the Bishop took your weapons,' Liá said.

Ardan grunted. The first time they'd gotten into a fight, the Bishop had confiscated their weapons. He knew their quarrelling was wearing on the Bishop's patience, but Regan was one of his father's murderers, and the debt had to be paid.

CHAPTER FIFTEEN: THE BURNING FIELDS

***

he humans were the ones that survived and eventually prospered under Eden's relentless onslaught. Power built up wherever they settled. They somehow drew on the energy of the world to create strongholds of Light, Darkness and the mysterious power of the Ancients. These places acted as buffers against Eden's wrath.
— Zadkiel, *Chronicles of Eden*

***

THE MIDDAY LIGHT shone through stained glass windows, illuminating the Cathedral hall in a beautiful collage of colours. Ardan and Liá stepped onto the white marble of the dais before moving down to the main aisle. They walked past the makeshift living quarters that had been set up between the pews. The refugees slept on stone floors and wooden benches. Even with the new buildings outside, housing would soon be cramped.

Liá brushed past Ardan, oblivious to his brooding, and straight into the transept. It brought him back to the present, and he followed her to the impromptu classroom.

Delaney stood in the centre, his pot belly barely held in by his leather jerkin. Twenty chairs were spread out in a semicircle, creating a small amphitheatre. The students were mostly around Ardan and Liá's age, but there were a few older people, including one wizened older woman hunched over in her chair.

'Some newcomers—fantastic,' Delaney said. 'We're taking a break from Waterlord numbers for a while. Instead, I've brought one of the few books I've got about the history of Barleron. I've always loved this city. It is the only place where the angels, demons and Ancients met without the intent to kill. We will cover it all, but where should we start?'

A general silence fell over them. There were rarely any comments; they usually let Delaney dictate the direction of the lessons.

'The civil wars,' Ardan said.

Delaney clasped his hands together as though he were about to receive a warm meal.

'I'd like to hear about that too,' said a man, folding his arms, emphasising his tanned, corded muscles.

'I assume you mean what we're going through at the moment?' Delaney said. 'Because when the angels, demons and Ancients were here, it was quite the—'

'The civil wars,' the man repeated.

'Of course, the relevance. I understand yes, indeed. The successions, or civil wars, have been going on for over sixty years. I trust we all know about the Purge?' Delaney looked around, his expression ever hopeful. No one said anything. 'Well, the nobles under Duke Widseth ordered the forest to be felled to create more farming land. The forest creatures didn't take kindly to it. Neither did the Children. They fought back, and the loggers started falling to raids and other nastiness. The death toll was high, and production slowed.'

'What does this have to do with this war?' the man interrupted.

'I'm always impatient to know more about history but understanding first needs a foundation. They pushed the peasants too far. A rebellion began under Áengus the Bloody. I could do a whole lesson on him, but I'll try to keep to the civil wars. They killed most of the nobles; the Countess and a few of the lesser gentry escaped. Blood literally ran through the gutters. I really don't think calling it 'the Purge' does it justice, do you? Anyway, the ruling class of the city was suddenly gone, a prime opportunity for anyone, including the religions of Dark or Light. It is quite curious—'

'Stick with the wars.'

Delaney's smile faltered for the first time. He turned his full attention to the man. 'You are new to my class and wish to learn, which is admirable. We show respect to everyone and listen to what they have to say. Is that understood?'

The man glared at Delaney, but the teacher took it, neither smiling nor backing down. Eventually, the scarred man broke eye contact, muttering under his breath.

'You are right, though; there is enough to cover with just the wars without getting distracted,' Delaney continued, his smile returning. 'Owing to the civil wars, the death of the nobility created a power vacuum. If Àengus had lived, it might have been different, but he didn't.'

'What happened?' Liá asked.

'Records during that time are scarce, so I don't know. Arguments started after his demise—his brothers and sons fought—and it began the first succession. None of his male kin survived, and the city was subjected to more death and destruction. Fiona the Beautiful was the one to bring stability. They say men were struck dumb by her beauty. Flawless skin, golden hair, a stunning figure and a voice that would melt the hardiest of men. She brought the city together, for a few years at least. Then she caught a sickness, which left her bedridden. As she was no longer able to control the masses, the next succession began.'

Delaney continued, his story going from one name to another. Sometimes the succession would last years, with different people controlling different parts of the city, in others control was seized within a month or two.

'The Magistrate held the rulership over this city the longest. Even the Cathedral and Temple of Darkness would answer his call and pay tribute. With his death, well, the power vacuum was back.'

'So, who's going to rule now?' the scarred man asked.

'It is always hard to know. Before the Magistrate fell, I would have said Amado of the Establishment, but he burned alive when his rivals torched the place.'

Ardan's jaw fell. They had torched the Establishment? He remembered there being dozens of guardsmen around the place. Lost in thought, he didn't hear what Delaney was saying.

'In short, all the major players are dead, fled, or in hiding.'

A hushed silence fell over all of them. Delaney didn't need to say it, but they all understood the implications. The war would drag out.

'Would the Countess take control?' Liá asked. All eyes turned towards her, and she flushed at the sudden attention.

'She'd want to,' the man said. 'Them nobles always want the peasants to suffer. Keep themselves in power.'

Delaney tapped a finger on his chin. 'It is possible, though I very much doubt it. We don't know who killed the Magistrate or why.'

Ardan thought back to the fishmonger's words. Had his mother been involved? And if so, where was she? He heard his father's voice float in his head. '*Keep your attention on the here and now, dream when you fall asleep.*' He returned his attention to Delaney. 'The mercenaries are a solid force, so someone would need to get them—'

'Who is most likely to take control?' the man interrupted.

Delaney paused, holding eye contact until the scarred man muttered an apology.

'The Ancient Quarter has no leadership yet. The Dock Master is keeping the Docks running as smoothly as he can, and Light help us, the Fiddler seems to be taking control of Ragtown. Both of them haven't been pushing too hard. One thing seems to be consistent: whoever acquires too much power quickly ends up dead.'

A heavy silence fell over the classroom. Ardan could see Delaney almost preening. He knew the teacher loved having an impact like this on his class. The teacher opened his mouth to speak again, but then there was raised voices coming from the courtyard.

It quickly devolved into yelling and shouting.

One of the side doors burst open and several guardsmen piled in.

'Stay where you are,' the leader commanded.

'Goodman, what is happening?' Delaney called.

'A demon, a demon from Hell is outside the walls of Barleron,' one of the younger guardsmen said.

There were gasps from the class.

'Don't be foolish,' an older guardsman snapped.

Ardan felt his heart sink. He had heard stories of demons attacking. *Were they under attack?* He thought about his conversation with the mercenary about fighting against Naberius. A three-headed dog as large as a draft horse and breathing demon fire. Gooseflesh rose all over his body as fear gripped him.

There was a heavy boom as the guards dropped a beam, barring the door. At the same time, the doors from the courtyard opened and guards, monks and refugees alike began filling the hall.

The Bishop entered the hall, a small glow of white light around him. He strode to the altar as people called out to him.

'Is a demon attacking the city?'

'The Light protect us.'

'Quiet,' Frederick called. His voice carried power, flowing through the hall, creating a stillness in Ardan and quelling his fears. He suddenly felt ashamed of how he'd reacted, getting caught up in everyone else's panic. 'A fire has started outside the walls. The fields are ablaze. I am locking down the Cathedral until we know more. Anyone not part of the church guard will stay inside the Cathedral. No one is to leave until we're certain what's going on.'

'Are we under attack?'

'No, but I am not taking any chances. For now, be patient and do not get in the guards' way.'

Someone else called out something, but Ardan nudged Liá and whispered, 'The tower?'

Her eyes widened for a second before she nodded.

The two of them slipped out among the confusion. They took to the spiralling staircase at the rear of the hall. It was eerily quiet as they climbed the stairs, circling the bell tower rope. Ardan's legs burned as they climbed. By the time they reached the top, he was breathing hard.

The bell tower offered a fantastic view of Barleron, the surrounding forest and the ocean itself. Its normally serene view had been shattered by an angry red glow illuminating the skyline. A column of black smoke simultaneously rose like a tower of darkness. A third of the fields outside Barleron were being consumed by flame.

Bucket brigades were mobilising, but the flame was moving too fast. Many quickly abandoned it, retreating inside the protection of the city walls.

A shout came from the courtyard. Ardan glanced at Liá, who was looking on in horror at the spreading fire. Church soldiers were pouring out from the barracks, forming up in their platoons. The Master of the Guard shouted orders, and soon the guards were marching out into the city.

They watched them go. There was little else they could do except watch, as the flames consumed the fields outside the walls, destroying buildings and crops in their destructive path. People were trapped out there, unable to get past the fires and to the city. One by one, they retreated into the forest. *Light protect them*, he thought.

Despite the distance, it felt as hot as when he worked the ovens, while gusts of wind brought up the acrid smell of smoke.

Ardan hated feeling useless, hated not being able to do anything. He wanted to go out there, but what could he do, even if he got past the church guards? In the end, he continued his vigil as night fell. Some spot fires made it inside the walls, but the bucket brigades stopped the flames from spreading.

The fire paused at the forest, as though the trees were resisting the flames. But eventually, the wood caught alight, the conflagration spreading out into the valley and up the escarpment. Thick black smoke blotted out the stars.

'Are we going to be okay?' Liá asked.

Ardan wanted to assure her, to say something comforting.

'I don't know,' was all he could manage.

CHAPTER SIXTEEN: EXPLOSION
AT THE BELL TOWER

* * *

hen Eden's fury finally abated, the world had changed. We had changed. Conquest was no longer at the forefront of our minds. There wasn't a peace, but we no longer attacked each other on sight. It is perhaps one of the most significant changes I have ever encountered.
— Zadkiel, *Chronicles of Eden.*

* * *

ARDAN SAT at the top of the bell tower with Liá, their feet dangling over the edge. It had been months since the fields had been torched, and they no longer beheld the orderly lines of crops inside of fences; instead, their view was filled with weeds and the burnt husks of buildings. If Ardan had to pick a point where things had changed, it would be that day.

Within days, refugees had arrived at the Cathedral in droves. Eventually, the Bishop closed the doors to all newcomers. The church soldiers had started coming back from their patrols bloody and wounded. When their numbers dwindled, all able-bodied men were conscripted to service. Oisin, the Master of the Guard, had taken one look at Ardan and said, 'We're not that desperate yet.'

Regan had smirked at him before he too stepped forward.

Ardan felt grim satisfaction when Oisin said, 'Same as him,' hiking a thumb at Ardan. 'I'll get you if we're desperate.'

The courtyard had been converted into a military compound. Ardan, Liá and anyone else not directly serving with the church guard had their living quarters shifted to the Cathedral.

The cramped confines made it difficult to move around. The bell tower was their last solace and escape. Ardan glanced at the harbour, hoping there'd be a trading vessel there. Their presence meant they'd get extra rations that evening, but there was no sign of ships there, nor sails on the horizon.

'You don't think that's our home, do you?' Liá asked.

Ardan's eyes darted over the city, scanning the Ancient Quarter until he spotted the black smoke. It was small; the red glow of the flames wasn't even visible. When the fires got bad, you could smell the smoke up in the tower. It penetrated their clothes, and the stench would follow them for days. When the fires threatened to get out of control, the major forces sprang into action. The standards of the mercenaries could be seen as they fought the blaze, coordinating like an actual battle. When he saw the flag of the Red Wolves, Ardan tried to imagine his brother down there. Still safe, still alive after all this.

'I don't think so,' Ardan replied.

'I hope no one was hurt.'

Their house was built into the side of a hill, making it impossible to see from the tower. He felt a pang of homesickness, missing his mother teaching him how to play Kings, and his father with his endless stream of advice and implacable patience. He looked over at his sister, sitting there in her brown dress. She was all he had left. Ardan made sure no one was coming up the stairs before he pulled out some flat bread from inside his tunic.

'Where did you get that?'

'Took it from Donnacha when he wasn't looking.'

'Oh Ardan, you mustn't. They'll kick you out if they catch you.'

Ardan shrugged. Everyone in the Cathedral was hungry. He understood Frederick restricting their rations. A single cart of fish would arrive most days, but it wasn't enough, and their stores were being ground away. He could see Liá clutching her stomach and curling into a ball when she thought he wasn't looking. Their kitchen shifts made access to the food easy but stealing it was harder than ever. People were always watching. He felt guilty taking the bread, but he would help Liá no matter the cost. He broke the bread in half and gave her the bigger portion. She looked at him reproachfully for a second but it didn't stop her from taking it. She looked at it before she took a huge bite out of it.

'You should take smaller bites,' he said.

'Brrres ors?' she said, with her mouth full of bread.

'What?'

She made eye contact and bit off another piece of bread into her already overloaded mouth, making a face at him. Ardan grinned. She had such difficulty chewing that it looked painful when she finally swallowed. Ardan laughed and her cheeks flushed. He took a bite of his own bread. It was a little stale, but tasted absolutely wonderful, like that first drink of water after a forest run. They ate in silence, but as they were nearing the end, Ardan heard a creak on the wooden stairs. He went still, straining his ears. Another creak.

'Shake off the crumbs, quick,' Ardan hissed.

Liá's eyes went wide, frantically brushing at her brown dress, but there were crumbs everywhere. Ardan went to stall whoever was coming.

It was Regan. Rage bubbled beneath the surface at the sight of his pointed nose. Turlach and Ultan were trailing behind him. Ardan wished he had his sword as he blocked the top of the stairs.

Regan's height brought him to eye level despite being two steps lower. His eyes brushed past Ardan to look at Liá. 'I thought I saw the two of you come up here.'

'What are you doing here?' Ardan snapped.

'So hostile. I was just coming up here for a friendly talk. No harm in that, is there?'

The other two joined him. Ultan was the bigger of the two. The way they looked at Regan made Ardan think of faithful hounds.

'So long as you don't murder more of my family,' Ardan said, stepping back, giving access to the platform.

'If you don't permanently cripple mine,' Regan said.

Ardan knew he'd used his knife to cut Cillian deeply, but permanently? He felt a grim satisfaction.

'Besides, we just came up here for some fresh air. It can get awfully cramped downstairs with all those people hemmed in. Not a lot of room for,' he paused, eyeing Liá up and down, 'Privacy.'

Both Ultan and Turlach laughed.

'We were just finishing up. We'll leave you to your privacy.'

Regan's face darkened. 'You can go, but Liá's staying.'

'It's Liádan to you,' Liá said.

'Maybe if we got to know you better, you'd let us call you Liá,' Regan said. His two dogs laughed dutifully behind him.

Ardan pointed out at the rising smoke. 'Do you think you could survive outside the Cathedral? In that? Frederick's thrown people out for less.'

Regan's eyes wavered between the rising smoke and Liá, but he didn't reply.

Ardan indicated for Liá to move forward. Regan watched with narrowed eyes while Ardan shouldered past him, trying to create a path for her. She was almost clear of them when Turlach's hand reached out and grabbed her arm. Her dress stretched as he dragged her back, revealing the pale skin of her shoulder.

'The Bishop doesn't need to know.'

Ardan lashed out. His fist hit Turlach's face hard enough that he let go of Liá and stumbled back into Regan. Then everything happened at once.

'Go!' Ardan screamed at Liá.

She took one terrified glance at them and started running down the stairs. Ultan made a lunge for her, but Ardan tackled him, the two of them crashing to the floor, dangerously close to the edge. He saw her reach the second landing, sprinting down. Turlach tried to jump over the two of them, but Ardan reached out and caught his ankle. It tripped him, sending him tumbling to land unceremoniously on the first landing. It was enough, Liá was away. She would be in the relative safety of the crowds soon. He disentangled himself from Ultan and got to his feet. By the time he did, Turlach and Regan were both blocking his exit.

'Broke my flaming nose,' Turlach said, wiping the blood that was coming out of his nostrils and looking at it on his hand.

'We've got to entertain ourselves somehow,' Regan said, advancing on Ardan.

Ardan barely heard them. Images were flashing through his head. The men that had killed his father. How helpless he had felt. He distantly felt his arms being restrained. He struggled weakly, but the two people holding his arms held firm. The same feeling of helplessness had fear coursing through him. The fear quickly transformed into anger. It welled up inside him and thundered in his chest.

'This is for my nose,' Turlach said and delivered a blow to Ardan's stomach.

He recognised the same flutter in his chest as when the Templar had calmed the horse. The power that had been threatening to overwhelm him for weeks. He let it flow freely. His vision flashed green and there was a roaring sound in his ears.

He was suddenly on his back, staring at the ceiling of the bell tower. Regan and the others were down, their chests rising and falling, but otherwise motionless. The large cathedral bell moved as though someone had just rung it. Ardan got to his feet a little shakily.

Blood was still coming from Turlach's nose. An image flashed in Ardan's memory of him reaching for Liá. The power welled up in him again, rage overriding thought. Ardan drove a foot straight into Turlach's stomach. His victim groaned and unconsciously curled into a ball. Something bestial had taken over as he struck his victim again. The conscious voice inside of him was screaming, trying to regain control, as he dealt out punishment to the three of them. He wasn't sure how long it might have continued if Regan didn't cough and stir, breaking the anger inside of Ardan. Fear coursed through him as he wheezed. What had just happened? He'd lost control and couldn't consciously control his actions. Without knowing what else to do, he started down the stairs. If he moved fast enough, he might outrun what had happened.

About halfway down he met with his sister hurrying up with the Bishop.

'Ardan,' she almost shouted.

'I thought you said he was being accosted by the other boys,' Frederick said.

'I was, sort of.'

'Well, where are they?'

'At the top of the bell tower.'

'And yet you don't seem hurt,' Frederick turned sharply to Liá, 'I'm disappointed in you.'

'No, it was more than—' Lia started.

But the Bishop interrupted. 'You know what I had to deal with this morning?' He didn't wait for an answer. 'Two of my soldiers were at death's door and I only had the strength to save one. I had to choose, condemning the other to death. I didn't have the strength to save him. Instead, I spend my days trying to keep the people in my quarter of the city alive. Which is becoming harder by the day. I don't need you adding to it. The next time you call for help, it better be an emergency.'

They watched Frederick descend the stairs, his increasingly threadbare sash adorning his shoulders.

Grimacing, Ardan felt the Bishop had just set a weight on his shoulders. He turned to Liá. 'Come on, let's find somewhere safe and I'll tell you what happened.'

Liá opened her mouth but thought better of it and nodded. He led her down into the main Cathedral hall. Groups of people were milling about in the open or seated in the aisles. The benches and floor space were all claimed. Refugees had put rough canvas up over various sections to give the illusion of privacy. They carefully navigated around sleeping spots to get to their own bench. Ardan relayed what had happened in a hushed whisper as they sat down.

'But....' Liá trailed off.

'I know. I don't know what happened, either.'

'You're not, you know,' Liá started and added in a whisper, 'a Shaper?'

'What? No. I mean, I don't think so. How would I know?'

Her face drew into a frown of concentration before she shrugged. 'Maybe it will scare them and they won't try it again.'

'Maybe,' Ardan said, unconvinced, 'But I don't think that we can go up the tower again.'

'I know,' Liá said, looking down.

He hated this feeling. He wanted better for her. He wanted better for himself. They were here, safe ... sort of, getting food ... sort of. One of their few freedoms that had let them enjoy their time was no longer an option. Now it was here or the stone courtyard. They sat in silence. Ardan's guilt at his actions against the three unconscious boys lessened the more he dwelled on it.

The moment was broken when Turlach appeared, holding his nose. Ultan was not far behind him, rubbing his head. Regan's lanky form and greasy brown hair appeared behind them. His eyes scanned the hall, his face red with anger. When their eyes met, Ardan could feel the hatred in the gaze as he stormed towards them. As he got closer, Ardan could see that the beginning of some impressive swelling was showing. Ardan knew they'd try to exact retribution. He didn't want to think of what would happen if they got Liá alone. He pushed that thought aside. There was nothing they could do in the crowded hall.

Regan stopped at the edge of the aisle. 'You will pay for that.'

'For what?'

'You know exactly what.'

'I'm not sure what you mean,' Ardan said with a perfectly straight face. He could see the cronies exchanging confused looks.

Regan bulled on. 'Watch your back. You're not as safe as you might think.'

With that, he turned and stalked away. Ardan watched him go. There was little any of them could do, hemmed into this place. But then again, he'd still thought his mother would return and save them. That expectation hadn't turned out well.

CHAPTER SEVENTEEN: THE FRAYING OF THE LIGHT

* * *

arleron was where we held the first talks. The forest surrounding the place thrummed with the power of the Ancients. We were cowed enough to listen. I sat across the table from Lucifer and Astaroth. We talked about establishing borders and treaties. For a time, there was hope.
— Zadkiel, *The Chronicles of Eden.*

* * *

A SHUFFLING of feet on stone woke Ardan. Instantly alert, he looked for the source. Some nameless person was walking wearily towards the outer doors to relieve themselves. He settled back onto the cold stone floor. Liá was sleeping on the pew above him, where it was warmer. Ardan pulled his cloak tighter to ward off the chill. He had been sleeping lightly ever since their encounter in the bell tower. They tried to avoid the trio as much as possible, but their cramped quarters made it virtually impossible. Ardan wondered where they'd go if they had to leave the Cathedral. Here was food and relative safety. Ardan felt like he had stepped into a snare and every time they ran across Regan, it tightened. Staring at the ceiling, Ardan felt help-less. The same power from the bell tower rose up. Panicking, he fought an internal battle, forcing it back from the surface. He breathed a sigh of relief.

Footsteps scuffled on the stone floor again. Another figure heading to the outer doors. As he got closer, a beam of moonlight illuminated his face. It was Regan. Ardan was on his feet in an instant.

'Easy there, friend,' Regan said softly, holding up his hands. 'I'm just heading to the outhouse.'

'It's a long way to come from where you're sleeping.'

'It is, isn't it?' He said, his mouth curving into a smile. He tried to walk past him, but Ardan shouldered into him.

'If you harm her—'

'You'll what? What will you do?' Regan snapped. When Ardan didn't answer, he continued, 'You are powerless here.'

'And the bell tower?'

Regan hesitated. 'I don't know what happened, but I don't think you do either. Can you pull that stunt again? It may be the only thing that saves you.'

Ardan glared at him.

The smile never left Regan's face as he walked past and headed outside.

Ardan lay awake, long after Regan was back in his sleeping spot. His sister never stirred. Her gentle breathing joined the hundreds of others, punctuated here and there with soft snoring to fill the hall with white noise. It was broken when the monks went for Matins. He only fell asleep in the last few hours before dawn. What felt like only a moment later, he woke to dawn's light. The sun was shining through the stained glass, illuminating the Cathedral in a collage of colour.

'Is it morning already?' Liá asked.

Ardan was working out the familiar aches that came with sleeping on stone.

'Another bad night? You should sleep better,' Liá said.

Ardan shrugged, saying nothing.

The two of them joined the others as they exited the main hall to the rear courtyard. As soon as they left the protection of the walls the winter wind struck, and Ardan pulled his cloak tighter while Liá shied into him. A queue had already formed that snaked around the courtyard. The smell of the morning porridge wafted over and his stomach gave an involuntary rumble.

They waited. It was some time before the church soldiers appeared. They looked little better than the refugees. Their tabards, once a vibrant white, had become grimy and tattered. Some wore bandages, while others grabbed several bowls to take to the traveller's lodge that had turned into a makeshift hospital. The rest of the soldiers walked wearily to the front of the line to collect their share. They got a bowl three-quarters full of the watery gruel. A soldier looked at the food, then back at Donnacha. The cook smiled gently but indicated at the rest of the people lining up. The church soldier glanced back and grunted.

Once the church soldiers were done, the line of refugees moved forward. By the time they reached the front, Ardan's hands were getting painfully numb. He shoved them under his armpits to keep them warm. When they got to the cook's pot, he picked up a nearby wooden bowl. Recognising them, Donnacha gave them a warm smile before filling half his bowl. Ardan smiled in return, though it didn't feel genuine. Liá got hers and together they went to the well. A guard stood on duty, ensuring no one could run the well dry.

They sat down with their backs against it and tucked into their food. Ardan took a generous spoonful. The warmth from it spread over through his mouth and down his throat. The rest of his body felt like it was thawing. As it went down, every fibre in his being wanted him to devour it quickly, but he forced himself to go slowly, to savour each bite. Dinner was never guaranteed. He took another bite, thinking it was the most wonderful food he'd ever tasted.

Liá had no such compunction and was eating hers at a breakneck pace. One spoon after another, she tried to stuff all her contents in her mouth before she swallowed.

'Take it slow, it will last longer,' Ardan said.

Through a mouthful of food, she couldn't quite respond but gave him a rude gesture, which he took well enough. He went back to his own bowl and took another careful bite, mulling it over in his mouth before he swallowed. Liá was using her fingers to wipe up the scraps. Her expression was forlorn as she looked at her empty bowl.

Ardan looked at his bowl. There were a few spoonful's left. He held it out. She looked down at the bowl, then at him.

'Go ahead,' he urged.

Her fingers inched towards the bowl, but she snatched her hands away, though it obviously pained her. Ardan took one more spoonful, then forced her to take the bowl.

'It's fine,' he insisted, overriding her protests. He hid the truth that his stomach felt emptier than before he had eaten. She finished his portion in under a minute, including wiping the bowl clean. They returned them to the kitchens, Ardan hoped he could help Donnacha again soon and get some more food.

They passed through the grey portals and back into the Cathedral hall. It was a welcome change to get out of the stinging cold.

They went back to the small pew that had become their home. Eventually, a monk came around and assigned them their tasks for the day. At first, Ardan was annoyed at the meaningless tasks, especially while cleaning the Archangel's aspect for the twelfth time. It was only when he was wiping the imaginary dust off the shield of Zadkiel that it dawned on him: Frederick was keeping them busy, stopping them from dwelling on other things.

Ardan kept watching for Delaney, hoping that today the man would make an appearance. When the schoolteacher was there to teach them, they were spared their chores. The man never lost his jovial enthusiasm and seemed impervious to the dangers outside the walls. It was one of the few breaks in their monotony.

Once their work was done, they'd join the line for their second meal. Sometimes food would come. It would depend on whether a ship was in the harbour. Afterwards, they'd retreat to their spots in the church pews.

Their afternoons were largely their own. Ardan would use them to sleep before the restlessness of the night set in.

Each day they woke a little hungrier. The chill of winter was more biting. Almost a week after the bell tower incident, Ardan was cleaning the Archangels again. He was stuck in the enclave behind the enormous statue of Zadkiel, wiping it down.

'So we're doing it tonight?' Turlach asked.

'What did I say about talking in the open?' Regan snapped.

'You said in front of other people.'

Ardan's eyes were wide, and he tried to stay stock still. He suddenly had a powerful urge to scratch his nose.

'Alright,' Regan said in a hushed whisper. Ardan strained against the statue to hear, 'Yes, we're doing it tonight. One of us will stay awake and wait until everyone's asleep. Then we'll do it.'

'But what about you know, if we're caught?'

'It'll be worth the risk. I don't think I can do it by myself.'

Ardan felt his insides constrict.

'How are we going to do it?' Ultan said, echoing Ardan's thoughts.

'We'll sneak across the Cathedral floor and...' but he stopped speaking suddenly.

'Have the two of you already finished your tasks?' Ardan recognised Frederick's voice.

'We had finished our duties early and were just admiring the Archangels,' Regan said.

'Really? You want to go with that one?'

'I ... uh,' Regan stammered.

Under different circumstances, Ardan would have found their predicament amusing, but fear overrode any sense of mirth.

'Go find Oisin. I'm sure he has some tasks that will keep you out of trouble,' Frederick said. The two of them groaned. Oisin's list of tasks never ended. 'Keep it up and I'll assign you to him tomorrow too.'

'Yes, Bishop,' they mumbled and shuffled off.

Ardan waited long after the sound of footsteps disappeared before extricating himself from behind the statue. They wouldn't take him by surprise. He needed to be ready for the three of them. He was tired of not being in control. If he had his sword, he could take all three of them. Whatever had happened in the bell tower might save him, but he couldn't rely on it. He wondered where Regan and Turlach were. Oisin often had people sent to him. *The man won't question it if I just turn up*, Ardan thought, a plan forming in his mind.

'Heaven's fire, you again. Horse shit useless the lot of you. What did you do to get sent here?' The grizzled Oisin said with a withering stare. Ardan found it difficult to meet it and knew better than to answer, 'No, I don't want to hear it. Go sharpen the cook's knives. The man has nothing to cut besides wheat and barley, but he still needs his knives sharpened, so you're getting that useless task for being useless yourself. Maybe that will knock some sense into you,' he said and before Ardan could respond, he spotted a church soldier turning to leave. 'No, you mother-loving idiot. That strap will wear at you all day, you'll barely be able to hold your spear up. Get over here, stupid hellspawn,' Oisin said, moving over to the guard, dismissing Ardan.

Ardan went to the weapons bench. It was easy to spot Donnacha's knives. They differed vastly from the weapons of war. He got a whetstone and sat on a stool, picking up the first knife. He worked out the burrs and imperfections until the knife could have split a hair. When he was done, he picked up the next knife, and then the next. His opportunity to hide one of the knives came faster than expected. Oisin had to step out of the room. Ardan quickly grabbed a rag and wrapped the knife, putting it inside his tunic. The hardest part was acting naturally when Oisin came back in. Ardan just picked up the next knife and worked away at the metal like he was whittling wood.

'I'd tell you I don't want to see you again, but you're too much of a goat-brained fool to listen. Get some water from the fountain and get out of here,' Oisin said in way of dismissal.

Ardan found his way back to their pew. Liá looked at him reproachfully, knowing where he'd been. He said nothing. If he got her involved, she would try to talk him out of it, or worse, try to help and get hurt. The rest of the evening passed slowly, another night with no dinner. He looked over to the corner that Regan had claimed. The three of them were huddled together, talking in hushed whispers. He caught Regan's eye a few times, but that wasn't unusual. Not seeing his customary smirk—that was unusual. Ardan returned his hand to the knife in his tunic. It had a reassuring weight.

Darkness descended excruciatingly slowly while the Cathedral's inhabitants began to fall asleep. Ardan lay down in his usual spot and waited. He could hear the occupants of the hall gradually descending into the even breathing of sleep, broken by the occasional snore. Time slowed to a crawl. The cold of the stone crept up and tried to inhabit his bones. He used the tricks his father had taught him: tensing and relaxing his muscles, keeping them awake and not letting them cramp up.

Every breath, every snore, every flicker of light made him tense. He forced himself to relax. Were they ever going to act?

There was a shuffle a few pews over. Ardan paused, moving carefully so he wouldn't be noticed. His breath caught. Their corner was empty. Resisting the urge to snap his head around, he kept his motions slow, raising his head slowly to peer over the benches. They were passing the altar and near the aisle that would lead them down to his and Liá's spot. Ardan got into a crouch, gripping the kitchen knife. Once they made their move, he would launch himself at them. Surprise was on his side. But they didn't turn down into his aisle. He sat there for a few moments as he processed what was happening. The trio disappeared through a portal towards the courtyard.

What in the nine hells were they doing? He got up to follow them. He stepped like a cat, fast, sure and soft. Soon he was out into the dark courtyard. The chilly wind wafted over him, and gooseflesh rose in its wake. He suppressed a shiver while he closed the door softly behind him. The three of them were huddled around the kitchen entrance.

There was no guard in sight.

He relaxed when he realised they were just hungry, exactly like the rest of the refugees. A dark thought entered his mind, and he entertained it for a moment. If they were caught out here, they'd be thrown out. But if he waited, he could get some food for Liá and blame it on them. He could feel his father's disapproving stare but shrugged it off. He waited. It didn't take long. The sound of splintering wood split the air, followed by a quiet cheer as the door swung open.

The three of them rushed inside, pushing each other as they did so. From this angle, it looked like street dogs quarrelling over a scrap of food. He waited and listened as he heard them pillage the kitchen. They came out with a leg of salted ham. There was little else that could be eaten without preparation. He could see them jostling each other good-naturedly as they walked, the ham being passed between them.

As they walked away, Ardan noticed the door was still ajar. How could they be so foolish? He waited until they had gone before he moved. He stepped softly, moving across the courtyard as quickly as a fox in the forest before he entered the kitchen. The place felt cold without the warmth of the cooking fire and the ready smile of Donnacha. Suppressing a shiver, he checked the holding hooks for ham, only to find them empty. He scrounged around, looking for anything edible, but there were only grains and oats. Then he remembered where Donnacha hid the cheese. He looked at the earthenware pots. Beneath a false bottom was almost a whole wheel of cheese. He grabbed the cheese and was about to leave when he heard voices. He froze. They weren't carried by the wind, they were close. *All the luck of Lucifer's horns,* he thought. He waited and cursed again. One of them was the Bishop.

Nine hells. He could hear the voices getting closer. If they found him here, they would throw him out and probably bloody him for good measure. His eyes darted around the place, looking for a place to hide. They slide from the jars to the oven, to the chimney. He needed to get out to hide. Then his father's voice intruded on him.

'If you're ever in a tight spot, take a deep breath and block everything else out. Then think.'

What he needed was more time. He leapt to the door, easing it shut. He waited behind the door with bated breath as they came around the side.

'I told you I heard something,' an unfamiliar voice said.

'Yes, yes, it seems like something has happened here,' Frederick said tiredly.

Ardan looked around the kitchen, hoping an option would appear, but nothing materialised.

'When you can neither run nor hide, then you must face it head-on. You won't have much chance, but it's better than before.'

His father's voice rang like a clear bell. He put the knife on the bench and reluctantly returned the cheese. He discarded everything that might be used against him.

He squared his shoulders, moved to the door, and opened it.

'Ah-hah,' the guard shouted. It was Corey, the young guard that had been on duty when he and Liá first came to the Cathedral. He looked thinner, with a wispy brown beard on his once clean-shaven face.

Ardan feigned surprise. 'I was about to come and get you.'

'You were about to come and get me?' Frederick repeated.

'Someone broke in here,' Ardan said.

'And yet here you are, in the centre of things.'

'Me?' Ardan said, feigning surprise. 'Oh yes. I guess it would look that way,' he said, trying to use the same bluff his mother had taught him during the game of Kings.

'Very much so. One of my charges, who I know is hungry, found in our food stores past a broken lock.'

'I was coming back from the outhouse and saw the broken door. I looked inside and you came along a minute later,' Ardan explained, trying to hold his mask as the epitome of innocence.

'Hmm,' Frederick said noncommittally.

'You don't actually believe this tripe?'

'We must not judge too quickly,' Frederick said, fixing Ardan with an owlish stare. 'But you realise this looks bad for you, yes?'

'It does,' Ardan admitted. 'But if it wasn't me, then surely something would be missing. You've caught me here and I have nothing on me besides what you can see. If something has been taken, then you know I wasn't the first here,' Ardan said and by the end, even he was surprised at how reasonable it sounded.

Frederick's stare stretched out and Ardan met his stare as innocently as he could. He resisted the urge to fidget. Instead, he employed some of his mother's tricks to keep calm. Long after he hoped it would stop, Frederick lifted the pressure of his stare.

'Corey, do you mind getting Donnacha? He can determine better than anyone if anything is missing. I will wait here with Ardan.'

Ardan tried to look at ease. He tried to imitate his parents, his father's casual nonchalance and his mother's unreadable expressions.

Frederick didn't question him further. He just leaned against the bench, his robes outlining his thin frame. At that moment, Ardan realised he was getting just as thin as everyone else. For the first time, Ardan really looked at him. Frederick rested his head against the wall, his eye closed. As he did, his constant frown of concentration eased, and his young features became prominent.

The door opened, and Frederick was instantly awake. Donnacha bustled in, his once portly stomach had sunk into an unhappy depression. He looked at Ardan and frowned slightly.

'It was bound to happen eventually,' Donnacha said.

'Breaking into the kitchen?' Frederick said.

'Can't give the people half rations and expect them to take it quietly.'

'But it's so we can all survive in the long run. It's—' Frederick's voice was rising, the lines in his face coming back.

Donnacha raised his hand to stall him. 'Your reasoning is sound, but it's difficult for folk to see that.' The cook turned his attention to Ardan. 'One of the last people I expected to see in here, me boy. What did you take?'

'Nothing,' Ardan said honestly, spreading his hands.

'Things will be easier if you tell the truth,' Donnacha said, stepping so close to Ardan that the man's hot breath washed across his face. 'It'll come out in the end.'

Ardan remained impassive. In response, Donnacha went about the kitchen, looking at the hanging racks, the condiments, opening every storage pot and jar. The entire process took well over ten minutes.

'There are two legs of the smoked ham that are missing,' Donnacha said, his eyes darting at the hidden cheese storage jars. His eyes narrowed for a moment as he went to inspect them. He harrumphed in surprise. 'The cheese is still here.'

Ardan's stomach growled at that exact moment as though to emphasise his point.

'It appears you were telling the truth, or at least part of it,' Frederick said, staring at Ardan.

'But you still caught him here,' Corey said.

'True, but he took nothing. No, I know,' Frederick said, raising his hand, forestalling the man. 'He may have taken something if left for long, but he wasn't the first one in here.'

'Who was then?'

'Could have been anyone, really.'

'I think I know,' Ardan said.

'Who?' Frederick said, then waved his hand dismissively. 'Of course, you two have been at each other since you got here. You'd say his name, regardless.'

'It doesn't mean I'm wrong.'

'No, it doesn't at that,' Frederick said, musing. His brow furrowed in concentration. 'It literally could have been anyone. Corey, get six guards up, the ones that don't have any duties today. You two go,' Frederick said, indicating Donnacha and Ardan. 'Get some shuteye until morning while I figure out what I'm going to do.'

Ardan followed Donnacha out and they went towards the open ground.

'I'm happy it wasn't you, boy.'

Ardan gave what he hoped was a sincere smile as he fought down a wave of shame. They parted ways and he went inside the Cathedral. It appeared he had gotten away with it.

CHAPTER EIGHTEEN: LUCIFER'S REACH

* * *

he forest around Barleron was wild and untamed. Only the Ancients could provide protection against the dangers of that place. It was enough for our followers, who built around us and our talks. Their works would provide the foundations of what the city would become.
— Zadkiel, *The Chronicles of Eden*

* * *

THE SUN SPARKLED through the stained glass, shining its light on the Cathedral occupants. Ardan woke up from a fitful sleep. The memory of the previous night came rushing back. He groaned, rolling over.

'Good morning,' Liá said.

'Is it?' Ardan asked, rubbing the sleep out of his eyes.

'I think they're going to give us bigger portions this morning.'

'I wouldn't count on it,' Ardan said as he sat up, his body protesting. He saw a glint of reflected light near the altar. He blinked, trying to clear his vision. There was a guard there. Surprised, Ardan looked around and found guards standing at every entrance. He watched one family walk up the doorway to the courtyard. The guard's hand tightened on his spear, and he shook his head. A man stepped forward, but the guard shook his head again and pointed at the altar. The family pulled away.

Ardan turned to his sister and could see the unspoken question on her face. Before she could speak, a loud boom interrupted her. Both of the main doors burst open as if struck. Ardan shivered from the onrush of cold air. A dozen more guards entered the hall, followed by the Bishop. The guards spread out into every section of the Cathedral hall. They looked like a pack of herd dogs, ready to snap at any foolish sheep that stepped out of line.

Frederick climbed the steps to his usual spot on the dais. There were bags under his eyes. He put his hands on the altar and paused for a long time.

'I want to start this by....' he trailed off.

It was so quiet you could have heard a feather drop.

'Last night someone plundered food from the kitchen,' he said at last. The hall broke out in exclamations as everyone turned to their neighbours. Ardan looked at Regan and his friends. They were looking distinctly straight ahead.

'*Silence!*' Frederick roared, slamming his hands down. His booming voice reverberated off the walls. Ardan brought his hands to ears, trying to block out the thundering voice. The sound echoed far longer than was natural and Ardan felt the now familiar stirring in his chest.

'That followers of the Light would steal food from their fellows, their protectors and, worst of all, from the house of Light itself ... the extreme betrayal had me deliberating whether or not I should turn everyone out,' Frederick said. There was a collective, almost melodramatic gasp as his gaze swept over the people gathered there. They knew how dangerous it was outside those walls. 'However, most of you have been trying to do right. You will be searched on your way out for breakfast. You will remain outside until we have conducted a thorough search of this place. If a scrap of food is found on you or in your things, you will be cast out.'

The eruption of whispers was more subdued. Regan went to talk to a nearby guard while Ultan and Turlach were being circumspect as they shifted through their belongings.

Ardan caught sight of a dull white bone as it disappeared inside Ultan's garb. Ardan watched it with narrowed eyes. It was his chance. He walked up the nearest guard, someone Ardan didn't recognise.

'Sir?'

The guard turned towards him, his lips thinning, but he said nothing.

'Over there. He's got ham bones, I saw him put them in his tunic.' Ardan felt no shame about ratting out the three of them. The faster they were gone, the better.

The guard eyed him for some time before he nodded. 'That one there!' The guard shouted, pointing at Ultan. 'Check him right now.'

Ultan's eyes went so wide he looked like a startled deer. Two nearby guards moved in slowly while the other patrons in the Cathedral pulled back, creating a space. Ultan ran. He rapidly changed direction when he got close to a guard, but the others cut him off. Ultan searched wildly for a way out. Eventually, he backed himself against the altar next to Frederick. With half a dozen guards blocking him in, he dropped to his knees and cried out, clutching at Frederick's robes. The Bishop made a scornful gesture, and the guards grabbed the prone Ultan, hauling him to his feet and dragging him away.

'And those two,' Frederick said, pointing at Turlach and Regan. 'I want everyone searched. I will banish anyone who has defiled the hospitality of the Light.'

Ardan breathed a sigh of relief. It was over, Regan would soon be gone and Liá would be safe. He found Regan glaring at him, his eyes seething with hatred. Ardan smiled. The Cathedral walls would soon separate them.

'We should get some food,' Ardan said lightly.

Liá nodded, looking away from Regan and Turlach being frog-marched to the Bishop.

They joined the line of people waiting to be let outside. Each person was searched before being allowed to go out. When they were nearing the front of the line, Ultan cried out, doubling over as a guard punched him in the gut.

Liá brushed imaginary motes of dust from her clothing, as though trying to clean the threadbare dress before stepping up to be searched by Corey. He eyed her speculatively but caught Ardan's glare and his hands were quick and professional. She was given the okay to proceed. She paused in the doorway to wait while Ardan took her place. Corey's hands padded his loose homespun, pulling out the purse and emptying its contents. Their house key, a few coppers, and a figurine of the Baron from their set of Kings came spilling out. Corey picked it up and eyed it curiously before shrugging, giving the purse one last shake. The silver coin of Lucifer dropped out. Corey dropped it as if burned.

'Bishop!' Corey's adolescent voice broke as he tried to shout. He stepped back and grabbed at the spear from the wall behind him. He wouldn't take his eyes off Ardan. 'Bishop!'

Frederick came over to them, eyeing Ardan. 'You had something, after all?'

Corey pointed at the ground with his free hand while he made sure his other gripped the spear. Frederick went still, staring at the coin for a long minute. He reached down to touch it, his hand slowing before it stopped completely. Instead, he reached inside his robe and pulled out a piece of cloth and used it to pick up the coin.

'This is yours?' Frederick asked, holding it out in front of him.

'Yes,' Ardan said. The likeness of Lucifer stared up at them.

'All free guards to me,' Frederick called. The guards were slow in moving. Ardan felt the stirring in his chest as the Bishop roared, 'Now.'

Half a dozen guards ran towards Frederick, their feet thudding on the floor.

The few remaining people didn't make any pretence of trying to move slowly. One started running, and they all followed suit, bumping into each other in their haste to exit the Cathedral.

'Let them go, we'll finish the search later,' Frederick called when the door guards moved to bar their way.

'Sir, I—' Ardan began.

'Quiet. The Devil has likely gilded your tongue,' Frederick said. He held the cloth-covered coin as though it might burst into flame at any moment.

The Cathedral had gone deathly quiet. Ardan was just realising that he may be in a great deal of trouble. It was at that moment that the Cathedral doors opened, interrupting them. The creak from the front doors echoed through the chamber, all eyes turning towards it.

Delaney walked in, his bald head shining like a beacon. He paused when he saw everyone scrutinizing him. He smiled and resumed his walk, ignoring the guards' stares, until he stood in front of Frederick.

'What happened?'

Frederick held out the coin in answer.

'Oh dear,' Delaney said, looking at the coin. Then up at Ardan, pointing first at the coin and then at him. Ardan nodded, affirming it was his. Delaney pursed his lips. 'That explains why you're so quiet.'

Frederick grunted.

'So, lessons cancelled this morning?' Delaney asked, his jovial manner undampened.

Ardan looked up, hoping that it had broken the tension, but he found Frederick staring at him, his brown eyes hard and unrelenting. Ardan fidgeted.

'Frederick,' Delaney began, 'he's just a boy.'

'He's almost a man. The doctrine is clear.'

'What? No, you can't—' Ardan said.

'Silence!'

Delaney motioned for him to be quiet. Fear gripped him as an unbidden memory flashed through his mind of a man tied to a stake. When his father had seen the kindling and wood being placed, he'd ushered them out of the square as quickly as possible. Before they got away, the flames were being lit at the unfortunate man's feet. The man's screams chased them down the street. Ardan's hands clenched. *Let them try it.*

'I believe it's only for those that have been corrupted. You can test for corruption, can you not?'

The Bishop didn't answer.

'Frederick,' Delaney said.

'I can try,' Frederick said at last. 'Hold him.'

Two guards stepped forward and grabbed Ardan. He winced as they manhandled him, holding his arms at painful angles. Frederick stepped close; he looked down at Ardan, his eyes narrowed. He brought both his palms up and placed them high on Ardan's chest. There was a peculiar queasiness that seeped in from Frederick's palms. That familiar stirring in his chest rose and pushed back. It felt like there was a battle going on inside him until Frederick pulled his hands back, surprise etched on his features.

'So?' Delaney asked.

Frederick's eyes searched him for a long time before he answered. 'I couldn't sense darkness in him, but there was something else. Something I've never felt before.'

'Great! No corruption,' Delaney said, slapping his hands together, 'he can stay here then, yes?'

'No,' Frederick said and Ardan's heart plummeted. 'I cannot allow the coin or its bearer to remain here. In better times, yes, I'd put him in the cells and destroy the coin. But here and now?' He gestured vaguely around them. 'I cannot. I barely have the resources to take care of the followers of the Light. He must leave.'

Delaney nodded his head slowly, 'I understand where you're coming from, but—'

'I will not be swayed. He is banished from this Cathedral, and I give leave for the guards to use whatever means they see fit to get him out of the Quarter of Light.'

'Surely the girl can stay though?'

Frederick looked at Liá.

'I'm going where he goes,' Liá said, standing straight despite her quavering voice.

'Very well,' Frederick said at last.

Both Ardan and Delaney spoke.

Frederick held up a hand, looking exhausted. 'Just go. You have a token of evil on you. One from the highest order of Darkness. You have left me little choice.'

'They're just children. Where will they go?' Delaney asked.

'I will pray for them,' Frederick said. The lines on his face were hard.

'Fine. Just flaming fine,' Ardan said, 'If you're throwing me out, then I want my things back. Including the coin and my sword.'

Frederick looked down at the coin, still clasped in the cloth in his hands.

'Light forgive me but yes, you can take it. I do not have the strength to destroy it and I fear its presence inside these walls. Take the coin and get your sword from Oisin. You two,' he said, indicating the guards, 'make sure they leave.'

CHAPTER NINETEEN: THE FIRE OF THE MOB

* * *

he truce crumbled once the Darkness realised how truly weakened the Light was. We had lost so many angels to Eden's uprising. Naberius struck first, but it was Lucifer who commanded the hound.

— Zadkiel, *The Chronicles of Eden.*

* * *

THE ASPECTS of the seven Archangels gazed down on them, while the Cathedral doors closed with a ring of finality. Ardan suppressed a shiver, averting his gaze to the surrounding area. It had been a long time since they had seen the outside of the Cathedral's halls. Despite the lateness of the morning, there were only a few people moving about, looking harried and clutching their clothes tightly, avoiding eye contact as they went past. The buildings near them looked forlorn, with all their windows latched shut and doors barred closed.

'We can't stay here,' Ardan said.

'But where can we go?' Liá said.

'We need to get away, and fast. Regan's going to be as mad as a slighted demon.'

'Oh. Oh dear.'

That's an understatement, Ardan thought as they started walking.

'Can we go home?'

Ardan let out a long breath. 'Maybe. We should try to head to Mercenary Square first and find Davan.'

'What if he isn't there?'

'Maybe we go home.'

'What then?'

'Then we go to the Dark Temple. See if this coin is worth anything,' Ardan said with forced confidence.

Liá swallowed before nodding assent.

The buildings they passed seemed almost normal beyond the occasional broken window or door hanging off its hinges. They continued on the road until it opened up to Zadkiel's Square. People were queued up, creating long snakes through the square. There were church soldiers everywhere, with even the smallest stall having two guards nearby. Ardan and Liá pushed through the throng. People in the queue began muttering, shooting them dark looks, while others shouted at them. Ardan held up his hands to show they were just passing through, not cutting the line. They quickly quietened down.

At the edge of the Square, a makeshift barrier blocked them. It was made of broken crates, overturned wagons and ragged pickets that created a wall between the Quarter of the Light and the rest of the city. There was only one clear passage with over a dozen guards milling about in their hard leather armour, armed with crossbows and spears. Most of their tabards were dirt-stained and tattered, bearing the holy silver flame at the centre. Some guards looked up as they passed, but none bothered them. They weren't there to stop anyone from leaving.

Ardan paused and stared. The nearest building was burnt down to its foundations, its pillars standing up like spikes aimed at the sky. As he looked along the barrier, he saw every single building close to it had been burnt or knocked down. Anyone trying to approach the barricade would have to cross a hundred feet of open ground. Unease washed over him, and they both moved quickly to get out of crossbow range. None of the guards paid them much attention, but it didn't stop Ardan from walking with his eyes cast over his shoulder.

Only once they were out of sight of the barrier did Ardan relax. They walked past a group of people and one of them smiled, wishing them a good morning. Startled, Ardan shared a look with Liá, who shrugged. They continued down one of the major streets and into a crowd of people. It was difficult to walk without bumping into some-one. Rubbish and debris had piled up in the alleyways. He realised that many of the alternate routes were blocked, forcing everyone to take the main street. The unwashed stench of bodies pressed together engulfed them as they slowly pushed their way along the street. Despite the smell, it was the first time Ardan had felt warm in weeks. Yet the crowd of people soon became uncomfortable, and he felt suffocated.

Suddenly, people started scattering in all directions. Ardan froze as he looked around wildly. Then he heard it. Hooves were thundering hard on the cobblestones. He recovered quickly and grabbed Liá, dragging her to the edge of the road where they flattened themselves against the wall. The hoof beats pounded like war drums, heralding the arrival of six men atop warhorses. He could see the warm breath of the horses funnel out as they charged. Each rider freely lashed out with his cudgel at anyone in range.

An elderly man was slow in moving, being caught directly in their path. The lead rider nudged his boots into the horse, causing it to speed up. They smacked the man into the ground like a sack of oats. He then continued to roll as the horses' hooves pushed and pounded him along the road until he eventually rolled to a bloody stop. The riders never halted, rounding a corner and disappearing.

The tide of people slowly returned to the street. The man lay on the ground, moaning for help while the people ignored him, moving around him like a river flowing around a stone.

Ardan stared at the man. He glanced at Liá, who nodded, knowing what he was thinking. But before Ardan could wade into the throng, a mercenary in a Red Wolf tunic got to the injured man first. He knelt down, gazing critically at the injured man. His movements were gentle as he grasped the man's hand. He then pulled a dagger from his belt. The old man tried to resist, but the mercenary pushed aside his resistance as easily as he would a child's. He put the dagger to the man's chest and pushed down. The old man gave one more fitful push, but his life quickly bled away. Once his struggling stopped, the mercenary pulled out the dagger, cleaned it on the dead man's clothes and then dragged the body to the edge of the road. He dusted his hands and re-joined the throng. Ardan stared, too shocked to move. No one had attempted to intervene. They all avoided looking at the body.

'Ardan, Ardan!' Liá said, grabbing his arm and pointing towards Regan. His matted and greasy hair was visible above the crowd, with Turlach and Ultan close behind. Ultan's eyes found them first, and he reached out to grab his companions.

Ardan didn't hesitate. He took hold of Liá's wrist and half led, half dragged her through the crowd. They stayed at the edges, where it was slightly less packed. Ardan was pushing people aside with abandon. He heard several curses and shouts directed his way, but he bulled forward, wanting to stay ahead. Inch by inch, they manoeuvred through the crowd, pulling away from their trio of pursuers.

They rounded a corner and Ardan realised they were in the Ancient Quarter, with the moss-covered stone buildings surrounding them. Here the crowds thinned, allowing them to move quickly. Dodging left and right, they weaved a path that would have been the envy of a drunk choreographer. They came across the park of the Ancients and darted inside and behind the vine-covered walls. Hugging the barrier, they avoided the large congregation of people near the Tree. Breathing hard, Ardan leaned against the damp wall. He could smell the moss and vines covering the stones. It was a welcome break from the stench of people pressed together.

They both jumped as an almighty roar erupted from the crowd of people. They were cheering. No, not cheering, they were howling, shaking their fists in the air. A man was standing on a bench near the

Tree of the Ancients. The bald man basked in the crowd's rapture. He raised his hand and the crowd dutifully quietened down.

'And the rich stay inside their walled houses in the Merchant Quarter. Do you know what they feast on? Crispy pork, roasted chicken and suckling duck,' the bald man said, punctuating each of his words, fuelling the crowd's anger. 'They hoard their food. While they see you out on the streets, hear your grumbling bellies and laugh at your starving children. Your families are hungry while they sit behind their walls and grow fat!'

The crowd's anger erupted like a thunderclap. Ardan shied away from the outcry, instinctively stepping in front of Liá. It took a full minute for the bald man to bring them under control again. Yet their anger was ready to boil over.

Few things in this world are as dangerous as the forest, but a mob when the fire is on them is one of them.

'We need to get away,' Ardan said, recalling his father's words.

There was only one exit in sight. The two of them ran for it, ignoring the bald man's words.

'*No!*' the crowd shouted.

They pulled up at the intersection just outside the park. One path led to Mercenary Square, the other to the Dark and Merchant Quarters. Yet another makeshift barrier blocked the way to Mercenary Square, manned by mercenaries with shields, spears and bows. Ardan looked back at the simmering mob, ready for the slightest spark before they burst into flame.

'Go then! Take what is rightfully yours! Go!' the bald man called.

The mob screamed their approval and turned towards where Ardan stood beside Liá.

CHAPTER TWENTY: A DARK
SAVIOUR

* * *

*O*utnumbered and outflanked, I went into hiding, gifting my power to worthy humans to continue the fight—and fight they did.

— Zadkiel, *The Chronicles of Eden.*

* * *

'No,' Ardan whispered.

Regan was between them and the mob. His grey eyes caught Ardan's. His smile was predatory as he called to his two cronies. They began running, keeping just ahead of the angry crowd.

With no choice, Ardan and Liá ran down the road towards the Merchant Quarter. Word of the riot must have gotten ahead of them, because the streets were mostly empty, allowing them to run unhindered. Yet after a few blocks, Ardan was breathing hard, his muscles burning. Liá looked no better. The weeks of half rations and the day's exertions were finally catching up. Their pace slowed to a jog and eventually to a staggering fast walk. Ardan kept stealing glances behind them. Regan, Turlach and Ultan had also slowed, barely keeping ahead of the mob.

They kept moving despite their exhaustion. Ardan eyed the side alleys and small streets. Could they run down them? They might lose Regan, but they might also end up trapped. His legs burned with every step, but it was Liá who was falling behind, heavily favouring one leg.

Regan was in front of the mob, instilling a motivational fear that forced each next step out of them. The streets were deserted, every door barred shut. Some people looked out cautiously from second-story windows. Ardan glanced back, realising they were losing ground. He grabbed Liá under the arm. Together they hobbled forwards.

Ahead was a sight that made Ardan's heart sink. Three ranks of guards dressed in the blue and grey colours of the Merchant Guard were blocking the street. Their large wooden shields overlapped to create a shield wall that was broken only by the shorthand spears pointing out from the gaps. Behind them was a line of archers with simple hunter's bows. One was in heavy plate armour, adorned with officer plumes, standing on a wagon at the rear. Next to him was a woman with silver hair that belied her youthful face.

The mob behind them did not slow or stop.

'Disperse!' the man on the wagon yelled. His voice was as clear as a bell, carrying over Ardan and the mob. 'Disperse or die.'

They were between a hammer and an anvil. Ardan grimaced. They'd have to chance the alleys.

The mob paused. A battle cry rose from the rear and the crowd resumed its advance. A man raised his makeshift club and yelled something, before charging the shield wall. His movements emboldened the others. The entire mob roared, running after the leader. The oncoming horde engulfed Regan and the others.

The guard captain nodded towards the silver-haired woman. She raised her hand, and a slight breeze buffeted them. Her loose hair flowed with the direction of the wind. The breeze quickly grew to gale-force winds. The mob continued to push forward.

Ardan pushed Liá into one of the bigger alleys and leapt in after her. A moment later, the onrush of bodies ran past, straight for the line of guards.

'Draw!' They heard the guard's voice spill out over the mob.

The mob took the challenge, yelling as they continued to charge. Their weapons were simple hand axes, spears, crude cudgels and the occasional sword. A rock was thrown. Others soon followed, creating a hailstorm. The wind grew fiercer, forcing the rocks back into the crowd.

'Loose!'

The wind abruptly stopped, and a succession of twangs from the guardsmen's bows punctuated the sudden silence. Cries of agony broke the angry chanting of the mob as the arrows found their mark. But the mass continued to press forward.

Ardan helped Liá to her feet as another wave of arrows fell among the crowd. The angry momentum transformed into a panic. The front was an impenetrable wall, the rear an unstoppable momentum, and the middle was the meat grinder.

They stumbled away from the battle, navigating the trash and refuse that littered the alley. Just as they reached the first bend, a shout behind them sent chills down Ardan's spine.

'I told you I saw them come this way,' Regan said.

Ardan stared at Regan in disbelief. *How in all the heavens did they get through the mob?*

'Run,' Ardan yelled, even though he knew the futility of it. Liá broke into an awkward shamble while he stayed a step behind.

They made their way down the twisting, turning points of the alley. It was so narrow in parts that Ardan had to keep his feet nimble to avoid his shoulders brushing the walls on either side. For one brief, glorious moment, Ardan allowed himself to hope. It was dashed as the dead end of a stone wall greeted them. It was a low wall, but it would take precious seconds to climb.

Regan stood there at the mouth of the alley, his hand resting on the wall as he panted. 'You led us on quite the chase.'

Ardan drew his sword in response. The exhaustion in him made it difficult to hold the blade steady.

'Get over the wall, I'll hold them off,' Ardan said, drawing his curved blade.

Turlach and Ultan joined them in the alley. *One against three.* He grimaced. *So long as Liá gets away.* The alley was narrow, forcing them to come at him one at a time. Regan drew a long dagger. Behind him, Turlach had a small woodcutting axe. Before he could see what Ultan had, Ardan felt a presence beside him. Liá was standing there beside him with a bit of cobblestone in her hand.

Regan took advantage of the distraction and slunk forward. Ardan saw it out of the corner of his eye and slashed wildly. Regan dodged, using the opening to slam into Ardan with his shoulder at the same time, using his dagger to lock his falchion against the wall.

Liá tried to strike Regan with her stone. He jumped back, letting Ardan get his sword free. He pulled it, and pushed Regan off, but realised too late the move put Regan between him and his sister. In the confusion, he'd forgotten about the others. He ducked instinctively as he felt rather than saw Turlach's axe swinging towards him. He sensed the whoosh of air as it passed him before hearing a dull scrape of steel against stone. He let out another wild slash behind him and was rewarded with a yell. A thin red line of blood appeared where his sword had struck. Turlach dropped the axe and stumbled back. Ultan took his place.

Regan stood there between them with his long dagger held in front of him. Before Ardan could make a move, he felt that very familiar stirring inside his chest. His vision blurred and suddenly he felt very dizzy. He tried to suck in a deep breath and that just made it worse. He stumbled and fell. What was happening was draining his strength.

Stunned, he watched as the light and shadows danced across his vision; the alley varying wildly in and out of focus. Liá tried to rush to his side but was quickly caught up by Regan. She struggled against him, and he tore the shoulder of her dress.

Ardan tried to get up, but the world spun alarmingly, and he fell.

What in the nine hells?

A slender figure in the black robes of the dark priesthood

appeared at the end of the alley. The hood was raised, hiding the face in shadows.

'Who are you?' Turlach yelped, still clutching his arm, his eyes a little wild.

The dark figure raised its hands to its head and lowered the hood. Lush red hair spilled out, framing a pixie-like face. *Is she really that beautiful or is my head still spinning?* Her hands lowered, saying nothing as she took in the scene with piercing blue eyes.

'We don't want any trouble with the black faith,' Regan said.

'She's not a priestess,' Ultan laughed. 'Far too pretty. Probably just come from entertaining some rich merchant with a fetish.'

'Ultan, don't,' Regan said in a low growl.

Ultan laughed again. He stepped in front of the priestess, reaching out a grubby hand to stroke her face. She didn't flinch.

'You're not any trouble, are you my dear?'

She lifted her fingers and grasped the hand that touched her face. Then her eyes rose and met his. Ardan almost recoiled from the glacial gaze. Even though he wasn't receiving the full intensity of it, he shied away. Ultan stood there, transfixed. He let out a whimper. His big shoulders shook, softly at first, then with greater intensity. He made some feeble attempts to twist away, but he couldn't break eye contact. The moment stretched, while Ultan's cries of terror grew until they barely seemed human. After what seemed an eternity, he crumpled to the ground. He scrambled back until he was pressed against the wall. He brought his knees up to his chest and cradled them, his arms shaking.

Ardan chanced a look at her again. The priestess' eyes had returned to a regular blue.

'Ultan, Ultan get up,' Regan said.

The priestess' eyes fell on him, and she spoke. 'You did this to her?' looking at Liá's exposed shoulder.

Regan stared at the priestess. He glanced at Turlach and his face grew a little uncertain. But he raised his chin and stared at her. His reply was ruined by the quaver in his voice. 'I did.'

The priestess stepped forward, but Turlach reached out to stop her. What happened next was so fast that Ardan barely followed it. She spun, grasped Turlach's shoulders, and kneed him in the groin. Turlach immediately crouched over in pain, and she followed up with a swift punch to his throat. His hands rose to his piggish face as he gasped for breath. She then grasped the front of his jerkin and pulled him forward, smashing his face with her forehead. He went down in a tangle of limbs, his face bloody. He wasn't able to cradle all of his injuries.

The priestess turned back.

Regan dropped the dagger and held his hands out. 'Please, don't hurt me.'

The priestess raised her hand and it pooled with blackness, the same darkness that Ardan had seen Esalon wield. Then it shot out like an arrow, hitting Regan like a battering ram. He was flung back and slammed against the wall with a sickening crunch. He fell down into a crumpled heap, unconscious.

The priestess walked over to Liá and looked her over. 'Pretty girl like you needs to watch her company,' she said, her voice soft. 'Find someone to protect you, or better yet, learn to defend yourself.'

Ardan's dizziness fought his balance, but in the end, he dragged himself to his feet. He knew it was futile as he grasped his sword.

'Young lover?' The priestess said, eyeing Ardan with distaste. 'Not the best bodyguard.'

Ardan's throat felt painfully dry, but he stepped forward.

'My brother,' Liá said.

The priestess asked. 'I expect you two will survive from here on,' she said as she turned. She stepped around a dizzy Ardan and past a foetal Turlach. Ultan still held his knees to his chest, muttering something incomprehensible. The priestess paused at the corner, her piercing eyes looking back at them.

'You will owe me for this,' she said before disappearing.

CHAPTER TWENTY-ONE: A BARGAIN

* * *

The Light, the Darkness and the Ancient strongholds in Barleron found a unique synergy. The fighting between them was relentless. Sometimes one gained the upper hand, but it would not last. By trick or chance, the three strongholds remained in the city as equals.
— Zadkiel, *The Chronicles of Eden.*

* * *

As soon as the priestess had left, Ardan's vision snapped back into focus. Liá's head was bowed, and her hands twined the pieces of her torn dress together. She preserved her modesty in a barbaric kind of way.

'You look like one of the forest people,' Ardan said lightly. Though he could see the swelling appearing on her cheek. His eyes shifted to the unconscious Regan.

'Just the look I was going for,' she said, dusting herself off. He saw her gaze wander to the end of the alley. 'Would any priest or priestess accept that coin you have?'

'I don't know, maybe?' Ardan said, still glaring at Regan's prone form. Then it dawned on him, 'Oh, oh!' Ardan was already turning but his head spun, and he stumbled into one of the walls. 'Let's find out,' he said once he had his balance under control.

'One moment,' Liá said and walked over to Regan. She stood there for a long moment before she drove her foot into his stomach. There was little visible effect on the unconscious Regan, but Ardan couldn't help but laugh. It rolled out of him in waves. Liá stared at him, her head tilted to the side, until it eventually subsided.

'I'm alright, just ... never mind, let's go.'

They followed the priestess' trail, but after a few streets they were lost in the maze of back alleys.

'Well, there's the Temple,' Liá said, pointing at the dark pyramidal structure towering over the surrounding buildings.

'Worth a try,' Ardan said. They tried to keep up a brisk walk, but with Liá's hobbling and their combined exhaustion, he doubted they were making good time.

After some wrong turns and backtracking, they broke free into the major street of the Dark Quarter. It led directly to the entrance of the Temple. The black structure rose like a thorn into the sky. The wide staircase led up the centre to the Temple's only entrance. Several Black Guards were milling around the base of the stairs. Ardan swallowed.

'There she is,' Liá said, pointing.

Halfway between them and the base of the Temple, he could see the red hair and black robe of the priestess. Without speaking a word, they both ambled towards her as quickly as they could. They caught her just as she reached the base of the stairs. Two of the Black Guards had already moved to intercept them. The setting sun combined to make odd shadows dance across their black armour.

'Priestess,' Ardan called.

The Priestess turned in response. She glanced at them before she flicked her hand at the guards. The black-armoured men stopped but didn't return to their posts.

'You two again,' she said, her glacial blue eyes regarding them.

'We need your help.'

'Greedy.'

Ardan reached into his purse with his fumbling fingers and spilled out what little coins they had before his hand eventually grasped onto the coin he was after.

The Priestess raised an eyebrow. 'You seek to tempt me with money?'

He said nothing as he held out the coin.

The effect was immediate. Her condescending smile vanished into a flat expression. She imperiously held out her hand for the coin.

Ardan drew back, shielding it from her. 'We seek sanctuary.'

'The coin first.'

Ardan looked at Liá. Her eyes were wide. He glanced back at the priestess but didn't move. The Priestess raised her hand and the Black Guards reached for their swords. Their expressions were as cold and dark as the Temple itself. He reluctantly put the coin into her hand.

She examined it for an exorbitant length of time. Throughout the exchange, the Black Guards stood there, still as statues, their hands resting on their swords. As they waited, a man walked past in a grey robe. He couldn't be much older than Ardan. He bowed to the priestess before moving up the stairs. She didn't respond, her attention fixed on the coin.

'I'll be damned,' she said, a pearl of laughter escaping her. 'It's from Esalon. How extraordinary.'

'So, you'll help us?'

Her hand closed around the coin, her smile fading. 'That depends.'

'But the coin?'

'Promises a bargain, nothing more.'

'Then we seek sanctuary inside the Temple until the city is settled.'

'I said a bargain. We are not the Light, to offer 'sanctuary'. You must offer something mutually beneficial.'

Ardan opened his mouth to speak and then closed it again. The priestess stood there, her hands clasped in an odd gesture. He thought about every story of deals with demons and the Black Clergy. They all carried the same warning. Be careful of what you say. Given the chance, they would honour the wording rather than the spirit. As he stood there, a woman in a grey robe curtseyed to the priestess. She had a clean face, straight teeth, and a robust figure, something uncommon in the Cathedral. He remembered the stories of the Black Clergy and the supposed evil behind them. Yet he hadn't witnessed it. At least they didn't burn people at the stake.

'We wish to become acolytes in the Temple of the Dark.'

The priestess smiled in a way that made Ardan distinctively uncomfortable. 'Before I accept, you should know that those who do not complete their training rarely survive long. You need to push through failure or weakness of spirit,' she said, but didn't elaborate further. 'Now, with one coin, I can only accept one acolyte. Who will take this bargain?'

The wildness inside of Ardan welled up in response, like a wolf squaring off against a wolf hound. Its power forced him to act. 'The coin is worth more than what you are offering.'

The side of the priestess' mouth quirked. 'What is your name?'

'Ardan, this is Liádan. And yours?'

'Orla.'

'I will accept the bargain of one acolyte, but you will need to provide something else.' the power inside of him was pushing aside cautious thought.

'Who will be the acolyte?'

'Liá.'

'Ardan, no! Ask for something else. We can figure this out,' she said, her hand grasping his shoulder.

His eyes fell on her bruised cheek and torn dress. He thought about the priestess' warnings, but Liá was tough. She'd proven that when she stood at his side in the alley. She had excelled in her studies under Delaney. He didn't think she'd have a problem in that environment.

The priestess gave Liá an appraising look before she replied, 'We take no prisoners or slaves. If she doesn't come of her own free will, then we cannot proceed.'

Liá was still clutching his arm.

'Liá, you must go.'

'No.'

'You saw what it was like out there. How many more close scrapes can we get out of if we continue like this?'

'I will not leave you out here.'

'I could have gotten away today if you weren't there,' Ardan said, forcing his voice to become harsh. If she got inside the Temple, she'd be safe.

'I know what you're doing,' she said, tears forming in her eyes. 'I'm not going. But if I did, what would you do? Where would you go?'

'Find Davan or Mother.'

'To survive,' Liá clarified. 'I need to know you're going to survive.'

'I'll farm the forest. Father taught me enough.' Ardan said, hiding the sudden pang of grief.

'I don't want to lose you too,' she said softly.

'You won't.'

Liá's eyes were glistening as she pulled him into an embrace. 'Visit me when you can,' she said when she released him.

Orla watched them, her face unreadable.

'You, Liádan, are entering the service of the Darkness of your own free will?'

'I am,' Liá said.

'That would conclude—'

'No,' Ardan said again. 'That is not enough for the bargain. I need more.'

Orla's ice-blue eyes regarded him. 'It is an even exchange.'

'I know the worth of Esalon's coin to you,' Ardan said, holding firm. 'If you want it, I will need something else.'

Orla pursed her lips. 'Like what?'

Ardan's mind raced. He tried to think of something he might need —silver? Food? Clothes? No. He knew. 'I would need supplies and traps to help me in the forest.'

'I am a priestess of the Dark,' Orla said incredulously. 'Why would I have those things?'

Ardan blinked, not really having registered before that she

wouldn't. They always had everything in the stories. 'Do you have dealings with Raigel? He would have it.'

'You wish to trade with Raigel?' Orla said, her mouth splitting into a smile. 'Very well. Tell him I will owe him one silver temple and a small favour. He will know its worth.'

'That's it then?'

'The bargain was opened with this coin and sealed with these promises,' Orla said, indicating towards the Black Guards. They stepped forward, one on each side of Liá. They didn't lay a hand on her. They didn't have to; they were as good as iron manacles. Together, the four of them ascended the stairs, with Liá turning to look back several times as she did.

'Ah, the card player,' an unfamiliar voice said behind him.

Ardan turned to see another black robe. The wild energy inside of him still blocked out any fear. The slight build, close cropped hair and almost black eyes registered in his mind. It was Esalon, the priest that had defeated him at cards all those months ago.

'I had worried something had happened to my fierce puppy,' Esalon said, walking towards him. 'Have you come to redeem your coin at last?'

Ardan shook his head.

'No? It seems like you could do with a good turn,' Esalon said, looking over Ardan's tatty clothes and various injuries.

'I already used it.'

'You what?'

Ardan retreated from the animosity.

'To whom?' Esalon said in a low growl as he stepped forward, his fists clenching in front of him. Ardan wasn't sure if he was imagining it, but the shadow behind the priest grew.

Ardan pointed, while his other hand found the hilt of his sword.

'Orla?' He peered up the steps. Esalon seemed to shake himself, and his shoulders relaxed like the lowering of hackles on a dog. He gave a mirthless chuckle. 'She would have pounced on it, and she'll probably want her own coin back in exchange,' he said, musing to himself, then returned his full attention to Ardan. 'Please tell me you asked something worthy of her.'

'She took my sister as an acolyte,' Ardan said, his hand still on his sword.

'Did she now?' Esalon said, stroking his chin. 'Bit of a gamble that one, but you do like to play high stakes. Don't you?'

Ardan didn't know how to answer, so he shrugged.

'Well then. I must congratulate her. She has outmanoeuvred me, even if it was through sheer luck. If nothing else, it will amuse the High Priest,' Esalon said, and started towards the steps.

'Wait,' Ardan said and Esalon stopped. Not inviting him to speak, but not objecting either. 'Will you accept me as an acolyte?'

Esalon laughed. 'Very bold. You impressed me with one coin, but I need something besides reckless courage. To gain another, survive this and prosper,' he said, gesturing at the city. 'If you can do that, we'll talk. Until then, I wish you Lucifer's luck, as you don't seem to have much of late.'

Ardan watched him head up the stairs. The sun had set, giving the horizon an orange blaze that offset the Dark Temple's ominous aura. Ardan walked away from the Temple. He wasn't exactly sure where he was going as he unconsciously headed towards the Tree of the Ancients. He walked past the intersection where the Countess' guards had stopped the mob. Several wagons were being loaded with the dead. There didn't seem to be any dead or injured guards amongst them.

Esalon had been right. He would need a turn in his luck to survive.

PART II

CHAPTER TWENTY-TWO: THE NORTHERN SLOPES

* * *

I always promised my father that I would keep a journal if I received an officer's commission. The great commanders do it, he said. I keep this journal out of respect for him and not belief in my own abilities.

— *Journals of Phillip, the twelfth Templar.*

* * *

THE RAIN PELTED DOWN HARD against the stone and burnt-out wood. The wind gusted, rattling the wooden windbreaker he was using at the entrance. Ardan pulled his blanket tighter, wrapping himself as though in a cocoon. The thing was filthy with soot and grime, but it was warm. His makeshift shelter was inside the chimney of a razed house. It was the only thing left standing amongst the rubble and charred beams. The place was dry and protected from the worst of the wind. He'd found it while running from one of the street gangs.

He knew he should get up, but the hammering rain had created a meditative feel. His mind drifted to months earlier, when a nameless mercenary had told him his brother was alive. It was the day after he had last seen Liá. He had hoped to find Davan and maybe get some help. As he'd gotten closer to one of the major intersections, he'd seen a roadblock had been erected with over a dozen mercenaries manning the barrier. A queue of people had been waiting to be checked through. One mercenary wore the Red Wolf sash. The man had been sitting on a barrel, his long brown hair hanging like a curtain, as he ran a whetstone down his sword.

'Hello there, Sir—'

'No beggars,' the man had said without looking up.

'I'm looking for my brother, Davan.'

The mercenary paused. He looked at Ardan, evaluating. 'You don't look much like him.'

Ardan sagged with relief. 'He's alive, then.' The pain of not knowing had been a thorn in his mind.

'Aye, he is. Least last I saw him.'

'Can I get through to see him?'

'Won't do much good. He's out of town for some time. Gone with a bunch of the wolves to Dentwall.'

'He's what?' Ardan almost shouted, 'Why?'

'Can't tell ya.'

'When does he get back?'

The man scratched the scruff of his neck as he thought about it. 'Hard to say that. He won't be back for at least a fortnight. Come back after that. Someone will tell ya then,' the man said, returning to sharpening his sword.

Yet every time Ardan returned, he was disappointed. They all said the same: 'He's not back' or 'I can't tell you what he's doing.'

Ardan's stomach growled, breaking his reverie. He grumbled, shifting. He pushed away the blanket, pulled aside the windbreaker and crawled out into the burnt-out husk of the house. It was early and dark, the storm clouds above making it difficult to tell the time. He muttered under his breath as he tried to use his tattered cloak to keep dry, no matter how futile it felt. The good thing about the rain was that it washed the city, and some of the stench away. He took the back streets towards the northern gate. In better times he'd take the main streets, but he didn't want to run into the Street King.

Yet despite sticking to the seldom used alleys, Ardan could feel someone watching him. His hand went to the sword at his hip, while his eyes searched the empty buildings. He kept moving, though his feet itched. So long as he didn't run into any of the Toughs he should be okay. He changed direction more than once to lose any tails he might have picked up.

Eventually, he made it to the north-eastern part of the wall and followed it to the northern gates. He looked at the nearby buildings and after making sure no one was watching the road, made for the wood gates that had rusted so they were perpetually open. Yet just as he slipped through, he stopped and cursed. In front of him stood six men armed with clubs, spears and swords.

The Street King stood out in front, wearing an iron circlet on his light brown hair. A little older than twenty, he was smiling, showing a full set of teeth. A trait not shared by his Toughs.

'Ah flaming hells Owen, what are you doing here?'

One of the Toughs stepped forward, taller than the others, 'You will address him as your Majesty.'

Ardan eyed him for a moment before returning his attention back towards the Street King. 'Of course, your Majesty,' Ardan said with such mockery in his voice that the Tough stepped forward, but Owen held up a hand.

'I like you Ardan, that's the only reason I don't have Noah here give you a lesson in decorum,' Owen said. Noah gave a grin, showing several missing teeth.

'I appreciate it,' Ardan said, ignoring Noah.

The Street King's mouth quirked, but his eyes flashed and Ardan decided to stop pushing.

There was no way around it, Ardan thought. 'If you're after your tribute, I don't have it.'

Owen paused, his hand going to stroke his goatee. 'Just like that?'

'No point in lying.'

The Street King eyed him for a long moment, before looking at his shoulder and brushing some imaginary mote of dust off his expensive blue jacket. 'What am I to do when one of my subjects doesn't pay his due?'

Ardan had to struggle not to roll his eyes. 'Let them off with a warning?'

The Street King brought a hand to his chin in an overdramatic gesture. 'My watchers have noted you going out into the forest and coming back with little. Should I still give you my protection?'

Ardan tried to bite his tongue. Despite the man's pomp, he was dangerous, but Ardan couldn't hold his tongue. 'Never really wanted your protection.'

Noah stepped forward again, raising a fist and Ardan shifted, a hair's breadth from bolting. The Street King held up his hand.

'Have I not made this part of the city a better place for everyone?'

Ardan thought about it. The streets were better. Those under his protection walked down the street with relative impunity. He had even organised some clearing of refuse and housing of the homeless. 'It is safer,' he agreed.

'But I didn't do it alone.'

The Street King eyed him. Ardan nodded, though he didn't know what the Street King was looking for.

'If you return to the city empty-handed, we will discuss making you one of my soldiers.'

As good a chance of that as hell freezing over, but Ardan nodded anyway.

The Street King gave a predatory smile. 'Excellent. I am glad we could have this little chat.' He said, moving past him, his Toughs spreading out behind him.

'You shouldn't be out here,' Ardan said.

The Street King raised his eyebrows.

'You know how dangerous it is for someone like you to be out in the open. You shouldn't have come here yourself.'

This time Noah put his hand on Ardan's shoulder and the size of it made him feel like a child. 'Are you threatening his Majesty?' Noah said.

Ardan did roll his eyes this time.

'Be easy. He isn't threatening me, just being cautious. If I do not come out in the open, people will think I am a coward. Who will fear and respect a coward?' Owen said.

'Running into a fire isn't bravery,' Ardan said.

'If the Prostitute can survive in the Ancient Quarter, so can I.'

Ardan went to say something else but shrugged, it was obvious he wasn't going to listen. When it was clear he wasn't going to say anything further, the Street King gave a regal wave and went back inside the city. Ardan headed out into the fields, feeling the eyes of some of the Toughs on his back.

'It's going to be a good day,' Ardan said forcibly, ignoring the dark clouds. 'I might even find some heartwood or Ancient ore.' As though the words would channel some of Liá's optimism. He continued across the fields, where the fire's destruction had made it difficult to tell where one field ended and another began. The rehabilitation had been disorganised and chaotic at best. All the fields were infested with weeds, while the charred remains of burnt-out farmhouses and barns stood as memorials. The only movement now was that of the coloured birds with their bright red tail feathers amongst the once bustling fields.

Ardan stuck to the northern edge where the fields met the forest. The surrounding trees rose like a wall as dark ominous thunderclouds sparked with lightning overhead. Ardan unconsciously swallowed. Did he really want to do this? His stomach gave a loud bellow of hunger. Then he remembered the Street King's threat of indentured servitude.

'Hard to argue with that.'

Steeling himself, Ardan pressed his way through the wall of trees. The world changed from grey to green as the carpeted forest floor and thick canopy spread out before him, giving him protection from the worst of the rain. He followed his trail markings while his eyes constantly scanned the paths, bushes and trees. His feet moved over a now-familiar way, careful in their movements. The wet foliage muffled the sound of his feet while the rain stirred up a mossy aroma.

He couldn't spot anything of worth besides the stubs of already harvested plants or droppings of game a week old.

His eyes caught something blue sitting on one of the nearby trees. It was a blue tree frog. Feeling a bite of fear, Ardan edged away from it, giving it a wide berth while his shoulder burned with phantom pain. He would have loved to harvest its venom, but trying to do it without a bow or glass vial would be damn stupid.

'I've done worse,' Ardan said aloud, 'but not today.'

The day is young—the thought came unbidden.

'Nope, staying cheerful,' Ardan said, quashing the thought, as he finished his circle of the frog and came back onto the path.

He continued on, his breath coming in heavier as he reached the foothills of the escarpment that surrounded Barleron. He moved towards a marked bush, finding the first snare he'd set. The thing was empty. Unperturbed, he kept on. Yet as he got higher in the hills and after nothing but empty snares and traps, he could feel his cheerfulness ebbing away. The trail he'd set out had been virtually barren the last few weeks.

'I warned you about overusing your runs. The forest will change its habits once it knows yours.' His father's voice echoed in his head.

'Yeah, yeah.'

The gradient steepened as he began to climb up the northern slopes, while his trail wound its way back and forth. The trees opened up more, their protection from the rain dissipating. A couple of times, he saw creeping vines heading towards him. He skittered around them but had his blade bared, just in case. The thunder crackled amongst the clouds.

'Uphill and getting wet, fantastic.'

He continued on, but after two more traps, he wondered if he'd find anything outside the Meadow. His last stop had never failed to catch something. He made his way further forwards, taking a glance back to see the valley around Barleron spread out behind him before pushing on, where he almost missed one of his trap markings. He pushed aside the brush he'd used to camouflage it, but the trap was gone, leaving drag marks in its wake. There were no footprints, tufts of hair or even a single droplet of blood left behind.

'Who or what has been messing with my traps?'

The gnawing of his stomach and the threat of the Street King played in on his thoughts as his mind warred whether he should follow the tracks or not. He knew he shouldn't but what choice did he have? He stepped forward, pushing some of the brush out of the way as he cautiously followed the drag marks.

He didn't have to go far. Past a small hedge, he found the metal and wooden remnants spewed over the place. It had been pulled apart and destroyed. As he was trying to figure out what had done this, he hadn't noticed the vine creeping through the brush until it had already wrapped around his leg.

'Shit—' he got out before the coiled vine tightened and with the strength of a charging horse, jerked him off his feet. Ardan landed hard, the breath driven from his lungs. Winded and confused, the vine dragged him towards the tree. He could feel dirt and leaves catching under his shirt and sliding across his skin while he dazedly fumbled for his weapon. Before he could grasp it, the vine hoisted him into the air and the world turned upside down. His shirt and cloak hung past his head while he dangled by his leg. He tried to grab his sword out to free himself but fumbled it and the whole weapon slid out and past him. He snatched at it, careless of the danger posed by the blade and caught the handle. His moment of triumph quickly faded.

Like the fingers of death, a dozen vines were coming towards him. They spelled certain death, whether they immobilised him or tore him apart. No one would be this way to save him and if he called for help, all he would attract would be predators.

The beating of his heart thundered in his chest. His breathing grew rapid, but his father's voice intruded in his mind.

'Panic helps no one. Close your eyes, control your breathing, then focus.'

'I am not closing my eyes.' Ardan said as the vines got closer. Though he slowed his breathing and got a lid on his feelings, the blood rushing to his head still disorientated him. The vines were like a green octopus as their tentacles stretched out. Ardan readied himself, focusing on keeping his sword arm free.

His first slash hit the closest vine. It immediately recoiled, vanishing back into the tree's canopy. His second slash only delivered a glancing blow, but it was enough to make the tendril retreat. The tree's other tentacles continued to come at him. Ardan hacked and slashed the best he could hanging upside down and though he kept most of them at bay, there were too numerous and persistent to give him enough respite to cut himself free. As he slashed at another vine coming for his arm, he could feel a second vine wrap around his other leg. He cut at another intrusive vine just as the vines on each of his legs began to pull him in different directions. Cursing, Ardan slashed at the vine creeping around his chest and throat. By the time that one released him he could feel a growing pain in his groin. The two vines were pulling his legs in opposite directions. In a wave of panic, Ardan curled up, hoping none of the other vines were close enough to grab him and slashed at one of the trapping vines. It released him, but the sudden lack of tension acted like a sling shot and he was propelled around the tree. Adrenaline pumping, he was out of danger, but he knew it'd be short-lived. A wild plan formed quickly in his mind and without thinking about the consequences, he curled up at the pinnacle of the swing and hacking at the last vine.

It released him, and for a moment, Ardan floated. Then gravity reasserted itself and the ground rushed to meet him. He hammered into it with a loud thud. His sword clattered away as the fallen leaves of the forest floor did little to cushion his fall. He gave a wounded groan. Chest burning, as his lung refused to function, and he could barely force a breath in or out. Yet the danger of the vines was still there and he forced himself to his hands and knees.

His hand fumbled for his sword. Panic crept in, as he couldn't draw any further breath. With the luck of Lucifer, he grasped his sword amongst the fallen leaves and in shambling movements, he forced himself away further from the trunk like a wounded dog. His breath was coming in small sharp gasps, and he chanced a look back.

The vines had disappeared into the tree as though they'd never been there. The surrounding forest looked calm and serene.

Ardan collapsed. After a moment, he rolled onto his back to give himself time to recover. Above him, the green canopy obscured the grey sky.

'Fuck this place.'

CHAPTER TWENTY-THREE: THE GOLDEN MEADOW

* * *

They have assigned me to the fortress at Jophiel's pass. My commission is the command of one hundred soldiers. They are good men and women, varied in both origin and experience. I feel blessed that they are my first command.

— Journals of Phillip, the twelfth Templar.

* * *

ARDAN SAT UP, groaning, trying to shake off the accumulation of leaves suddenly sticking to him. There was a break in the trees above him, allowing the continual pattering of the rain to hit him unabated. He considered going back. But that would mean dealing with the Street King. And he had no food. With a curse, he knew he needed to eat and find something to pay the Street King. He had to keep going until he got to the Golden Meadow.

Ardan hobbled gingerly back towards the trail markers, working the kinks out as he did, until at last he was able to walk normally but he kept his pace slow and cautious. He eyed every vine suspiciously.

None tried to kill him, but it didn't stop him from grasping the hilt of his sword tight enough that his knuckles were turning white.

Ardan could hear the river long before he saw it. He felt relieved when he saw its wide banks, breaking the monotony of the forest, its water twisted and turned, creating white caps amongst the rapids as it flowed out of sight. In the distance he could hear the crashing of the waterfall.

He knelt down on the bank and used his hands to cup the water he drank. It was cool and refreshing, one of the first welcome things of the day. Once he had his fill, he got to his feet and followed the river's edge, his feet sinking into the muddy ground. Up ahead was the bridge he used to get to the Golden Meadow. It was the remnants of a gigantic tree that had fallen, bridge the rapids that high enough to tickle its base.

Grasping the slippery surface of the fallen tree, Ardan hoisted himself onto the damp surface of the wood, but as he did, his pants caught on a loose splinter, dragging them down. He managed to retain some measure of dignity as he got to his feet atop the tree and pull his pants back up. As he did, he eyed the belt critically, making a mental note to add another notch to accommodate his thinning waistline. His stomach gave a grumble of agreement. *Nearly there*, he thought to himself as he moved across the bridge, his steps small and sure. If he fell, the water would carry him off to Light knows where.

At the opposite end, Ardan leapt from the tree and onto the soft soil. *It isn't far now*, he thought as he followed the small trail towards the Meadow. The first time he saw it, he thought it might be a circle of stones, but there wasn't anything magical about it, just a natural and beautiful space, open to the sky. Daisies littered the Meadow, making the clearing look golden.

He had eyes for only one thing. His last trap, that he left near some rabbit warrens. It was past the small rise on the opposite edge.

A bird squawked overhead. Ardan glanced up, making sure it wasn't one of the wide-winged eagles. Relieved it was just a carrion bird, he continued forward. He'd clear the trap and be gone. As he got closer, he could see it had been sprung, but something was off. Trepidation swallowed the brief elation he felt. As he circled the small hill, he could see the remains of a rabbit in the trap, covered in blood, gore and broken bones. Ardan gripped his sword, looking about.

The bird called again. He looked up and could see the black silhouettes of more carrion birds. Six of them, circling the clearing.

'Stupid, stupid, stupid,' Ardan swore at himself and sprinted back towards the river.

A brown and grey dog with short ears stepped from within the foliage. It resembled a weasel but was as large as any street dog.

It let loose a deep-throated growl.

More dogs appeared around the clearing, their fur colours and patterns varying between brown, black and grey. Ardan slid to a stop. At least a dozen of them surrounded him. He drew his sword, cursing himself for a fool. He should have abandoned the run after his encounter with the vines.

The lead dog took another step towards him; its growl was like the shaking of the earth. Its mouth twitched, revealing white, pointed fangs. The other dogs paced towards him, tightening the noose.

Ardan felt panic and fear rising in him, the emotions opening up the well to that primal feeling inside. Anger at his helplessness. He thought of the bell tower; the last thing he needed was to knock himself out with predators around him. Yet the anger, fear and rage rolled through him in waves, his emotions feeding on themselves. He felt his hand tightening on the leather grip of his sword. There was no easy escape. Exhaustion threatened to overwhelm him.

'To the hells with the lots of you,' Ardan yelled, and filled with power, he charged. The dogs stood stock still. The growling ceased. Just as it looked like Ardan might strike the lead dog, it leapt away, dodging the wild strike. But Ardan was already moving, heading for the next nearest dog. He kept his forward momentum, zigzagging aggressively, trying to get closer to the nearest tree. The dogs exchanged yips before they were moving, running, circling, and growling around him. Coming close enough to be tantalising targets, to distract him, while another would snap at his heels. Ardan swung wildly at any of them that got close, while continually trying to move forward.

The trees were getting close, but the wild slashing to keep the dogs at bay was taxing. He didn't have long. The tree and its escape were almost in spitting distance. A dog yipped, darting in. He slashed, not realising it was a feint. Razor sharp fangs pierced his calf like tiny daggers.

Ardan swept the blade behind him, but the other dog was already gone. His next step caused his leg to buckle, and he fell to one knee. He flailed with his sword, trying to keep them back. A dog lunged from the side. He brought the blade up, but the angle was awkward. The dog crashed into him, sending him sprawling. Several brown and black blurs charged towards him.

He couldn't control the panic. The power rose up. Ardan scrunched his eyes, trying to force the power down. Its energy flowed up his arm and erupted out of his palm in an explosion of green fire. The force flattened him against the ground as though he had been struck by hurricane-force winds. The dogs were flung violently away from him, their forms crashing and skidding across the clearing.

The pressure lifted.

Panting, he cautiously opened his eyes. The dogs were there, but further back. Ardan scrambled to his feet. They began circling him again but kept their distance. With his injured leg he wasn't getting away, but he'd take as many of them with him as he could.

'Is that all you've got? Come on!'

There was an answering roar. Its sound echoed through the forest, washing over the clearing like a tidal wave. The circling carrion birds immediately squawked, flapping their wings in panic. The dogs started to yelp and wail in terror, running away from the roaring with their tails between their legs.

The sound reminded Ardan of a bear baiter at the festival of the Ancients, if the bear had its roar infused with the same power the Bishop used.

'Thank you, ominous beast, for your timely roar,' Ardan said. It didn't stop him from shuffling away from the sound and towards the river.

Another roar soon followed the first. This time, the ground shook. It wasn't an earthquake; the thunder was too regular.

Gooseflesh appeared on Ardan's neck and shoulders. The shaking ground was caused by the footfalls of whatever was roaring. Ardan kept running, ignoring the wound in his leg as best he could. As he reached the log, he stole a glance behind him. A giant shadow towered behind him, like a moving mountain.

The next roar was much closer. The thing had reached the clearing quickly. Whatever it was, he didn't want to meet it. He took one look at the rushing river and knew which one he'd rather take his chances with.

He gripped his sword hard and jumped. Rushing water engulfed him, causing the world to go momentarily black while the chill stole his breath. When he broke the surface, the log bridge was rapidly fading into the distance. Ardan tried to flatten himself close to the surface, as his feet kept brushing rocks as he passed.

Trees and bushes obscured his view as the river turned around a bend. When he heard the next roar, it felt more distant. He tried to swim towards the shore, but the power of the river sucked him back in, the pace of it speeding up. White water foamed and frothed amongst the rapids. Twisting vortexes of water spiralled like pitfalls. It sucked him up a mound of water and dumped him on the other side. The water pulled at his legs while it pushed at his torso. Ardan went under. After twisting and turning, his foot caught on a submerged rock wall. For a panicked second, he thought his leg would break, but there was a slight give, and his leg came free. He came to the surface for a second, spluttering for a breath.

Ahead, all the trees and brush had vanished. He could see clearly out over the valley and on to the ocean. It took a moment to realise why.

'Are you flaming kidding me?' Ardan yelled. The sound of the crashing waterfall rapidly approached him. He tried to swim for the river's edge, but the aggressively flowing water forced him forward. He hit the edge and was propelled out over the waterfall.

The world slowed as he hung in mid-air.

Well, if I'm going to die, at least the view is superb, Ardan thought as he looked across the beautiful green valley and across the ocean. The moment of beauty gave way as gravity reasserted itself. The world sped up, and he fell. Wind rushed in his ears as he flailed, looking at the fast-approaching lake.

His feet struck first, and he sped into the water like an arrow. The sudden compression of his body stole any semblance of thought and time. When he finally slowed, he tried to reorient himself. The light gave him an upwards direction. He swam, but the light looked impossibly far away. There was a shooting pain in his right calf and a burning in his chest as he kicked and paddled. He felt a panic build up, his movements becoming more frantic. He got closer and closer, but the need for air was unbearable.

Ardan burst through the surface like a whale. He gasped deep, golden lungful's of air, keeping his exhausted body from sinking through sheer force of will. Without realising it, he was being pushed by the flow of the waterfall towards the nearest shore. He let it carry him. His feet eventually touched smooth pebbles under the shallow water. On unsteady feet, he waded out to collapse on the bank. The worn gravel felt better than the softest bed.

For the first time, he fully appreciated why forest stalkers were treated with such healthy amounts of fear, reverence, and incredulity. Only a madman would do it. He knew he might die here, that he needed to move, but he couldn't do it—at least not yet.

He waited until the burning need for air had completely subsided.

Ardan tried to say, 'One more time, I can do this,' but all that came out was a mix of mumbles and groans. He ignored his protesting muscles and pushed himself to his feet. Water started draining down his clothes, causing him to shiver afresh.

Then Ardan froze. In front of him was a massive tree with a wide trunk, large protruding roots, and arching branches that created an umbrella of protection. It could have been a twin to the Tree of the Ancients, albeit significantly smaller. The entire scene emitted a peaceful serenity, something so contrary to the rest of the day's events, Ardan wondered if he had become slightly delirious.

CHAPTER TWENTY-FOUR:
HEARTWOOD

* * *

he fortress at Jophiel's pass was larger than I could have imagined. Banners of the Light fly atop the battlements. The Iron Gates are scorched. Its walls are marred and dented from the ceaseless Northman attacks. Though I wonder why they bother; they would need an incredible host to even consider breaching the walls, let alone taking the keep.
— Journals of Phillip, the twelfth Templar.

* * *

ARDAN AWOKE A FEW HOURS LATER, stirring as though having slept on a feather mattress. *That isn't right*, he thought. His eyes slowly opened. Where was he? The green and brown of the forest was illuminated by the brilliant orange of the setting sun. Darkness was coming.

'Oh, nine hells!' Ardan spat, sitting bolt upright.

'What we deal with during the day within these woods is nothing compared to what roams at night. No man or woman has survived an hour after darkness falls, let alone a full night outside the stones.'

How could he be so careless as to fall asleep, so close to dark?

Barely registering his tired and stiff muscles, he pushed himself to his feet. He'd never make it back to Barleron. He needed to find safety. He...

He was already inside a circle. The pale stones of varying sizes, little higher than his ankle, surrounded the tree in a haphazard circle. He was safe inside the stones.

A sharp breeze brought him back to reality. With a shiver, he realised how damp his clothes were. The stones protected him from the horrors of the jungle, but from little else. He needed firewood and food.

Judging by the colour of the sky, Ardan had maybe half an hour before darkness fully set in. Leaving the safety of the circle, he went to some nearby saplings. He bent and twisted the plants into traps. They were rushed jobs, but he had the more pressing need for firewood. Cursing, he moved as fast as his injured leg would allow. He looked for any wood protected from the rain and carrying as much as he could before the sun dipped behind the horizon.

Ardan threw the last bit of wood down. *It'll have to be enough*, Ardan thought. He took out his sword and began to shave the nearest piece. While he worked, the stars began dotting the darkening sky like fireflies. He started scraping branches against each other, as his father had taught him. The sound of scraping competed with the birds and insects of the night. Sweat beaded on his forehead as he worked on the wood. His father had always made it look so easy. After half an hour of cursing angels, demons and everyone in between, he saw small, barely visible tendrils of smoke rising from the wood. With careful movements, Ardan knelt down and blew on it. As the glowing coals flared up, he carefully added kindling in small amounts until a flame burst up. As the flame grew bigger, he progressively added wood until it was a respectable blaze. The soft glow of warmth washed over him, and the open flame felt like a luxury.

With his immediate needs taken care of, Ardan examined himself for injuries. *Light, I've been lucky*, he thought. The only real damage he'd taken was the bite marks in his calf from those damned dogs.

They still stung. He tore off the edge of his pants and made a makeshift bandage. *I hope I can make it back before it festers.*

His stomach reminded him he'd gone another day without eating and he sighed. Tomorrow would be better. He lay against one of the larger roots. The sounds of buzzing insects and nocturnal birds filled the air as he slowly fell asleep.

Despite his exhaustion, he woke up whenever the coals burned too low. The fire kept him warm, while the tree kept the worst of the wind out. By the time the sun rose, he was feeling considerably better. He rubbed the sleep from his eyes but froze when his vision cleared.

'Well, I'll be damned.'

There was a hare stuck in one of his roughshod snares.

Ardan moved towards it. The creature struggled fitfully, but the sapling held firm. With an efficiency born of his father's training, he snapped the hare's neck and used his sword to skin it. The size of his sword made it cumbersome, but the carcass was soon roasting over the fire.

The aroma of cooking meat filled the air. Ardan cut slivers off the roast, his hunger giving it such a seasoning that it would be worthy of a king's table. He was soon licking the juices off his fingers, wondering where all the meat had gone.

He had the hare skin. It was worth enough to keep the Street King off his back. At least the trip hadn't been a complete loss. He was getting ready to leave but something in the fire caught his eye. There was a single stick in the fire without a single blemish or mark of char-ring. Ardan used another stick to pull it out, sending small sprays of coals everywhere. Tentatively, he touched a finger to the unmarked branch. The wood itself was cool. Was it heartwood?

'No. No, don't get your hopes up.'

He had to be sure. He drew his sword and ran the blade across the wood, trying to chip or cut it. But the blade would cut, chip or mar the wound, not a single mark. Could it be heartwood? It had to be. Ardan tried not to get too excited. There was a literal fortune in heartwood lying around. He immediately searched for every piece of wood that fit the profile.

Raigel had been asking him about heartwood and Ancient iron ore every time he'd come into the demon's shop. Was this where heartwood came from? He thought about why the Tree of the Ancients shed none of its branches—a thought for another time. He went around the clearing, picking up wood and testing each stick one by one. Once he had a respectable pile, he tore the bottom of his other pant leg to create a sling and tie. Once he'd bundled everything together, he swung it over his shoulder and set off.

As he walked, he felt the sting of the dog bite, but he pushed forward, following the river and marking trees as he went. Occasionally the foliage became too thick, forcing him away from the river, but these meanders were short. He kept his pace measured, making sure not to let impatience get the best of him. He carried a fortune with him, something that should give him some breathing space. His trip back was unhindered by vipers, dogs, vines or any other nasty surprises. It helped bolster Ardan's mood to the point he started to whistle.

Eventually he broke free of the dense jungle, the expansive ocean spreading out before him. Small waves were breaking on a white, sandy beach.

'It's been fun,' Ardan said, with a salute to the trees.

He could see the Cathedral bell tower jutting out from the skyline and walked towards it, leaving a trail of footprints imprinted in the sand.

By the time he reached the city walls, his limp had become more pronounced and his wound ached. The battered gates looked just the same, but he felt they should have been different after he'd gone through them yesterday. Had it only been one day?

The gates were unguarded. Curious, he stepped under the stone arches. As the moss-covered buildings spread out before him, he couldn't see a single person. A sense of unease filled him, and his hand unconsciously reached for his sword. His first thought was to run, but he remembered the wound in his leg. Should he go to another entrance? But he didn't know who controlled the other entrances.

Ardan swallowed and continued on, creeping around corners and walking silently up the side streets. As he moved, he got the distinct smell of carrion. He tried not to gag as he pressed on, using the back alleys to get to the Street King's 'manor.' He peeked around a corner and stared in horror.

Bodies of the Toughs littered the streets. Flies buzzed around the corpses, the warriors holding their weapons even in death. Some of the bolder street urchins were already picking over the bodies, rags tied around their faces to block the smell.

Ardan stepped around the corner. At his appearance the urchins scattered, disappearing over walls and into buildings within seconds. He ignored them, limping forward. He knew what he'd find, but he had to see it for himself. In front of the two-story ersatz manor, was the Street King himself. His blue coat stained red with blood, the iron circlet lying on the ground next to him.

It wasn't the best time to say I told you so.

'I flaming told you so.'

For the first time in several days, Ardan was glad it hadn't stopped raining. It was helping to wash all the blood away. He reminded himself to not stay in the open. A pang of regret filled him, and he muttered a quick prayer for the Street King before pushing on.

The image of the body-carpeted street chased Ardan through the Ancient Quarter, through the streets and all the way to Raigel's shop. The demon was out front, hanging herbs on some drying racks. His red scales glittered in the afternoon light. Ardan recognised some of the silphium he'd brought a few days ago.

Raigel glanced at him from his green eye. He finished tying up the herbs before turning towards him, his long, pointed teeth stretching across his entirely too-wide mouth as he smiled. Ardan had never gotten used to the terrifying sight.

'You made it through. I had wondered. Though you have seen better days, son of Tristan. Did the Dark Clergy do this?'

'That's who massacred those people?' Ardan demanded, ignoring how he must look.

The demon fluttered his wings, reminding Ardan of a shrug. 'Who else? They approached the Street King for some sort of agreement. He did not take them seriously, insulting them with his refusal. They could not let it stand.'

'So they killed everyone?'

'I am not privy to the details. It isn't like the Dark, so I believe something else was going on.'

What have I gotten Liá into? he wondered.

'If not the Clergy, is the forest the reason for your state?' Raigel said, his eyes trailing over Ardan's injuries and torn clothes.

'You have no idea.'

'I trust you have not come for a sympathetic wing to cry on.'

'No, I've come to trade. I've found some heartwood.'

The side of Raigel's mouth quirked, his eyes looking at the bundle still being carried over Ardan's shoulder. 'Indeed? Come inside—I would like to see it.'

Ardan followed the demon inside his shop. Small items, weapons, goblets and trinkets lined the shelves. Ardan followed Raigel down the short aisles, ignoring the curiosities, and put a piece of wood on the counter.

'Raigel, how long have you lived in this city?'

The demon's green and red eyes were focused on the wood. 'Many generations.'

'Then you've lived through the previous civil wars.' Ardan continued at the demon's nod: 'Has it always been this bad?'

Raigel paused in his examination. 'This is one of the worst. Only the Purge involved more bloodshed. I do not think anyone expected it to continue as long as it has. Yet I predict it will draw to a close soon. The people are becoming weary of the power mongering. They will soon band around some of the more powerful candidates. Now, a moment please,' Raigel said, taking a piece of wood from the bundle. The demon's long, spindly fingers ran along the edges while he brought it close to his eyes to inspect it. He drew a hand back, and a small spurt of oily black fire erupted from his palm, striking the wood.

Ardan jumped back, startled. The demon's attention had not left the wood. It was still completely unmarred.

'You are Tristan's legacy, of that there is no doubt. This is indeed heartwood. I shall set up a meeting with the buyer.'

'You're not buying it?'

'No. This way is easier,' Raigel said, but didn't elaborate further.

Ardan stared at the demon suspiciously.

'You need not fear deception. No one else can shape the wood, at least in this city. That service does not come cheaply.'

Ardan's suspicion faded. 'So, how do we do this?'

'I presume you mean meet with your buyer?'

Ardan nodded.

'The Inn is at the end of the street. It is under my protection and, as such, quite safe. I will grant you a few days of free food and board.'

'No, thank you. I'd prefer to pay. I have this hare skin,' Ardan said, untying the skin from his belt and placing it on the table.

'That will grant you some coins, but barely enough for one night.'

'And people say demons don't have a sense of humour.'

The red scales of Raigel's mouth pushed together as his lips opened into an unnatural smile. 'You amuse me. Very well, the hare skin will suffice. Tell Gael I sent you. Stay at the Inn until the buyer arrives. You may leave the wood here with me.'

Ardan eyed the demon. 'I need your word.'

The demon inclined his horned head. 'And you are right to insist. Your items will be in my safekeeping until next we meet. I give this protection freely and without seeking recompense.'

'Thanks, Raigel. You know, you're alright for a demon.'

The demon stared at him for a long time, its green and red eye penetrating. 'That sentiment fills me with—what is it you humans call it? The warm and fuzzies?'

Ardan couldn't help it. He burst out laughing.

The demon returned to sorting the wood, but Ardan could tell he was secretly pleased. Raigel paused with one of the branches between his long fingers, meeting Ardan's eyes. 'Are you aware of its worth?'

'Like a hundred silver temples?' Ardan blurted.

'A reasonable assumption, but who can afford it? You should consider an alternative form of payment.'

'Like what?'

'That is for you to decide.'

Ardan mulled over it. 'How long will I have to wait?'

'I do not expect it to be long. The buyer knows its rarity and will be eager to obtain it,' Raigel said, then reached under the counter and pulled out a small bottle. 'And take this. It should help with that wound of yours. It is given freely.'

Ardan stared at Raigel, who had returned to inspecting the wood. He took the bottle, unsure of what to make of him.

CHAPTER TWENTY-FIVE: AN OLD FRIEND

* * *

*R*efugees flood the pass. They fill the halls and hostels to bursting. They speak of fleeing a nameless horror, consuming them in war. The commander is old and cautious, refusing to let me scout past the Mountains. He assures me it is Astaroth who is stirring up the northern kingdoms. I cannot find ease in these words.

— *Journals of Phillip, the twelfth Templar.*

* * *

ARDAN WALKED down the narrow alley from Raigel's shop. The directions had been easy enough: follow the alley until it hits Forest Way. The Inn was at the corner. It was a two-story building with weathered, flowing patterns etched into the stonework. The ground floor was raised off the street level by a few steps. A man sat by the entrance, sharpening his long sword. He watched Ardan with beady eyes beneath a bushy black beard.

Ardan nodded to him, stepping through the doorway and onto the polished wooden floors of the Inn. Tables were spaced evenly inside the room, a cheerful fire crackling at one end. This place yelled at him; it was too warm, too nice. He felt like an interloper. The few people inside wrinkled their noses, but otherwise ignored him. A woman, carrying several plates of food, wove between around the benches, dropping off the plates before coming to stand before him. Her iron-grey hair was tightly bound, and she gave him a once over, her mouth thinning.

'Raigel sent me,' Ardan said before she could speak.

She raised her eyebrows, her eyes going over his clothing, lingering on the pants torn at the knee, stopping briefly at the sword on his belt. She crossed her arms. 'Did he?'

'He did.'

'Raigel the demon?'

'Yes,' Ardan said, trying to keep the edge out of his voice. What unfortunate child would be named Raigel?

'Are you sure? Because the last time someone tried to use his name in vain, bad things happened.'

'Look lady, he sent me here for a bath, clothes, some food and to get my wound fixed up. Is this the right place or not?'

'Alright, alright, no need to get snippy. I was just asking. From my experience, Raigel has little to do with foul-smelling men in rags. I will sort your bath first, but it will take a few minutes. Until then, find a seat. I'll bring you out something to drink in the meantime.'

Ardan took a chair by the fire. The flames were warm and crackling. He tried to let the warmth wash over him, thaw out some of the more frozen parts of his body. The Innkeeper gave him a mug of warmed mead. He took a sip, enjoying the honey flavour. People that went by gave him a wide berth. *Maybe I really do stink*, Ardan thought ruefully.

'Ardan, is that you?'

Ardan's head snapped up, searching for the speaker. It was a mercenary. He was barrel chested with thick red hair and a full beard. The familiarity practically screamed at Ardan, but his feet itched to run, to move, to get to safety. Then the memory hit him; the mercenary's face had lost its sickly cast.

'Riordan.'

The man stepped forward, lifting Ardan in a crushing bear hug.

'Ooof,' was all Ardan could manage.

'Sorry,' Riordan said, putting him down. 'I prayed for you. And Light above, lad, you've had a growth spurt or two since I last saw you. Gotten a few scars too.'

'To impress the ladies.'

Riordan laughed, then looked down at him. 'Are you living on the streets? Gael? Gael!'

The iron-grey haired Innkeeper appeared. 'No need to shout the house down.'

'Ardan here is an old friend. I'll pay for his food, a bath, some clothes and whatever else he needs,' Riordan said with a sweeping gesture.

'That's not necessary,' Ardan said.

'Nonsense. I won't see someone I've shared a span in a sick room with live like this. I insist.'

Ardan shared a look with Gael and shrugged. The Innkeeper understood. 'I have a bath ready and some second-hand homespun that my son's outgrown.'

'Sounds like just the thing. Don't worry lad, I'll be here when you get out. Now go, go,' Riordan said, not letting Ardan get a word in, a wide smile splitting his bushy red beard.

Gael led Ardan to a small room near the rear of the building. It held a basin, a small mirror, a bench and a wide half-barrel, large enough to submerse himself in. The barrel was full, with small tendrils of steam coming off its surface.

'There's soap, a scrubbing brush, and a hairbrush. I'll be back shortly with the clothes. Is there anything else you need?'

'No, thank you.'

After Gael had left, Ardan stripped down and tentatively tested the water. The temperature verged on painfully hot. He eased himself into the barrel. Warmth permeated his bones, and he sighed contentedly. After an indulgent length of time, he grabbed the brush and soap. He scrubbed through layers of dirt and grime, rubbing his skin raw. He checked on the puncture wounds on his leg, finding them a healthy-looking pink. His hair was a different story. After washing it, he stood in front of the mirror and used the brush. He winced as he tore through tangle after tangle, often pulling out large chunks of his own hair. In the end, his black hair was straight, hanging past his ears. He looked at the reflection, really studying himself. He had his father's hawkish face, the tanned skin of living in the outdoors, and the black hair of his mother.

There was a polite knock at the door. Ardan hastily grabbed a towel before Gael came in. She placed the clothes on the bench and left without a word.

Ardan dressed in the loose-fitting clothing. Her son, possibly the hulking man out front, was considerably larger than he was. He had to fold the tent-like shirt sleeves several times to make them fit. He strapped his sword belt on and headed back out to the common room.

Riordan was in the same spot. In front of him were two bowls of stew. He looked up, his whole demeanour radiating approval. 'What a transformation. Come eat, eat!'

Ardan sat down in front of the mercenary. Small tendrils of steam spiralled up from the stew. Picking up his wooden spoon, he took a bite. The gravy was warm and spiced, while the meat chunks fell apart in his mouth. After months of living on a diet of cold, scavenged, near-rotten food or roasted trail game, the warmth and flavour of a properly cooked meal felt fit for heaven's tables. He could barely shovel it in fast enough. A hunk of freshly baked bread was placed next to him. He snatched it up, tearing off a piece and throwing it into his mouth. It had been an age since he'd had fresh bread. A small amount of butter was included. He tore off another piece and hastily chewed while he slathered the remaining bread with butter. Biting off an enormous piece, he leaned back and closed his eyes. When he opened them again, he saw Riordan staring at him.

'No one's going to take it from you, lad.'

Ardan forced a smile. That hadn't been his experience. He used the stew to soak some of the bread before taking another bite. It was one of the best meals he'd ever tasted. He looked enviously at Riordan's food.

'Best not, lad. I've lived through a particularly rough siege. Too much at once and it'll go poorly for you. I'll give Gael some money for a few more meals. Maybe I can help you get off the streets.'

Ardan didn't answer but stared at him suspiciously. Who would be this nice to him without wanting something? Riordan was wearing a rich burgundy cloak that clashed horribly with his hair. The man's leather armour smelt rich, earthy and sweet, very different to the rancid oil most mercenaries used.

'You're doing well for yourself.'

'All thanks to my new employer. That blasted venom kept me bedridden for weeks. When I could finally leave, I did the rounds. I considered applying to one of the bigger mercenary guilds, but she approached me. It was a stroke of luck, really,' Riordan said, sitting back, a faint smile pulling at his lips.

'What does she get you to do?'

'Guard her, mostly.'

'That's it?'

'It's much more lively than I expected. I've fought harder protecting her than in some of the wars my Da and me were in.'

'Really?'

'Aye. It's part of the reason I'm here. We had a couple of close calls with some Shapers. One run-in with the Dark Clergy—that one was nasty. I'm meeting someone here to get a few special materials. We need to hold our own when it happens again.'

Ardan realised Riordan was here to meet him. But before he could say anything, four heavily armed men entered the Inn. Each wore similarly unadorned, toughened leather armour. The first three had spears and shields, with swords strapped to their waists. The fourth carried a loaded crossbow. *Ancients, it's ready to fire*, Ardan thought. Like Riordan, they were well-fed, with well-maintained equipment. None of them wore any identifying markers. Ardan immediately looked for a way out. Soldiers always meant trouble.

'It's clear, lads,' Riordan called with a wave.

They waved back at Riordan, most of them sitting down at their table. The crossbowman stood near the door as another mercenary entered. Behind him came a woman. Her blue garments were tailored to accentuate her slender figure, and her blond hair cascaded in soft waves over her shoulders. It was her eyes that caught Ardan's attention. They were a startling green. Something about them seemed familiar, though he couldn't place it. After seeing her, the large contingent of armed men suddenly made more sense.

'Quite the escort,' Ardan said. Though they appeared at ease, their eyes were constantly assessing the surrounding people. The crossbowman's hands tightened on his weapon when two newcomers entered, and he didn't relax until they sat down.

The woman came towards them after conferring with Gael.

'Taking in more strays?' the woman asked.

'You know me,' Riordan said.

She smiled. 'I think this one is fine. He's our contact.'

CHAPTER TWENTY-SIX: THE DEAL

* * *

*T*omorrow I will ride north with my company. I tried to go alone, but they learned of my plans. At a hundred strong, we will learn more about this threat. We will be branded as renegades and traitors.
— *Journals of Phillip, the twelfth Templar.*

* * *

'You?' Riordan said incredulously. He looked back at the blond woman. 'Him?'

Ardan gave a sheepish smile.

'It appears that way,' the woman said, sitting down. Something in the lilt of her voice tickled at his memory. Why was it so familiar?

'You just let me....' he trailed off, going red. He cleared his throat, looking around. 'Gael, some ale for the lads and some wine for the lady.'

'Wine? We haven't had wine in months.'

'Ale will be fine,' the woman said.

Riordan was getting over his shock. He looked between the two of them. 'I was planning on introducing you anyway, but my lady, this is Ardan. We spent a week in the same healing house. Ardan, this is—'

'Marion,' Ardan interrupted, the memory hitting him like a sledgehammer.

'You've met before?' Riordan said.

Ardan gave a harsh laugh. 'You could say that.'

Marion's green eyes suddenly became wary.

'You saved me from the four men that killed my father and took me to the healing house, most likely saving my life,' Ardan said. Realisation dawned on her face. 'Then you stole all my coin.'

Marion went still, but she met Ardan's stare evenly.

'Is what he says true?' Riordan asked slowly.

'It is.'

'And?' Riordan prompted.

'It's not something I'm proud of. I needed the money, more than you know, and saving him cost me a good deal.'

Ardan rose, fists clenched, but Riordan held out a placating hand without taking his eyes off Marion. 'How much did you take?'

'Not enough to matter.'

'Not enough to matter?' Ardan said, incredulous, anger rising within him. If he'd had that money, everything would be different. Liá would have been safe in Mercenary Square. He might not be living in a hell-blasted chimney. The rage built up so much that a peculiar tingling in his chest burst the anger-filled bubble.

Suddenly, the mug in his hand exploded, showering everyone in frothy ale.

'What in the Light's name was that?' Marion exclaimed, trying to brush the frothing liquid off her dress.

Ardan stared at the mug, just as dumbfounded as the others, his anger fading. The sensation in his chest left him. It had happened again, just as at the bell tower and the Golden Meadow. The fury had found an outlet.

'*Lad,*' Riordan said loudly.

Ardan stared, realising Riordan had been talking to him.

'Can you go get us a rag to clean this up?' Riordan said, before leaning forward and whispering, 'Make sure you take your time. Couple things I'd like to discuss with the lady.'

Ardan nodded, too lost in thought to question it. He blindly walked towards the bathroom again, just glad he'd locked down the power inside him before it could do any damage. Ardan stood in front of the bathroom door, his hand on the latch. *What is happening to me?* It was as though the power was alive, resisting any form of control.

'What are you doing, wandering around back here?' Gael said, interrupting his thoughts.

'Oh, I was—uh—just looking for a rag. I spilled my drink, and we need something to clean it up.'

'Of course you did,' she said. 'I'll be out shortly to mop it up.'

Ardan made his way slowly back to the common room. Marion and Riordan had moved to a different table, away from the guards. They both went quiet when he sat down at the table.

'I may have been mistaken when I took the purse from you,' Marion said. Riordan grimaced, but Marion kept her eyes on Ardan. 'For the harm it has caused you, I apologise. I had reasons, but that doesn't excuse what I did. I owe you more than money, and if you require aid, know that I will come.'

Ardan raised an eyebrow. He caught himself before saying he didn't need the help of a thief. He looked at Riordan's hopeful expression, considered the amount of guards she had, and decided it might not be a bad idea to be owed a favour. He nodded.

Riordan breathed a sigh of relief. 'Can we sit again? Let's get this business done, then we can properly catch up.'

They sat and began talking. Marion kept her gaze on him, her eyes assessing.

'Raigel said you've found a decent amount of heartwood.'

'Enough for a standard-sized shield. Maybe some extra,' Ardan said.

Riordan's eyes brightened.

'That's it?' Marion said.

'It's more than anyone else has found,' Ardan said.

'I have twenty silver temples,' Riordan said.

Ardan tried to keep his face passive. That sort of money would change everything. Hells, he'd be off the streets and living in luxury for months with that sort of money. Yet Raigel's advice echoed in his head, and he restrained himself.

'Are you trying to lowball me?'

'Twenty silvers for a shield is already outrageous,' Marion said.

'Is it?' Ardan said, keeping his face blank.

Marion went to respond, but Riordan shifted his weight. She looked at him.

'It isn't unreasonable,' Riordan admitted. 'It is worth more, much more.'

'Then why offer me twenty?' Ardan said, his suspicion returning. He knew no one was that nice without an ulterior motive.

'Because it is all I have,' Riordan said earnestly.

Ardan sighed; he was inclined to give it to Riordan, but Raigel's advice kept rattling around in his head.

'It's not enough.'

'If I was in your state, I would gladly accept twenty silvers,' Marion said.

'Or steal it if it wasn't offered.' Ardan said.

Marion's lips thinned.

'That was beneath you, lad,' Riordan said.

Anger bubbled up inside of Ardan, but he pushed it down. He breathed out, calming himself, remembering his mother's lessons. 'You are right. I apologise, Lady Marion, for any offence given. Twenty silvers is a fortune, but not what the wood is worth. If you cannot offer me more, then I will have to look elsewhere.'

Riordan stared at him, conflicting emotions warring across his face, then his eyes widened while he looked Ardan up and down. 'I have an idea, but I need to discuss it with Lady Marion first. We will be back soon, lad.'

Marion looked surprised, but she followed Riordan until the two of them were out of earshot. Ardan could read their body language like a book. Riordan was imploring, then explaining, doing some dramatic renditions while Marion watched on, a smile playing on her lips. In the end, she nodded.

'Riordan says you're quite proficient at Kings. I propose we play a game,' Marion said as the two of them sat down.

'Why?' Ardan blurted.

'To get the measure of you.'

'What's in it for me?'

'Lad,' Riordan admonished.

Marion held up a hand, her green eyes drilling into Ardan. 'Riordan's proposal presents a quandary, and this game might help.'

What in the nine hells? Ardan thought. He glanced between the two of them, trying to figure out their angle.

'It'll be worth it,' Riordan said.

'Alright,' Ardan said with a shrug.

Gael brought out the game and a new round of drinks. The three of them took turns with the dice, rolling for their avatar. Ardan drew the Baron, Riordan the Archbishop and Marion the Waterlord.

Ardan kept his face still as he drew some phenomenal cards. As the game progressed, his luck continued, and he could turn it into a landslide if he wanted to. Riordan played as he usually did, gambling wildly by charging ahead, and over the next two turns Marion and Ardan cut him down.

'By the hells, I hate this game sometimes,' Riordan said, draining his cup and going to the bar to get a refill.

Ardan knew Marion was studying him intently as the game continued. He did the same in return, watching as she moved slowly, taking every opportunity to stall. With grim determination, he forced her hand by increasing his forward momentum until she could no longer ignore his advance. She laid her cards down and he countered them easily. He won the game after two more turns.

'Interesting,' Marion said. 'May I see your other cards?'

Ardan reflexively pulled them closer, but after a moment, he reluctantly lowered them.

'As I thought. You drew well and could have finished the game long ago. Instead, you used it to get a better read on us, or at least, on me. Either that or you wanted to draw out your victory,' she added as an afterthought. She rose and went over to Riordan, conferring with him.

Ardan began to pack up the game until they returned.

'Riordan has made a suggestion that may benefit us both,' Marion said, clasping her hands together.

'What is it?'

Marion looked at Riordan and motioned him to take over.

'How would you feel about training to become a mercenary?'

'You want me to become one of her guards?'

'You'd need to train up first, but it'll keep you off the streets at least. You'll learn how to use all the weapons needed to be a good mercenary and have lodgings and armour. It'll come out of the price of the heartwood.'

Ardan looked between the two of them. Something about Riordan just seemed so earnest. 'We never agreed on a price,' he said at last.

'You're right, we didn't. What I'm offering is more than just coins. Marion could lend me the money, but I want to give you some stability, and skills that will last a lifetime. So you won't end up in the state I found you in.'

Memories flashed through Ardan's head of the last few months in the forest. The more time he spent in there, the more dangerous it became, while his trail was becoming more barren than Barleron's fields. He looked at Marion's other guards. Their clothes and armour were in good repair, and they smiled while they ate and drank. He thought about Riordan saying how dangerous it was, but then he remembered his last foray into the forest.

'What would I be doing?'

Riordan beamed. 'To begin with? Training, learning how to fight and take care of yourself. I'll have to work out the details, but it'll be great.'

Marion kept her eyes on him. 'We are taking a chance on you. Riordan vouched for you, which doesn't mean much. The man would vouch for Naberius himself if the demon bought him a beer.'

Riordan gave a dry chuckle.

Marion continued. 'I hope you don't disappoint him.'

Ardan met her stare evenly. 'I guess we'll have to wait and see.'

Riordan grinned. 'Great. The Lady and I have business this evening, but we can start early. We have nothing planned for the morning, right?' Riordan said to Marion.

She inclined her head.

'Then we will be up early. You can stay here for now until we can find something more permanent,' Riordan said. 'Gael,' he yelled.

'Will you stop shouting? You can just wave if you like,' the Innkeeper said in an equally loud voice.

'Young Ardan will need lodging here for a few nights. Maybe longer. Cheapest room you've got,' Riordan said.

'A few silver pennies per night should do it if you want me to feed him as well,' Gael said.

'That much?'

'Food's expensive. It's like they're selling from Lucifer's table.'

'A temple for the week,' Riordan said.

Gael barked a laugh. 'I'll have the boy do some of the dirtier jobs around the place for that sort of price. And he gets the loft. No customer wants that place, anyway.'

'Done. Let him know what needs to be done and he can do it in his spare time. I will need him at odd times, though.'

'Good enough,' she said before turning to Ardan. 'You'll be on the top floor, doesn't have much head room but there's a cot in the corner. You'll have to keep it clean yourself,' Gael said. Then she gave him a meaningful look. 'The cot is a single.'

Ardan cleared his throat uncomfortably while Riordan grinned.

'That'll be it from us then, lad. I'll see you bright and early in the morning. We're already late. Thanks, Gael.'

'Come on,' Gael barked once Marion, Riordan and all their guards had left. He followed her up to the second floor, down the long hallway, and up a small ladder. The roof space was small, and he had to crouch over while he brushed away dust and cobwebs. There was a small, latched window at one end.

'Open that thing and let some light and air into this place,' Gael commanded.

Ardan did as requested, although it took a couple of tries to push the window open. It had a cot in one corner and a tiny desk and stool at the other. There were several barrels stacked up against one wall.

'You'll be living here. Cleaning this place is the first of your chores. I'll wash the sheets for a half copper. Don't touch the barrels. You do, and I'll be charging the Lady and Riordan for the cost of the entire thing. They're beer,' she said, answering his unasked question. 'Hard to get in times like these, so worth plenty. Right then, any questions?'

Ardan shook his head. Gael handed him a few rags and then disappeared down the hole.

He began trying to remove the months of accumulated dust from the small space. As he worked, he couldn't help but wonder at his change in fortune. This morning he'd been living in a makeshift hovel on the verge of starvation. He'd had two square meals in one day, a warm and comfortable place to sleep and the promise of better things to come. For the first time in months, he felt optimistic. He started to hum while he cleaned.

CHAPTER TWENTY-SEVEN:
PRACTICE AND PAIN

* * *

We have scoured the outskirts of Astaroth's domain, penetrating as far as we dared. The number of refugees arriving here rivals those at the Pass. It is clear Astaroth is not the cause. Tomorrow we continue north, though our supplies are dwindling.

— Journals of Phillip, the twelfth Templar.

'Boy!' he heard Gael's voice shouting imperiously. 'Get up. Riordan will be here any moment.'

Ardan's hands shot to the sides of the cot. Uncertainty filled him at the unfamiliar surroundings. It came rushing back to him: where he was, and Gael's shrill voice. He languished in his cot; though it was a simple affair, he felt like royalty. Despite that, he hadn't slept well. He tested his leg, found he could walk with barely a limp, and made his way downstairs.

'How'd you sleep?' Riordan asked.

Ardan shrugged.

'Beds take getting used to after sleeping rough for a while. Tonight should be better. First, we'll need to find you a suitable weapon.'

'I already have a weapon,' Ardan said, indicating the sword at his side.

'That thing? It doesn't look like much.'

Ardan pulled the blade in response. Despite the tattered state of the scabbard, the sword came out looking pristine.

Riordan's jaw dropped. 'That looks like a mighty fine blade. May I?' he said, taking the hilt from Ardan's proffered hand. He ran his finger along the edge. He drew back, rubbing the finger and smearing blood. 'Hell's fire, it's sharp. I'd bet a pretty penny that it's Ancient steel.'

'I thought so too,' Ardan said, taking the weapon back.

'Where'd you get it?'

'My father,' Ardan said softly.

Riordan nodded thoughtfully but didn't press further. 'How much do you know about the old weapons, those of Ancient steel or heartwood?'

'Besides how much it's worth?' Ardan shrugged.

'You haven't tried to sell it, either. I'm guessing it's worth more to you than coin?'

Ardan clutched the blade tighter. It had crossed his mind to sell it on the nights when the hunger pains had felt overwhelming. Or he was shaking from the cold so much he was damn near convulsing. But it was the last piece he had of his father. 'No.'

'Ancient steel is rare, but not unheard of. Has it already started showing its powers?'

'What?'

'Ancient steel is great, no doubt about it. It obviously doesn't need much maintenance, but the real draw is that weapons made from it start developing powers of their own.'

'What?' Ardan asked again, feeling stupid.

'I don't rightly know myself. It just happens after a while. A man in my unit had a war hammer of Ancient steel. Not much of a companion, but real handy in a fight. He saved my ass from the fire plenty of times—my Da too. We were trying to cause an avalanche at Jophiel's pass, to try to block some of the enemy. The man's hammer packed a punch. He smashed some boulders the size of houses down the mountain. It gave the lads some rest, helping us hold the line.'

'You're saying I could do that?' Ardan said, looking at the weapon.

'Maybe,' Riordan said with a shrug. 'I'm not the right person to ask. I didn't ask our companion much, he was fairly prickly. I'm here to teach you to be a soldier. Speaking of which, we need to move. We're already late.'

'Where are we going?' Ardan asked, following Riordan as the man started walking.

'Mercenary Square, one of the best places to learn how to fight. Oh, and keep the fact that the sword there is Ancient steel to yourself. Best to keep it as low profile as you can,' Riordan said.

Ardan nodded. He had already decided the same thing, hoping no one could spot it as easily as Riordan had.

They kept silent as they walked, passing through the barricade without being challenged. Eventually they arrived at Mercenary Square. It was an enormous open space, covered in sand and dirt. Multiple troops of horsemen could practice different manoeuvres with room left over. Over a hundred people were already milling about, checking on their horses, chatting idly, haggling with merchants, or doing weapons drills. The entire Square was lined with a collection of Inns, weapon smiths, armourers, farriers, stables, general stores, tap houses and semi-permanent residences, making the place a city in itself.

Ardan followed Riordan over to an area where a group of thirty men and women were training with their weapons. They watched as the group drilled repeatedly while a limping older man moved around them. He leaned heavily on his cane as he walked, but it doubled as a discipline stick whenever he saw sloppy work. The cane didn't discriminate as it found flesh, eliciting yelps of pain while he yelled at the soldiers to turn their feet or move their bodies, not just their arms.

'What are you doing here, you giant cow shite?' the limping man said when he noticed them.

'Visiting a tired and grumpy old has-been,' Riordan said affably.

'Old!'

Riordan shrugged.

The man grinned. 'What brings you around here? I'd be interested in a few drinks, but not until I finish training these useless whelps.' He turned and spat on the ground. 'Who said you could stop?' he shouted when he saw the practice had slowed. 'Get back to it!'

The group hastily got back to practising.

'Ardan here needs to be taught how to fight,' Riordan said.

'You sired a bastard?'

Riordan laughed. 'No, Marion wants him trained. Ardan, this is Seamus, probably the foulest-mouthed lecher in the city, but not a half-bad teacher.'

'What does he need?' Seamus asked, sizing Ardan up.

'Someone to teach him a solid foundation in sword work and some unarmed combat. I couldn't think of anyone decent to teach him, so thought I'd settle for you.'

Seamus grunted. 'What of the spear?'

'We're going to be doing mostly personal guard work. Not a lot of use for spears.'

Seamus spat on the ground. 'The Prostitute still alive, I take it?'

Riordan's lips thinned.

'Just asking. The new city lords die at an alarming rate, though yours seems to be pretty good at avoiding it. You sure you don't want spear training?'

'Maybe later,' Riordan said.

'You'll regret it, but you're paying,' Seamus said. He turned to yell at his students. 'Alright, you worthless pieces of demon shit. Take a rest and get some water. Pray to whoever you have to for some flaming improvement, or I'll give you all a good hiding!' He turned back to them. 'What's he know already?'

'Knife and bow,' Ardan said.

'Hunter's bow, I take it?' Seamus said but didn't wait for an answer before he continued: 'Makes sense; Tristan probably taught you that one.'

'Eh?' Riordan said.

'He's one of Tristan's boys. I'm getting old not seeing it right away. Tristan was a forest stalker, and a good one too. It makes sense he taught him some tricks. He didn't teach you much else, though.'

'He taught me—' Ardan began.

'That wasn't a question,' Seamus cut in, 'I know where his strengths lay. He could shoot a bull's eye from a hundred paces but could barely hold a sword without cutting himself. Your mother, though, she was a different story. A real talented fencer.'

'My mother?' Ardan said. *She was a fencer?* he thought incredulously.

'Aye, though I don't think your father ever knew.'

Ardan opened his mouth to object, but the old man's cane swept out and slapped him across the thigh. It took a moment before the pain blossomed and he started hopping, crying out in pain.

'Don't interrupt me, boy. I'm here to teach you how to fight, not hold some lengthy argument. You'll do as I say, and you'll get better. Any back chat or arguments and you'll get welts. Understand?'

Ardan nodded, trying not to whimper.

'Answer—yes, sir.'

'Yes, sir.'

'Good choice for a weapon, that,' he said, pointing at Ardan's falchion. 'Takes into account your size. It's made for slashes and cuts; takes a bit of skill to use well, though, and speed. You'll need to be quick. It takes plenty of practice. You can use it on horseback too, although from the looks of it you can't even afford a one-eyed, lame pony. You'll start on practice weapons till I think you're ready. Get to the shed and pick out a sword that looks and feels like yours. Go,' Seamus said impatiently, angry that Ardan wasn't already moving, although he hadn't stopped talking.

Ardan turned to run.

'Stop,' Seamus snapped. 'Give your sword to Riordan.'

Ardan handed over the sword in its crumbling sheath and ran to the shed. It stood near one edge of the yard and was one of the few structures to occupy a space inside the Square. Across the walls were hundreds of wooden practice weapons. He bypassed the wooden pikes and spears, heading for the sword section. There were broad and bastard swords by the dozen. He shifted through the racks of short swords and sabres until he found one similar to his. It had a less pronounced curve, and weighed more, but it was close.

By the time he returned, the trainees were already exchanging blows. Seamus moved between the different groups, shouting at them. Riordan watched the whole thing with a bemused smile.

Seamus barked an order and every one of his trainees stopped and quickly gathered around him. 'We've got someone new joining us,' he said, and sixty-odd eyes glanced at Ardan. 'Okay, so let's see if you got any mongrel in you. Try to hit me.'

A couple of them snickered.

Ardan just stared at the man.

'Use that sword, you useless gutter shite, and cross weapons with me,' Seamus said, brandishing his cane in front of him. 'Bring your best.' He had turned side on to compensate for his bad leg.

Ardan approached hesitantly. His wooden sword was raised at mid-point in front of him, but he stayed out of range of the old man. He knew a trap when he saw one.

'Grow a pair,' Seamus bellowed.

Ardan's eyes narrowed. He used what his father had taught him. Look at the animal's stance, watch their body language. Seamus's good knee was bent and leaning slightly forward. *What the hell*, Ardan thought and swung. Seamus stepped back, and Ardan's sword swished through the air, meeting no resistance. Ardan then saw his opponent step forward and the cane swing towards his head. He ducked and caught a look of surprise on Seamus's face. The cane was already circling back before he could regain his balance. Instinct took over.

He lunged forward, shoulder barging into Seamus. It knocked the old warrior back off balance, but that barely slowed him. He swung his elbow, catching Ardan in the head. The blow sent him sprawling, stars erupting in his vision. The next thing he felt was the cane under his chin.

'Look at that, boys and girls. No matter how little training a person has had, they can still surprise you. Sometimes that can mean death. It's one of two important lessons,' he said as Ardan got to all fours. He slammed Ardan with his cane, making him collapse again. 'Don't leave a foe alive and behind you if you can help it.'

When the world stopped churning, Ardan hesitantly got to his feet. The grizzly instructor showed no remorse, just pointed at another trainee. He was a medium-height, stocky man, edging into his middle years. He trotted over, showing a friendly grin beneath thick blond hair. The smile immediately put Ardan at ease.

'Everyone else split up, new partners,' Seamus said. They all slowly paired up. 'By the hells! Move, you useless lumps!' he roared and began swinging his cane at anyone who was close enough to hit. The students ran to the nearest person and immediately started sparring.

Seamus hobbled over to Ardan.

'Eamon is an old hand, having trained others and survived a scrap or two. He's better with the shield than most of these poor excuses for fighters,' Seamus said, standing between the two of them. 'And because, like you, he can't use that sword of his worth a damn.'

Eamon grinned and shrugged, as though to say it was a fair assessment.

'Use your speed to avoid getting hit. Use your sword to strike. Only use it to block if you're desperate,' Seamus said, standing closer and bringing the cane up under Ardan's arm, so that he raised the weapon. 'It's a finesse weapon, and like you, it's not made for hacking. You've got a light build, good for speed. If you're good enough, you might not get yourself killed in your first battle, understand?'

'Yes, sir.'

'Eamon, just block to begin with. While I want you,' Seamus said, pointing at Ardan, 'to hit him any way you can. It's not a trick. I want to see your form.'

Ardan raised his sword hesitantly and brought it down on Eamon's shield with a dull thud. He quickly looked to Seamus for the man's judgement.

'Where in the heavens did your fire go? Your attack was as fierce as a washerwoman's. By Lucifer's backside, I wish I could have one decent swordsman come to me. Again.'

Ardan attacked with more vigour, striking first from above, then shifting to the side. Eamon barely shifted his shield to block it.

'Better,' Seamus said. 'Stay on the balls of your feet, keeps you nimble. Don't draw your blade back so far, tells your opponent what you're about to do. Quick slashes. Got it?'

Ardan nodded.

'Today you're just getting used to the weight of the weapon. Tomorrow we'll begin the foundations of your training,' Seamus said and hobbled off.

'He's a little gruff but he knows his stuff,' Eamon said cheerfully. 'Ready?'

Ardan nodded, and they began. Their swords went back and forth, the clanging of the wood filling the air around them. It didn't take long before Ardan felt tired; the sweat seeped right through his clothes. It felt like hours before Seamus made it around to them again.

'Not very fit, are you? Soon you'll be able to keep up with the demons of hell.' He paused, sizing up Ardan. 'Then again, maybe not.'

Ardan moved to leave.

'Where in the blazing hell of Lucifer's ugly red member do you think you're going?' Seamus roared.

Ardan froze.

'You leave when I *say* you can leave. Get back in front of Eamon. I want to see you two fighting until the sun sets. If you're lucky, it will be the one that sets today.'

Eamon shrugged and raised his sword and shield to let Ardan know he was ready. They began again, while Seamus limped off. His weapon felt as heavy as an anvil. He found it easier to step out of the way of Eamon's attacks rather than parry.

'Good!' Seamus yelled. He was so close that Ardan jumped. He hadn't noticed the man sneaking up on them. 'Did I say you could stop?' he shouted and struck Ardan across the arm with his cane so hard he dropped his weapon. 'Pick that thing up before I give you another love tap.'

Ardan picked it up. The muscles in his arm and body protested every movement, but he got the blade up and in front of him again. Then he and Eamon went back to trading blows.

It was barely past midday when the Square seemed to become hazy. Ardan squinted as the world churned around him, and he stumbled, finding Eamon's wooden sword at his chest again. Breathing hard, he stepped back and tried to raise his sword, his entire shirt drenched in sweat. Ardan hated that Eamon only had a light sheen of perspiration on him.

Seamus clapped. 'Enough. Get a drink and some slop. Can't have any of you passing out on me. I'll begin again at first light tomorrow,' he said, then looked at Eamon and Ardan. 'You, new boy.'

'Ardan.'

'I don't care. Be late again and I'll make the fires of hell seem like a walk in the park. Understand?'

'Yes, sir.'

Seamus nodded and walked off.

'It might seem hard, but he's trained some outstanding warriors and been in some serious wars,' Eamon said.

'He has?' Ardan asked, then thought about it. The man had been through everyone, correcting their form no matter their weapon. 'How'd he get injured?'

'Oh, I'm not brave enough to ask that,' Eamon said. 'You can, though.'

'Thanks,' Ardan said wryly, knowing he'd probably end up with another welt or two.

Eamon waved and jogged towards the weapons shed. *How does the man have the energy to run after this?* Ardan grumbled to himself while he tried to follow.

Riordan intercepted him before he got there. 'You'll need to oil that before you put it away.'

Ardan let out a heavy breath.

'It's all part of it. You want to make good coin, this is part of it. Oil it and I'll take you back to the Inn and you can get some food. Get some water in you before we head off.'

It took what felt like an age, but Ardan went inside the shed and oiled the practice sword at the workbench before replacing it on the rack. He stopped by one of the rain barrels and used the ladle to drink. It felt like liquid gold was being poured down his throat and he went back again and again. Riordan grabbed his arm, shaking his head gently. Ardan understood he shouldn't drink too much too quickly and the two of them left the Square together.

They arrived at the Inn a little after lunch.

'You did well today,' Riordan said once they were settled. 'And old Seamus spoke well of you. He rarely does that.'

Ardan felt a warming in his cheeks but was saved from thinking of a reply when Gael arrived and put the bowls down in front of them. He immediately started eating the warm stew. The faster he ate, the faster he could get upstairs and get to sleep. He finished it so quickly even Liá would be impressed. He got up to leave, but Riordan held up a hand.

'What?' Ardan asked abruptly.

Riordan gave him a flat expression.

'Sorry.'

'If you're going to work with the nobility, then you need to abide by their rules, and as such manners are essential. Ask if you may be excused.'

'Why?'

'It is one of the games they play. If you want to play rough, then you'll never be able to expect more than a halfpenny for your work. But if you show you are a man of refinement,' Riordan said with a flourish of his hand, 'well, then they will pay you as such.'

'May I be excused?' Ardan said.

'You may.'

Ardan went up the stairs, then up the ladder and collapsed on his bed. He was asleep as soon as his head hit the pillow.

A moment later, Riordan was shaking him awake. Exasperated, he was about to ask why, but then he saw that the sun had set ,and it was dark outside. The hours had passed like minutes. The mercenary got him to get up and follow him outside. There they stretched. Ardan's muscles protested loudly at the simple movements. Riordan did them easily, while Ardan struggled not to stumble. He hated it and he hated that he felt better and more limber. He looked at Riordan and grumbled his thanks.

The man gave a knowing smile.

They didn't speak after that. They ate dinner in silence before Ardan headed to the third floor and his bed.

He had barely shut his eyes before he was being woken by Gael's shrill voice telling him he was going to be late for the practice yard again.

Ardan groaned.

It only took him a few days to begin to dread the sound of her shrill call, because it heralded another day of practice and pain.

CHAPTER TWENTY-EIGHT: AIR AND POWER

* * *

*E*ntire towns lie completely deserted. The farms have been harvested
and left bare. Theory and history books do not prepare you for the
lifeless countryside of a nation at war.
— Journals of Phillip, the twelfth Templar.

* * *

A LOUD CREAK at the bottom of the ladder made Ardan's eyes snap
open. It was too early for it to be Gael. The ladder creaked again. And
it was too loud for it to be the Innkeeper. Acting on instinct, he rolled
over and slid out of bed, grabbing his sword on the way. He hadn't
lost the skill of creeping quietly that his father had taught him.
Moving in a measured manner, he kept the weight on the balls of his
feet and stuck to the shadows. The ladder groaned as a shadow
appeared in the hole.

'Oi, lad,' the shadow whispered.

Ardan's shoulders sagged with relief. It was Riordan. Who else
would it be?

'Over here,' Ardan said.

'*Ahh!*' Riordan yelled as he jumped, then lost his footing. His shadow disappeared down the hole and there was a loud thump as he hit the second floor. 'Hell's fire,' he groaned.

Ardan popped his head over the hole and saw Riordan's sprawled form. The man sat up, shook his head, and gingerly got to his feet. He looked up at Ardan in disbelief.

'Get dressed, put on your leathers and bring your sword. We're needed and fast. I'll meet you downstairs after my heart stops pounding.'

Ardan grabbed his leathers, tightening their straps. Riordan had said he'd have to grow into them. He belted on his sword and hurried down the ladder. *I've only been training for two months—are they that desperate?*

He made it downstairs and found Riordan stretching his lower back into a half moon shape. Ardan walked over and Riordan jumped.

'Holy shite lad, that's twice. Announce your presence for the Light's sake.'

'I'm not doing it on purpose,' Ardan muttered.

'Marion is mobilising everyone she can. We're meeting at the Tree of the Ancients,' Riordan said and then held up his hand to stall Ardan. 'No, don't ask me any more, because I don't know. We need to move.'

Ardan stayed silent as he followed the mercenary. It wasn't easy, as he was practically dying from curiosity by the time they got to the Tree. Eden's two moons shone light down on the dozen figures standing around Marion. She wore a practical dress of blue and white, with the hem high enough that you could make out her leather boots. She was pacing back and forth, constantly looking towards the different entrances.

A woman, with hair that was silver despite her youthful appearance, joined them. She looked familiar, but Ardan couldn't remember where he'd seen her.

'Bree, I'm glad you could make it,' Marion said, before turning to the rest of them. 'I know it's early, but something has just been called to my attention. I'm sure you're all aware that the mercenaries have banded together until the city settles down.'

Ardan nodded along with the rest of them as she continued, 'Over a month ago, they sent large caravans to Dentwall to secure grain and livestock, enough to flood the markets with food.' Shocked gasps met this announcement. 'I can't overstate the implications; it will change the dynamics of everything in the city. The first carts are arriving as soon as today. I need to arrive in Mercenary Square with a show of force. I expect a lot of sabre rattling, and I need your support. There shouldn't be any bloodshed.'

'What's your plan?' Bree asked. Her voice was like a violin, sharp and pleasant.

'To call them to account,' Marion said firmly. 'They made an agreement with me, one that they have broken. I want them to know that they cannot proceed without consequences. The rest will happen on the wind.'

Bree tilted her head for a moment before inclining her head. No one else spoke.

'Alright, if there are no more questions, let's go,' Marion said.

Ardan fell in beside Riordan. Besides the odd street urchin, the roads were empty. Before long, they had arrived at the north entrance of Mercenary Square.

Scores of mercenaries were up and moving. Seamus's class didn't begin for hours, but even then, it wouldn't account for this many people.

Marion strode straight for the largest group. There were a dozen soldiers standing in a haphazard circle around a single man with short, cropped grey hair, dark leather armour, a short sword at his side, and a large wooden shield on his back. He wore the Red Wolf armband. He saw the group approaching them and held up his hand. The group fell silent as he stepped out in front.

'Lady Marion, you look as beautiful as ever.'

'Thank you, Captain Dásun,' Marion said with mocking courtesy. 'I believe we should talk.'

'Later. There are things in motion,' he said, gesturing around the courtyard.

'I am aware of what you are doing. I have waited this long in the hopes that you would honour your word. But it has been in vain,' Marion said, stepping in front of their own group, her head high.

Dásun paused, his eyes assessing, but he said nothing. The mercenaries behind him shifted uncomfortably.

'Captain, did we not strike a bargain? That my protection was contingent on information being filtered through me?'

'The other captains and I have all agreed to stay quiet on it. We agreed before you and I struck any bargain.'

'Irrelevant. There were no contingencies or loopholes in our agreement. If you had given me word, I could have used my people and made this whole transition easier.'

'If I thought you had any actual power, I would have. You are a woman, not a military man; you wouldn't understand,' Dásun said, with another wave of his hand.

'Do you have no honour?' Marion challenged.

'What would a whore know about honour?' Dásun snapped.

Riordan growled, his hand snapping to his sword. Marion made a hushing gesture. He held the hilt but didn't draw the weapon.

'Then perhaps you could explain something for me?' Marion said in a sweet voice. Ardan could practically feel the venom laced into it. 'What would happen if I suddenly sent my people to every corner of the city, to tell everyone what you're doing? They'll yell it on the streets. What if I send messages to the Fiddler and the Dock Master about it?'

'Do it, I couldn't care less. We're giving it to the people.'

'But how do they know that? You've kept it very quiet. For all they know, you'll be hoarding it.'

Dásun stared at her, his eyes incredulous. 'That would mean, they would ... you wouldn't dare.'

Ardan remembered the desperation of the people during the riot as they charged the Merchant Quarter. Their hunger-fuelled rage.

'Wouldn't I?'

'You told us you'd give us protection,' Dásun said, grasping for something.

'And you expect me to honour my word?' Marion asked innocently.

Dásun eyes narrowed, his eyes darting to the people around her.

'You think I came here unprepared? I have orders in place and the entire city will know by midday unless I stop it. Do not test me, Captain.'

Dásun's jaw seemed to have stopped working. He stared incredulously at her. 'You would destroy everything out of spite?'

'I'm here to make sure you keep your word, Captain.'

Dásun looked behind him again. The mercenaries had spread into a semicircle around them. Riordan drew his sword, and this time Marion didn't stop him. The other members of their party drew their weapons and fanned out. Ardan followed suit, holding his falchion in front of him. So much for not having to fight, Ardan thought. He looked at the gigantic figure directly before him. His features were hidden in the morning gloom, but something about him was achingly familiar. Ardan watched him draw the axe in the way he'd seen a hundred times.

'Davan?'

The axeman slowed his draw. Ardan stepped forward with a few tentative steps until he was close enough to see his brother's features. When they became clear, Ardan's sword slipped from his grasp, and he charged forward. His brother's eyes widened in alarm, but then recognition flickered in them, and he dropped his axe and opened his arms. They collided in a rough embrace. The contact drove the air from Ardan's lungs.

'Ardan,' Davan said after they separated. 'I was so worried about the two of you. I looked everywhere but...' he said and Ardan could see his eyes were glistening. 'Where's Liá?'

'She's safe,' Ardan said, and his brother visibly relaxed.

'I got sent to Dentwall, I asked people to look, I—' Davan stopped, looking at the surrounding people. Suddenly transported back to the tension of the confrontation, Ardan hesitantly looked around, but everyone had lowered their weapons.

'Maybe we can come to an arrangement,' Marion said quietly.

'That would be wise,' Dásun agreed. The other mercenary captains took his lead, and suddenly Marion was giving orders and a few of her party ran off.

A troop of men arrived on horseback. Ardan recognised Lachlan, their leader, with his long blond hair and warrior's build.

'Davan,' Lachlan began, but stopped, his eyes widening. 'Ardan! You're alive, it's good to ... have I interrupted something?' he asked, looking around.

'Nothing that can't wait,' Dásun said.

'Excellent. It's good to see you alive, Ardan. We prayed for you. I am sorry, Davan, but it can't wait. We need to go.'

'I'll find you tonight, once this is all over,' Davan said, grasping Ardan on the shoulder before mounting the horse Lachlan held for him.

'Stay safe,' Lachlan called as he nudged his horse. The rest of the horsemen followed him out of the square.

'Your brother, eh? Did you have the same father?' Riordan said. Then he immediately raised his hands in front of him defensively. 'I'm just joking, lad. You're just an average Barleronian, maybe a tad taller. Him, though? He'd be big even in the Empire.'

'He is at that,' Bree said admiringly.

'We have the same father,' Ardan said flatly. The pang in his chest flared at the mention of his father. How long had it been since Tristan had died?

'I'm just joking, lad. You share too many similarities.'

Ardan forced a smile. 'I haven't seen him in over half a year. I didn't even know he was still alive. They told me he was, but that's different to knowing, you know?'

'Aye, I get that.'

'So, what now?' Ardan asked.

'Well, after our tense morning, we'll stay near Marion as she goes around and works her own special brand of magic on this place.'

'I'm surprised she didn't take charge of the entire operation. Isn't that what she's aiming for?' Ardan asked.

Bree laughed. Riordan peered at him for a long time before he answered. 'Watch her for the next few hours, lad, and tell me she isn't running things.'

Ardan sighed. He hated when the man wouldn't give him a straight answer. Nevertheless, the three of them followed Marion. He had nothing else to occupy him, so he watched her. She was speaking with Dásun, and he focused on their conversation.

'We've coordinated with the other bands, and we will escort the wagons to the distribution points. We'll keep enough men on guard to stop anything underhanded from taking place.'

'How much are you passing out?' Marion asked.

'We are treating this as a siege. We will be giving rations of food out sparingly, enough for the people to eat, but we will keep the majority here in the Square.'

'Smart thinking,' Marion said, and though Dásun tried to appear nonchalant about it there was a prideful shift in his body language.

'Have you any objection to me spreading word through my channels? That the mercenary bands will be handing out food to everyone for free?'

Dásun paused for a moment to consider. 'It should be obvious soon enough.'

'It should be, but you know how the masses can be. If our word gets there first, then the people will be much more amenable because they know they won't be cheated.'

Dásun nodded. 'You're right.'

Marion wasted no time in sending a couple of her retainers running out of the Square with instructions.

'Fancy a drink?' Riordan said to Bree.

The woman appraised Riordan, her blue eyes sparkling. 'Sure, why not?'

Ardan looked up at that.

'Not you, lad. You're Marion's shadow, someone needs to be. We'll be over there,' Riordan said, pointing to one of the many Inns lining the square. It had empty tables out the front. 'Signal if you need us.'

Ardan grumbled but he did as he was told, while Riordan and Bree left. He tailed Marion as she went around to each of the mercenary leaders. He started noticing a pattern in the way Marion handled the situation. As she approached them, the captains would stiffen or cross their arms or some variation of defensive body language, while she questioned what they did. She would always compliment what they had put in motion and appear to be an attentive audience. It never failed to disarm them. Then she would offer some tidbit of advice or assistance, and invariably they would agree. Ardan tried to consider if she had done this to him. He conceded she probably had.

It was well into the afternoon before the first wagons started rolling into the square, along with six guards. Marion dismissed him as they came to report to her. Ardan made his way over to Riordan and Bree. He was so deep in thought that he didn't notice what Bree was doing until he was almost on top of them.

He stood stock still when he did. Her silver hair, although tied tightly back in a ponytail, was spinning and twirling while the wine spiralled upward out of her glass and hung, suspended in mid-air. Bree then made a gesture and her hair seemed to flow with the wind, while the suspended wine flowed in a tiny stream straight into her mouth. She stopped sipping and let the wine flow back into her glass. Once the wine had settled, she smiled at Riordan who roared with laughter.

'That's where I've seen you before,' Ardan exclaimed.

She raised an eyebrow at him.

'You were there, that day on Merchant Street. Where there was a riot of hundreds of people. You were deflecting the stones being thrown,' Ardan said.

'I was,' she said with a shrug, 'Not a lot of work for a sail master when few ships are coming into Dock. I take work where I can find it, and that day it was protecting the Merchant Guard from missiles, rocks or otherwise.'

'So, you can control the wind?' he said, pulling out one of the wooden chairs and sitting down.

'I can influence its flows and direction to a certain extent. I usually use it to bring in ships safely during high winds or to protect the ports during storms. Long nights, those.'

'How?'

'First time meeting a Shaper?'

Ardan hesitated before nodding.

'Buy me another wine and I'll tell you.'

Ardan looked at Riordan. The man sighed.

Once her wine arrived, she started.

'It's quite simple to understand the basic concepts. I'm just not exactly sure where to begin.'

'How did you learn how to control the elements?'

'*Element*,' she corrected. 'Any decent Shaper can influence only one element. I'm not sure of the full ins and outs of it, but when your communication skills with that element increase, you seem to lose the ability to communicate with the others. At least that's how it was with me. Murieen, my mentor, tried to teach me to communicate with water but I had a much higher affinity for air, so I eventually started to communicate with it and shape it.'

'Communicate?'

'The elements aren't passive things. They're alive. I can't talk much about the other elements, but trying to communicate with air—well, it's like communicating with a toddler, I guess. I've got to use simple commands and focus on it. It needs lots of direction.'

'What about during a storm—is it throwing a temper tantrum?'

Bree smiled. 'Yes, exactly that. Air is not one single element, it's a combination, a herd of like-minded, related beings, similar but not the same. Like twins, but there are millions of them.'

'That's ... not very clear,' Ardan said.

'Have you ever tried to describe sex to a virgin?'

Ardan gave an awkward shrug as his cheeks turned red.

'They understand the concept, but the feeling, the intimacy of it ... well, it's not something easily conveyed until it's experienced,' Bree said, and the whole time she was staring at Riordan. Then she gave an exaggerated yawn. 'We should probably rest up for the evening in case Marion needs us.'

Riordan stared at her blankly for a moment, 'Oh, *oh!*' he said and stood up so fast his knees knocked against the table, making the glasses rattle.

Ardan was left alone on the porch with three empty wine glasses while he watched Marion move like a bee between all the different mercenary bands. It had been an instructive day.

CHAPTER TWENTY-NINE: THE HUM OF THE TREE

* * *

I have seen it with my own eyes—Lucifer's three-headed hound is unmistakable. Naberius, a High Demon of Hell, leads a great host of men and women.

— *Journals of Phillip, the twelfth Templar.*

* * *

ARDAN WATCHED as the procession of wagons entered the Square. Their contents were unloaded, and they left again. He couldn't help but feel sorry for some of the wagon masters, as they could barely flick the reins on their horses without being shouted at to move somewhere different. A competition was raging between the different mercenary captains, as though whoever yelled the most was winning. The gridlock of wagons made it difficult for people to walk through. A large group of Red Wolf mercenaries was walking towards the worst of the wagon jam with Lachlan in the lead and Davan a step behind him. Ardan got up from his seat outside the Inn and edged closer to them.

'No, no! Ignore everyone but the Quartermaster. They work around you, understand? So do as he commands,' Lachlan was telling the wagon drivers. He then turned to the nearest and loudest Captain. 'And you, Cillian. Weren't you tasked to guard the approach?'

Ardan froze. Cillian was one of his father's murderers. He and Regan shared the same sharp nose and smug smile. Ardan felt a grim satisfaction to see his knife cut had left a jagged scar on the man's arm. His left hand was crooked, as though he couldn't fully open or close it.

'It's Captain Cillian.'

'Well, Captain,' Lachlan said scornfully, 'get back to the approach while I try to clear up this demonic cluster you've created. From now on, all your decision-making privileges have been removed. Nine hells, I've seen pigs make less of a mess than what you've done here.'

'How dare you talk to me like that?'

The deputy captain of the Red Wolves smiled ruefully, stepped forward, and punched Cillian in the mouth. The man went down, his lip split and bleeding. 'Flaming hells, if my mother was bollocking things up as bad as that, she'd receive a similar tongue lashing. I'd never hit her though. I reserve that for demon-brained fools, now get back to your post before I knock some more sense into you.'

Cillian scrambled to his feet, looking mutinous.

'Your men have already left.'

Cillian glanced behind him to see his men had indeed scrambled off. Still cupping his bleeding lip, he turned with as much dignity as he could muster, making for the entrance.

'Davan, how many have we got?' Lachlan asked, his gaze still on Cillian's retreating form.

Davan's eyes were scanning the Square. 'We're four short.'

'Light, give me strength,' Lachlan said. 'Alright boys, I'm sorry but we need to find those wagons. Get your shit together, because we need to hit the edge before dusk.'

'Captain?' Davan asked.

'What?' Lachlan said and noticed Ardan standing there. 'You have two minutes.'

'I might have to miss the feast tonight,' Davan conceded.

'I'll figure something out,' Ardan said.

'I hope the Prostitute has something organised for all of you.'

'It's Lady Marion,' Ardan amended.

'I mean no offence. It's just what everyone calls her. All the city lords have nicknames, like the Dock Master, the Fiddler and … Lady Marion. It's only a matter of time before they duke it out. Try to keep yourself safe, and Liá too,' Davan said. The two shared a rough embrace. 'It's good to see you wearing that. It suits you,' Davan said, indicating the sword at his belt before turning and jogging off.

Ardan watched as his brother joined Lachlan and his squad. They led their mounts between the wagons and out of the Square.

Feeling homesick, Ardan had a sudden urge to visit Liá. Yet when he looked around ,he couldn't see Marion, Bree or Riordan.

To the hells with it. Nostalgia drove him towards the Black Temple, where he hoped he could see Liá. The Black Guards hadn't run him off in weeks. Why not try it again? The looming Temple didn't dampen his spirits as he climbed the steps to the top.

Four Black Guards barred the entrance, their eyes barely visible behind their faceplates. Two lowered spears to show that they knew he was there. He walked closer and smiled.

'Gentlemen.' He spoke more confidently than he felt. 'My sister's a trainee. I'd like to see her.'

'Name?'

Ardan paused, not having gotten this far before. 'Liádan.'

'I will send word. Wait here,' the Black Guard said.

All the Black Guards shared the same emotionless tone. Ardan moved to the edge of the Temple while he waited. He looked around across the city, past the Tree of the Ancients, whose branches jutted across the skyline, to the Cathedral's tinted windows sparkling in the day's dying light. He shifted his gaze to the orange line on the ocean, shining from sun to shore.

'Ardan?' a voice said behind him.

He turned and saw two hooded figures. One wore a grey robe, the other was draped in black. The grey-robed figure lowered her hood. It was the first time in six months he'd seen his sister. She had grown taller, while her face had lost the starved, gaunt look. Her raven black hair spilled out over her shoulders, around the silver symbol of Lucifer hanging from her neck.

'Liá, you're all grown up,' he said, and stepped closer to hug his sister. The Black Guards shifted, but the other priestess held up her hand. Liá froze, but Ardan just hugged her tighter.

'It is you,' she said into his ear, pulling him into a tighter embrace. Ardan felt a budding sensation of warmth inside him, seeing both his siblings on the same day.

'I've been trying to see you for months,' Ardan said after they broke apart.

She smiled, and he realised she hadn't just grown physically. There was a confidence in how tall she stood. 'During the training, I wasn't allowed outside influences. There were … things they had to teach. I don't think I would have learned it with family around.'

'But you're out now?'

Liá looked at the priestess.

'She has moved onto the next stage of her apprenticeship,' Orla said. Even with her hood up, her red hair was unmistakable.

'Next stage? How many are there?'

She ignored him. 'Liá, remember your time.'

Ardan looked between the two of them, 'What?'

'I have one more stage to go before I can leave and return as I please. The Temple will let me know when I have to return.'

'The Temple?' Ardan said.

'I can't speak much about it, at least not yet. Even this kind of visit is irregular,' she said, with a glance at Orla.

'I don't understand—but I do, in a way,' Ardan said. 'Davan is alive and with the Red Wolves.' This elicited a smile from her as he continued talking: 'How are you going in there? Are you happy?'

'The training is hard, but Orla is kind and knowledgeable. She reminds me of Father. The more she teaches me, the more I realise how much I don't know. I can do certain things now, but I can't tell you about it until the next stage of my training.' She continued in answer to his unasked question: 'I don't how long that will take. Orla will let me know when I'm ready. Have you found Mother?'

Ardan shook his head. 'I searched when I was living on the streets, but I didn't know where to start outside of Ragtown. Inside Ragtown ... well, the Fiddler is likely to indenture you if you go in there.'

Liá sighed. 'I hope you find her. The Black Guards often come back with blood on their armour, and I am worried about how dangerous the streets are. It is a relief to know you and Davan are okay.'

'I'm fine,' Ardan said, smiling broadly. Well, he was now. She didn't need to know about before. 'I've gotten an apprenticeship and am learning the sword.'

'Another mercenary in the family,' Orla said. Ardan couldn't tell if she approved or not.

Liá ignored her, 'Ardan, that's great. Where are—' she began.

A giant gong sounded from deep within the Temple. It seemed to reverberate off the stones. Ardan glanced around wildly, his hand immediately going to the hilt of his sword. He realised he was the only one that was reacting; everyone else was unperturbed.

'It's time,' Orla said, and indicated the large ornate black doors at the entrance to the Temple.

'For the one you spent on me,' Liá said, handing him something. On reflex Ardan took it. Both she and Orla raised their hoods and entered the Temple.

After they'd gone, Ardan looked down at the token she'd given him. It was a coin of Lucifer. The too-beautiful face, framed by demon wings, was unmistakable. Bemused, wondering if it would be like the last coin that had brought disaster and relief in equal measure, Ardan put it in his pocket. It made him feel light as he started down the Temple steps. His brother and sister were safe. For the first time in a long time, he felt a great weight lifted off his shoulders, making him walk taller. Once on the streets, he drifted towards the Tree of the Ancients as he always did when he started to wander. Two of Eden's moons were shining brightly tonight, illuminating the city as he walked. There were plenty of people out on the streets, sitting on the front steps of their homes, eating, talking and laughing.

As he got closer to the park of the Ancients, he could hear music. A huge bonfire illuminated the entire park. The Tree seemed alive as the shadows danced in the fire's flickering light. The music floating through the air had a light, moving feel. Dozens of people were up and dancing. There was something wild and primal as they danced around the flames. The smell of cooked pork wafted to him. Ardan joined the queue that had formed in front of the roasting pig, hoping he had enough coin for a small piece. When it was his turn, the man simply cut off a generous slab and passed it to him, smiling as he waved the next person on. Ardan picked up the warm, slightly sizzling meat and took a bite. The succulent flavour washed through his mouth. As he swallowed the first piece, he noticed mugs of beer being passed around and he took one. Before he'd even finished half the cup, he started feeling pleasantly happy.

He wandered over to the base of the tree. He passed a hand over one of the many vines that were hanging down from the branches. It responded, twirling around his hand as though grasping it. The vine felt friendly, unlike the creeping vines in the forest that would crush you if they could.

He eventually found an unoccupied part of the Tree's trunk to sit against. As soon as his back made contact, the whole Tree seemed to hum. He sat up as though struck by lighting and looked around. No one else had noticed; their singing and dancing hadn't abated. He tentatively put his hand back on the trunk. Now that he was ready for it, the hum wasn't as jarring. A sense of contentment swept through him, a similar feeling to the one that he felt when holding his sword. Out of curiosity he drew the weapon. The hum immediately intensified, surging through his body. His hand instinctively tightened on the hilt. A light green flame erupted along the edge, covering the entire blade in a transparent green glow. Ardan dropped the sword onto his lap and immediately scrambled back, pushing himself to his feet. As soon as the sword left his grip, the green flame vanished.

He stared at the sword so long that he started to wonder if he'd imagined it. He touched the blade with a tentative finger. It felt cool. He picked up the blade gingerly and after some swinging around and testing it, he wondered what had been in that beer. He put the sword back into its sheath and decided it was probably time for him to head towards his bed. It had been a long day.

He didn't remember much of the journey home, but he distinctly remembered putting the sword in the corner of his room, away from himself and his bed, just in case. He thought it would take him a long time to fall asleep, but whatever the Tree had sent through him was still there and he fell quickly into a deep, contented sleep.

CHAPTER THIRTY: A BROTHER'S FURY

* * *

*T*he army of Naberius is an ocean of people, their numbers spanning the horizon. The Fortress of the Light cannot stand against such numbers. I have sent riders to the Pass and beyond to prepare.
— *Journals of Phillip, the twelfth Templar.*

* * *

WHEN ARDAN AWOKE the next morning, the hum from the Tree was gone. He sprung bolt upright. *What in the nine hells happened last night? Did I leave a burning sword in the room?* The sword leaned against the wall, still in its scabbard. He tentatively touched it, but the leather on the grip felt normal. He drew the weapon and saw curved lines near the hilt, too regular to be a blemish. The more he studied them, the more they looked like vines with budding leaves. The sword didn't burst into flames again, but he was still wary, electing to carry it rather than strap it to his waist. As he looked up, he could see light was shining through his small window.

'Hell's fire,' he cursed. He'd have to run to make it to training on time.

Ardan was breathing hard as got to the Square. Seamus' practice group had almost doubled in size, with a lot of fresh faces. Most of them had an armband representing one or other of the mercenary groups. He froze. Amongst their number was Regan. The tall boy's hair was sleek and wavy again. They stopped and stared at each other. The last time Ardan had seen him, Orla had knocked him unconscious.

'Bad blood between you two?' Seamus said.

Ardan tried to answer, but Seamus slapped him with his cane. He yelped, pain blossoming in his thigh. Regan smiled cruelly. Seamus smacked him too. 'Now you two have something in common. One week you fight against each other, the next side by side. It is our lot. Have either of you killed friends or family of each other?'

'Close enough,' Ardan said.

'It's a yes or no answer, you goat-brained fool,' Seamus said. 'I don't expect you to be butt buddies, but you will work with all types. I will pair you against each other, and soon. If we have a problem, you will duel me to first blood.'

Ardan swallowed. He'd seen Seamus do it several times; the instructor used nothing but his cane, a blunt weapon, against a blade or spear. Whoever was foolish enough to take on their instructor never came close to winning. Seamus was careful to beat and bruise them until he deemed they'd had enough. Then his precision strikes would eventually draw blood, often after they'd already tried to concede.

Regan hadn't seen it, but his smile faltered none the less.

True to Seamus's word, they weren't paired together today. Instead, Ardan fought against Saoirse, a pretty brown-haired woman a few years his senior. She fought with a medium length slender blade and was exceedingly quick. By the end of their session, Ardan had the usual number of welts from Seamus' cane and felt pleasantly tired.

He replaced the practice sword and picked up his own, then went looking for Riordan. Yet he was barely halfway across the Square when he could see Davan coming towards him. The way his brother was moving made Ardan think of an angry bull.

Oh shit, I know that look, Ardan thought as he spread his hands wide to appear as nonthreatening as possible. His brother threw a punch at him as soon as he got close. Without thinking, he brought his arms up to block the blow. It was still powerful enough to send him reeling.

'*Liá is a black acolyte?*' Davan roared. He stepped closer and delivered another hit. Ardan blocked this better and kept his balance, skittering back. 'You've condemned our sister to a fate worse than death,' he continued as he stepped forward and laid out several quick snaps. Despite his size, Davan moved smoothly. Ardan ducked and weaved his way backwards, only taking a few glancing blows. 'What in the Light were you thinking?'

Suddenly Riordan was there, standing between them.

'This is between him and me,' Davan said, towering over him.

'You need to calm down.'

Davan said nothing as he drew his axe. 'Last chance, old man.'

Intricate vines twirled around the haft and spilled out onto the steel of his brother's axe, just like on Ardan's blade.

'Don't do anything foolish, lad,' Riordan said, pulling his shield off his back.

'Move.'

Riordan drew his sword and shook his head sadly.

Ardan held the hilt of his sword, but he didn't draw. He didn't want this to escalate any further. He opened his mouth to say something, but then Davan swung his axe at Riordan and the two of them were fighting.

'Stop, stop you flaming demon shit,' Ardan yelled.

Davan ignored him as he pressed forward using the superior reach of his axe to attack, while Riordan used his shield and sword to deflect. Riordan moved expertly, never taking a hit directly. Davan kept trying to scare or fight Riordan out of the way so he could get to Ardan, but the warrior kept getting between them.

'Stop, you stupid fool!' Ardan yelled, but the two continued back and forth. He gripped his sword tightly. He didn't know how to intervene.

At first Ardan thought his mentor was taking it easy on his brother, but his brother wasn't giving him any openings even if Riordan wanted to fight back. His strikes never overextended, and he never exposed himself. The rage was there, beneath a mask of intense focus. Davan struck hard, getting Riordan full on for the first time. The axe sunk into the shield with a dull thwack. Davan yanked back, pulling the shield out of Riordan's grasp, leaving him with only his sword.

Riordan didn't hesitate. He stepped neatly forward into the opening. Davan brought his axe up to block, but the shield was still lodged on the axe and it slowed him down. Riordan grabbed for the shield and grasped the handle. He used the leverage to tilt Davan off balance and used the split second to slam the hilt of his sword into Davan's face, sending him stumbling back. The axe dislodged from the shield, and Riordan was fully armed again.

The fight had attracted a crowd of onlookers, with more arriving every second. Davan spat blood onto the ground. He smiled, showing bloody teeth.

'Davan, stop before this gets any worse,' Ardan said.

His brother ignored him, keeping his attention on Riordan. 'You have some skills, old man. I'll give you one last chance to leave, but if you stand between my stupid brother and me one more time, I will kill you.'

'Lad, this isn't the way.'

The spectators were growing to include Seamus' class and scores of mercenaries.

'So be it,' Davan said and charged, his axe raised.

There was something different. Ardan felt a familiar internal rush in response to Davan. As Riordan brought his shield up, the axe let out a pulse of invisible energy. Even from this distance, the power of the strike caused Ardan to stumble.

Riordan caught the full brunt of it, and it sent him flying back. He landed hard on the gravelly surface of the square. His breath was expelled from his lungs, and his sword skittered away. With effort, Riordan stumbled to his feet, still holding his shield.

Davan advanced. He drew his axe back in a mighty swing. Riordan just got the shield up in time, but the axe blasted it apart and sent Riordan sailing through the air again. He crashed into some wooden training equipment, scattering it. He groaned, trying to move, but it was clear he wasn't getting up again. Davan came towards him, his axe held like a waiting executioner's.

'No!' Ardan shouted, running to intercept him. He drew his sword, and he instinctively funnelled his internal power into it. The blade burst into brilliant green flame. He didn't pause as he ran, but before he could close the distance, a blast of wind hit him and he stumbled, barely keeping his feet. He looked up, fearing the worst, but his brother had been affected too.

Ardan spotted the source. Bree's silver hair was unmistakable as it twirled and spun while the wind cascaded around her.

'Stay out of this, witch,' Davan said as she squared off against him.

Bree lifted both her hands, her expression thunderous. In response, her hair whipped forward as a gust of wind shot from her. The dirt spiralled up in its wake before it centred on Davan, lifting him into the air. He looked around him, trying to get his bearings. He tried to shift his weight but remained suspended above the ground. The look of confusion left his face, and he narrowed his eyes. He still held his axe and swung it awkwardly. A pulse of energy ripped across the ground and struck Bree. She was launched backwards into the air. Her hands whipped back, and the wind picked up. Her arc through the air slowed until she was gently lowered back down to the ground, the wind settling.

Davan crashed onto the sand and gravel practice yard, the woman's spell broken. He sprang to his feet and whipped his axe forward, sending pulses in controlled motions. Bree shifted her hand back and forth, the wind rising in response. Gravel and sand rose and spat and shattered as the two fought their invisible battle. Davan advanced with each axe swing, and the closer he got, the harder the axe pulses hit Bree.

Ardan ran forward. He would not let his brother do this to him and to his friends. He had no right. How dare he question what he had done in that desperate time? The anger fuelled whatever energy fed the sword and the flame rose.

Davan saw him coming, his eyes taking in the flaming sword, and he swung his axe through the air. Without thinking, Ardan slashed at the air in front of him and the green flame cut through the pulse and engulfed it in a fiery flash of green.

Davan looked shocked. His face set and he gripped his axe. Yet they kept their distance; neither wanted to take the first step that would cement their fight. His brother's chest heaved from the exertion, his eyes shone beneath the bloody face, but then his brow furrowed in confusion. His eyes widened as he tried to draw in breath. He dropped the axe and started pointing at his throat, panic entering his every movement.

Ardan took a step towards him, and the flame on his sword immediately vanished. It made him pause but seeing his brother down on all fours forced him to take another step forward. He hated his brother for what he had done, but he didn't want him hurt. Then it hit him too—he tried to breathe, but there wasn't any air to draw in. Panic welled up in him. He searched around wildly, his eyes settling on Bree, her hands spread.

Ardan realised the problem and immediately took a step backwards. Golden air filled his lungs.

'Enough!' a voice roared. The crowd that had been watching the fight so intently suddenly looked for other things to occupy them as a score of Red Wolves ran past. Lachlan was in the lead, his face red with rage.

Bree lowered her hands and a great whooshing sound could be heard as air filled the void she had created. Davan, now prone on the ground, drew in ragged breaths.

'What in the nine hells happened here?' Lachlan said as his men surrounded the four of them. Riordan got groggily to his feet. Davan followed a moment later. Bree smiled wearily while Ardan stood stock still. Riordan tried to answer but Lachlan held up a hand.

'Let me guess. You,' he said, pointing at Davan, 'came here in a hissy fit because you found out your sister has joined the priesthood. You attacked your brother and then these two,' he said indicating Riordan and Bree, 'went in to defend him. Considering the state of them you must have used the unique powers of your axe. We spent weeks making sure we'd trained you in secret, that your powers were a hidden weapon until the Trials. But you ruined all that work and for what? To sate your anger? I thought better of you. You are a disgrace to the Red Wolves. I'm sorely tempted to rip that tunic off you right now.'

His brother shifted his feet, staring down.

Lachlan rounded on the other three. 'Riordan, get the blazing hells out of here. I'll deal with the rest of you later.' Then he turned to the waiting crowd, his face still furious. 'What are the rest of you gawking at? Clear off!'

The onlookers quickly busied themselves in other parts of the Square. Riordan was moving with the help of Bree. He gathered up his fallen sword and after a few awkward attempts he managed to sheath it. The three of them left the Square quietly. Lachlan's rage could still be heard several blocks down.

CHAPTER THIRTY-ONE:
PERSPECTIVE

* * *

*W*e stole uniforms from Naberius' dog army and began ransacking local towns. We did terrible things to frame Lucifer's hound. It roused the smaller kingdoms to stand united against the High Demon. It's a victory for the Light, but the blood of innocents stains my hands and tarnishes my soul.

— *Journals of Phillip, the twelfth Templar.*

* * *

ARDAN, Bree and Riordan sat in the common room of Gael's Inn. Ardan's mind was flittering between Bree almost killing his brother, his brother almost killing Riordan, and his own sword bursting into green flame. He nursed his ale as the three of them waited.

'Well, your sword finally manifested its power,' Riordan said.

'I had been meaning to ask. Why can his sword catch on fire?' Bree asked.

'It's Ancient steel,' Riordan said. When Bree looked confused, he continued, 'Weapons with special properties. His brother's axe is one. How they work, I don't know. I'm just a simple soldier.'

Bree gave a soft laugh, her hand reaching up to stroke his cheek. 'Does anyone really believe that?'

Ardan took a sip of his ale, struggling not to roll his eyes, feeling irrational anger at their happiness. Riordan already had bruises appearing on the side of his face.

'So these people are weapon shapers?'

'As good as explanation as any.'

'You've got to give me more to go on.'

Riordan sighed, looking down at his ale. 'The weapons are rare, as in I've only encountered one other. I believe it is related to their material origins. Places of power, like the forest. Once they're forged into weapons, they can exhibit powers.'

'Like mine?' Bree asked.

'Maybe.'

Ardan didn't feel the need to join in the conversation. His mind was a torrent of frustration at the disaster Davan had caused. The power inside of Ardan welled and tumbled, taking any spare attention he had to keep it under control.

His thoughts were interrupted when Marion came into the Inn. She wore a green dress of casual elegance and was flanked by several guards. As she approached them, she took in their injuries and her face grew soft.

'You've seen better days, my friend.'

'Bah, I've had worse in bar fights. The young lad got lucky that Lachlan turned up before I could lose my temper.'

Bree snorted.

'You mean the walking mountain with the magic axe?'

'Yeah, he got lucky.'

Marion's smile faded. 'I've smoothed things over with Lachlan. However, I'd like the three of you to make yourselves scarce for a while.'

'What? What did I do?' Bree asked, standing.

Marion tsked. 'The city's peace is tenuous, a hair's breadth from erupting in fire. We can't risk anyone causing that. No one blames you, because without your intervention things would have been much worse,' Marion said, mollifying Bree enough that she sat down. 'I want the two of you on the next caravan to Dentwall. Keep you out of trouble and away from the city for a couple of weeks.'

'I'm not going into the forest,' Bree said. 'The wild air makes me feel like I'm suffocating.'

'No, I figured you wouldn't. I need all the wind masters here for when more ships arrive.'

'And to use me as a bargaining chip with the Dock Master?'

'Blunt, but true,' Marion said easily. 'We have a real chance here to restore peace. Make the city safe enough to walk the main streets without an armed escort. With so few experienced Shapers, you'll be an essential asset.'

'I assume I'll be paid extravagantly?'

'Of course, I've even organised new rooms for you in the Merchant Quarter.'

Bree's eyebrows rose. 'Getting me out of the Ancient Quarter?'

Marion sighed. 'That's the problem I've created by surrounding myself with perceptive people. They see through everything I do.'

'Close enough. And I trust my new accommodations will be nice and grand.'

'Grander than your current one.'

'That is something I can drink to.'

Marion tried to hide her amusement. 'I'll open a tab with the Innkeeper. Riordan and Ardan, you need to be at the eastern gates before first light. I need you to stay clear of Mercenary Square for a while.'

'What about the trials?' Riordan asked.

'The caravan master is desperate, and he'll want to make the return trip as quickly as possible. You'll be back in time.'

'We'll need to make some preparations,' Riordan said, getting up. Ardan rose with him.

'There isn't much to do. They know you're coming. I've had your things brought over—bedroll, weapons, supplies and so on. I'd prefer if you two were to lie low until you leave.'

Riordan looked like a startled deer, a smile spreading across his face. 'Lying low doesn't mean staying sober, does it?'

Marion closed her eyes for a moment. 'Just don't miss the caravan.'

Riordan grinned and got up.

'I would like to have a private word with Ardan,' Marion said.

Riordan shrugged and glanced at Bree. She smiled in turn and the two of them got another table together.

'A game of Kings?'

Ardan shrugged, wondering where this was going. He retrieved the game, and the two of them set up the board. Ardan got the Water-lord while Marion got the High Priest.

'Has your brother always been a devoted follower of the Light?' Marion said as she moved her piece.

Ardan rolled and put some cards down. 'I never thought so. I mean, our father tried to make us go to the local church of the Light. We both said our prayers, but I never thought he took them too seriously.'

Marion nodded, as though expecting that answer. She took up the dice. 'You should know that your sister is quite good looking—stunning, in fact.'

Ardan blanched.

A peal of laughter escaped Marion. 'If she were in my profession, she would have done well.'

'Alright, alright, enough about that,' Ardan said, putting some cards down to distract from that train of thought.

'I understand your brother has been looking to offer her hand to someone suitable.'

'Her hand?'

'In marriage.'

Ardan rose, feeling anger bubbling inside his chest. 'He has no right.'

'Why not? Davan is the oldest male in your family and head of the household. He would have picked someone who could provide for her.'

'But she's just a girl.'

'She's on the cusp of womanhood. The proper forms would be adhered to; they would be betrothed and only married when she came of age.'

Ardan laid down several cards in quick succession. He wasn't sure what Marion had in her hand. But anger bubbled inside him, and he wanted to hit something. She looked surprised and put down a few cards in her defence. They were darkness cards, ones that complimented her High Priest avatar.

'I think he's practically promised her to someone,' Marion continued, 'but when he got back to the city, he discovered that as a Dark priestess, her fate is now her own. Well, he had to rescind the offer, to some embarrassment. I also think he might take the Light seriously, and to find his sister is now part of the Black Clergy, well,' she shrugged, 'you can see the source of his anger.'

By now, Ardan was seething. 'That is so stupid,' he said as he laid down each card. He could feel the anger welling up in his chest. Davan was the one who had abandoned them. He had chosen the Red Wolves over his family. They had fought and nearly died trying to stay safe. Then his brother's audacious anger had almost killed Riordan.

Marion put the High Priest down. All her cards of darkness had been defeated. Ardan put down his last card despite her already being beaten.

'By the Light, I hope I never make you angry at me,' Marion said, looking down at the Tidal Wave card.

'Is that why he attacked me, because I made a choice to protect her and his precious reputation is ruined?'

'I think it runs a little deeper than that,' Marion said gently. 'With your parents gone, I think he saw himself as the protector of your family. He had worked himself into a position where he could finally save you both, but by the time he had, you had already helped your sister and advanced yourself. I think he was angry and felt helpless. Who else could he take it out on except you?'

'By the blazes of hell, he is such an asshole.'

Marion ignored his language as she continued, 'I just thought I'd offer you a little more perspective on what happened. A seed that might bloom into forgiveness. Let you cool that hot head of yours.'

Ardan resisted the urge to argue. If he did, it would just prove her point. She watched him struggle with a knowing smile.

'It is unusual, but when the two of you get angry, it seems to sharpen your focus. The difference is that you seem to have better control over its direction,' Marion said as she rose.

He stood, feeling about as graceful as a pack mule next to her, and escorted her out. Instead of being an unwanted addition to Bree and Riordan's party, he went upstairs to his room to think. He was certain of two things: Davan was an asshole, but also, he was still family.

CHAPTER THIRTY-TWO: THE DARK FOREST

* * *

Our time in the northern kingdoms has ended. Naberius has crushed all those who oppose him. We ride for the Pass, torching every field and food silo we come across. As we move, our numbers have grown to almost a thousand strong. I fear the demon's advance elements may catch us, but I cannot abandon my people. Enough blood stains my hands without adding them to my conscience.

— *Journals of Phillip, the twelfth Templar.*

* * *

THE TWO MERCENARIES waited at the eastern gates. The streets were otherwise dark and empty. Ardan glanced up at the stone archway, the same one he and his father had run through the better part of a year ago. He tried to focus on something else, knowing conversation with Riordan would be one-sided. The man's bloodshot eyes bespoke his hangover. Ardan looked around the empty streets again. If the carts didn't arrive soon, it would be difficult to reach the edge before sunrise.

He heard the convoy before he saw it. They came trotting around the corner, a single horse drawing each light, narrow, manoeuvrable cart. Mercenaries walked next to the caravan on both sides and Ardan was glad none wore the Red Wolf tunic.

'You're the last of my guards,' the lead driver said as he pulled up next to them. He was a portly, balding man.

'That's us,' Ardan said.

'I'm Conner, and this is my caravan. We're behind, so jump on the wagons until we get to the edge.'

Ardan climbed on the back and helped pull a groaning Riordan up with him.

'Good, let's go,' Conner said, flicking the reins. The carts pulled off and soon they were at a steady trot. 'First time in the forest?'

It took a moment for Ardan to realise the question was directed at him. 'I've been there a few times.'

'Ah, of course,' Conner said, clearly unconvinced. 'Always good to have experienced hands along.'

Ardan shrugged and didn't answer. His eyes wandered to the fields, noticing those closest to the walls had had their weeds cleared and the soil tilled. He wondered if the forest would have reclaimed them if they'd been left untended.

The treeline rose like a green wall in front of them just as the first rays of sunlight crested the horizon. The road disappeared inside a narrow portal amongst the greenery while the guards dismounted, milling about. None wanted to be the first through.

'Get on with it!' Conner yelled.

The first guard visibly tensed his shoulders before passing into the darkness. The threshold swallowed them one by one. Ardan didn't pause as he stepped into the familiar jungle, slowly adjusting to the new light. The forest floor stretched out before him, weaving between the close-knit trees that fought each other to reach the sun. It felt like coming home. The steady beat of the horses' hooves filled his senses, broken by the occasional bird cry and distant sound of running water.

He kept his own eyes moving as they walked, never letting them settle on one thing for long. His eyes unconsciously did the work while his mind wandered. There was no friendly chatter amongst the guards, and he knew his father would approve of the silence.

It was about midmorning when he spotted something that snapped him to attention. A creeping vine had slithered from the brush, primed to tangle the cart wheel. Without thinking, Ardan dashed forward, sword in hand. He slashed it. The thing immediately retreated, disappearing back into the trees.

'Quick moving, lad,' Riordan said in a croaking voice.

The entire caravan paused. Two mercenaries raised eyebrows at each other. Conner nodded his approval before he flicked the reins of his cart. They continued up the winding path of the escarpment. The vines approached their caravan a few more times that day, but the mercenaries handled them efficiently.

The day stretched out, until eventually the sun descended towards the horizon. The mercenaries kept trying to walk faster, but Conner yelled at them to slow down. He kept the lead cart plodding along at the same pace, worried that they might hit some ditch in the road if they went faster. As the light disappeared and the darkness in the forest grew, Ardan could feel the tension rising.

There were audible sighs of relief as the large clearing finally came into view. Devoid of trees and canopy, it was completely open to the sky. A ring of stones surrounded it, and in the centre stood a stone altar, adorned with a moving, shifting, spherical piece of liquid stone. As least, that's what Ardan thought it was. The only other one he'd seen was in his father's glade. If you focused on the idol, trying to determine its size, shape, or matter, you only ended up with a headache.

'We've got about ten minutes until dark,' Conner called out, once the last caravan had pulled inside the stones.

Most of the guards were already outside the circle, gathering wood as quickly as they could. They dashed back into the clearing to throw it down haphazardly before running out to repeat the process. Ardan joined them, filling his arms before heading back to the stones. The last of the guards leapt over the boundary as though the whips of hell were behind them.

'Did your father ever teach you about the circle of stones? Why they protect us?' Riordan said once Ardan had calmly stepped over the stones.

'He said they're a remnant of the Ancients,' Ardan said, thinking about the times they'd stayed in his father's glade. He had usually been too tired to ask questions.

A nervous energy filled the clearing, which only dissipated once the fire was going. Rather than heat his rations, Ardan followed Riordan's lead and just ate them cold. As he took a bite of trail bread, a familiar figure came towards them, a wiry frame with blond beard and ready smile.

'Eamon,' Ardan said, ignoring the glares of the mercenaries for breaking the silence. 'I didn't know you were here.'

Eamon sat down with them. 'Didn't know you guys were here either. I was trapped as the rearguard with Sean. Boringest man on Eden.'

'Sod off,' one of the other guards yelled. Eamon grinned.

'How's your farm?' Riordan asked.

Eamon's smile dimmed a little. 'You saw the fields. I'm doing this run so I can afford to sow the fields again. Ate all my seed grain through the troubles.'

'Lucky our fat little caravan master pays well,' Riordan said.

Eamon winked.

They ate the rest of their rations in silence, adhering to the other mercenaries' glares and mutters to keep quiet.

Ardan and Riordan drew the first watch. They sat on one of the empty wagons, their backs to the fire. The red flame barely held the darkness back, and the flickering light made the shadows dance and Ardan's imagination flare.

A loud scream echoed out of the darkness. Ardan leapt to his feet, his hand reaching for his sword, but he felt Riordan's hand restraining him.

'It's trying to attract prey.'

'What is it?'

Riordan shrugged wordlessly.

Several mercenaries snuggled harder into their bedrolls or pulled covers over their ears. Ardan released his grip on his blade and slowly sat back in the cart. On the second cry, Ardan knew he would have charged out if not for Riordan's warning. He wondered why he'd never heard the noise before, thinking it was just another thing he couldn't ask his father.

He continued to watch the darkness while Riordan was whittling away at a bit of wood with his knife.

In the distance, they heard the crunching of sticks. Then another log-splintering crack. Leaves high in the trees were moving, despite the stillness of the air. Riordan reached for his shield.

Was this the same thing he'd seen near the Golden Meadow? Ardan's hand clenched on his sword again. Little good it would do. The thing was massive.

They waited there, tense, listening hard as the sounds stayed in the distance, eventually fading away.

Riordan resumed his whittling.

Twice, a member of their party would wake up, sitting bolt upright, their eyes wide as they looked at the engulfing darkness. Then they would calm themselves, but it took a long time before the steady breathing of sleep overtook them again.

With their watch at a close, they went to their bedrolls. Still, to be properly clothed and have a blanket that wasn't covered in filth was a luxury. Ardan quickly drifted off.

He woke to feel Riordan shaking him. He blinked and could see the darkness of the sky slowly retreating. It must have been close to dawn.

'I'm not sure I've ever seen anyone sleep that soundly on their first run through the forest,' Riordan said. 'Nor many experienced people, now that I think of it.'

Ardan yawned as he sat up and rubbed his eyes. 'I spent a lot of my childhood following my father around the outskirts of the forest. It's like a second home.'

'But he never made you stay the night, did he?'

'Sometimes.'

Riordan stared at him as though not sure if he was joking.

'Come on, you lot,' Conner said. 'We don't have far to go today, but I'd prefer to make it to the second clearing before mid-afternoon.'

There wasn't much to say after that. The fire was doused, their belongings gathered, and the remaining wood left in a pile for the next group to pass through. They all gathered at the road leading out of the clearing. The caravan master flicked his reins once the sun cleared the horizon and their caravan moved past the stones.

The first part of their journey proceeded without incident. There were a few creeping vines, but the mercenaries cut them out of the way before they could get to the carts.

It had gone past midday when Ardan started to wonder how soon they'd reach the next clearing. He snapped himself out of his wishful reverie and focused back on the road. As he did so, he saw a small sprout off to the side of the path shift. He focused on it and saw green glittering scales slither out. It was a forest viper and it was heading straight for one of the mercenary guards.

'Look out!' Ardan shouted.

The snake struck at a familiar face. It was Eamon. The man did an odd dance, as though barefoot on hot coals. Ardan ran forward, pulling his falchion as he did. He didn't think as he swung the sword in a broad arc. The snake turned towards him, but the blade caught it on the neck, its head toppling to the ground. Dropping the sword, he shouldered Eamon to the ground and started grappling with the boot. Two holes had punctured the leather, with a drop of venom running down the side.

'Steady on,' Eamon said in dismay.

Riordan came up beside him.

'Riordan, hold him.'

Riordan obeyed without question and together they pulled off the boot. There was green liquid on the man's foot, and his skin was already blistering.

'Hold still.'

He did exactly what his father had done, using a rag to wipe the excess liquid away, before flinging it to the ground. Then he alternated between a second rag and diluting the wound with water. Eamon squirmed despite Riordan's effort to hold him down.

'Good,' Ardan said at last. 'The puncture wound looks tiny, and I think little venom got inside. You need to stay off it until a healer can check you out. You'll likely be sick and weak for the next few days, but you should be fine,' he said, and stood up. It was only then that he looked around to see everyone was staring at him. 'What?'

It was Riordan who broke the silence first. 'You're just full of surprises, lad.'

CHAPTER THIRTY-THREE: THE CALL OF THE ANCIENTS

* * *

I held the rear-guard against Naberius' advance elements. I lit fires, held phantom lines, and assailed them from afar. It gave the young and elderly time to get through the iron gates. Once they were safe, we retreated into the fortress.
— *Journals of Phillip, the twelfth Templar.*

* * *

THE SECOND CLEARING was large enough to house half the Ancient Quarter. Sunlight shone on the grass inside the stones. On the opposite side of the clearing was a small army of church soldiers, the holy fire insignia emblazoned on their tunics.

The clearing had a shifting idol on a pedestal, identical to the last one. A priest and an armoured warrior stood near the stone altar; the priest was red in the face, gesturing wildly at his companion. With a start, Ardan realised the second man was Templar Phillip, the holy warrior they had met on their first day at the Cathedral.

'Father Walter. We've been over this. These keep us safe from whatever prowls this forest,' Phillip said.

'Pagan relic! They represent dead gods and a lost religion. They should be cast from the path of the Light.'

'Maybe, but we need them.'

'You are a representative of the Holy Order of knights. You should not allow such a symbol of blasphemy to stand. It is repulsive to the Light and all it stands for.'

Ardan wondered if the priest was about to burst a vein.

Phillip sighed and leaned back. 'I could find worthier things to die for.'

'The Light will protect us from the evils of this forest.'

'Zadkiel himself had trouble moving through these woods. What chance do you think we have?'

Walter opened his mouth to reply.

'Enough,' Phillip said, holding up a hand. He spoke as though to a child. 'You've forgotten who's in command. You think this is a discussion, but it isn't. You think you have a say, but you don't. My duty is to keep you and everyone else from making decisions that will get us all killed. We're not in the Citadel anymore. The idol stays.'

'I refuse to believe you are one of the Archangel's chosen.'

Phillip shrugged, turning away from him.

Walter, noticing them, pushed past Phillip to stand in front of Riordan.

'Are you men from Barleron? How is the Light there? Has the city descended into a hell-torn place?'

'Father Walter,' Phillip snapped, forcing the priest to turn back to him. 'I think it's time you checked on the men. Now.'

Walter glared at the Templar before throwing up his hands and muttering as he retreated to the camp the church soldiers had set up.

Phillip clasped hands with Riordan. 'My old friend, what are you doing here?'

'Saw enough killing at the Pass. Wandered around looking for the quiet life. I eventually ended up here.'

'Travelling through the dark forest is the quiet life?'

'I never could get things right.'

A smile split Phillip's face. 'Protégé?' he said when he spotted Ardan. Then his brow furrowed as the man tried to place him. 'Have we met before?'

'You saw me outside the Cathedral when the civil war started,' Ardan said. 'You were about to ride off, worried Naberius was loose south of the Pass.'

'*What?*' Riordan shouted.

Phillip made a hushing gesture. 'I don't want to create a panic. We can't find him, but the church of Zadkiel is taking no chances—which is why I'm leading this pack of green horns. I just pray to the Light that I can keep them alive.'

Now that he'd mentioned it, Ardan noticed that all the soldiers weren't much older than he was. All on the cusp of manhood and huddled together in tight packs. They whispered to each other as they stared out into the forest.

'I'd hoped he was dead. Especially after I saw you and a hundred others take him down.'

'Many Templars and soldiers sacrificed themselves that day,' Phillip said, bowing his head. 'I'd hoped we killed him, but the Darkness is ever cunning. The Citadel won't sit idly by, so they've sent forces to every major city. They even sent an emissary to the Waterlords.'

'Wow,' Riordan said.

'Exactly. I'm part of this contingent, shepherding these people through the jungle. I'm mostly trying to curb their behaviour so that it won't get them killed here or in Barleron. Father Walter makes it harder, but he's one of the few who have been willing and strong enough to come.'

Riordan gave a grim smile. 'You always seem to take on impossible tasks. Although you'll be happy to know that the city has settled down. With any luck, it might recover sometime soon.'

'It's nice to hear some good news for a change. Naberius has me more worried than I'd like to admit; he's more cunning than most people realise. Something has been growing in me, a feeling that we're approaching something awful like the Iron Gates all over again,' Phillip said, but then he forced a smile. 'But enough politics. Tell me, have you decided to settle down with a nice woman?'

'Not exactly,' Riordan said, shifting uncomfortably.

'Easy women always lead to trouble.'

'I think I'll help set up,' Ardan said, walking away from Phillip's interrogation.

Ardan went outside the ring of stones to collect some firewood for the night. As he was loading his arms with sticks, he felt a stirring in his chest. He glanced back at the Templar, but he was still talking to Riordan.

Then the stirring rose to a torrent, followed by a flash of pain. Staggering, he reached for the nearest tree to steady himself. He barely felt the rough bark as a sensation of panic and fear coursed through him.

'What the hell?'

Ardan stumbled towards the clearing, but the fear thrummed inside him. He had to force himself forward. He stepped over the stones, the pain and panic immediately vanishing. It was as jarring as the initial burst had been. On a hunch, he crossed back over the stones. The sensation returned, worse than before. He focused on it. Something was projecting to him, calling out for help. He could sense the direction, if only vaguely. He looked at the sky, judging what hours of sunlight remained. *To the hells with it,* Ardan thought.

He marked the trees the further he went. Twilight was descending, and he briefly considered turning back, but the call was getting more powerful. He pressed forward. He knew he should turn back, but the pull felt strong enough to yank him off his feet. Darkness filled the woods. He stumbled over unseen roots and uneven ground. Just as the need to turn back became insurmountable, he stepped on something soft. There was a responding snarl.

Ardan jumped back, drawing his falchion. His father had talked about the larger predators of the forest; shadow beasts that blended in with the trees. He held the sword in front of him, ready to slice anything that moved. In vain, he tried to ignite his sword into green flame. It took a moment for him to collect himself. After he got his breathing under control, he saw something at his feet. A pair of emerald eyes were staring up at him. It was a cat with midnight-black fur and red markings across its side. The cat hissed again, but it was weak. He pushed aside the bush that was camouflaging the feline. It was larger than any street cat he had ever seen. He sheathed his sword and knelt down, tentatively reaching out a hand to touch it. His hand skimmed the soft black fur and a responding surge of triumph flowed through his chest. Whatever had pulled him here had wanted him to find this cat. He'd have to question it later. What he'd first thought, the markings were actually caked blood, dried over claw marks that ran down its side.

The cat gazed at him before lying back and closing its eyes. Only a weak orange light illuminated the forest and Ardan knew he'd stayed far too long. He picked up the creature, holding it awkwardly in his arms. Its lips twitched but it ultimately surrendered, its head lolling back against him. He followed the same path back. The light was fading too quickly, and he couldn't make out his trail markings.

Oh, Light and Darkness.

He tried to still the rapid beating of his heart. There was nothing for it. He headed in the direction he thought the clearing was in. He kept his legs at a fast walk, despite their incessant need to run. A twisted ankle would be a death sentence.

Darkness fell over the forest, and Ardan felt despair grip him.

What's that? he thought, staring at a faint glow in the distance. He hoped it was light from the campfire. With no better options, he headed towards it. He kept his movements careful, hoping not to attract any attention. The calls of birds echoed in the surrounding trees. The large, luminescent eyes of an owl stared down on him. It opened its beak and let loose an ear-piercing screech. Ardan shied away from it, almost dropping the cat in his need to block his ears. The eerie note continued on, long and loud.

A monstrous roar answered in the distance. All the birds and insects ceased their calls, creating an ominous silence. Ardan knew that roar; it was the same one from the Golden Meadow. He darted around trees, getting closer to the fire and protection of the stones. He stumbled over the unseen ground, but he thought he must have the luck of Lucifer in keeping his feet. The creature was giving chase, its heavy footfalls sending reverberations through the forest, shaking the threes. Ardan needed to get inside the ring, to get past that barrier of safety. The creature's next roar was so loud that it shook the very earth beneath his feet. Ardan barely kept his balance as he ran. Breathing as hard from fear as from exertion, he kept the orange glow in sight. The soldiers' silhouettes were moving in front of the bonfire. A quick glance behind him revealed the shadow rising like a mountain. He urged himself to run faster.

'It's me, it's me!' he shouted as he ran.

There was a thundering behind him, and he felt a hot wash of air as the creature's breath engulfed him. He didn't stop but just kept running, willing himself to go faster. The circle of stones was a dozen feet away. Another step shook the ground behind him. Eight feet to go. The mercenaries and church soldiers who were inside the circle cowered away. He leapt the last six feet. He sailed through the air as something collided with his side. Pain exploded across his ribs and sent him spinning mid leap. He cradled the animal to his chest before he hit the ground, rolling and tumbling a few times before he came to a stop. The cat gave a soft hiss of displeasure.

He looked up and saw the creature. Cascading shadows completely obscured its features as it roared again, furious that its prey was behind the stones. He could feel the hatred oozing out of it. It raised a limb and crashed it down. Ardan tensed at the impending blow, but it struck the barrier the stones had erected, shimmering an iridescent blue. It roared again and Ardan got to his feet, knowing that if the barrier failed, it would likely get them all killed.

'No!' Phillip shouted, charging forward. His shield and the tip of his spear shone with pure white light. 'Begone, foul creature of the night. By the power of the Light, I cast you out.'

Even the Light couldn't penetrate the darkness surrounding the monstrous thing. It gave a hate-filled bellow and threw its entire body at the barrier. The iridescent blue flickered, the barrier bending, but then the Templar's glowing shield seemed to lend strength to it, and it halted the creature's movement. Phillip took the opportunity to stab the thing with his glowing spear. It roared in pain and stepped backwards. It roared again, before rushing forward and crashing against the barrier so hard that the shield shimmered, the blue fading. The light on Phillip's shield held it at bay but the creature kept pushing, making the barrier bend further. Ardan knew in his heart that the barrier and the Templar would fail. But then Father Walter was there, one hand on the Templar's shoulder. Light was passing from him and into the Templar. The light brightened so much that Ardan had to shield his eyes. The creature pulled back as if burned; it stood at the edge of the stones and gave another roar. The blue of the shield was getting stronger. The creature bellowed in frustration.

It stalked back and forth in front of the barrier. It stopped and gave one monstrous roar. Ardan shielded his ears but could feel the hatred from the creature tearing into him. The cat brought its paws up to block its own ears. With a huff, the creature retreated into the forest. The ground trembled because of its footsteps; they could hear it circling their camp. It wasn't until the sound of its footsteps grew weaker and weaker that some of the tension lessened. The soldiers gave a ragged cheer. Phillip turned towards them, but his expression was off. He stumbled. He would have fallen, but Walter caught him, easing him onto the ground. Riordan was there with a water flask.

'Phillip, you've got to expel some of the Light,' Riordan said.

The man looked up at him. His face split into a grin and some drool escaped his lips.

'Priest, you need to siphon the power out of him.'

'What would you know of transference?' Walter snapped.

'I fought at Jophiel's Pass in the Dog War. All the Light from transference was like fireflies in the night.'

Walter stared at him before giving him a slight nod. He knelt down and put his hand on the Templar's chest, drawing Light out of him. The glow on the man's shield and spear died down, returning to a metallic grey.

'Are you well, Templar?' Walter asked.

Phillip looked up at them before giving a weary nod. Then he closed his eyes. The priest ordered some of the church soldiers to take him to his bedroll.

Riordan rounded on Ardan. 'What in all of Hell's demons were you doing outside the stones after dark? You almost got us all killed!'

Ardan held out the black cat. It was breathing but was clearly unconscious.

'You went out there for that?'

'It felt like the right thing to do,' Ardan said, knowing how stupid it sounded.

'The right thing to do ... the flaming Hells, the right burning thing to do,' Riordan said, his voice rising. He held a finger in front of Ardan. 'I want you to promise me you will never, ever, do anything so brainless or foolhardy again.'

'Can you help me save it?'

Riordan glared at him a moment longer before switching his gaze to the cat. His eyes softened. 'Wait here.'

'You brought a great evil upon us,' Walter said to Ardan. 'You will have to stand trial for this transgression.'

Great, Ardan thought. He had angered more of the Light's Clergy. He knew the Bishop would not be lenient with him. One of the church soldiers stepped forward to arrest him.

'Enough of that,' Riordan said, returning with a wineskin, needle and thread. 'He was attacked and ran to the Light for help.'

'Regardless, he put a Templar in danger.'

'We are not in the Citadel of Light, priest. You will need the Bishop's approval to bring him to trial.'

Walter glared at him. 'I will get it. Do not think this is over.'

Riordan shrugged and deliberately turned his back on him. 'Hold it down.'

Ardan placed his hands on the unconscious cat and waited. Riordan poured wine over the animal's wounds. Its eyes sprang open, and it squirmed to get out of Ardan's grip. The black paws extended and swiped at them. Riordan was quick enough to avoid the claws.

There was something about its terror that touched the primal part in Ardan. It was the sensation that had drawn him out into the forest in the first place. He acted on instinct, sending a feeling of calm through his hands. The effect was immediate; the cat's struggles slowed into acceptance. It turned its head and the emerald eyes pierced Ardan's soul with their judgement. Before Ardan could fully comprehend what happened, the animal's eyes closed, and it went limp.

'It's not dead, is it?'

'No,' Riordan said slowly, 'It's still breathing, but keep your grip firm, just in case.'

Ardan held the cat as Riordan stitched its wounds. The cat didn't stir again. Riordan gave him instruction on how to keep the injuries clean. Once finished, Ardan was suddenly aware of how exhausted he felt. Holding the feline, he headed towards his bedroll.

'Where do you think you're going?' Riordan said. 'You've got triple watch because of your stupidity.'

Knowing better than to protest, Ardan set out his bedroll for the cat and then sat up to watch. He watched the darkness outside the stones, weariness filling him.

CHAPTER THIRTY-FOUR:
DENTWALL

* * *

They arrested me before the gates finished closing. The commander promised to protect the refugees from the more zealous priests. I now sit in the dungeons and am allowed the small comfort of my journal and writing materials.

— Journals of Phillip, the twelfth Templar.

* * *

ARDAN WAS UP EARLY the next morning despite only having gotten a few hours of sleep. The cat's breathing seemed easier. He kept his bedroll in the wagon and moved the cat, so she wouldn't be too jolted by its movements. The feline's green eyes regarded him coolly before it lowered its head back onto the blanket.

Riordan came up and wordlessly handed him a small bowl carved from wood. The man had obviously spent his time on watch making it. Ardan nodded his thanks before filling it with water from his skin. He woke the cat and held the bowl to its head. With effort, she lapped the water before collapsing back into the blanket.

Ardan left the bowl, positioning it in the corner so it wouldn't tip from the bumps in the road, then he quickly joined in the preparations for the next leg of their journey. The two parties were positioned at opposing sides of the clearing. Riordan had said his farewells to the Templar before joining them. As soon as the sun crested the horizon, both parties were on the move.

Ardan stayed at the rear, keeping his eye on the cat in the last cart. The day passed slowly, creeping vines slithering across the road to tie up their wagons, but little else crossing their path. Ardan guessed the shadow creature had scattered anything living as the wagons manoeuvred along the narrow forest road. He tried to ask Riordan about it but received such a glare that he kept quiet for the rest of the trek. He avoided the others, figuring it was probably best to stay out of their way.

They reached the final clearing a couple of hours before nightfall. The stones surrounded a much smaller field of lush grass. The shifting and changing idol sat in the centre beneath the forest's open canopy and blue sky. As they set up, Ardan realised the mercenaries were avoiding him. *I guess they did almost die because of me*, he conceded. He pulled some dried meat out of his pack, taking a bite and giving the rest to the cat. She ate quickly before pawing at the bowl. Ardan smiled when he realised what she meant. He poured more water into it. The cat closed its eyes with pain, hauling itself up and over the bowl. It lapped at the water until it was gone, before collapsing back onto the blankets.

'It seems to be recovering,' Ardan said when Riordan joined him.

The man grunted. Ardan couldn't blame him for still being upset. Whatever had called him out there had made him forget the consequences of being outside the stones.

Nightfall came slowly as Ardan sat alone in the back of the wagon. Riordan had gone to spend the evening with the others, leaving Ardan to spend his multiple watches alone.

The next morning, Ardan was looking forward to getting out of the forest. He liked the place, but his companions' silent stares were wearing on him. The edge of the forest couldn't come fast enough.

When they escaped the green jungle, Ardan had to shield his eyes from the light and the openness of the plains. Rolling green hills spread out before them, while gusts of wind sent ripples along the ocean of grass. Through the haze, Ardan could see the mountain wall to the north.

'Dentwall,' Conner proclaimed, raising his arm grandly, 'a hubris of trade and a place where anything can be bought, provided you have enough coin.'

'Why are you trying to sell the place like it's one of your wares? It's a grubby town that's been conquered more times than Riordan playing Kings,' Eamon said.

'Hey!'

'It has many aspects that appeal to me, but seeing it means that we're out of the forest.'

All the nearby mercenaries murmured their agreement as their party progressed forward.

The city of Dentwall stood in the centre of a small hill. A wooden-staked wall surrounded the place, with watch towers positioned along the edges. A coloured flag went up, followed by a shout from a tower.

'Signals for the gate to expect us,' Riordan explained. 'This place has its own complex systems to keep the peace. Difficult, considering everyone who comes here.'

'Who is 'everyone'?'

'Northern kingdom refugees and traders, Waterlords, people from the Citadel and the Empire, travellers from the coastal cities,' Riordan said. As he spoke, a dozen horsemen rode out of one of the city's gates. They wore furs and leathers, their dark hair elaborate with braids and buns. Every single one of them carried a bow. 'Kurks are welcome here, too.'

'They are?' Ardan asked. The Kurkistanis in stories were the warlike nomadic horse tribes that lived on the sea of grass.

'The mayor organised it. The man has enough courage to match an entire continent of soldiers. He rode out to meet them, his horse loaded with gold. Everyone thought he was mad, that the Kurks would take his gold and his life. Yet within a week he'd brought some

chieftains back and made a pact. After that, he had everyone's attention. It was shortly after the Dog War and the place hasn't been
conquered since. The man brought everyone together.'

They were just passing through the gates when Riordan finished.
The wooden doors were big, swinging on large hinges. Their own
carts looked comically small passing through them.

The caravan master didn't pause as he flicked his reins, steering
their carts through the myriad of streets. Every building looked to be
a store, with living quarters above it, and Ardan realized how few
were solely residences. They passed some workers mixing crushed
stone into the dirt road and it forced them to take a detour, but
Conner barely hesitated before taking the alternate route.

'We'll be staying for a few days, so try to enjoy yourself,' Riordan
said.

'So long?' Ardan asked him. He thought they would have loaded up
and headed back in the morning.

'People need a chance to rest, lad. The forest is an exhausting
place,' he said, then eyed Ardan. 'For most people.'

'But—' Ardan stopped as they pulled into a street. There were six
men standing in a defensive semicircle around a woman. There were
at least twenty church soldiers and a priest surrounding them in turn.
They had the same look as Phillip's cohort, the same holy flame
insignia.

'Children of the Ancients,' Riordan whispered. Then amended
when Ardan looked confused, 'Forest people.'

The six men in the centre wore loose-fitting pants with massive
belts. Their heavy cloaks were fastened together with a bone just
below their necks. Beneath them they wore no shirts, displaying
different tattoos etched across their chests. They had an odd assortment of swords and spears, while the man at the front had four
hatchets in his belt.

'Lay down your arms, Pagans, and repent,' the priest said. There
was a feeling of 'or else' laced in there.

Ardan studied the forest people. He could see the scars and relaxed
manner that marked their experience. If anything, they looked

completely at ease. While if these soldiers were anything like Phillip's, then they'd be greener than fresh grass.

The woman in the centre moved forward, squeezing between two of the warriors. She had auburn hair tied back into a ponytail. She was young, her lean muscles tattooed with vines weaving up her sleeveless arms before disappearing beneath her green garb. She was wearing the same style pants with a large, sheathed dagger in her belt. The warrior with the hatchets reached out to stop her but she slapped his hand away before he could touch her.

'You're one of the Light's holy men?' she asked brightly, walking up to the priest.

'I am,' the priest said haughtily.

'Do you believe it is your right to stop the innocent?' she asked. Ardan could hear the dangerous gleam in her voice. He waited, while Riordan grabbed the hilt of his own sword. It felt like an impending storm.

'It is my right and my duty to spread the Light to all corners of the —' the priest began, but the woman suddenly stepped forward, hooked a leg around his and shoved him to the ground. The priest went down in a tangle of limbs, his brown habit getting caught up as he tumbled. She was down beside him in an instant, her knife out and held dangerously close to his throat.

The forest warriors stepped forward, their weapons ready. The church soldiers took longer to react, slowly drawing their weapons and looking around for directions, unsure of what to do.

Riordan drew his weapons too. Ardan followed suit.

Some of the church soldiers stepped forward.

'Stop,' the woman shouted. The church soldiers were not cohesive. While some had been moving forward, others were looking about, while a couple had stepped backwards. She looked down at the priest. 'Tell them to stop.'

The priest remained silent, whether from terror or stubbornness, Ardan couldn't tell.

She pressed the knife closer. 'Tell them,' she said, and a thin line of red appeared at his throat.

'Stop,' the priest croaked.

The church soldiers looked confused, some still stepping forward.

'Back, you louts!' Riordan shouted.

The soldiers took a few steps back.

'We are free, and we don't answer to you,' the woman's voice was low, but it carried over to everyone. 'We are the Children of the Ancients. We came here to trade and to talk. How dare you accost us.'

'Infidels,' the priest said, then his eyes went wide when he realised what he'd done.

The woman laughed, but before she could say anything else a contingent of guards came trotting around the corner. They wore the same grey as the guardsmen at the gate. A man with golden epaulets on his shoulders stepped forward.

'What is going on here?'

The woman pulled her knife, wiped it on the priest's habit, and stood. 'Just exchanging cultural customs.'

The constable looked at the priest and back at the woman. 'Perhaps you should do that without so many weapons drawn.'

The priest got to his feet, pointing a condemning finger at the woman. 'I demand you take her into custody. She attacked us.'

The watchman looked at the thirty church soldiers and the six forest warriors with raised eyebrows. 'That seems unlikely.'

'Are you questioning a man of the cloth?'

The constable ignored him, his eyes scanning further. They settled on the caravan.

'What happened?'

'We're not getting involved,' Conner said.

'The church soldiers were stopping the forest people from leaving,' Riordan said, despite a glare from Conner. 'I don't think it would have been long before blood was spilled. The woman took aggressive actions to stop that from happening.'

'Well, no one has been permanently injured,' the city watchman said. 'I think you've blocked the streets long enough, move along.'

'You can't just...' the priest began.

'You've probably had worse cuts from your barber. My job is to keep the peace. The peace hasn't been broken.'

'Let's go, Talon,' the woman said. The lean man holding a hatchet in either hand nodded, slipping them back into his belt. He signalled the others to start heading down the street.

'Stop them,' the priest demanded.

'No,' the watchman said. 'That is breaking the peace. You, forest woman, you'd best leave. I'll handle them.'

'You'll *handle* us?' the priest spluttered.

The woman nodded and they continued, leaving the busy street.

'Us too,' Conner said and flicked the reins. Their caravan moved along the streets, following the woman and the six warriors.

Ardan began to wonder if they were following them, as they progressed along the same hardened dirt roads of Dentwall.

'Well, this is going to be interesting,' Riordan said.

'What, why?' Ardan said.

'It appears we're both staying at the Gilded Branch,' Riordan said as the carts pulled up in front of a large Inn with a sign of a large golden tree limb.

The six forest warriors entered in front of them, while the woman looked back at them curiously before disappearing inside.

CHAPTER THIRTY-FIVE:
MISHIPESHU

* * *

*V*isitors have kept me sane during my incarceration. They tell me
*the northern road is completely cut off and the major elements
of Naberius' army are only days away. My frustration and fear grow. I want
to meet the enemy, not sit locked in a cell, alone and useless.*
— *Journals of Phillip, the twelfth Templar.*

* * *

THE INN of the Gilded Branch was a large four-story building. The
arched windows, from the second floor up, were uniformly sized and
spaced. Ardan glimpsed the food hall, guessing it took up most of the
ground floor, as the unique white noise of people talking, eating and
moving emanated from it. Their caravan went around the building
and up the gravel and mud driveway.

The rear yard had its own fully manned stables, farrier, workshop,
vegetable garden, bath house and several smaller buildings that Ardan
guessed were more accommodations. They got to work storing the

wagons and stabling the horses while Conner disappeared inside. Before they were done, he reappeared.

'I've started up a tab to cover your meals and a few drinks. I'll need some of you tomorrow to join me at the morning markets. The wagons need to be filled and ready to go in two days' time. Speak to the Innkeeper for your room. Riordan, can you sort it out?'

'Not a problem,' Riordan said.

'Until morning, then. Enjoy yourselves.'

Ardan gently picked up the cat before following the rest of the party inside. The common room could have rivaled the Cathedral hall for size. Over a dozen large tables were sprawled out over the floor, with smaller ones filling the spaces in between. An army of serving men and women moved between the tables, serving drinks, tending the fires, mopping the floor and wiping down tables. Off to one side was a stage, where two musicians tried valiantly to perform above the noise of the hall.

Riordan spoke to the Innkeeper before splitting up the mercenaries and giving out keys to the different rooms. In the end, it was just Ardan, Riordan, and Eamon left. Their room was on the second floor. It was a simple affair, with three cots squeezed into the relatively small space.

'I never properly thanked you for saving me from that snake,' Eamon said, putting his travelling pack down.

'Don't worry about it.'

'They're saying you're a forest stalker.'

'My father taught me,' Ardan said, his voice catching slightly. It had been some time since he'd thought about him. 'How's the leg?'

'The healer dismissed me pretty quick. Gave me something foul to drink and said if I wasn't dead, I probably wouldn't be.'

'I can relate,' Riordan said.

Ardan created a small bed out of blankets for the cat. The feline barely stirred as he laid her down, while Riordan told Eamon about his own snake bite.

'Come, lad, let's leave Eamon to get some shuteye before dinner.'

Ardan looked over at the cat's sleeping spot.

'I'll look after it. Besides, I think we'll both be sleeping the night away,' Eamon said, settling under his own blanket.

The two took one of the smaller tables in the common room. A server brought them some ales. Ardan took a sip, enjoying the frothy bitterness of the ale. He looked up to see Riordan looking away, clearly not inviting conversation. They drank in silence. It stretched, and Riordan did not break it.

'I'm sorry Riordan, I really am,' Ardan said. He wanted the gap between them to pass.

'I know, lad. You and me are fine, truly. It'll take me and the lads a day or two to get used to it.'

Ardan took a drink of his ale, trying to enjoy it, and after a glance at the other caravan guards, he hoped that it was true. He sighed.

A woman, well into her twilight years and wearing a barrage of blues, greens and greys that reminded Ardan strongly of the ocean walked over to their table. Her grey dreadlocks were lined with seashells. She stopped in front of Riordan and dropped a folded letter on it.

'Did you deliver this?'

Riordan nodded.

'Excellent,' the woman said, plonking herself down on one of the empty seats.

Ardan looked questioningly at Riordan.

'Bree asked me to deliver a letter when we arrived. I gave it to the Innkeeper less than an hour ago. The man obviously works fast.'

'I'm staying here, you big dolt,' the woman said. Her tone didn't imply an insult, more that Riordan simply was a dolt and couldn't help it. 'My apprentice warns me it isn't safe to go back to Barleron, but I'd like to hear it straight from the sea urchin's mouth.' Her grey eyes focused on Riordan.

Riordan looked thoughtful before answering. 'No one is starving and there's less killing in the streets. Trade and farming are fledgling, but they're starting.'

The woman started fingering one of her dreadlocks in thought. 'Good enough. I miss home. I left the city when that buffoon Magistrate got himself killed. When are you leaving?' she asked, as though it was a forgone conclusion that she'd be joining them.

'Two or three days from now. We're not sure yet, Mrs...?'

'Murieen, and it's Miss, though don't get any ideas.'

Ardan had to stifle a laugh while Riordan stared at her. She had to have at least thirty years on Riordan.

'What's your relationship with my apprentice?'

Riordan sat there, his mouth opening and closing a few times.

'I'll give you time to gather your wits. Go get me a drink. I'll take a large cup of caudle.'

Riordan looked thoroughly confused at the exchange but still made his way towards the bar, leaving Ardan alone with the eccentric woman. She appeared completely at ease, looking at the stage. Ardan followed her gaze. A large barrel of water sat in the centre.

'Water dancers,' Murieen said, answering Ardan's unspoken question.

'What?'

'Never seen water dancers before? Even the untalented ones can be entertaining.'

The room fell silent when five people walked out onto the stage. Two men and a woman sat on stools, dressed in blue and white uniforms. One man was empty-handed, the other held a flute while the woman had a handheld drum.

'Is that a bodhrán?' Ardan asked, looking at the drum. His father had played one occasionally, though his had been larger.

'How in the shape of water would I know?'

The two women who remained standing wore skirts that stopped above their knees with long stockings underneath. Their bright green tunics held twisting and turning golden patterns. Their respective blond and black hair had been curled to shoulder length.

Riordan dropped the caudle in front of Murieen and sat down quietly.

A slow, methodical beat filled the room. The two women began the dance, their legs moving in time with the drum, while their arms remained largely immobile. The beat quickened and the speed of the dancers matched it. A light melody carried from the flute, filling the gaps between the drumbeats. The dancers responded by moving faster, weaving around as they spun and jumped in perfect harmony. The beat sped up and again the dancers responded, their legs moving impossibly fast.

The last performer raised his hands, and the water rose like a pillar. He clapped, and tendrils shot out, hovering in the air. The water spun, the tendrils twirled and twisted with the music, and the two women moved between them, weaving amongst the water tendrils while they spiralled around them. The music sped up, and the dancers and the water moved faster and faster, blurring in their speed. It seemed inevitable that one of them would make a mistake. Ardan held his breath at the beauty and thrill of it.

The woman struck the bodhrán with a hard note of finality. The dancing stopped.

Silence settled over the room. The women curtseyed, and the water slipped back into the barrel.

Like the rumblings of a bear, the entire hall's approval began slowly, but soon rose to a roar as cheers and clapping erupted all around them.

Ardan released the breath he hadn't realised he'd been holding. 'That was incredible.'

'It was adequate,' Murieen said, taking a sip of her caudle.

'I always thought it a shame they've never travelled through the forest. Be nice to see them in Barleron,' Riordan said.

'Most are trained by the Waterlords. They find the water at Barleron too wild. Same way I find the water here too tame—not enough character.'

Before Ardan could question her any further, he saw Eamon coming towards them. He was carrying the cat at arm's length.

'It wouldn't be quiet after you left. I tried to calm it down but then it pissed on everything, so now you need to sort it out,' Eamon said before turning and heading back towards the stairs.

The cat immediately started yowling. Ardan tried to hush it, but that just made the cat louder. The surrounding people shot him annoyed looks as the beat of the bodhrán started up again.

'I'll take her out back, see if she's hungry.'

'Kitchens over that way,' Riordan said, pointing.

Ardan left quickly, finding a cook around the back. He was a smiling man with a thick black beard splattered with scraps. He listened to Ardan while stirring a cauldron of bubbling stew.

'What does she normally eat?'

'I rescued her out of the forest a few days ago and only had trail rations. She nibbled at some of the dried meat, but nothing otherwise,' Ardan finished with a shrug.

'Hmm, give me a minute.' The man rummaged through the kitchen, soon loading Ardan with a bowl of milk and cuts from the roasting meat. 'That should do the trick. Come back if you need anything else.'

Ardan thanked him before leaving for the rear of the Inn. He went to one of their parked carts and set the cat down there. He put both food options down, letting her decide.

She sniffed them both before dipping her tongue tentatively into the bowl. Within a moment, she was lapping it up noisily. Soon the bowl was empty, while her face and whiskers were covered in milk. She meowed loudly.

Ardan couldn't help but laugh.

'Another plainsman taking something that isn't his.'

Ardan spun to see the speaker, it was the forest woman from earlier. She was still in her green garb, revealing tattooed shoulders and arms. Standing further back was the tall warrior with four axes in his belt.

'Can't see an animal without trying to subjugate it...' she trailed off as she frowned at the cub. She strode forward, her hand snapping out to push Ardan. On instinct, he slapped her hand away before it connected. She glared at him. This close, he could smell the faint aroma of sage and sweetgrass on her.

'Talon.'

The warrior stepped forward, his hand resting on his axe. Ardan stepped back, wary. The woman ignored him, bending at the waist. Her unbound hair cascaded like an auburn waterfall as she examined the cat. 'Ancients,' she breathed. 'It's a Mishipeshu.'

'And I won't let you interrupt her recovery,' Ardan said, keeping an eye on Talon.

'So you can cage a great water lynx? I don't think so.'

He recognised her tone and would not end up like the priest. Observing her movements, the steel behind her brown eyes and false smile, he waited. When her eyes flicked to his feet, he knew what to do.

Her leg went to hook around his, and he moved in response. The unexpected motion caused her to stumble. Her arm, originally meant to push him over, was now using him to stop her from falling. He grasped her wrist, twisted it around and in a moment, he had her arm behind her back.

She let loose a cry of pained surprise. *And I thought the unarmed training wouldn't be useful. Yet here I am, subjugating a woman. What a hero.*

Talon was already moving, his axes out. His legs quickly covered the distance between them. Ardan used his leverage to put the woman between him and the warrior. Talon's footwork shifted, circling and moving, as he looked for an opening.

Instinct took over. Ardan shoved the woman forward, the movement giving him enough time to get his sword out. Talon recovered, a predatory gleam in his eyes. In that moment, Ardan wondered if he were looking at his impending death.

A mug of ale sailed through the air, directly towards Talon.

The man moved impossibly fast, cloak flaring as he spun, smashing the mug out of the air with his axe. He immediately looked for the offender.

At the doorway stood Riordan. 'You attack him, and you'll be dead before morning.'

'He laid hands on the Lady Koira.'

'Yet who will the guards believe? How many fights have you started since you got here?'

'It doesn't...' the warrior began.

'Talon, stop,' Koira said. She had adjusted herself, straightening her clothes. 'He's right. We're not here to make enemies.'

'Could have fooled me,' Ardan said. He still held his sword out in front of him. He was acutely aware of how close Talon was with those axes of his.

'You have stolen one of the great hunting cats from the forest. It is a great crime amongst our people.'

'Punishable by death or dismemberment,' Talon added, his mouth curving like a blade.

'What are you waiting for, then?' Ardan said, feeling the strange sensation rising in him. It was tangible enough he could funnel it to his sword, causing the green flame to appear. He wasn't giving up the cub.

Riordan barked a laugh. 'The lad almost got us all killed saving it. What's one more time?'

Koira looked at Talon, who gave a slight shrug of his shoulders.

'You saved it?' Koira asked.

He kept his mouth shut. He didn't owe her anything.

'If the lad hadn't taken it in, the cub would be dead.'

Koira looked between Ardan and Riordan, then at the cat, who was chewing on the meat rather enthusiastically. The scabbed wounds on her side were clearly visible.

Something unseen passed between the two of them and Talon lowered his axes.

'Even if you saved her, it doesn't give you the right to keep her.'

'She would die on her own,' Ardan snapped, his sword hand shaking.

'It is not for you to decide,' Talon said.

'I'm not letting her go,' Ardan said, trying to still his sword. At that moment, the cub meowed loudly, looking at the empty milk bowl.

Ardan could feel the eyes of the others on him. He sighed, sheathed his sword and went to pick up the cat, feeling horribly exposed as he showed them his back. The feline reached out with a paw. He pulled her into his arms, careful of the wounds on her side.

Koira's brown eyes softened as she looked between the cat and Ardan. She turned to Talon and said, 'Let's go.'

Talon huffed, aggressively replacing the axes in his belt before following Koira back to the Inn. When they disappeared inside, a great flood of tension left Ardan's body.

'Light, lad. I leave you alone for five seconds and you find yourself in a scrap. Lucky I thought you could use another drink.'

'Well, you are my mentor. Every time you leave me alone, I go off trying to find trouble. First Davan, then the Shadow beast, now the forest people,' Ardan said. The encounter had left him feeling giddy.

'You didn't back down, either.'

'I couldn't.'

'In a lot of ways, it's a good thing but know Talon would have sliced you up like a hunk of meat. Words can be as powerful as any weapon. Try to remember that.'

'Didn't work with Davan.'

'Nothing is perfect for every situation,' Riordan said. He tried to scratch the cat's head, but she swatted at his fingers. 'Mishipeshu, eh?'

The cub squirmed, wanting to get down. Ardan obliged, letting it move around the courtyard.

'It's a bit of a mouthful. What about Mish?' Ardan said. The cat was focused on a bug, not even glancing at him. 'Well, I like it.'

Mish suddenly bounded after the bug, her movements blurring between graceful and adolescent. She didn't look like a great water lynx. Then it made him wonder how big they got—what was he going to do when she was fully grown?

CHAPTER THIRTY-SIX: THE SHADOW AND THE WILD

* * *

he Archangel himself came to my cell, arriving with the army of the Light. We spoke for hours before Zadkiel absolved me of my sin. He gave me the greatest honour of all, direct access to the Angel's light. I am now a Templar.

— Journals of Phillip, the twelfth Templar.

ARDAN AND RIORDAN closed the door as they left their rooms, muffling Eamon's snores. They walked down to the common room. A couple of the staff were diligently mopping the floors around the mostly unoccupied tables. Loud cursing was already emanating from the kitchens. The empty, lifeless feel was a sharp contrast to the atmosphere surrounding the water dancers the previous night.

Mish stirred in her makeshift carrier. It was Ardan's spare shirt, turned into a sling. He'd thought it was a place she could sleep, though she was doing anything but that, constantly twisting and turning. Ardan gave up and put on her the wooden floor. She immediately started exploring, though she quickly retreated when her paws touched areas the staff had been mopping.

'Duties today. We're taking turns heading out with Conner into the markets, while he buys what he needs. Mostly grain and livestock, but I think he wants to bring back some fine wines, trinkets, and the like.'

'When is my shift?'

'The first one. We'll be leaving late morning, but once we're done, you're going to be stuck back here. Unloading the wagons back into our carts.'

Ardan looked suspiciously at Riordan. 'Am I still being punished?'

'A few extra watches and everything is forgiven?' Riordan laughed, sitting down. 'Good joke.'

'Why can't we just take the carts with us?' Ardan muttered as he sat heavily in the wooden chair.

'One wagon can hold the load of two or three carts. It's easier, trust me,' Riordan said, leaning back as a server arrived with two bowls of thick, steaming porridge.

'Sounds fantastic. Nothing I enjoy doing better than loading some carts,' Ardan said, blowing on the food.

'That's the spirit.' Riordan's eyes caught something. 'I might take my breakfast outside. I'll meet you out front in a few hours,' he said, moving quickly away from him and outside.

Ardan twisted in his seat, spotting Mish at a nearby table. She was swatting at something while Murieen sat opposite her, flicking her fingers back and forth.

'You're up early, boy. Come join me.'

She looked the same as she had the previous night, wearing an odd assortment of blue and green clothing, her hair a tangled mess of grey. Her adornments were seashells, shark teeth, and a single white feather. She was playing idly with the bowl of water in front of her. The water would spiral out of the bowl, hypnotising Mish. Ardan grabbed his porridge and went to her table.

'There's more I want to know about Barleron before I return. Your friend was too enamoured with my apprentice to tell me anything but pleasing platitudes. Sit and talk to me of the city.'

Ardan hesitated. 'What do you want to know?'

Murieen stopped playing with the water and stared at him as though he were daft. 'Who controls the city?'

'Well, there are the six Quarters—'

Murieen brushed her hand through the air. 'Yes. Yes, Barleron is ridiculous, but who's taken the Magistrates' place?'

'Uhhh—'

'There are three of them, yes? The Fiddler, the Dock Master and the Prostitute.'

'Her name is Marion.'

Murieen smiled, and he realised he'd been baited.

'It's early for these sorts of games.'

'Games? Now, that is an excellent idea. How do you feel about a game of Kings? It'll give us something to do while you tell me about the city,' Murieen said, and before Ardan could speak she was already calling over one of the Inn's staff, requesting a board.

Ardan sighed, trying to finish his porridge while he had the chance. It would be nice to play against someone besides Marion even so.

Talon and Koira came down the stairs just as they'd finished setting up.

Her auburn hair was back in a warrior's braid, accentuating her sharp features. Talon was scratching at his shirt. *Wait, the man is wearing a shirt?*

Koira spotted him and immediately turned to Talon, whispering.

'Got a crush on the savage forest people?' Murieen asked with a sly smile.

'The opposite. We sort of got into a fight yesterday,' Ardan said, not taking his eyes from them as they made their way towards him.

'Did you now? Well, this should be interesting,' she said, leaning back, her green-grey eyes dancing as she watched them approach.

Ardan's hand itched for his sword. The power inside of him rose like the tide. He desperately grappled with it, not wanting to lose control now.

The two of them stopped in front of the table. Where Murieen greeted them in a different tongue. It sounded old and musical. Talon and Koira stared at her, dumbfounded. Koira eventually responded in the same language.

'Do you speak the common tongue? I'm afraid I know little of the Ancients' language beyond the greeting,' Murieen said, her hands resting in her lap.

Koira nodded, though her mouth was still slightly agape.

'Splendid, I thought I'd help break the ice. Let you get your thoughts together.'

'We were just surprised, that's all.' Koira swallowed, stole a glance at the ceiling, before she focused on him. 'I wanted to apologise for my actions yesterday. They were ... done in ignorance.'

It was Ardan's turn to be shocked. 'It's fine.'

'That's it?' Murieen burst out. 'I thought you two were going to duke it out.'

Ardan sighed. 'Ignore her. I think she's bored.'

'I... see,' Koira said.

Ardan felt something hit his head. The old woman was glaring at him, a glob of water floating near her outstretched hand. With a start, he realised she used the water to slap him.

'Why don't you join us? We're just about to play a game of Kings,' Murieen said, as one of the Inn's servants arrived. The man had a large, curling, orange moustache. He opened a small wooden chest and took out a well-used board, deck of cards, and game figurines. He passed the dice to Murieen, smiled, making his moustache to curve with it, and left.

'This is a game?'

'Aye, tricky but fun. The people of Barleron love it. If you wish to move among the upper class, you'd best learn it,' Murieen said. Koira looked startled. 'That's what you're trying to do, isn't it? Be an ambassador for your people?'

'In a sense.'

'Great, a third player. What about your tall, brooding friend?'

'Absolutely not,' Talon said.

'Not fond of anything that isn't sharp or pointy?' Murieen asked.

Ardan held his breath, looking between the two. Did this woman have a death wish? Then he saw the glob of water hovering just above the bowl. It was like an arrow taut on a bowstring.

'No, I am not,' Talon said, walking to another table.

The water flowed back into the bowl. Ardan released the breath he hadn't known he'd been holding. He could see the corners of Koira's mouth were quirking upwards. Murieen began walking her through the rules as Ardan took the deck of cards and shuffled. They rolled the dice for their avatar. Ardan got the Waterlord, Murieen the Baron, while Koira got the Ancient. She inspected the figurine shaped like a man with roots for feet and branches for arms.

'This is an Ancient?' Koira asked.

Murieen peered at her. 'Aye, because we don't know what they looked like. Try not to take it personally. '

Koira pursed her lips as she placed the figurine down.

The game was slow as they explained the rules to Koira. They played with their cards face up, explaining what they were doing and why. Ardan had just picked up the dice.

'Let us start the game over. I believe I understand the rules now,' Koira said. They were barely halfway across the board.

Ardan looked at Murieen, who inclined her head. They reset the board and began anew.

As she didn't have to explain the rules, Murieen began pestering Ardan with questions about Barleron. As he was answering her questions at every turn, making it difficult for him to concentrate, he turned to the old woman.

'Why all the questions?'

'I want to go home,' Murieen said, but when Ardan raised an eyebrow, she continued: 'I left the city when the Magistrate kicked it —I've dealt with too many successions already. But that's the problem; I'm old and I miss my own comforts. I want to make sure it's safe before jumping on your caravan back to Barleron.'

'Even with the city still in upheaval?'

'The Fiddler concerns me, no doubt about it. Someone who press-gangs others to fight for him needs a quick walk off the deep end of the Docks in full mail armour. The way you and Riordan jump to this Marion's defence tells me she's decent enough.'

Ardan caught Koira following the conversation with a forced casualness. She was trying to not appear too invested in it. 'And the Dock Master?'

'Now him I know. Smarter than I gave him credit for, walking around in torn clothes and cursing like the drunken sailor he is, but he's kept the Docks running despite everything.'

'These are the royals fighting for power?' Koira asked.

'Royals? No, lass. Barleron has no use for nobility. People rise there by the sword and the power of their connections.'

'I see.'

'Now that you've gotten what you need out of us, tell us why you're out of your forest home.'

'We want to seek alliances and trade with plainsmen again. We believe we can achieve—'

'Can you save me the rehearsed speech? Sounds too unnatural. I didn't ask the boy questions I already knew the answer to. What's the real reason you're here?'

Ardan watched Talon stiffen at the end of the table and he wondered how Murieen got away with talking like this. The old woman continued: 'I know what it's like to be a proud outsider. You've got to know when to lower your barriers and seek help.'

Koira's grip tightened on her cards, but she otherwise gave no tells. The three of them waited in silence until Koira eventually spoke. 'The power that resides inside the forest is becoming restless. Something or someone is attacking it.'

'And you want to find it and stop it? I thought the power of the Ancients was limitless? Murieen asked.

'The mightiest oak can be felled from rot.'

'A ship is sunk from the tiniest hole,' Murieen agreed. 'Well, you won't find it here. Whatever's doing it is likely in Barleron.'

'That's a stretch of reasoning,' Ardan said.

'What better cover than a city in chaos? It would give them access to the forest, while the amount of blood spilled there would throw anyone off.' As Muireen spoke, Ardan suddenly had a vivid flashback of the road filled with the corpses of the Street King and his Toughs.

'Who would do such a thing?' Ardan asked, feeling sick.

Murieen looked between them as she answered: 'Of the people at Barleron? Bishop Frederick and High Priest Guillamere have the power. Raigel—maybe, and Templar Phillip. Or one of the surviving angels or demons hiding in that place.'

Koira's face had gone ashen during the exchange. 'So many endanger my home?'

'I was just naming powerful people in the city. Outside of shaping, I have little knowledge of the three powers.'

Koira's eyes went distant. 'I appreciate your candour. You have given me much to think on.'

You and me both, Ardan thought.

CHAPTER THIRTY-SEVEN:
UNEXPECTED ENCOUNTERS

***

I cannot help but feel a certain amount of satisfaction that the commander who ordered my incarceration must now bow to me.
— *Journals of Phillip, the twelfth Templar.*

***

YAWNING, Ardan adjusted the makeshift sling that housed Mish. Her weight was a comforting warmth while they waited in the brisk predawn air. Some of the other guards muttered while Conner walked amongst them, snapping at his drivers to check their loads one more time. They tightened the ropes, rocked the barrels and shook the crates. When they were confident nothing was loose, they mounted up and started through the streets.

Murieen was bundled in so many blankets that she resembled a cloth hamper. She had bullied Conner into letting her sit on the lead cart with him.

They took a shortcut through one of the Squares. The day before, it had held hundreds of market stalls and thousands of people. He had seen the Kurks in their thick leathers, church soldiers and priests, fire and water Shapers, horse dealers, weapon merchants, and more fruits and vegetables than he even knew existed. Riordan had to nudge him more than once to focus on their task.

Only the bakers inhabited the Square this early. Their ovens cast a faint light across the empty stalls, the aroma of baking bread filling the air.

The creaking of the wagons' wheels and the beat of the horses' hooves broke the stillness as their party passed. They exited the city unchallenged, taking the western road.

As they pulled up near the edge of the forest, figures materialised from among the trees. Someone gave a shout of alarm, and there was a flurry of movement as swords rasped out of their scabbards. Murieen suddenly had several globes of water about the size of fists levitating in front of her.

'Good morning gentlemen,' Koira said from amidst their group. She stepped forward, her hands raised in an open gesture. The faces of her six guards behind her were only just recognisable in the early morning gloom.

'Light, you gave me a fright,' Conner said.

'My apologies,' Koira said with a bow of her head.

'I thought you weren't coming when we didn't see you in the yard this morning.'

'The men of the Light were getting persistent. We left the city late last night.'

'Some warning would have been nice,' Conner muttered.

Koira gave an apologetic grimace.

Conner looked over at the forest warriors, raising his voice to carry over everyone. 'Keep pace, don't slow us down, and I'll take you to Mercenary Square.'

'Thank you, master merchant.'

Conner grunted.

No one spoke as they waited for the first rays of sunlight. When it was time, Conner gave the signal. The guards tensed, going through the invisible barrier, but the forest people kept up their casual stroll.

The carts creaked as they navigated the twisting and narrow forest road.

Several hours had passed and they had yet to encounter a single creeping vine, viper, or any other forest surprise. At first Ardan thought they were merely lucky, but he grew suspicious as the hours continued to pass by. The forest people were doing something. No one was this lucky.

A little before midday, they passed another caravan heading to Dentwall. Conner and their caravan master spoke briefly, but soon both parties were moving again. A couple of hours later, they pulled up to the first circle. The guards commented on the good time they were making.

Ardan sat down near the edge, letting Mish out. She immediately bounded back and forth, playfully pouncing on small bugs in the grass. After a spectacular leap and subsequent crash, she looked surprised to find Ardan there and immediately acted more dignified. As she did, Ardan noticed a figure over her shoulder. In the afternoon light, he had to make sure he wasn't seeing things. The figure was a man, standing stock still, watching them.

'Hey, there's a man out there,' Ardan called.

Riordan came over to him. 'Aye, that's Hadwin. The shadow beast probably scattered him last time.'

'You know him?'

'No, that's just what we call him. There's a sweet-scenter out there somewhere.'

'A what?'

Riordan glanced sideways at him, 'You haven't heard of 'em?'

Ardan shook his head.

'I haven't met anyone that's seen one up close. Don't know if it's a plant or a tree, but they release a sweet, intoxicating aroma. It's meant to be different to each person, but I'm not getting close enough to test it. If you do, you lose your mind, forget everything you've ever known. The others might know more. Talon!' Riordan shouted the last.

The tall man looked at Riordan, his face unreadable. 'Do you know anything about sweet-scenters?'

Talon ignored them, going back to the small circle of forest warriors. It was Koira who rose, leaving the six warriors as she walked towards them. 'What do you wish to know, plainsmen?'

'Ardan was asking about sweet-scenters. I know little about them besides to steer clear, and that they make you forget everything.'

Koira knelt in front of Mish with a tiny piece of wood tied to a bowstring. The black cat could barely contain herself as she leapt at it, swatting wildly. 'Not *forget*; the smell overrides everything else— loyalty, duty, love. Only the sweet-scenter is important. There were several drug addicts in Dentwall. Their affliction is the same. Look,' she said, pointing at a stag with a magnificent set of antlers. 'There's another one of its slaves.'

'It works on animals too?' Ardan asked.

Koira nodded. She looked out across the Meadow. 'It works on many things. If we come across one, we mark it on our maps and do our best to destroy it. Assuming there isn't collateral damage, we burn entire sections of forest to get it.'

'They're that dangerous?'

'They're a disease, a remnant from when Eden unleashed its wrath. There's no cure, although some seek it as a release. A man lost his wife and son in childbirth. After several weeks, he left without a word. We later found him at the edge of one of the known sweet-scenters.'

'Is that him?'

Riordan shook his head. 'An unlucky guard from a while back. Word is he went into the woods to relieve himself and a gust of wind caught him.'

'How does he survive out there?'

Riordan shrugged.

'Any way they can,' Koira answered.

'Has no one tried to get close to it, just blocking their nose?' Ardan asked.

'Are you volunteering?' Koira said.

'The lad is not,' Riordan said quickly.

'We have not tried. It's dangerous, for so little gain.'

Ardan studied the man and the stag in the distance, feeling the icy grip of fear, and shuddered. To have everything you'd ever known suddenly mean so little—was death preferable to the complete loss of freedom? Ardan wouldn't wish that fate on his father's murderers. *Well, maybe Verrick.*

After that, they sat in a circle and ate their trail rations in silence. Ardan sought his bedroll early, but sleep proved elusive. He glanced over to the area of darkness where he'd seen Hadwin and the stag, imagining their eyes on the party. His sleep was fitful, and he was glad when they had to get up for the next leg of their journey.

Like the first day, their passage passed without an incident, leaving little for the guards to do. Some of them cast furtive glances at the forest people. Ardan stayed at the rear with Eamon and Riordan.

'No use staying back here,' Eamon said as he limped along at a fast shamble. 'Nothing for us to do. Go up and have a chat with your lady friend.'

Ardan stared at the grinning man. 'She'd gut me before that happened.'

'If I weren't married, I know I'd be trying my best to woo a woman like that.'

Ardan remained silent.

'Could be a good reason to increase relations between their people and ours.'

Ardan rolled his eyes.

'Let me help,' Eamon said with a wink that immediately made Ardan nervous. The man picked up his pace. It was almost painful to watch his limping stride, but he caught up to Talon and Koira. Ardan couldn't hear what he was saying, but he was pointing at his foot, moving it back and forth. She shook her head. He looked back at Ardan, who immediately tried to appear nondescript, looking out at the forest as though it was the most fascinating thing in existence. By the time he looked back, Eamon was waving him forward.

Riordan was barely holding back his laughter.

Ardan suddenly felt annoyed; he disliked being forced into things.

Riordan gave him a shove, and he sucked in a deep breath and made his way there. *I shouldn't have saved that ass*, Ardan thought as he got closer. Talon watched him coolly as he joined them.

'The Lady Koira wanted to know what type of snake bit me,' Eamon said, a twinkle in his eye.

'A green forest viper. From the size of it, probably an adolescent,' Ardan said, feeling very mechanical.

She nodded. 'How did you treat it?'

Ardan told her.

'If you're still walking on it, it is a gift from the Ancients,' Koira said to Eamon.

'I think they can keep their future gifts,' Eamon said, giving his foot a shake.

Koira smiled. 'Now that I have answered your questions, will you answer mine, plainsman?'

'Ardan's probably better at it than I am.'

Ardan shot him a glare while Eamon smirked. Their caravan had just come to a point where two trees crowded the road. Ardan stood with Koira as the cart drivers navigated through the narrow section.

'What do you want to know?' Ardan asked.

The woman was silent. Ardan was about to repeat himself when she finally spoke. 'We haven't dealt with plainsmen for over a genera-tion, beyond an unfortunate forest man. There are pitfalls in your speech and mannerisms I do not understand. I would like to learn more and avoid future entanglements.'

'Like attacking me?'

Koira averted her eyes, and Ardan felt a stab of guilt. She had already apologised, he reminded himself.

'When you're talking with people, try to use their name or title, but generally don't call them 'plainsman'.'

Koira nodded thoughtfully. 'We use tribal names unless we are known to each other.'

'Like you and Talon?'

'Yes.'

'Should I call you by your tribal name?'

'I have no tribal name.'

Ardan frowned. No tribe? Before he could question it, the last of the caravan had cleared the chokepoint and their party progressed on.

'Is it true that you brought the shadow beast down onto a circle?' Koira asked, giving him a sidelong glance.

Ardan shrugged. 'It felt like the right thing to do.'

'Explain that further, plainsman,' Koira said, then caught herself. 'Ardan.'

Ardan smiled. 'There was a feeling inside of me, pulling me towards Mish,' Ardan said, nodding towards the lynx cub. 'It was like she was projecting towards me, and I had to go to her.'

Koira stopped, staring at him. He paused too, as though waiting for her to catch up. Yet when he saw her face, he couldn't read her expression. She blinked and her features smoothed. No more questions came, and they lapsed into an awkward silence. Eventually, Koira slipped away, and he felt strangely disappointed.

The caravan rolled through into the second clearing around midafternoon. Another party had come from Barleron with their own convoy of carts and guards. Ardan scanned their faces, trying to see if there was anyone he knew. None wore the markings of the larger mercenary guilds. But he recognised one man. He was sitting by the cook fire, skinning a hare. He was thinner than the last time Ardan had seen him, but he still looked like a weasel. It was Verrick, his father's murderer.

CHAPTER THIRTY-EIGHT: FIRE OF THE ANCIENTS

***

I walk the battlements. Barrels of arrows line the parapets, while siege engines are checked behind the walls. We prepare as best we can. I wear a brave face. We are too few to stand against the oncoming horde.
— Journals of Phillip, the twelfth Templar.

***

ARDAN'S ANGER cascaded into fury and a deep desire for retribution. He drew his sword. His conscious thoughts were drowned out by the power welling up inside of him. It screamed for justice. He stalked towards his target. The power that welled up in him fuelled his rage to higher levels. Nothing else mattered.

Verrick saw him coming, his weasel eyes darting to the sword and back to Ardan. Realisation dawned on him, and he jumped back, dropping the half-skinned hare in the dirt.

'Lad, what are you doing?' Riordan called out to him.

Ardan ignored him. There was only his father's murderer, and the vengeance that drove him. The man's greed had caused every woe that had befallen his family. He let the power flow into his falchion, the green flame bursting into life.

There were curses and exclamations of surprise as he advanced. Ardan laughed scornfully as Verrick retreated, ducking and weaving around the camp, keeping the skinning knife in front of him as though the pitiful thing would protect him. He kept putting people between himself and Ardan. Most people scampered away when they saw the flaming sword. But the clearing wasn't big enough for him to run away for long. Ardan had almost closed the gap when Riordan and Eamon appeared in his way. The two mercenaries stood shoulder to shoulder, blocking him. They both had their weapons out.

'Move,' Ardan growled.

'No.'

'You must not defy the sanctity of the circle,' Koira said, her voice commanding. It gave him pause, but then he saw Verrick standing behind Riordan and Eamon, a sneer on his lips. Memory flashed of the knife plunging into his father's chest.

The green sword flared up, becoming blindingly bright. Ardan slashed out in front of him, not intending to hit his friends, but expecting the flame to scatter them. Riordan stepped forward, his shield catching the sword. Eamon moved before he could recover, slamming his shoulder into Ardan, taking them both to the ground. Denied his prey, he felt his anger blaze, and the sword responded in kind.

'Hell's fire,' Riordan cried out, throwing his shield down. The thing had been engulfed in green fire, mirroring the sword's heat.

Ardan felt his wrist slamming against the ground again and again until he released the sword. The flame vanished instantly. He struggled, trying to force his way up but Eamon was bigger and had the right leverage point. Try thought he might, Ardan couldn't break free.

'Absolute madman. What he's doing coming at me like that?'

Riordan walked calmly over to Verrick and put a comforting arm on the man's shoulder before driving his fist deep into the man's stomach. His cavalier attitude caught Verrick completely off guard, and he doubled over, collapsing onto the ground.

'I know the reason; I know the lad. You're lucky we're in the forest, otherwise I'd be helping him.'

The blow caused the rage inside of Ardan to feel mildly sated. It was enough that he was aware of his emotions; inch by inch, he clawed control back from the rage that fuelled him, and the fire of his sword. By the time he'd recovered, he looked over at Verrick.

The man had risen to a sitting position, coughing as he tried to catch his breath. He watched the three of them warily. 'I killed a thief. I did it the legal way,' Verrick said between breaths. 'If that's a problem, take it up with me in Barleron. Or keep doing it the coward's way, while I'm sitting down and unarmed. Or hitting me without warning.'

A crowd from the two caravans had gathered, some muttering at Verrick's comments.

'Did you beat children the legal way too?' Riordan asked.

'Were you there?' Verrick snapped.

'He was,' Riordan said, pointing at Ardan. 'I think he expressed how he felt about it. Next time, I won't stand in his way.'

'He can find me in Mercenary Square when he needs to,' Verrick said, getting up, still clutching his stomach. He moved back to where his caravan had made their camp, keeping his eyes on them.

Something about Riordan's measured responses made Ardan considerably calmer. Eamon noticed the change and tentatively let him up. The insane rage had left him feeling weak and empty. He wanted to hurt Verrick, but he knew it wasn't the right time. He slowly got to his feet.

'It's okay. I'm fine,' Ardan said. He looked at his weapon, then up at Riordan, who nodded. He grabbed his sword and as he sheathed it, saw the burnt remains of Riordan's shield. 'Sorry about that.'

'The sooner Raigel finishes my shield, the better. See if you and your brother can break that one.'

It brought the ghost of a smile to Ardan's lips and released a lot of the tension. He avoided looking at his father's murderer. It helped. They stayed inside the circle, going to the furthermost point from Verrick.

Conner came over to talk to Riordan, his face sombre. They eyed Ardan, speaking in hushed whispers. Eamon joined them. While they did, Koira and Talon came over to him. His face was still stony, but hers was fierce. He hadn't seen that expression since she'd downed the priest of the Light.

'You almost broke the sanctity of the circle.'

'I wish I had.'

Talon's hand went to rest on the edge of one of his axes.

Koira glared at him. 'The circle is a safe place. From animals, creatures and humans. No blood is spilled here. It is one of the fundamental rules of the Ancients.'

Ardan shrugged, not wanting to deal with this right now.

'Now I demand to look at your sword.'

Ardan stared up at her, not fully comprehending. 'What?'

'Your sword is unnatural. I demand to see it.'

'No.'

Talon stepped forward, but Koira put a hand on his arm. Her glare next left across her face. 'Do you know what you did?'

Ardan was too weary to care. 'Is this going to take long?'

Talon stepped forward and slapped Ardan. Pain exploded in his cheek as he collapsed to the ground. Tasting dirt and blood, he looked up at the tattooed man. 'Sanctity of the circle, huh?'

'Enough,' Koira snapped. 'You used the power of the Ancients. A plainsman, wielding their fire. Do you know what this means?'

Ardan got to his feet and dusted himself off. 'It means you're not leaving me alone for a while.'

Koira's brown eyes hardened, her fist clenching and unclenching. She let out a curse in her own tongue and turned, stalking off.

'You've got a talent for destruction,' Eamon said once she was gone.

Despite Ardan having control of his emotions, the power inside of him was still there, a constant pressure ready to boil over. Despite their distance, a glance towards Verrick was enough to make the power rise, trying to get out and break free. It wanted vengeance, regardless of the consequences.

'Riordan, I need help.'

'Obviously.'

'The power inside of me. It threatens to overwhelm my actions.'

Riordan stroked his red beard. 'That's an excuse I haven't heard before.'

'Riordan, please.'

He looked at Ardan with genuine concern. 'You don't want to kill Verrick?'

Ardan gave him a flat look. *Of course I want him dead.* 'The power is urging me to do it now, trying to force my hand.'

Riordan paused his hand halfway through his beard, brow furrowing. 'It's this power that gives you that green fire?'

'Yes.'

Riordan mused on that. 'Does your brother have the same problem?'

'I don't know.'

'Can you keep a handle on it until we get back to Barleron?'

The inner turmoil was bouncing back and forth inside of him like a tempest. 'Maybe.'

Riordan paused. 'There's one person who might help.'

Ardan followed his gaze, then shook his head. 'I don't think she'd be willing.'

'You know, I always thought I was bad with women. Yet you've known her only three days and got on her bad side quite spectacularly more than once.'

Surely I haven't been that bad, have I? He thought but remained silent.

'Think on it—but if it's as bad as you say, I can speak on your behalf. It might be beneficial,' Riordan added with a shrug.

Ardan found a space near one of the larger stones, as though their proximity might help him. He didn't shift from his spot all night. He didn't eat, just kept his focus on not losing control. Eventually, the members of both caravans sought their bedrolls. Soon Eamon's soft snoring filled the air, punctuated by the sound of night owls and buzzing insects. Ardan kept looking towards the forest. Trying to keep the power under control was a constant battle for him. He could imagine his father's eyes on him, telling him that revenge helped no one. It did little to aid him.

It turned out to be one of the slowest, most arduous nights of his life. He couldn't help but breath a sigh of relief as the dark sky slowly gave way to the orange hue of dawn. With it, the camp began to move. The horses were hitched to the wagons, bedrolls were packed up, and within short order, both caravans were ready to leave. As soon as the first ray of sunlight shone through the trees, they left.

Ardan looked back, finding Verrick. The weasel face bastard smirked at him. He immediately felt the power well up, threatening to overwhelm him. It was like trying to stand against a hurricane. Step by step, he pushed back and regained control. It helped when Verrick was finally out of sight. Yet exhaustion reigned. He knew if he ran into Verrick again, he would lose control.

'Riordan.'

'Mmm.'

'Speak to Koira.'

Riordan beamed and almost said something but nodded instead. He went over to the forest woman as the caravan had followed the road. The trees spread out allowing a view of a hundred yards in any direction. The carts rolled by as he waited, their wheels crunching the dry leaves and twigs of the forest.

He could see Riordan speaking to Koira. More time with the forest woman, *flaming wonderful*. She was as volatile as the forest itself. Their discussion continued for a long time. Ardan wondered if she could help him but discarded the idea. He'd be no worse off if she couldn't. But what was taking so long? Was she reluctant? Had he broken one of their taboos? He felt sheepish, especially after remembering how he'd spoken to her last night.

It was midmorning when they came to some sort of agreement. Riordan came back to him.

'It wasn't easy. The woman's got a natural fire in her. You threw lamp oil on it last night with that little stunt.'

'Then fanned it,' Eamon said.

Riordan ignored him, focusing on Ardan. 'She will teach you.'

'Thanks,' Ardan grunted.

Riordan grabbed him by his arm, his grip firm. 'I had to give up a lot of concessions to make this happen. As in, I don't know if Marion can keep them all. Learn what you can from her. Be respectful.'

'Or don't,' Eamon interrupted. 'Maybe throw in a viper, spice this run up.'

'Thanks, Riordan,' Ardan said.

Riordan let him go, but his blue eyes remained intense. 'Don't want to lose you, lad. Now get up there, time's wasting.'

Ardan took a deep breath, berated himself for being a coward, and walked faster, going past the carts and catching up with the forest warriors. As he got closer, talk between Koira and Talon ceased. The warrior's face twitched into a sneer as he moved away.

'Uh, Riordan said you'd help me with my problem?'

Koira's face was flat and impassive. 'I will.'

They continued walking for some time. At first Ardan thought she just needed time, but the silence stretched out for a long time.

'I am trying to gather my patience. The Wild is often unpredictable, and it likely guided your actions. But you almost broke the sanctity of the stones.' Koira kept walking as she spoke, her face focused on the ground in front of her, deliberately not looking at Ardan.

'Like you, I might need etiquette lessons. I do not know the forest people's—'

'We are the Children of the Ancients.'

Ardan swallowed. Then he remembered his mother's lessons about how to read people and adjust to a situation. 'I do not know the Children of the Ancients' customs. If I give offensive, it is out of ignorance, and not intent.'

Koira eyed him suspiciously for a moment before accepting his words. 'Then we will begin there. The stones are a gift from the Ancients, one of their last. A place in which to escape the nocturnal predators. Extreme violence must not be done except in the most dire of circumstances.'

'I'm sorry.'

'I do not think that you are,' Koira said matter-of-factly. 'But the sanctity was not broken, thanks to Riordan and Eamon.'

The silence was back, worse than before. Ardan's eyes fell on a nearby Ramón tree, its small breadnuts littering the leaf-covered ground.

'What is happening to me?'

'You have tapped into the power of the Ancients.'

'I've what?'

Koira paused, looking back at him. 'Are you hard of hearing?'

'No, it's just ... I didn't know that was possible.'

'Is it so hard to believe? Priests tap into the power of Light and Dark.'

'So I'm a priest of the Ancients?'

Dimples appeared for a brief instant but vanished as quickly as they had come. 'No, you are not. The Wild just *is*—having access to it does not make you an elder, a priest, or wise. Obviously.'

Ardan stopped himself from retorting. She watched him struggle, the corners of her mouth turned up.

'Alright, so I can tap the power of the Ancients.'

'Yes, and you seem to do it directly, something that is very unusual. If you are left without guidance, this power will likely get you killed.'

Ardan was about to ask how, but then he remembered losing control with Verrick. And blowing himself up in the bell tower, and again at the Golden Meadow. He didn't need to stretch his imagination.

'How do I control it?'

'You don't.'

Whatever brief humour he'd wrung from her vanished, replaced by a flat expression.

'I said something stupid, didn't I?'

She exhaled, her face softening. 'It is the plainsmen's need for control. You do not control the Wild.'

'How do I stop it from killing me, or controlling me, then?'

'That is a better question,' Koira said. 'It is like stopping a falling tree from crushing your home. You might stop it for a while, but eventually, you will lose. Yet if you redirect it, you may save yourself and your home.'

'So it's like surviving a storm?'

Koira's mouth pursed and the expression made him realise how striking she was. Ardan tried to shake off that train of thought. *She'd likely gut me if I complimented her, probably for breaking some tradition of the fallen tree gods or something.*

'Think of the Wild as a feral beast. If you work with it, convey your intent, and the Wild listens—well then, then you can achieve something wonderful.'

Ardan watched as her tone took on something wistful. He waited for her to continue, but she was lost in her own thoughts.

'I don't want to sound ungrateful, but I'm stuck. How do I stop it from crushing me?'

Koira stretched out her hand, the tattoos of vines stopping at her wrist as she twisted her palm. A tiny green flame appeared in her hand, floating above her palm. It flicked and danced, but a moment later, it burst into a small green explosion. She looked at him, her brown eyes hard.

'You need to release it in short, controllable bursts. Can you achieve that much?'

'With or without the sword?'

'What do you mean?'

Ardan pulled out his falchion and funnelled the power into his sword. It burst into green flame. The relief was immediate, the internal pressure lowering.

Koira's face had gone white as she stared at the blade.

Ardan cut off the flow to the blade, letting the flame wink out. The blade was unmarred, shining in the morning light.

Koira's eyes shifted between him and the weapon. 'Talon!'

What have I done now? Ardan thought as the tall warrior stalked towards them with the casual grace of a predator.

CHAPTER THIRTY-NINE: THE POWER OF THE WILD

* * *

*N*aberius has arrived with his army; they clog the Pass like *locusts. They are led by the High Demon himself. The three-headed dog stands there with its oil-like fur, letting loose a howl that echoes down the pass. The fear that has haunted my dreams now faces the walls of the fortress.*

— Journals of Phillip, the twelfth Templar.

* * *

'Give me the sword,' Koira said, holding out her hand.

The carts continued past them while she waited. Ardan glanced at the blade, then at her. His stomach dropped. Then Talon walked over, hands resting on his axes. They were in the forest; there was nowhere to run. His hand tightened instinctively on his sword.

'Why?'

Talon leaned forward, looking menacing. 'The weapons are relics of my people.'

'My father had it made,' Ardan said, stepping back.

'Ardan, please,' Koira said and the pleading in her voice moved him. 'This is important. I need to see that weapon.'

Ardan gripped the sword tightly, looking her in the eyes. 'As long as you promise to give it back.'

Koira nodded impatiently and snatched it from him the moment he held it out. She examined it closely, her eyes lingering on the budding vine patterns visible partway up the blade. Looking puzzled, she passed it to Talon. The weapon looked small in his hands. The warrior hefted it while the caravan passed steadily behind them, their wheels crunching over twigs and leaves.

'It's not one of ours,' Talon said.

'You're sure?' Koira said, looking up at him.

He nodded. 'Nor do I think it is a weapon from the Ancients.'

'Then who?'

Talon stared at the weapon. 'I do not know, but we should take it to your mother. She might know.'

'You're not taking my weapon anywhere,' Ardan said flatly.

Two pairs of eyes snapped towards him. It was Koira who spoke: 'We must know how it was forged. We cannot let the technique fall into plainsman's hands.'

Unease filled Ardan. He couldn't lose his father's sword. 'It is too late for that. My weapon is not the first made from Ancient steel.'

The two forest people shared a look. 'We should bring it to the elders,' Talon said.

The last of the wagons was disappearing amongst the trees. Ardan suddenly felt alone. He wouldn't let them take his weapon without a fight. 'I gave you the weapon in good faith. Did the Ancients not teach you about honour? Are you nothing more than savages who live in trees?'

Talon growled while Koira looked startled. Her hand tightened on the weapon. Her brown eyes regarded him with an expression he couldn't read as she held out the weapon.

Ardan took the hilt of the sword, his father's last gift. He felt his eyes watering with relief. He looked away, ashamed. It was Mish who came to his rescue, butting her head against his leg before reaching out, wanting to be picked up. He sheathed his weapon and obliged. Her purring started immediately.

'You are right, I forgot myself,' Koira said, looking down. Talon didn't meet Ardan's eyes. 'It is just that these weapons—they are sacred to us. They're a remnant of the Ancients. I did not know new ones could be made.'

'The materials were taken from this forest. Mine by my father,' Ardan said. He breathed a sigh of relief when they started on the trail again.

'He did?' Koira asked.

'Yes, he was a forest stalker.'

'Means he's one of the plainsmen trappers,' Talon said when Koira looked confused.

'Surely he wasn't...' Koira said and paused. 'Where is he now?'

What she had been about to say? 'Dead. Murdered by the man I tried to kill last night.'

There was a significant pause before Koira spoke. 'That explains much.'

They continued on, a lull in their conversation. It was Ardan who broke it. 'Why is the sword so important?'

Talon gave Koira an unreadable look, but she shrugged. 'The Wild is unpredictable at the best of times. The sword provides protection, but it comes at the cost of scope. To wield the Ancients' flame through a weapon is unheard of.'

'And the sword can do more than spurt green fire?'

Koira stared at him as though he'd been dropped on his head as a child. 'The power of the Wild was virtually limitless, at least before the arrival of Heaven and Hell. Since then, it has been abused and tormented into becoming the feral beast you now sense. You sword is limited but it is up to you to find where that line is.'

'You speak as though the Wild is alive.'

'Do you not feel it?'

Ardan thought about it. The emotions that flowed in with the Wild weren't always his. It caused him to act irrationally, as he had when chasing Verrick. He knew the man deserved to die, but the method had been unlike him.

'You do see it,' Koira said, her soft brown eyes watching him.

They continued to walk along the path, eventually catching up with the rear of the caravan. She had given him a lot to think about. She was obviously lost in thought, too.

'How was the sword forged?' she asked at last.

'There's a merchant in the city that knows how.'

'A merchant?'

'He's a demon,' Ardan admitted.

Talon stared at him in disgust and spat on the ground, then sped up to rejoin the other forest warriors. As he left, Koira was watching Ardan curiously. She opened her mouth to speak several times before adding, 'I will try to reserve judgement. Plainsmen words and actions are confusing.'

They continued on for a while as Ardan chewed over what he'd learnt. 'Can I use the Wild without the sword?'

His question was met with silence. Koira continued on the trail, her eyes on the ground. Ardan didn't press her. They continued like this for close to twenty minutes until she spoke. 'I can teach you, but I want something in return.'

Ardan's hand unconsciously went to the sword. 'Yes?'

'There is much about plainsman culture I do not understand. I need you to explain things to me, so I do not....'

'Make a fool of yourself?'

She raised an eyebrow and clarified: 'Unknowingly make enemies.'

Ardan could think of a hundred people better suited, but if she'd teach him to handle his power.... 'Me? I mean, I'll try.'

'That is enough. Let us wait until we get to the next point of safety. There we will begin your lessons.'

Ardan shrugged and nodded. Since he'd released the pressure through the power of the sword, he had a much better handle on the Wild inside of him. They continued on and their caravan was not attacked or abused, allowing them to make good time.

They arrived at the last clearing before Barleron not much past midday. It was empty. Mish sniffed the idol in the centre before bounding towards the edges of the clearing. Ardan joined the others to help set up, but once he was done, he went looking for Koira. Her auburn hair was easily identifiable amongst the other forest warriors.

'Come, let us find an open space. Just in case,' Koira said.

They stood in a free part of the Meadow. She stepped in front of him and said, 'You can feel the Wild already, and you know how to push it into your sword. Now, what you need to do is focus on the same flame your sword creates. I want you to create that fire without the weapon as a buffer. Let the power flow. Don't let it get too big, and don't force it. Both will end up causing the backlash,' Koira said as she raised her hand. A small green flame appeared, dancing and flickering above her palm.

Ardan reached for the power inside him, trying to follow the contradictory advice. Yet it felt like trying to eat soup with a fork. *Are you flaming kidding me? The first time I actually want you, you're gone.* He cursed, his frustration building. Koira took a few steps back.

Alright, breathe, Ardan told himself. He thought of Verrick and his weaselly smirk. Anger filled him, and with it, the power of the Wild. It fed off his emotions, cycling and rising. He thought back to the wild dogs and tried to emulate funnelling the Wild down his arm and out onto his palm. A small flame spluttered to life in front of him, undulating in size. He could feel the pressure from the Wild but tried to keep the flame steady.

'Hey, I'm doing it,' Ardan said, looking up at Koira. As he did, the restrictions he'd put on the power buckled and failed. The Wild rushed out like a bursting dam. Green fire filled his vision, and he was flung across the clearing. He tumbled and crashed, barely managing to stop without seriously injuring himself. Pain flared in his chest, his arms, and he opened his eyes to see the trees and sky spinning. He groaned, but the sound was strangely muffled.

'Lad, are you okay?' Riordan said.

A moment later, he could see Koira above him. 'You lost focus.'

Ardan pushed himself up, lights appearing in his vision. *I probably shouldn't have done that so quickly.* Head spinning, he tried to get to his feet, until he felt a hand on his shoulder.

'Take a moment,' Riordan said. His red braids were spiralling around. Ardan concluded it was sage advice.

He looked at his right palm. It was sore, and he could smell singed hair on his arms. 'It went better last time.'

'Last time?' Koira asked.

'I used it unconsciously, and it came out as raw force.'

Koira considered his words before answering: 'The Wild can be used in many ways, but we should stick to fire. Be warned that the more you use the Wild, the more easily it will come to you. If you do not learn focus, these explosions will grow.'

'Should I try not to use the Wild then?'

Koira shook her head. 'It is no longer an option.'

Ardan grimaced as he got to his feet. 'It's worse than a lesson with Seamus.'

'You'll be a right old Ancient sorcerer in no time,' Eamon said.

'Shut it, Eamon.'

The man grinned.

'Enough for one night,' Koira said.

'No, let me try one more time,' Ardan said.

'Can you find the Wild again?'

Ardan felt for it. He searched, but the well inside of him felt empty. At the bottom, he found a smidgeon—but it felt tumultuous. He looked up to see Koira's knowing gaze. 'I guess tomorrow is soon enough.'

They drew their billets for the night and Ardan had to share a watch with Talon. He looked at Eamon accusingly. If mischief had a grin, it was Eamons'.

He muttered under his breath but went about putting some more wood on the fire, while the others sought their bedrolls. Talon sat with Koira in sight. His dark eyes followed Ardan until he sat down and made himself comfortable.

'You've known Koira for a while?' Ardan asked.

'All her life.'

'You're her guardian?'

'Yes.'

Ardan tried to elicit conversation a couple more times but got little more than one-word answers. *Like getting blood from a stone*, Ardan thought. With no chatter between them, the watch stretched out. He didn't think he'd ever been happier to see his relief. When Ardan found his bedroll, it was only to stare up at the night sky. Sleep eluded him for hours.

He was woken by Riordan. The entire crew was already up, despite the dawn still being half an hour away. Everyone in the caravan moved with purpose and their morale was high. They were getting back to the city today.

Almost before light pierced the horizon, the caravan was moving. Ardan fell into his space near the centre, but the atmosphere was relaxed. He smelt sweetgrass and sage in the air a moment before Koira stepped up next to him.

'Can you tell me about your father?' she said.

Ardan looked sideways at her. 'Like what?'

'He patrolled this forest and was never killed. How?'

'He was extremely careful and paranoid beyond belief,' Ardan said. She looked pensive at his answer. 'How do you people do it?'

'We are the Children of the Ancients,' Koira said, looking out amongst the trees.

Ardan waited for more, but it didn't come. 'And?'

'And what? We are born of this place. It is our home and only we know how to respect and navigate it.'

'Alright then.'

The silence held as they began the descent on the last leg of their journey. At some points there were breaks in the canopy, revealing the expansive green valley, broken only by the fields that surrounded Barleron. The Tree of the Ancients, the Cathedral of Light and the Temple of Darkness were distinctive amongst the small buildings that lay sprawled within its moss-covered walls.

'That is your city?' Koira asked.

'That's Barleron.'

'I did not expect it to be beautiful,' she said, pausing on the roadway.

'What about your cities?' Ardan asked when she started walking again. Surely the Children of the Ancients would have stone cities hidden amongst the trees, or maybe tree houses. She ignored the question, continuing to take in the valley as they moved downhill. The path narrowed, forcing them to walk in single file. The cart drivers expertly drove their horses, keeping them on the path as it zigzagged down to the floor of the valley. As they progressed, they encountered another caravan heading up. *Hell's fire, what are we going to do now?* Yet the drivers knew their business. They squeezed onto patches of dirt that overhung the steep drop-off, while the other carts drove past. The cartwheels sometimes clipped each other, but the drivers were quick to recover. Soon they were past the others and continuing their journey down.

When the ground had levelled out again, he knew they were nearly there. Yet the final part of the journey stretched out. The more he wanted to be home, the longer the trip felt. Ardan wondered if they had taken a wrong turn.

Then he could see it, the pathway leading to the fields. As they left the forest, Ardan had to shield his eyes from the late afternoon light. A hive of activity greeted them, as men and women were clearing weeds or ploughing and sowing the fields.

There was a contingent of mercenaries ready to meet them at the gates. They fell in beside them as the carts made their way towards Mercenary Square. Ardan wondered how necessary they were as passers-by waved at them and smiled while women could be seen hanging out laundry from their windows, instead of having bolted their houses up tight.

'Are we not going towards the Tree of Ancients?' Koira asked. She was looking up at the Tree. It towered over the other buildings in the Ancient Quarter.

'Riordan, do you need me?' Ardan said.

His mentor quickly understood what he was asking. 'You'll owe me for this. Heavy labour, no-questions-asked type of owing, but alright. Take her to the Tree. I still need to figure out what I'm going to tell Marion.'

CHAPTER FORTY: STALKING THREAT

* * *

*R*ichard, the first Templar, is like a hero of legend. Everywhere he walks the soldiers brighten and stand taller. He welcomed me with open arms but meeting him has only heightened my sense of inadequacy. I do not understand the Archangel putting me in the same league as titans like him.

— *Journals of Phillip, the twelfth Templar.*

* * *

ARDAN LED the forest warriors through the stone and mortar jungle. People would stop and stare at the bare-chested warriors with their exotic tattoos. It didn't stop, even once they got to the vine-covered walls of the park.

As soon as they stepped onto the grass, he could feel it. Like the warmth from a fire, the calm that surrounded the Tree immediately washed over him. Even the Wild inside of him was stilled. He glanced back to see Koira and Talon exchange an unreadable look. The other forest warriors moved into the park, tentatively, sharing looks of wonder.

'Is this tree so unusual?' Ardan asked.

'What do you know about the Ancient Trees?' Koira asked.

'They're old.'

It looked as though Koira was struggling not to roll her eyes.

'Their significance would take weeks to tell and even then, I am not sure you would understand.'

'And this one is different?'

'Very much so.' She didn't elaborate further, walking through the park with the other warriors. They treated the place with a spiritual reverence similar to the way Bishop Frederick handled relics of the Light.

He went over to the large roots of the Tree, running his hand along their rough bark. The Wild leapt from his constraints straight into the Tree, creating a connection. It was like being suddenly and violently thrown into the ocean. He was engulfed; sight and sound were muffled in the expanse of his new consciousness. Despite the jolt, he didn't feel threatened, not directly. He could suddenly feel the pulsating heart of the forest, the power that linked the Trees together, their community. They stood together, while an encroaching power sought to split them apart. There was a sickness outside the wall of trees. It would engulf them one by one, like the rising floodwaters. Yet the barrier of trees looked impenetrable.

He pulled his hand back, and the connection broke. The sensation vanished and his mind snapped back. Losing the communion of the trees jarred him so that he stumbled and fell, plopping down on the grass and fallen leaves.

Ardan lay on his back, staring up at the brilliant skyline of blue and pink. A pair of emerald eyes appeared, and Mish meowed loudly in concern. Ardan smiled, forcing himself up to scratch her behind the ears. She butted her head against his hand in affection.

Koira was watching him. 'Did you connect with the Tree?'

'Is that what the hell just happened?'

She shook her head in disbelief. 'It took me years to do what you've done by accident.'

Ardan brushed himself off, ignoring Talon's glare. 'I've always been gifted.'

Koira ignored that comment, her expression remaining serious, 'What did you see?'

It took him a moment to gather his thoughts. 'A great expanse. The trees, all of them like the Tree of Ancients. Yet there was something outside trying to harm them. The trees stand together but there is an underlying fear. That it won't be enough.'

Instead of answering, Koira went up to the Tree and placed her hand on it. Her eyes closed, her face frowning in concentration. He watched her as her eyes moved rapidly beneath her eyelids. It took a few minutes before she withdrew her hand.

'It is as you felt, but the power threatening my home is here. In the city.'

'Where?'

A gust of wind picked up, sending leaves swirling through the park. Koira cut a dramatic figure, her silhouette sharp against the expanse of the Tree. 'That, I will have to find out.'

'You seem awfully calm about it.'

'Now is not the time for rash actions.'

That's a bit rich, coming from you. Ardan restrained himself from saying it aloud.

'Come, let us meet your benefactors. There is much to do,' Koira said. Though it was obvious some of the warriors wanted to stay, they obeyed Koira without question. *Who is she?* he wondered, as he led them back to Marion's mansion.

The building took up half the city block. The stone once had intricate carving, but it had long weathered away to form indistinct patterns. A short staircase led to the double-door entrance and balcony, where several people were playing cards.

'You did *what?*' Marion demanded. She and Riordan were near the bottom of the stairs.

Riordan spread his hands. 'I did what I had to do. Otherwise, I'd have been scraping Ardan off the ground.'

'Take me through what you promised her. Do it slowly,' Marion said, her green eyes glaring at Riordan.

Heaven's above, that woman can glare.

'I thought it was a bargain, actually. Ardan's learning something few can, and all you have to do is—'

'Show her hospitality and grant her a few favours that hopefully aren't too taxing,' Marion finished.

'They will not be too taxing,' Koira said joining in.

Marion spun, her eyes immediately taking in Koira, the half-dozen warriors, and their dress and weapons. In less than a second, she had collected herself, spreading her skirts in a curtsey. 'My apologies, Lady Koira. I did not mean it as a slight against you, but I rarely find myself unknowingly indebted. Know I will honour whatever my manservant has offered.'

'Manservant?' Riordan said indignantly.

Koira smiled. 'Just some rooms to stay, and a guide through the city.'

'There are rooms here. Ardan knows the city well enough and can act as your guide if that's agreeable?' Marion said.

Talon scowled while Koira looked him up and down. He met her steady gaze, until she nodded. 'That will be acceptable.'

'As for rooms—Aofie!'

'Yes?' The voice came from a woman at the card table. Her bright yellow dress swept before her as she descended the stairs. A faded, jagged scar stretched from her mouth and halfway across her cheek, yet her smile was warm and inviting.

'Lady Koira and her retinue will stay with us indefinitely. Can you show them around?'

'Of course. Come in, be welcome!' Before Aofie could say anything else, Mish, who'd been crouched at Ardan's feet, suddenly bounded forward towards the woman. Startled, she laughed, kneeling down in front of the black feline. 'Aren't you just beautiful,' Aofie said, scratching her behind the ears and on the neck. Mish purred loudly. 'I'll have to get you some fish tonight.'

Traitorous little cat, Ardan thought, as Mish pranced away, following Aofie.

As the forest people started up the stairs, Riordan pulled Ardan aside. He waited until they were inside before he spoke, his face serious. 'Don't mess this up.'

'Stop believing in me so much, Riordan. My ego is big enough.'

'It's been over a generation since anyone's spoken to the Children without a weapon being drawn. Try not to offend them, or get on their bad side,' Riordan said. 'Any more than you already have.'

'Not a problem. You know me.'

'That's exactly why I'm warning you. Especially with the two of you making calf eyes at each other. Your weapons training will be put on hold, at least until your power is under control. We'll figure something out once we know how long they're staying.'

Ardan gave an exaggerated bow and followed the others up the stairs. The entrance room alone was bigger than most houses. There were multiple doorways and a large staircase that dominated the room.

'How many people live here?' Koira asked.

Aofie paused at the bottom of the stairs. 'Oh, that's tough to say. Maybe twenty of us girls, twice as many guards. A few guests important to Marion, not including yourselves. So seventy, eighty?'

Mish was having trouble with the polished wooden floors, sliding on the sleek wood, but she found her footing and kept on Aofie's heels as their party got to the second story. A large balcony opened up before them, with an open-air centre overlooking a garden.

Their party followed Aofie into one of the balcony suites. The drawing room was adorned with cushioned couches and small table. A dark wood dining table dominated a wall in front of drape-covered windows. Opulent Rugs carpeted the floor, and paintings hung from the wall.

'These are your rooms, Lady Koira. The dining hall is near the bottom of the entrance stairs. If you get lost, anyone you find will be happy to help,' Aofie said, rubbing imaginary dust off the table. 'There's enough bed space here for several guards or servants. Though it might get a bit cramped. The soldiers' quarters are below the first floor, near the kitchens, and they can stay at either. Though if there's one thing I know about soldiers, food is near the top of their minds. There's companionship available if any are so inclined. There are enough girls here that would happily join them.'

Ardan stared slack-jawed at Aofie. Had she really just offered that?

'Some guards might warm their beds if your men are so inclined,' Aofie said, stepping around Mish, who was pawing at the rugs. 'I've got the fabric to tailor any dress or garb you might want. Now here is your bedroom, Lady Koira,' she said, opening to a room that held an enormous four-poster bed.

'Where will you be staying, Master Ardan?' Aofie asked.

'Separately,' Talon said.

Aofie didn't bat an eye at his tone. 'There's a room two doors down. The first one's a broom closet, the second isn't much bigger, but it's comfortable,' Aofie said, as she went over to the drapes and yanked them open, exposing a stunning view of the sprawling city, dominated by the Cathedral of Light and the Temple of Darkness. 'I'll head down and organise your evening meal. Is there anything else you need?'

'Do you need payment?' Koira asked.

Aofie's smile stretched even further. 'No, you are our guests.'

Koira weighed the words carefully. 'So no payment?'

'No. Guests invited freely do not pay.'

Koira considered. 'Do you have the game called Kings?'

'Of course. Shall I retrieve it for you?' Aofie asked, and on receiving conformation, promptly left the rooms.

Once she was out of sight, the forest warriors inspected the room. They pushed at the cushions suspiciously. Talon picked up the bell and gave it a small shake. The tinkle had every head turning towards him. Shock and disgust played across his face as he put it down.

'What is this?' Koira asked, circling a large porcelain bathtub.

'It's a bath. You, uh, wash in it.'

'How?'

Ardan involuntarily wondered how far those tattoos went. *Focus, you idiot, or she'd kill you if she could read your thoughts.* 'It gets filled with water, and you wash yourself in it. The water is warm.'

He was saved from further embarrassment when Aofie returned with a small army of people, carrying in trays of food. They were filled with cuttings of roast chicken, cheese, bread, and some dipping sauce. The trays were placed on the centre tables. Like a pack of ravening wolves, the forest warriors descended on them.

A meow filled the room as Mish danced back and forth, almost tangling Aofie up as she put down a plate of fish.

Ardan waited for an opening at the table. He saw it and got his portion before being pushed back. The chicken dipped in yellow sauce was warm and succulent. Anything after trail food always tasted amazing. All too soon the plates were empty, and everyone was licking their fingers once they were done. Well, all the warriors were, anyway.

'You will teach me to play this game better,' Koira said. She had somehow kept herself completely clean throughout the ordeal. She seated herself at one of the smaller tables and began opening up the game.

'Alright,' Ardan said, sitting across from her and helping to set up the board.

'I will not roll for a piece. I wish to play with this piece,' she said, taking the Ancient avatar.

Ardan shrugged. It was easier to learn the game if you stuck with one piece. He rolled anyway and ended up with the High Priest of Darkness.

They played, and Ardan continued as he normally did—equal measures of building up his offensive and defensive capabilities, while keeping his piece moving at a reasonable pace on the board. During Koira's turn, she barely moved her piece, instead focusing on getting her cards down.

Over the next few turns, Ardan quickly outpaced her while she continued to build up her deck. He knew the strategy, and he put down his Demon and Priests of Darkness cards. They were powerful enough to stop whatever she was planning.

The next turn she went on the offensive, throwing a lot of cards at him, but his defences held. As he got closer to the throne, he saw she was becoming increasingly distressed by her inability to take him down. In the next round, he slowed his piece's movements and held back on his attack, stopping the fleecing that this was turning into.

Over the next few turns, she clawed back, her piece gaining ground. Then she rolled high and smiled, locking eyes with him as she played the Queen of Autumn Leaves. It was a powerful card in its own right, but with her Ancient avatar, it made the card incredibly strong. She swept his Demon aside. Her next card, the Forest Warriors, slew his Priests. Her Armies of the Light clashed with his Mercenaries, wiping each other out. He stared at her accusingly. All signs of distress had vanished.

'Foolish plainsman.'

Ardan couldn't help but laugh. 'Clever.'

She tried to hide her smile, but he could see the dimples.

'It's getting late,' Talon said from the doorway. He was eyeing Ardan, his lip twitching.

Taking the not-so-subtle hint, they packed up the game. As Ardan was leaving, he looked back. Koira's soft brown eyes held his gaze. He felt a sudden flutter in his stomach.

He closed the door and went to the balcony edge that overlooked the garden. In the centre was a stone table and benches. He pretended to study them while he searched through what he was feeling for Koira. There were a hundred reasons warning him against it, but he couldn't help but hope she felt the same. Nevertheless, he doubted it. Frustrated, he sought his room.

Aofie was right; it wasn't much bigger than a broom closet. A small cot occupied one wall, but there was a washbasin and a tiny wardrobe squeezed in.

Ardan sat heavily on his bed, ready to take his boots off. Yet he'd sat on something that crumpled. Puzzled, he pulled out a piece of paper. He opened the shutters, thankful the moons were bright enough to read by.

'*Mother has been spotted near the Cathedral. I cannot leave the Temple, and Davan won't look. Please find out what you can.*

– Liádan'

CHAPTER FORTY-ONE:
REVEALING LIGHT

* * *

Richard called a meeting with the other Templars. He spoke of the danger Naberius posed, and how we needed to convince Zadkiel to leave. He united us in this. We could die, but the last Archangel had to survive. Together, we approached him. At first, the Angel outright refused, but Richard made him see reason. The Angel would return to the Citadel.

— Journals of Phillip, the twelfth Templar.

* * *

ARDAN WOKE before the sun rose, his bed a tangled mess. Thoughts of his mother flooded his mind. She was alive, and she had been seen in the Light Quarter. He'd almost gone searching in the middle of the night. Yet a moment of clarity had struck: what was he going to do? The Light Quarter might still be off limits, and the Cathedral was closed to him. Eventually. he'd come back upstairs, but sleep was slow in coming. *Where has she been? What has she been doing? Why did she abandon us?* These thoughts plagued him throughout the hours of darkness, his imagination growing worse as the night went on. His fitful sleeping caused Mish to retreat underneath the pallet, her tail swishing with displeasure.

When the skyline at last lightened, he got up. He dressed in his leather armour, belted on his sword, and opened the door. As he did, Mish scampered out between his legs and went straight to the edge that overlooked the garden, giving one loud meow.

Ardan started down the stairs and Mish somehow got between his legs as he did so. He reached the front door, without her killing him, and opened it. The cat immediately shot out to one of the garbage-filled alleys and squatted. *Right, she needed a place to do her business.*

'Ardan, I'd like to speak to you for a moment.'

Riordan was there, in leather armour, sword at his belt and spear in hand. His red braids had been redone. He was dressed for war, though he didn't carry a shield.

'Yeah?'

'I think it's best you don't come to the Trials today.' It took a moment to register. *The Trials.* He blinked, realising they were today. Riordan continued, 'I'd like you to get your power under control before we involve you in any battles—real or otherwise.'

Ardan's mind was sluggish. It took him another moment to realise. 'Yeah, that's okay.'

'It is?' Riordan said, ready to launch into another explanation. He'd obviously been preparing for this.

'Yeah, I understand,' Ardan said, though it was one of the furthest things from his mind. Besides, the man was right. He barely understood what the Wild was doing, and he didn't want to accidentally set someone on fire. 'How's your shield going?'

'Raigel has finished it, so I'm going to get it now,' Riordan said, his demeanour changing instantly. 'Let's see you burn this one.'

'Maybe let's wait to see it develop its powers first.'

Riordan's smile didn't fade. 'Try to keep yourself out of trouble,' he said, and patted Ardan on the shoulder before heading outside. Several other soldiers followed him, all of them leaving for Mercenary Square.

Ardan felt a pang of regret watching them go, he still hadn't seen the Trials. Riordan said it was meant to be a proving ground for guild hopefuls, and freelancers wanting to showcase their skills but that was just the premise whale on each other for fun and the celebratory drinks afterwards. He sighed, as his thoughts returned to his mother.

Ardan headed back inside and towards the breakfast table. Koira and the rest of the forest warriors were already in the dining hall, loading up on bread, sausages, and fried potatoes. She looked at him, her auburn hair hanging free.

'Today we will begin our search for the sickness that haunts this place,' Koira said, buttering a piece of bread. The other warriors were devouring their food as only soldiers can.

'How will you find it?' Ardan asked.

Koira paused, staring at the bread in her hand. 'When I am close enough, I will know,' she said, taking a bite.

'Where do you want to start?' Ardan asked.

'Places of Power. Marion has informed me that the Dark Quarter is closed off at the moment, but she is trying to gain access. For now, we must visit the Cathedral of Light.'

Ardan nodded, feeling a well of emotions bubbling to the surface that they would be going to the Cathedral of Light today. Koira's brown eyes searched him, seeing entirely too much. Ardan felt exposed, and he shifted his attention to the breakfast table.

'There's something else you're not telling me,' she said.

Ardan froze. He thought about lying but after some quick back and forth, he couldn't see any benefit in hiding the truth. He swallowed, having trouble getting the words out. 'My mother was last seen at the Cathedral of Light.'

'You are here to be our guide and nothing--,' Talon started.

Koira held up her hand. 'She has been missing?'

'For almost a year,' Ardan said. Shortly after his father's death, he thought bitterly.

'It is important to you,' Koira said. It wasn't a question. 'Very well. It will not slow our task,' she said before Talon could interrupt. 'Take us to the Cathedral first, from there we will search for the source of the attack, and you can find your mother.'

Talon looked mutinous, but Ardan ignored him, gratitude almost overwhelming him. 'Thank you,' he managed at last. He grabbed a sausage to try and mask the overwhelming of emotions he felt, but after one bite he found like he couldn't eat any more. Instead, he waited until the others were done. It took an eternity but what was likely less than half an hour and they were walking through the streets and towards the Light Quarter. Some of the abandoned houses had already been repaired. The people were no longer scurrying about or peering suspiciously at passers-by. Their group still drew cautious looks, as an armed group rarely meant anything good, but no one ran from them.

Ardan felt heartened by it adding to the torrent of emotions as fear, hope, trepidation and longing rotated to the forefront of his mind. They fed into the Wild and the power fed off them. Instead of feeling overwhelmed, the Wild's power made him feel better.

He questioned Koira about it.

Koira grimaced as she answered: 'Sometimes the Wild will create a loop off your emotions, amplifying them. The Wild used to be more balanced between positive and negative emotions. Not so much now. It will feed off your negative emotions much more readily than your positive ones. You are lucky to have your sword—a safe outlet for you to release your power.'

They continued in silence for a while. Mish was following along behind them. The feline was keeping to the shadows, not exposing herself as she followed them, but he could sense exactly where she was.

'How do I stop the flow?' Ardan asked after a while.

'The flow? You mean the Wild?'

Ardan nodded.

'It is difficult. If you hold it back, it will stop it, at least for a while, but the pressure will build, eventually overwhelming you. In the end, you have to communicate with the Wild.'

'I . . . what?'

Koira stared at the ground ahead of them, a telling sign she was deep in thought. 'These Shapers, they communicate with the elements—it's a watered-down version of communicating with the Wild. Think of it like that, communicate with it. If you try to control it and the Wild feels disinclined or forced, it will strike back.'

'Alright, so how do I communicate with it?'

'How does one court a mate?'

Ardan opened his mouth before closing it again. 'So the Wild is a living thing?'

'Yes and no. It is a force of nature, with the emotional range of a child. Imagine your greatest swordsman,' Koira said, looking at Ardan and waiting.

Ardan's thoughts flitted through different people—Davan, Riordan, Oisin, Lachlan—until they eventually settled on Seamus. Despite his injury, he'd been a match for anyone.

'Now think of that skill in the hands of a simpleton. One who has been beaten and abused for half his life.'

Talon growled behind them. 'You should not speak of the Ancients' power so.'

Koira didn't glance back. 'It is not disrespectful to call a sword a sword, nor an angry fighter an angry fighter. If I were to call Hoof a firebrand, none would dispute it.'

'*He* might,' Talon muttered.

'How does...' Ardan started but let himself drift. The barricade between the Ancient and Light Quarters was still up. They joined the queue of people passing through the checkpoint. There were at least eight guards carrying crossbows on the barricade. Several tensed when they saw the forest warriors, but they didn't shoot.

Though it looked as though they were getting ready to deny them entrance.

Ardan stepped forward. 'This is Lady Koira, Ambassador from the Children of the Ancients. She is seeking an audience with Bishop Frederick.'

The guards looked at each other. Ardan couldn't see an officer insignia anywhere. No one spoke.

'Maybe you should get Oisin?'

'He's at the Trials,' one corporal said. He had to be younger than Ardan, his armour fitting loosely on his scrawny frame.

'Then can we get through?'

The corporal looked unsure. A few of the crossbowmen exchanged glances.

'What's your name?' Ardan asked.

The corporal stuttered. 'Jason.'

'Jason, we're going to see the Bishop. If you don't want to let us through, find someone who can. The longer we wait, the more unhappy the Ambassador will be.'

Jason looked around, as though an answer might appear. Eventually, he gave a shaky nod.

A wry smile played on Koira's lips as they went through the checkpoint.

Their party continued up the main road, Heaven's Way. The Cathedral commanded their attention long before they got to its doors. The likeness of the seven Archangels was carved above the double door entrance, their eyes looking down on those who passed beneath them.

As they got closer, they could see Walter the priest out in front, speaking with Bishop Frederick. Frederick's eyes flicked over and he recognised him. He frowned.

'You,' he said. He looked like he'd aged ten years since the Magistrate's death. His eyes were sunken, and grey dominated his head. 'I thought you understood that I never wanted you near this place again.'

Ardan stuttered, not prepared for such animosity.

'He is my escort and guide,' Koira said, stepping forward. In that moment, she commanded everyone's attention. 'Are plainsmen ready to turn away peaceful envoys now?'

Bishop Frederick took in Koira for the first time, trying to compose himself. 'You should take better care with your guides. He is not to be trusted.'

'He was the one who suggested I come here and speak with you.

That you were kind and wise. Was he mistaken? Should I have gone elsewhere?'

Ardan stared at her. She wasn't lying, but she was close. He managed to compose himself in time to see the words had touched Frederick. The man looked faintly ashamed.

'You were right to come here. I should not let past actions completely cloud my judgement. Please come and speak in my chambers.'

As they were turning to go inside, a stray dog appeared. Its fur was matted, and its ribs were showing. It sniffed at something near the main gate of the courtyard.

Mish snarled, the hackles of her back rising. The dog took one look at Mish and yelped, his claws scrambling to find purchase on the stone. Mish immediately set off in pursuit.

'Damn it Mish, get back here,' Ardan yelled, but the lynx kept going. He gave chase. 'I'll meet you here later,' he called over his shoulder, careening after them.

He ran around the corner, and the dog kept running, heading straight for the stables. The dog disappeared inside, but before Mish could screech in after it, a large sack of grain was slapped onto the ground in her path. She skidded to a halt, looking up at the offender.

He was a large man, carrying a second bag of grain over his shoulder. It was Liam. Ardan hadn't seen the man since the night of his father's murder; he was the one who had carried Ardan to the healer. A tumble of emotions suddenly burst through him.

'Aren't you a pretty girl?' Liam said, his voice gentle. 'Do you want some milk?'

Mish, who had been about to resume her chase, paused. Her hackles lowered. *How much could the damn cat understand?* She meowed loudly.

'What are you doing here?' Ardan said, surprised he hadn't reached for his sword.

Liam looked up, his eyes taking in Ardan, and like a candle being blown out, his smile faded. He looked away, unable to meet Ardan's eyes. 'Trying to atone for my sins.'

The Wild inside of Ardan trembled but didn't spit or tumble. There was something about the man's demeanour that didn't invite violence. Yet Ardan's tongue still ran away with him. 'Nothing you do will ever be enough.'

Liam scratched Mish's head and the cat's eyes closed contentedly. He glanced at Ardan. 'There is not a day that passes by that I do not feel guilt for the part I played in Tristan's death. Not a single day.'

Ardan stared at the man. He felt some vague sense of pity, and he tried to quash it. Yet it was persistent. Ardan had imagined this meeting many times, but it had never gone like this. 'Why?'

'Does it matter?'

Ardan hesitated. 'It might.'

Liam still wouldn't meet Ardan's eye. His words were halting. 'I hadn't been doing forest stalking long, and I didn't understand the woods as well as your father did. My wife's morning sickness and our one-year-old kept me up more nights than I care to remember. I stuck to the same paths and brought home less each time. From the way Verrick spoke when he came to me, it was easy to believe that your father was stealing from me.'

Ardan stared at him. The hunched form, the ragged clothes. He was already beaten. His father's death hadn't done all this.

'What led you here?'

Liam let out a weary sigh, glancing up towards the sky before answering. 'I had nowhere else to go. Things were getting worse, even before the field burning. My home was raided while I was out in the forest. My wife and child did not survive.'

What little remained of Ardan's anger died at his words.

'I cannot blame anyone but myself. It is a punishment for my sins against you and your father.'

They fell into a long silence. Mish butted her head against Liam, and he resumed patting her.

'As someone who misses their family every day,' Liam said. 'I think you should make up with your mother sooner rather than later. She seemed rather distraught over your and your siblings' wellbeing.'

CHAPTER FORTY-TWO:
DIPLOMACY OF THE SWORD

* * *

*B*ulwarks and engines of war are being built. A large host with limited stores does not have the luxury of time. The assault will come soon.

— *Journals of Phillip, the twelfth Templar.*

* * *

ARDAN STOOD STILL SUDDENLY, feeling disconnected from everything around him. The stone courtyard felt alien, the Cathedral obscure and the surrounding forest distant. He looked at the large man kneeling in front of Mish, petting her gently.

'What did you say?'

Liam's hand stopped mid-stroke, and he looked defensive. 'Your mother, the lady Alaine came here looking for you.'

'When, where?'

'Over a week ago. We were building sleeping quarters for all the extra soldiers when she entered the courtyard like a tornado. She's a terrifying woman, your mother. Once she found out what happened to you two, well, her words cut sharper than most blades and she eloquently skewered the Bishop with her tongue.'

Ardan felt a flash of pride. 'Where is she?'

She was looking for us, he thought, over and over.

'You don't know?'

'I didn't know she was alive,' Ardan said, not realising he was shouting.

Liam's mouth formed an O of surprise. Mish raised a paw, pushing him. Liam resumed stroking her. 'I had assumed … well, she didn't say. Eight of the Countess's personal guard turned up, escorted her back.'

'The Countess—but that would mean…' Ardan began, but his voice trailed off. He didn't know what it meant. He looked over at Liam. 'Thank you for this,' Ardan said, and meant it.

Liam nodded, trying to keep his head down.

Ardan glanced away to give the man some privacy. His mother was alive, and he knew where to find her. 'I've got to go.'

Liam nodded and opened his arms, giving Mish one final scratch. The lynx gave a satisfied wriggle of her body before trailing after Ardan.

Ardan moved around the courtyard, oblivious to the church guards, heading for the Cathedral entrance. He was looking for Koira but instead he found Father Walter. The priest eyed him up and down, frowning in disapproval, saying nothing as he stalked away.

Probably for the best, he thought, looking at the man's retreating form.

Luckily, it wasn't too long before Koira and Talon reappeared.

'It's not here,' Koira said. 'There is power here, but it doesn't have the right feel.'

Ardan wanted nothing more than to run straight to the Merchant Quarter and the Countess' palace, to find his mother and demand answers. Yet he paused. Despite the urgency, he didn't think he could get access on his own.

'With the Dark Quarter closed, we could visit the Countess' palace. Someone of power might hide amongst the wealthy.'

Koira frowned at him. 'And the real reason?'

He hesitated. 'My mother's there.'

'The power of the Ancients is in turmoil,' Koira said. 'We cannot be side-tracked; we must locate the source of the attacks. However, we don't know where they're coming from. The Archangels and High Demons can take human form, can they not?'

Why is she speaking so oddly? Ardan thought, then realised the speech was meant for the forest warriors. 'Oh yeah, umm, they can, and what better place than there?'

'Indeed,' Koira said.

'Thank you,' Ardan mouthed at her. She nodded and gestured for him to lead the way. Some of the forest warriors glanced at each other but stayed silent.

The Merchant Quarter was on the other side of the city. Koira looked offended when Ardan asked if she wanted a carriage, so they walked. Mish quickly found her way onto the rooftops, following along. The streets were sparser than usual, and Ardan assumed most people were at the Trials. When they got close to the principal thoroughfare through Ragtown, they encountered a score of armed men and women on the street. One of them immediately ran towards the crumbling remains of the Keep, shouting for help. It forced them to circle around through the Docks.

They encountered a second group, larger than the first armed with sabres and small arms. A couple of them trailed their group, but otherwise didn't bother them. More than six ships were anchored in the harbour as they walked past. Koira and the others paused, amazed at their number and size. There hadn't been many ships in the harbour since the Magistrate had been killed.

'How has word gotten out so fast?' Ardan said aloud.

'What?' Koira said.

'Nothing, just talking to myself.'

The Docks eventually gave way to the Merchant Quarter, the roads changing from packed dirt to cobblestones. The debris and rubbish that plagued the rest of the city was conspicuously absent here. Some of the shop fronts had glass windows instead of stout wooden shutters.

The streets were heavily patrolled by the Merchant Guard. They were easily distinguishable, their breastplates glinting in the afternoon light. They would pass in groups of spearmen with a few bowmen amongst their number. Every few blocks they would encounter at least a guard or two. At first Ardan wondered at the necessity, but then he realised that none of the streets were deserted, that none of the buildings were abandoned. Though the guards eyed them, there was no suspicion in the air.

They passed the plot where the Establishment had been. A master builder was yelling himself hoarse at the construction crew, while stone and mortar were being brought in on wagon beds. In the unused space, several large tents had been set up, surrounded by men in black uniforms. Inside were tables where men and women were playing cards.

Ardan slowed their pace, allowing the forest people to take in all the sights as they walked. It gave him time to figure out their path to the Countess' palace. He knew its general direction but hadn't been able to spot it yet. The closer they got, the larger the buildings became and the more expansive the surrounding grounds.

At last, they came to the Countess' palace. It had once been a large manor house built on a small hill, but it had suffered numerous renovations and extensions over the years. It was now an over-compensating, sprawling residence, and Ardan wondered who had paid for the expensive eyesore.

They continued walking around the ten-foot wall until they came to the gates. The Countess' guards stood there, similarly armed to the Merchant Guard, but their cloaks were a heavy, darker blue. Some of them even wore mail. On seeing the group of forest warriors, they immediately sprang into action. One of them ran off while the other four grouped together, shields coming up as they got ready to repel the possibly hostile force.

'State your business,' one guard yelled in a deep voice.

'I'm looking for my mother, Alaine.'

The man's hostile exterior faltered, his shield lowering as he looked at a fellow guard, who shrugged.

Ardan felt a wave of relief at the exchange. She was here; she was alive. An overwhelming longing to see her struck him while, simultaneously, accusations sprang into his mind. *Why was she here? Why hadn't she searched for them earlier?*

Before he grew too lost in thought, he saw twenty soldiers running out from one of the Palace's extensions. Almost half of them had bows, while the others moved in orderly formation, carrying large shields and short spears.

'That was fast,' Talon said behind them.

Past the walls, on the grounds of the Countess' palace, there were several women walking along a garden path. They watched the soldiers jog past them and then looked at the gate. A woman with the same hair as his mother's watched the commotion. She headed for the gates, but one guard blocked her path.

Ardan moved closer to the gates, trying to get a better look. He could see the woman push at the guard, and for one brief shining moment, he saw her. It was his mother; her face a mix of anguish and hope. Before he could shout to her, the sound of hooves on cobblestones filled the air. A troop of men on horseback arrived. The lead man was clean shaven, with strawberry blond hair and blunt features, while his chain mail lacked rust spots. Ardan knew Captain Callum by reputation, only having seen him once when he'd commanded the Merchant Guard against the rioters.

'I will give you one chance to leave,' Captain Callum declared, his hand resting on his sword hilt.

Talon whistled and the forest warriors fanned into an arrowhead, with Ardan and Koira behind their line.

Callum looked a lot less sure of himself as he tried to manoeuvre his horse backwards.

Ardan glanced over at his mother, who was being dragged away, while the guards behind the gate formed up, archers nocking their bows. He looked at Callum, whose hand was tight on the sabre at his waist. The Wild inside of Ardan tumbled. He looked at his mother and he remembered one of her lessons.

'When the cards are about to be played, govern thoughts and fears.'

'I am sure you didn't mean to insult the Lady Koira, Ambassador of the Children of the Ancients, first of her people to pay a courtesy call to the Countess in several generations, did you Captain?' Ardan asked loudly.

Callum looked at Talon and the other forest warriors before shifting his gaze to Koira. His hand came away from the sabre. 'You arrived with no letter of introduction, no warning, just an armed escort? There are processes, proper ways to do these things. This isn't how it's done.'

Ardan tried to speak, to talk about different customs, but the frustration was growing inside of him. He was barely a hundred feet from his mother and still, he was being held back. The Wild fed off his hope, his anxiety, and his anger that he was so close but still might be denied.

Ardan tried to rein the Wild in, stop it from overwhelming him, but it broke through the dams he'd set up and the last thing he remembered was an explosion of green as he was flung back.

CHAPTER FORTY-THREE: THE MURDER OF THE MAGISTRATE

* * *

heir siege engines pound our walls like the beating of a drum. They seek to demoralise our forces; we can see their siege towers being built like a wall of trees. I march along the battlements to bolster the men's spirits, but they are afraid. So am I. The fortress will fall before the end.

— Journals of Phillip, the twelfth Templar.

* * *

THE WORLD slowly came into focus. In front of him two green orbs slowly materialised into Mish's emerald eyes. He slowly sat up, trying to take in everything that had happened. The gates, the armed guards, Koira and Talon. Had he been out long? Everyone was still where they'd been before. Except for Talon and Koira, who were now next to him.

'Captain Callum,' a voice rang out. It took him a moment to realise it was his mother speaking. 'Regardless of how I have been treated,' Alaine said, glaring at the guardsmen blocking her path, 'I am the ranking nobility here. For this, I insist you escort the Lady Koira to the palace. Anyone of lesser rank might be an insult.'

How hard did I hit my head? Ardan wondered. Was that really his mother beneath the blue silk dress and elaborate makeup, or was it Liá? He shook his head and really focused. No, it wasn't Liá—it was definitely his mother.

'Lady Koira, I apologise for any implied insult, as it is the standard practice to come here with a referral or a letter of introduction. However, as the Lady Alaine has pointed out, it is not my place. I will escort you inside the grounds, but I am afraid I cannot allow you to take an armed escort with you without permission from the Countess.'

'You can escort me inside the grounds, Captain. I will take one guard with me,' Koira stated as she strode forward. The Countess' guard immediately made way for her, while Talon fell into step behind her. 'Please, see to my men,' she said without turning her head.

Callum scrambled into action, ordering the majority of the guards to stay while taking four men with him.

Ardan regained his feet. He realised the gate was open, and his mother was standing there. Beneath the blue silk and finery, it was her. Ardan came forward, getting closer but suddenly feeling self-conscious. Mish needed little encouragement, charging forward, past the guards and straight into the manicured garden amongst the trimmed hedges.

'The cat is yours?' Alaine asked.

'Where have you been?'

'Not here. Follow me for a moment, please.'

Still somewhat dazed, Ardan followed as she led him into the low hedge maze. They walked past beds of flowers and sweet-smelling roses. She eventually stopped in the circular clearing in the middle of the garden. Her immaculate sapphire silk dress stood like a barrier between them, the makeup around her eyes as a mask. It was like the afternoon he'd come home early to discover her looking like one of the rich merchant wives.

She glanced around, and realising they were out of earshot of the others, her facade broke. She swept forward, and Ardan almost took a step back as her arms wrapped around him. The embrace was achingly familiar. The smell of pressed wildflowers wafted up to him. He tentatively hugged her back. His mother was here. She mumbled something and pulled him tighter. He wasn't sure how to deal with the influx of anger, confusion, longing, and love. Her body was silently wracked with sobs. By the time they separated, her tears had caused her makeup to run.

'I have missed you all so much.'

Ardan took a step back. Whatever wall she had broken down now felt taller than ever. She was here, at the palace. He looked at her dress, the gardens, the surroundings. 'Why are you here?'

She leaned back at the terseness in his words. The mask sliding back on, but they couldn't hide the tear-streaked makeup or the red outline of her eyes. He met her dark eyes and held them for a long time. She looked away first.

'I am sorry I wasn't there for you, that you lived on the streets, surviving the Light knows how. I never wanted the three of you to go through this.'

Ardan didn't answer. He didn't trust himself enough to respond without anger.

'I tried to get out, to help you, but ... but I just couldn't.'

'Mother, enough. What are you doing here?'

She stopped, took a moment to gather herself. 'You've grown,' she said at last. 'You were forced to, which is my fault. I guess you've earned the right to the truth,' she looked down before continuing, 'The Countess and I are distantly related.'

Ardan blinked. Some of his anger gave way to confusion.

'It's true. I've known her since I was a child,' Alaine continued.

'How did I not know this?'

She adjusted some invisible foible on her dress. 'I kept it from all of you, including your father. For your own safety.'

'I—what?'

'My old life wasn't all peaches and cream.'

'Maybe you should start at the beginning,' Ardan said shortly, some of his anger returning. He knew he shouldn't take it out on her. She was trying, but he felt abandoned, betrayed. It was obvious that it wasn't her fault, but it didn't stop the onrush of emotions.

'I guess you deserve to know,' Alaine said. She smoothed her dress and took one last look at the garden before she began speaking. 'My parents are second cousins to the Countess. Normally that wouldn't mean much, but the purge changed everything. My father survived, in part because he was incredibly poor. We had little more than our names, but it bought more than you might think. I could read, was educated in the arts and conversation, I could walk with the higher classes, know which fork to use. Everything the rich found important. We frequented parties because my father couldn't always keep food on the table. He was too proud to take work he thought was beneath him. Tired of being hungry, I started stealing small things at these parties, like a bit of jewellery or silverware.'

'You stole things?' Ardan said, thinking about when he'd taken a sweet tart at the market and the subsequent beating she had given him. He'd had trouble sitting down for a week.

'That and worse. I got caught, as we all do eventually. I thought she was a sycophant trying to climb the social ladder, looking to black-mail me. She had plans for me too, but not in the way I had imagined.'

'She was a thief?'

A small smile played on her lips. 'She invited me to join her crew, people casing out the richer places to rob. I was sceptical at first, but eventually she introduced me to a whole new world, and I became the front woman. I would charm and wile people, usually older men, while setting them up to be robbed. It was all done under the pretext of me moving in high social circles.'

'How did that work, exactly?' Ardan said. His mouth moved while his mind tried to grasp the person behind the woman he'd known his whole life.

'I'd enquire about their social calendar and then steal a key here, unlatch a window there. Our crew earned quite a reputation, but no one ever suspected me, a noble from birth.'

'And you made money?'

'Enough that I could set up a dummy business for my father to run. He thought he was finally getting his due. He was terrible at business, but I hired the right manager who made it profitable, and my father thought it was all his doing. I didn't stop performing my role; I couldn't. I loved the thrill. At least I did before I met your father.'

She sighed, leaning back, her eyes somewhere else. Ardan didn't interrupt. It gave him a moment to take it all in. His mother, a genteel thief? He had to stare around the garden to reassure himself of reality.

'Before the Magistrate was the uncrowned king, the underground was split into several factions, as it is today. One leader was the Butcher. My crew and I were there to pay our tribute. I wanted to leave as quickly as possible; the smell of the carcasses always put me on edge. While we were there, your father came in, bold as you please. He was something else, even back then. He told the Butcher he wanted to farm the forest. The Butcher laughed, telling him if he wanted to get himself killed, he'd need to pay for the privilege.'

'Father paid to farm the forest?' Ardan said, thinking about how he had paid the Street King.

'Everyone pays tribute. He did it then to avoid trouble in the future. Even though he didn't have the right sense of decorum for the situation, his calmness at the Butcher's laughter caught my attention. He gave the Butcher two silver temples. The Butcher stared at the coins, his laughter cut short, not quite sure what to make of him. He let your father go, and he would return every few weeks until they worked out a more permanent arrangement.'

'That led to the two of you getting married?'

She laughed. 'I was intrigued by him and made sure we were introduced. I knew he was too honest to approve of my line of work. He suspected, I think, but he never pressed me. What he didn't suspect was that there was another suitor,' Alaine said, anger flashing across her face.

'Who?'

'The Magistrate.'

'Him?' Ardan said, incredulous.

'I hadn't told him no, but his cold ambition had already put me off.

He was one of the main reasons I left that world. I constantly worried that he would somehow take it out on your father. The more power he got, the further I distanced myself from my old life.' She paused for a moment, her eyes glistened before she continued. 'When your father was killed, we had little money. I started looking for work because I knew we needed more.'

'What about your parents? My grandparents?' Ardan said, suddenly hit by a stark realisation that he might have more living relatives.

'My Father never forgave me for marrying beneath my station. They eventually sailed off to the Empire. I haven't seen or heard from them since.' There was a tightness around her eyes, but her voice never wavered. 'I found some old friends and got back in the game. While I was doing this, I crossed paths with the Magistrate. He had much younger and prettier girls at his beck and call, but I used some connections and old tricks to get an audience with him.'

'Tricks?'

'Played the part he expected of me,' Alaine said, but when he still didn't understand she continued, 'My husband dead and three children to look after, however would I have enough money to support them? Who would help a poor old widow like me?' she said, giving a shrill sniffle. The mask of a bereaved, helpless widow was so complete that Ardan blinked, reassuring himself it was still her.

'He said we would talk, organise a private arrangement,' Alaine said, her mask dropping, and her mouth curved with distaste. 'He had grown too comfortable in his power. Lost his edge and forgotten who and what I was. But I erred too. I had forgotten about my temper, been too long with your father and his calming nature. I had always planned to kill him, but at a point of my choosing,' she said, gripping her dress tightly.

'What happened?' Ardan asked softly, suspecting the answer. He knew about the need for revenge. The Magistrate was his Verrick.

'He never forgave your father for stealing me away from him. That was the main reason he allowed a mark to be taken out on him,' Alaine said, staring off into the distance before continuing: 'He never said it, but I read between the lines. Once I realised it, well, I saw red. My knife was through his ribs before I even knew what I was doing.'

'You killed him?' Ardan asked loudly.

'Shh, keep your voice down. It's not common knowledge,' Alaine said, her neck swivelling to make sure no one was in earshot.

Ardan felt a flush of embarrassment. He'd suspected she'd had him killed but hadn't realised she'd done it herself.

'But yes, I did. He was old and fat, not the fighter he used to be. It was only then, when I was covered in his blood and staring down at his corpse, that I realised the full implications of what I had done. Standing in the centre of his home in Ragtown, I knew I had to move fast. I couldn't risk leading his followers back to you three. I went to the only place I could think of,' she said, making a sweeping gesture at the Countess' palace.

'And she just let you in?'

'Light, no,' Alaine said with a laugh. 'I was a complete mess when I turned up. My clothes were covered in blood and my makeup was a fright. They thought I had been attacked, bless them. They took me into their guard house and out of sight. I believe people were already looking for me. There I could calm down a little. I convinced them I was related to Aine. They were reluctant to wake the Countess, but eventually went to get her. I was taken around the back of the house to the kitchens with several guards nearby when my dear cousin came downstairs.' Alaine gave a wry smile as she continued, 'Her first words were 'Alaine, what in the Light have you done now?''

'She remembered you?'

'We'd kept in contact. I would write to her a few times a year. She wouldn't always reply, but often enough.'

'You ... were corresponding with the Countess,' Ardan repeated.

'Yes, dear,' Alaine said. 'After she learned what happened, she confined me within these walls. For my safety, she said. Had me forcibly restrained when I tried to leave anyway. Eventually she locked me in my room. She told me she sent guards to our home, but the three of you slipped away from them.' She smiled ruefully. 'Never have I been more proud of and exasperated by my children. Yet I still escaped, but by that point you hadn't been back home in some time. I had planned on going to Mercenary Square after that, but her guards caught me shortly thereafter.'

'Why was she so determined to keep you inside the walls?' Ardan said.

'I think originally it was part family affection. She didn't want to see me strung up. Later, I think it became a matter of pride. The harder I tried to get out, the more she sought to imprison me. Lately, though, I think she has realised my value after I got certain pieces of information from key members of the Merchant's Guild. It helped her with a few matters that were hindering her here in the Merchant Quarter. I had hoped it would garner me enough credit that I could send a message, but no, she wouldn't let me go. I pestered everyone who came for news. There were enough stories about a bear of a man wielding a two-handed axe to know Davan was okay, but you and Liá...' she said, and he could see her eyes watering again.

'It was hard,' Ardan said. Despite the story, he still felt a lingering resentment. 'We made it through, but it was hard.'

The tears in her eyes grew, threatening to spill over. 'I was supposed to be there to protect you. I knew of no one who would cross the Countess for me. They dragged me back here from more than a dozen escape attempts. They got good at tracking me whenever I got out.'

'Liá was the one that led me to you. She heard about the disturbance at the Cathedral.'

'So that's how.' Alaine smiled faintly.

'You've been prisoner here since the night you killed the Magistrate.'

She grimaced. 'Yes, after I did that.'

Ardan said no more. He'd known there was more to her; it had been obvious from the way she played Kings and the effortless grace she possessed when wearing expensive clothes, but he hadn't expected quite this much. He thought about Barleron's civil war, the men ransacking their home, and later living on gruel. He tried to feel angry, especially when he remembered the rotten and mouldy food he'd eaten, but memories of his doting mother kept intruding any time he tried to hold on to his anger.

'So now you know.'

Ardan could see she wanted to say more, but she kept her mouth closed, though it obviously pained her.

'Do you want to know how Liá and Davan are?'

'Light, yes,' she breathed.

So he told her, answering all her questions about their health and wellbeing, including his own. He had exhausted all his answers long before she stopped asking questions. When he could finally leave, she pulled him in for an embrace. He tensed at first but slowly he leant into it, really hugging her back, and the pain and anger that had become a constant companion finally eased.

CHAPTER FORTY-FOUR: MANNERS AND CLOTH

* * *

Their armies crashed against our walls relentlessly. Without the Templars, the walls would have fallen days ago. We forced the enemy off the battlements any time a breach was made. My hands no longer wash clean of blood. Their horde seems endless, while we grow weary and few. The men have stood tall, but we cannot prevail. It is only a matter of time.

— Journals of Phillip, the twelfth Templar.

* * *

ARDAN WANDERED with his mother through the palace gardens in comfortable silence. Mish was charging ahead, jumping into the hedges. Though she still had her kitten enthusiasm, he could see her movements were becoming increasingly graceful.

Koira strode out of the palace entrance, her back stiff, while Callum and Talon trailed behind her. She spotted Ardan and immediately made a beeline for him. She clutched an envelope in her hand.

'The Countess has invited me to a ball.'

Ardan couldn't help it; he laughed.

Koira crossed her tattooed arms and glared at him. He stifled his laughter with mixed success, imagining her twirling about the ballroom in a dress.

'I apologise for my son's rudeness. When is it?' Alaine said.

'Tomorrow night!'

'Tomorrow night...' Alaine murmured, frowning. 'But there's been nothing planned. It means she's going to try and trap you, in trade or militarily or with something else. Have you already accepted?'

'I didn't know there was a choice,' Koira said, throwing up her hands. 'This Countess, I dislike her. She does not think much of me or of the Children. I was so fearful of offending her that I let her lead me right into a Mishipeshu den. This is your fault,' she said, pointing at Ardan.

Ardan pointed at himself, 'Me?'

'Yes! You've drawn me into plainsman politics.'

'Ardan, be quiet. I'm trying to think,' Alaine said, rubbing her temples. 'What you need are allies. How many people can you bring?'

'One escort,' Koira said.

'Of course, one guard will do little to protect you. I'll be there, but I'm sure she'll limit what I can do. You need someone unfettered in this kind of fight, something that can distract the Countess and the other vultures...' Alaine pondered. She looked directly at Ardan. It was the same look she'd given him just before she'd hit him with something unexpected in Kings. 'Yes, I'll give you an invitation.'

'Me?'

'What good will that do?' Koira demanded.

Ardan's mind was already racing; he'd never dealt with this kind of party before. Ancients, most people he didn't even like. Then what could he bring to help Koira—or who? Riordan was friendly enough, but Ardan didn't think he'd fought on this kind of field before.

'You're letting me bring a partner, aren't you?' Ardan asked, everything coming together at once. Alaine smiled. Koira looked impatient. 'Marion will be my partner,' Ardan said at her unasked question. 'She's

335

handled these situations before. If anyone can help you get through this, it is her.'

'Why not invite Marion directly?' Koira said, looking between the two of them.

'My son has some claim to nobility by blood; Marion does not. It is a flimsy claim, but we can get away with it without much scrutiny. It's not just Marion's political prowess that will come. Oh no, it will be so much more,' Alaine said, her smile looking absolutely malevolent.

'Marion is one of the three individuals left vying for power. If she turns up when the Dock Master and the Fiddler do not...' Ardan explained.

'Two things distracting a viper are better than one,' Koira finished, her eyes narrowed at Alaine. 'You are a dangerous woman.'

'In some ways; in others, I am horribly powerless,' Alaine said, with a furtive glance at Ardan. 'Go to Marion. She will help you prepare, and I'll send the invitation when it's ready.'

They stood there for an awkward moment before Ardan spoke. 'I'll see you tomorrow night, then.'

Alaine gave him a sad smile that he couldn't read. The two of them embraced before she left for the palace doors.

'We are here to stop the threat, not attend a dinner party,' Talon said behind them.

'We will stop it when we find it. This is a good place to search until we get access to the Temple,' Koira said. 'Unless your men have already gained access?'

Talon looked towards the gate, held his hands up to his mouth and gave a shrill whistle that sounded like a forest bird call. The returning call was long and low.

'Then the dinner party it is.'

Talon scowled.

What in all the Hells? Ardan thought.

'The sooner we get back to Marion's place, the sooner we can prepare,' Koira said, looking pointedly at Ardan.

'Right,' Ardan said. They headed back to the gate, the other warriors falling in behind them while Callum watched them go.

Ardan pushed his mother to the back of his mind and was grateful Koira didn't press him as they walked. Her mind was also occupied.

They found Marion and Aofie playing a game of Kings in the mansion gardens. The sun shone down on them, illuminating them like a beacon of light.

'What's happened? Is everyone okay?' Marion said, standing.

'The Ancient-cursed countess invited me to a hell-spawned ball,' Koira said.

Ardan kept a straight face, if only barely. Aofie had a half smile, trying to understand the joke.

'You're also invited,' Ardan said to Marion. She froze in astonishment. 'It's because—' Ardan began, filling them in.

'Aofie, can you make something for them by tomorrow night? Maybe Riordan too, when he gets back,' Marion said.

Aofie looked thoughtful. 'I'll have to steal some girls to help, but yes, I think so.'

'I'll make it up for them,' Marion said. 'It'll have to be something they can move in. I will have to teach them some basic dances and I don't think they're ready for the full formal wear just yet.'

'Dancing?' Koira said, her eyes lighting up. 'Maybe you plainsmen aren't so uncouth after all.'

'Ardan, can you clear the smaller dining room? We will need the space. I'll meet you there shortly.'

'I'll get my things,' Aofie said.

Ardan led Koira and Talon to one of the smaller dining rooms. It was still larger than Ardan's old home, with a long, polished table, individual chairs and an enormous fireplace.

They spent the next few minutes shifting the chairs and table off to one side. As they were almost done, Aofie arrived with several men at arms, each of them loaded with sewing equipment and rolls of cloth. She began laying them out, taking up half of the table.

'Ardan first,' Aofie said, stepping forward with some tape. Ardan stood there while she measured him and gave a running commentary. 'Medium height, although you've got a bit of growing to go yet. Those shoulders of yours, yes, definitely a fighter. Nothing too restrictive, we need to let you move freely. Green silk will suit you, I think,' she said and got some of the material off the table, pinning it around Ardan. He stood there, a human pincushion, while she worked. He tried to scratch his nose, but Aofie gave him a warm smile and an unspoken message of 'don't try that again.' After what felt like an age, she finished and Ardan was free.

'Alright, my Lady Koira, it is your turn,' she said.

Koira's sense of amusement during Ardan's ordeal suddenly vanished. 'I have my own clothes.'

'As do I,' Talon said.

'I'd prefer to see you out of your clothes, big man,' Aofie said.

Talon opened his mouth and then closed it again, his cheeks going red. Ardan laughed. He'd never seen the warrior flustered before. Talon glared at him.

'But you, my Lady, are turning up at a ball hosted by the Countess. It is a high honour. I want to give you clothing that will adhere to our customs but honour yours. I will make a dress that will shout to the world of the fierce beauty and legacy of your people. Allow me a chance to make it come alive and I promise you won't be disappointed.'

'Your words are honeyed,' Koira said, eyeing Aofie up and down. 'If the dress is as good as you say, I would be honoured to wear it.'

Aofie's face lit with delight, and she immediately came forward to measure Koira. As she was working, Marion came in with two other women. The first was small and petite, her blond hair tied into one solid braid. The second was Bree, her long silver hair hanging freely over her shoulders. They carried a violin and flute, respectively.

'Well, Aofie?'

Koira let out a yelp.

'Sorry,' Aofie said, pulling out a pin. 'The outfits will be ready by tomorrow.'

'Excellent. You have saved me a lot of headache. Now, ladies,' Marion said, addressing the two people with her. 'There is a ball tomorrow night. We need to practice some of the courtly dances.'

The woman with the violin frowned.

'It'll be alright, Niamh,' Bree said. 'The slow dances help us appreciate the taprooms when we get back to them.'

Niamh didn't look pleased as she tuned her violin. Aofie took the marked cloth to her workstation at the edge of the room. Her needle and thread flashed.

Marion moved to the centre of the room. 'The dances of the rich require partners, so Talon, will you please join me?'

Talon's expression didn't change as he removed his cloak, showing ripcord muscles beneath his tattooed chest and back, and went to join her in the centre of the room. Marion looked tiny next to the forest warrior, but she took his hands, correcting their position, and then nodded to Bree. The air Shaper lifted her flute and played. Niamh raised the violin to her chin, nodding to the beat before joining in. The wind and string instruments melded together, filling the room with a slow, soothing melody.

Ardan had never seen dancing that wasn't being performed on a stage before. The two began, Talon stepping with surprising gentleness, picking up the dance moves quickly. Talon led Marion around the room while she flowed from one move to the next. Sometimes they'd separate, while at other times they mirrored each other. By the time the song finished, Ardan thought he had the pattern.

'This is plainsman dancing?' Koira said. 'Where is the fire? Where is the passion?'

'This is the high court style of dancing,' Niamh said. 'You want real dancing, then come to the dockside taprooms. The rich like to castrate themselves and bleach their fun.'

'That is certainly one way of putting it,' Marion said. 'Now you've seen the basics, it is time for you two to learn.'

Talon immediately went to Koira's side.

'I'm afraid I'm still your partner, Master Talon,' Marion said.

'No, I am the Lady Koira's partner.'

'They are the ones who will dance together.'

'Why?' Talon said, his eyes narrowing.

Marion smiled patiently. 'The short version is if you danced with Koira, it would be an insult to the Countess' hospitality. Ardan here falls under the banner of acceptable partners. There are a thousand other rules that govern this, but for now can you take my word for it?'

Talon glowered but didn't object further.

Ardan walked up to Koira, feeling remarkably self-conscious. As he got closer, he realised the top of her auburn hair would tickle his nose if they stepped closer. *Focus, you idiot.*

'Follow our movements and I will correct you if I can,' Marion said, taking Talon's hands.

Ardan copied the stance, holding his hands out for Koira. She put her warm, calloused hands on his. He could smell her perfume of sage and sweetgrass. Their eyes met as the flute and violin played. Then they were dancing with the music.

'The woman follows while the man leads. Let him push you into the movements. The man doesn't need to merely know the steps, but he has to be sure and confident,' Marion said as the four of them continued around the room.

Bree and Niamh played their instruments. Ardan moved with the rhythm in the music as he led Koira around the floor, his feet stepping with the beat of the woodwind and stringed instruments. Koira smiled as they moved, enjoying herself. He got so lost looking into her eyes that he ended up stepping on her foot. It broke their trance.

'That will happen,' Marion said sympathetically. 'If some of the older nobles get you on the dance floor, they'll step on your feet enough to flatten them.'

Koira gave a wry smile. Ardan, feeling bashful, took her hands. He was acutely aware of their closeness, the warmth as her body pressed against him as they resumed their dance. The movements became more natural as they continued. The feel of her in his arms was comforting. They'd stop occasionally, while Aofie measured them for adjustments in whatever she was working on, but the breaks were brief.

'Is it time for dinner yet?' Bree asked, lowering the flute from her mouth.

Koira looked up at him, her smile as beautiful as a sunrise. She slowly released his hands and stepped back, a light sheen of sweat on her forehead. His muscles ached, unused to the motions of the dance, but he still felt regret the dance was over.

'It is close enough,' Marion said. 'I am sorry, Lady Koira, but the lessons don't stop here. We have to show you how to eat the way plainsmen do.'

'I knew things were getting too simple.'

Ardan smiled as they followed Marion to the main dining hall. The long tables were laden with a banquet of spiced duck, grilled fish, roast potatoes, bread, cheese, assorted vegetables, and a large bowl of soup.

'Do they always eat like this?' Koira asked.

'It'd be nice, but no,' Marion said, leading them to the end of the table. 'This is to prepare you for tomorrow's fare.'

In front of Ardan, roast potatoes surrounded a golden and slightly charred duck, sprinkled with herbs and lemon juice. The smell of it wafted to his nose, warm and intoxicating.

'Ardan, you can't afford to make mistakes. Koira's cultural heritage will give her some leeway, but you will be heavily scrutinised on a first official outing,' Marion said.

Ardan nodded sagely. He went next to the nearest chair and pulled it out, waiting for Marion to sit. She looked surprised, but soon took the seat. When he pushed it in for her, before sitting in his own chair, Marion appraised him for a moment. 'Your mother's training. Well, that makes things easier. Talon, you will need to do the same to seat Koira.'

'She can seat herself.'

Marion didn't bother to argue. 'Fine. Maybe your customs will let you get away with it.'

Once they were both seated, Marion kept up a steady commentary.

'Wine will be on your table, but you must not drink it until the Countess has made the first toast. The Countess will be seated last, so you must not touch your food until she has given her consent. You'll be expected to take a bite of each course, so pace yourself because there will be a lot. Ignore the commenters; they will make disparaging remarks about the Countess, the food she sets or others at the table. The sycophants will relay anything you say, hoping to gain favour.'

'They insult their host's hospitality while enjoying it at the same time?' Koira asked.

Talon grunted with disapproval.

'One of their more distasteful customs,' Marion said.

As they continued to eat, Marion continued to sprout advice on table manners. Fortunately, Ardan remembered the lessons his mother taught him, suddenly appreciative of the rules his mother had enforced.

When they were done, Marion led them back to the dancing room. Ardan was grateful to see Bree and Niamh weren't joining them this time. Instead Aofie was measuring Riordan, flicking one of his red braids out of the way while she pinned on his coat.

'Ow.'

'Hold still,' Aofie commanded, as she went about pinning the cloth around his shoulders.

'How'd the Trials go today?' Ardan asked Riordan

The man didn't answer right away, instead looking at Aofie's pins apprehensively. 'Good. Found some new blood that should help to bolster some of Marion's forces.'

'Anyone I know?'

His hesitation was more noticeable this time. 'Maybe; it's hard to know.'

Yet before Ardan could question him further, Aofie jumped in: 'Alright, I've got what I need. You can go eat, big man.'

'Finally,' Riordan said, shrugging out of the clothing and practically running from the room.

What's he not saying? Ardan wondered.

'Strip,' Aofie said.

'Here?' Ardan said, looking behind him to see Koira and Marion standing nearby. Talon was leaning against the wall. Aofie inclined her head, so he shrugged and took off his shirt, dropping it to the ground.

Aofie made an appreciative noise.

'Aofie,' Marion reprimanded.

'What? He's a bit young but can't deny he's got a good physique to work with.'

Ardan's face reddened, and he was grateful that he still had his underclothes on. He noticed that at least Koira had looked away.

'Aofie can work wonders, but she'll likely need to make more alterations tomorrow. You can still enter armed; we'll put it down to Children customs. You too, Ardan. Your sword is exotic enough that the Countess and her lackeys will accept it for its unique style,' Marion said.

A sudden prick in his underarm caused Ardan to jump. He looked down at Aofie, who'd barely noticed, already using more pins for different parts of the cloth.

'Alright, get out of here. It's time for me to measure up the ladies,' Aofie said.

Ardan left, replacing his shirt, and headed upstairs. As soon as he was out of the room, he suddenly felt incredibly weary. What had he gotten himself into?

CHAPTER FORTY-FIVE: DINNER
WITH THE COUNTESS

***

oday I watched as a small band of mercenaries scaled the cliffs. Working together, they brought down half the mountain. An avalanche of stones, rocks, trees and mud crashed into half of Naberius' army, blocking the Pass. For one shining moment, I was filled with hope. Then I realised the remnant's only escape was through us.
— Journals of Phillip, the twelfth Templar.

***

ARDAN ADJUSTED the cuffs on his suit one last time, staring at himself in the mirror. He wore a long green jacket over a white frilly shirt. His black hair had been combed, falling almost down to his shoulders. He had a new leather scabbard fitting snugly at his waist. *If I'm going to have to do this, I may as well look dapper doing it,* he thought as he went downstairs.

Before he'd made it halfway down the stairs to the street, he stopped and stared. Marion was dressed in a red and white flowing silk dress. It left the fair skin of her neck and shoulders bare except for a silver necklace. Her blonde hair was sleek, bound in an elaborate floating style and held together by a silver brooch resembling a sailor's knot.

'By your expression, I guess I do look okay,' Marion said.

Ardan shut his jaw.

'I told you,' Riordan muttered.

Marion's answer was interrupted as the carriage pulled up. Riordan stepped forward, opening the door and placing the stool, before standing back and holding out his hand. Marion took it, stepping gracefully into the carriage. They were every bit a picture of the upper classes. Riordan gestured for him to get in.

'Where's Koira?'

'She has her own carriage and escorts. Now get in with Marion. Only escorts get to sit outside of the carriage.'

Ardan grumbled but climbed into the carriage. Marion's dress was already splayed out on the bench. After some difficulty in adjusting his sword, he sat down opposite her. She withdrew a small pocket mirror and inspected her face. They rode in silence, and despite the rocking motion, Marion smoothed out the thousand imperfections that were visible only to women. Ardan stared out the windows as the archaic stone buildings were replaced by the modern constructions of brick and wood in the Merchant Quarter.

Soon they arrived at the Countess' palace. Callum stood at the entrance, his polished armour gleaming in the torchlight. The Captain nodded in recognition of Ardan, but kept his face professional, taking their invitation and waving them through the gates.

They joined the slow procession of carriages that were emptying their passengers at the entrance to the palace. When it was their turn, Riordan helped Marion down and Ardan took her hand, escorting her into the entrance hall.

His mother was there, in a beige dress of a similar style to Marion's. She stood with several other women behind a lady who had to be the Countess Aine. At first, he thought she was incredibly pale, but as he got closer, he realised it was the sheer amount of makeup she had on. Her gown was a rich purple, and she bore a small fortune in jewellery on her person.

'Countess, thank you so much for the invitation,' Marion said with a courtly curtsey.

'You are most welcome,' Aine said behind a furrowed brow. She clearly didn't recognise them but waved a hand to the main room. 'All our guests are in the drawing room, so be sure to help yourself to the refreshments. I am sure we will have an opportunity to speak soon.'

Marion curtseyed again. Ardan followed her lead, but he glanced back to see Aine round on his mother. She wore an innocent look. Ardan had to stifle a laugh. The Countess had had no warning of Marion's coming.

He scanned the room but didn't recognise anyone. Not that it really surprised him. Every single person probably had more money in their pocket than he'd had in his entire life. Riordan had already helped himself to some of the cut-up fruit. Marion was speaking to a merchant like an old friend.

Ardan stood nearby, figuring one of them should stay near Marion. An elderly gentleman passed them with his wife. It was hard not to gawk at their gaudy jewellery, thickly oiled hair and the way they held their noses in the air. Then Ardan smelt them; the perfume was worse than frog venom. He felt as if he were choking as he tried not to gag.

Luckily it wasn't long before the Countess entered the room, letting him move away from the couple. As she stepped forward, Ardan studied her closely. She welcomed everyone and thanked them for coming. He thought her vanity was a good mask, hiding her accomplishment of surviving the purge as a teenager and then every subsequent succession. Despite being in her seventies, she still stood tall.

'Ladies and gentlemen, we have a very distinguished guest. The Lady Koira,' Aine said.

Talon appeared first. He wore a tight-fitting coat, similar to Ardan's, but his was a stark black. People near him drew back, the colour making him look even more intimidating. Behind him Koira came out. She had adopted the fashion of the merchants, with a deep décolletage that exposed her tanned skin. The sleeves were artfully slashed to show the vine-like tattoos beneath the sleeves. Her dress was black with white patterns scattered over it and she wore a belt, adorned with a knife, cinching it closely about her waist. Her auburn hair was artfully loose over her shoulders, accentuating her exotic heritage. Her gaze passed over them all and then quickly darted back as her eyes found his.

Koira looked beautiful and fierce, just as Aofie had promised. Riordan elbowed him and he grunted. He'd been staring. He smiled and gave a small wave. Her eyes widened, and she was suddenly looking everywhere but at him.

'Oh, you *are* in trouble,' Alaine said from just behind him.

'What?' Ardan said.

'Just like your father. Falling for someone who is distinctly bad for you.'

'She'd just as soon gut me as kiss me.'

'Exactly like your father. But the question is, are you interested in her?'

'I, uh … no,' Ardan said, though he could feel the blood rushing to his cheeks.

'Uh-huh,' Alaine said, unconvinced. 'Well, at least you're motivated to see she doesn't get into trouble tonight.'

'How?' Ardan said and was struck by the realization that despite his hard won independence, his mother filled a space in his heart that he didn't know he'd been missing. It helped.

'We need to work the room. Marion will stick by her, and we'll help. When we aren't around your lady friend, we'll steer the conversation away from her. Keep it general. The less they think about her, the less the people here will gossip, cause trouble and try to corner her.'

'Alright, but how?'

'Talk to everyone and anyone, make small talk, get people interested in what you know.'

'But I don't know anything.'

'You work for Marion, one of the few remaining contenders for control of the city, and you've been on the ground throughout the succession while they've been behind their walls with their perfumed handkerchiefs. You've lived in the Cathedral of Light, conversed with priests of the Dark and just returned from going through the forest. Play the right card at the right time, keep your face unreadable and remember your manners. A genteel fighter intrigues these people. I'll show you—just follow my lead,' Alaine said.

She immediately picked up a few cups of ale from the refreshment table and walked over to a group of mostly younger merchants. Ardan breathed in for a moment, watching his mother, the Lady Alaine. She had been born to this, moving easily in these circles, inserting herself while distributing the drinks. Soon she'd created an opening for Ardan. He tried to join as gracefully as he could.

'Real Children of the Ancients,' one said. 'Has anyone spoken to her yet?'

'No,' another laughed, 'she's barely been here ten minutes. Give her a moment to settle in.'

'It's great news that she's here,' Alaine said.

They all turned to look at her.

'It means that the Countess is confident enough that the streets are safe. Trade should increase as word gets out.'

'I don't know about that. No one has claimed the city or made any overtures to the Merchant Guild,' the first one said.

'I heard the Dock Master has the most power,' one ventured.

'The Fiddler has control of Ragtown.'

'Hardly compelling evidence that the streets are safe again.'

His mother caught his eye and made an expression that he should join in.

'Lady Marion has made a deal with the mercenaries,' Ardan said, a little softly. Suddenly, every eye was on him. He swallowed. 'Consistent food runs are coming through the forest and the fields are now being worked.' His voice gained traction as this was new information to some of them, while others nodded in agreement. 'The city has become less dangerous since that has started happening,' Ardan said, although he wasn't entirely sure how much of it was truthful.

'Marion?' one asked.

'She's the one that the ... lower class refer to as,' one man coughed, 'the Lady of the Night, but much less politely.'

'Oh yes, I've heard of her. She has control of the Ancient Quarter.'

'So there's what, three people vying for control?'

'Yes, but Marion is the only one here tonight,' Alaine said, nodding to the corner where Marion was talking.

'Is she now?' the older gentleman said.

'Papa, I don't understand,' a small girl said. She was dressed in a similar style to his mother's, if much more conservatively.

'The Countess knows something we don't. She probably invited Marion so that we could make her acquaintance,' the older gentleman said. 'Tell me, young man, how do you know her?'

Ardan caught his mother's eye. She mouthed the word 'Kings' at him. Ardan straightened. *Just act like you hold all the cards.* 'I was originally hired for this,' he tapped his sword lightly and ignored the inner voice telling him he was a liar. 'But since then, she has invited me to do specific tasks for her.'

'Like what?' the girl asked. It felt a little disconcerting to feel her unblinking eyes on him, but he kept his mask.

'We had to go through the forest to get the supplies. Then while we were there, we escorted the Lady Koira back here,' Ardan said.

One man whistled. 'You went through the forest?'

Ardan shrugged noncommittally.

So it went. Alaine led the first few introductions, and he inserted himself into the conversation and steered it away from Koira. After a few tries, he was confident enough to lead the conversation without his mother's help.

'Should we help Koira?' Ardan asked between groups.

'I've been watching. Marion has intercepted most things directed her way, but your lady friend is far from defenceless. We're trying to keep people focused on other things, and so far, you're doing well.'

A small chime echoed through the room.

'The banquet is served,' an obsequious-looking servant said.

The entire room began to shuffle towards the proffered doors. Ardan followed his mother into the dining room. Four large tables had been set up in a rough square. Two enormous fireplaces adorned opposite walls, complemented by candle chandeliers hanging from the ceiling. Together they cast a warm light over the room. Rich tapestries covered most of the empty space. A small troop of musicians stood off in one corner, waiting for the word to begin playing. The tables were set with pristine white cloths and precious metal plates, each one having individual chairs. Several people walked around with incense bottles, wafting a pleasant aroma throughout the place. Ardan had never seen such wealth in one place. It was probably the hardest he'd had to fight to keep his face impassive. The wealth here could have kept families from starving, stopping fights and raids. *Maybe the Fiddler is onto something*, he thought.

'Try to act natural, dear,' Alaine said while excusing herself to find her seat at the Countess' table.

Ardan forced his incredulity down, schooling his expression and taking his own seat while Riordan helped Marion to hers. It seemed to take an age for everyone to find their place. It appeared the social dance extended to every facet of the evening. At one point, the gaudy older gentleman from earlier insisted he should be at the main table, but after some complaints, a few adept servants managed to politely but insistently get him to a chair at one of the regular tables.

At an unseen signal an army of servants came out, carrying pitchers of wine. With an efficiency that bordered on magic, everyone's glass was soon filled. The wine was giving off slight tendrils of steam and a faint smell of cinnamon. *Who in the nine hells heats wine?* Ardan thought.

The Countess stood, and a hush immediately fell over the hall.

'Thank you for coming during this difficult time. We have been fortunate to avoid the worst of what has befallen our beloved city,' Aine said. Her voice, though not loud, carried clearly through the room.

Her speech droned on about the horrors the Merchant Quarter

had had to overcome. Ardan couldn't help but wonder if these 'horrors' were the rich not having their favourite food every night or having to drink ale and mead instead of wine. *It's a wonder these people stay as well adjusted as they are.* He didn't voice his thoughts. Alaine would be proud that her lessons in courtly manners had paid off.

Long after he'd hoped she would finish, Aine's speech finally seemed to wind up.

'With a delegate from the Ancients, it seems to herald that peace may have finally settled over Barleron. I believe that trade may soon open up again and we will return to normalcy. With that, I would like to propose a toast,' she said, holding up her glass of wine. Chairs scrapped around the room as people stood. 'To peace in Barleron.'

'And good wine!' one man yelled.

Aine smiled indulgently while the rest of them intoned, 'To peace.'

Ardan took a sip of the mulled wine and tasted cinnamon and orange. *Unusual,* he pondered, taking another sip. *Maybe the rich might be onto something,* he thought grudgingly as he swirled it around his mouth and found he liked the sweet, spicy flavour of the warm wine.

The small troop of musicians played, washing the room in pleasant white noise, while the army of servants reappeared, carrying trays of food. It was a procession of roasted venison, pork, geese, chicken, and pheasant. There were plates of root vegetables, along with peas and beans. His stomach gave an involuntary grumble as the smell of cooked meat filled his nostrils. The servants placed the food at the central table. From there, several of the servants appeared with large knives and cut the meat. Ardan was entertained by the showmanship but found the other members of the party were ignoring them and he tried to adopt their air of nonchalance.

'It appears even the Countess' table is affected,' Ardan heard one guest pronounce. 'Pheasant?' he asked with disdain.

Ardan stared at him, then at the food. It was the most lavish meal he'd ever seen. One servant brought Ardan a generous portion of roast chicken. He quickly cut a slice, practically throwing it in his mouth. As he chewed, the succulent flavour of the tender meat filled him. It was unusually spiced. There was something enhancing the lemon and garlic. It was slightly spicy, leaving a pleasant aftertaste. With his next bite, he caught a whiff of something that teased at his memory. Then he realized—it smelt like blue frog venom. He took another bite and immediately understood why they liked the venom so much. It was delicious. It was a shame he couldn't just pick it up and eat with his hands; instead he had to put the utensils down between mouthfuls, respectfully chew his food and swallow before he could pick up the knife and fork and repeat the process.

As soon as he'd finished the chicken, it was replaced with pork, then venison, followed by a portion of the goose. When the pheasant came, he could barely look at it without his stomach protesting.

Leaning back in his chair contentedly, he took a sip of the excellent wine. His eyes instinctively sought Koira. She was surrounded by the Countess' retinue; every time she tried to take a bite of her food, something would require her attention and she'd put the fork down. He could see her lip twitching in irritation, and he wondered if she'd got a morsel in. Their eyes met for a moment, and he smiled, but she glanced around her and grimaced. The night would be much longer for her than it was for him.

Ardan saw her distress and moved before he fully thought it through. He made his way over to Koira's table. There were enough people and servants moving around that none challenged his break in protocol. She eyed him curiously while Talon watched with a barely concealed sneer.

'I think it's time we give the Lady a chance to finish her dinner,' Ardan said. There were a number of affronted gasps at this, as they shifted their attention to him. 'We don't want to show an ambassador of the Children of Ancients what a lavish feast the Countess can put on and then deny her the opportunity to eat it, do we? It would be an offensive to both her and the Countess,' Ardan said, though he thought it was a considerable stretching of the truth.

With that he bowed and returned to his seat. When he sat down, he could see the silent warring going on between those around Koira. Some glared at him, while one of the others opened his mouth, glanced at the Countess, and closed it again. But none bothered her.

Koira gave him a warm smile of gratitude before being able to take a bite from the roast chicken.

He inclined his head, glad she could at least have some pleasure from the evening. Where she could eat her fill, until the food was eventually cleared, and the musicians relocated to a more central position. The dancing would soon begin.

CHAPTER FORTY-SIX: THE MELDING OF POWER

* * *

I stand on the crumbling battlements, surrounded by scorch marks and bloodstains. Naberius' army is preparing to charge. The three-headed dog stands in front of the cavalry, larger than any horse. The sunset will bring his end or ours.
— *Journals of Phillip, the twelfth Templar.*

* * *

ARDAN STOOD and strode across the open centre of the hall. This time every eye on him as he approached the head table as everyone else was seated and the servants had retreated to the edges of the room. *Heaven's above, I didn't realise everyone would be staring.* Still, he went through the motions, bowing to the Countess before turning to Koira.

'Lady Koira, may I have the pleasure of this dance?'

It went so quiet you could have heard a feather drop. The Countess looked over at Alaine, then searched the room, her gaze falling on Marion, her mouth curving with displeasure.

'You may,' she said, rising to take his hand as he led her to the dance floor.

Here, he could smell her perfume of sage and sweetgrass. The musicians took their cue and played. The music filled the hall like the first warmth of spring. Ardan held out his hands and waited. She eyed him up and down, before placing her hands in his. Her mouth quirked at the edges. They fell into step, he led and Koira followed, like a beautiful duet.

'Glad to be out of there?'

'Like leaving a Mishipeshu den,' she said in a low whisper. 'The elders were less condescending when I was a child than these cretins are. I was asked if I could read. I'm never accepting another invitation. Ancients curse their courtesy and politeness.'

Ardan smiled. 'No trade agreements then?'

Koira almost sneered. 'They were as obvious as a snake in the water. They think me simple and my lack of answers as obedience. Foolish plainsman.'

Fortunately, other people joined them on the dance floor, taking the focus off of the two of them. It also helped distract her and the rising tide of her anger. He pulled her into the last part of the dance where they finished with a foot stamp. It was customary to switch partners, but Ardan found himself reluctant.

'How about something a bit more lively?' someone called.

The Countess rose, everyone falling silent as her gaze fell on Koira. 'My servants have been searching through every historical record we have. They've found sheet music from the Children of the Ancients. What we don't have is someone to show us the dances—do you think we can impose on our guest?'

There were mild cheers, and polite clapping to this announcement as every eye was drawn to Koira. Ardan suspected the Countess was trying to embarrass her, but oh how little she knew the forest woman.

The pounding of the percussion echoed through the room while the string instruments filled the gaps. The combination sounded earthy and powerful, but there was an alien cast to it.

The Wild inside of Ardan rose in response. It wasn't angry or vengeful. That alone surprised him enough that he allowed it to swell to the rhythm of the music.

Koira looked startled, but her mouth curved into a wicked grin. 'They wish to play games? So be it. Let the power flow,' Koira said, her hand finding his. 'It will guide you.'

Ardan looked into her eyes. In their brown depths, he found trust. He let the Wild flow; it rose like a mountain. Then Koira began to move. Ardan followed, letting the Wild extend to every part of his body, feeling in concert with it like he never had before. His movements were strange and hypnotic, the primal powers pushing and pulling while Koira spun, the hem of her dress spinning out with the motion. Her face was flushed with excitement, and he could see her genuinely smile as she moved. When their hands touched, he felt a spark of electricity as the Wild inside of him met the Wild inside of her. They joined, the power welling up and spilling out among the guests. Their energy spread out, invisible as it drew people into the dance. Nothing specific could cage or define it, but everyone was pulled in. The younger participants were enthusiastic, while the older ones were more graceful.

As they danced, Ardan felt an urge. He watched Koira, how her figure moved with the beat of the drum. Her eyes were alight with passion, while her smile brightened her face. He had a sudden need. As the intensity of the dance rose, so too did the Wild and the power that filled the room. He pulled her close, his arms wrapping around her waist. For a moment his felt the back of mind warn against the power's influence, but he lost all resistance when his eyes met hers. He forgot the dance, the surrounding people and the turbulent Wild inside of him. He wanted this. She closed her eyes as he drew closer. Their lips met. Passion and power rushed through him. The Wild exulted in the connection. The song continued, and he felt the heat rise, his arms trailing up the sides of her body. Their kiss ignited the power that had been filling the room. It rose with the music, matching its beat and rhythm, As the music faded, so too did the Wild.

Ardan leaned back but kept his hands on Koira's hips. She regarded him, the corners of her mouth twitching upwards.

Around them, there were gasps of surprise and shock. Those enthralled by the amorous dance were waking from their trance. Everyone else stared in slack-jawed amazement.

A resounding slap echoed across the room. A younger woman had slapped the older man she'd been kissing. A different woman confronted the man.

'But honey—' he began.

'Don't you *honey* me!'

Everywhere people split apart, trying to figure out why they had lost all sense of decorum.

Ardan felt eyes on him and found Talon glaring at him with outright hostility. The man looked menacing despite his finery. *Did he learn that trait at birth, or has it taken him forty-odd years to perfect it?* Ardan thought.

Someone started to blame the musicians, and the servants quickly created a barrier, allowing them to leave before things could get violent.

Koira returned to her place at the Countess' table. Whereas she had been accosted before, now those around her avoided eye contact and stayed quiet.

Nearly half the guests made their excuses and headed for the door, while a large number of them came up to Ardan. Wanting nothing more than to be left alone, he had to put on his game-playing mask, answering questions about Koira, his mother and Marion with disingenuous honesty. He exaggerated Marion's importance and downplayed his relationship to one of the Countess' ladies. During it all, he was stealing glances at Koira.

Ardan found himself crowded, as those intimidated by the forest woman looked to him for answers. They blocked him in and suddenly Ardan wanted to leave. He saw Koira heading for the door. Ardan made his excuses, pushing through the people, trying to catch her before she left. He almost ran into Marion and Countess Aine. They were speaking together in low voices right at the gap between the two tables, making it impossible to get around them. Talon was ushering her out, glaring at him as they went.

Finally, Ardan thought as the Countess and Marion parted. Yet, to his horror, the Countess moved to intercept Koira and caught her just before she was about to get into her carriage.

He resigned himself to knowing that he wouldn't speak to her again this night. He sighed and turned to Marion, seeing a bemused smile on her face.

'Sorry,' he said, realising she had been trying to speak to him.

'No need to apologise.'

Ardan grunted. 'Can we get out of here?'

'We are nearing the end of our welcome.'

Despite Marion's words, she still spent half an hour saying farewells to various groups. Ardan was ready to leave long before the carriage arrived. He felt such relief, climbing inside the cramped confines and collapsing on the bench.

'What happened in there?' Marion asked.

Ardan's mind was immediately on kissing Koira, but he frowned. She wouldn't be asking that. 'You mean the dance?'

Marion smiled patiently. 'Yes, the dance. Something that will become legend, I think.'

'A few relationships may be over too.'

Marion shrugged. 'These people don't suffer from the burden of fidelity.'

Ardan smiled wryly. 'I don't know how to explain what happened. My power acted differently to the music, and it met with hers, twined together and just kind of spilled out.'

Marion was playing with her silver necklace. 'It made me feel much younger. This power can do some unexpected things. Perhaps it is good you are learning to control it after all.'

Ardan said nothing, instead looked out the carriage window as it jostled along.

'I have much to thank you for this evening,' Marion said.

'Huh?'

'I saw you going around to the different merchants, promoting my cause. It made my job much easier. I gained the support of a few key members of the Merchant Guild, and that eventually resulted in the backing of the Countess.'

'Really? I thought the Countess stayed out of politics.'

'Normally she does, but I think the dance unbalanced her. I now have more support than the Fiddler and maybe even the Dock Master. All from a single dinner invitation...' Marion said, and added with a sly smile, 'even if it was forged.'

'Yeah,' Ardan coughed, uncomfortably. 'My mother is full of surprises.'

'Oh yes. I had never heard of her before, but the older players remember. She has quite the reputation. I am now in a position to make some real, positive changes in Barleron.'

'How are you planning on getting rid of the Fiddler and the Dock Master?' Ardan asked.

Marion stared at him for a long time before answering: 'I'm not. It isn't all or nothing. I want people safe and fed. We don't need more bloodshed.'

'And you can convince the others of that?' Ardan asked dubiously.

'The Dock Master—yes, I think so. About the Fiddler, I am not so certain. But I just need one and the other will follow.'

'Bold plan.'

'Anything worthwhile always is.' Marion didn't speak after that, which let Ardan's mind wander to Koira. *Had she wanted to kiss him, or was it the dance?* He hoped it was the former but if not, he'd just have to dance with her more often.

CHAPTER FORTY-SEVEN:
MANIFESTATION WITH MISH

Naberius himself charged the wall. The surviving Templars and the Light's Clergy went to meet him. We fought for hours, the three-headed demon slowly cutting us down. Any time we got the upper hand, he would retreat to his lines. In the end, we had to pursue him into the heart of his army. Several Templars sacrificed themselves to pin Naberius down. Our light-infused weapons pierced him again and again until he no longer healed, but we were forced back. We did not see what became of him, and I pray to the Light he is dead.

— Journals of Phillip, the twelfth Templar.

* * *

ARDAN WAS ROUSED EARLY the next morning by Riordan. The mercenary was already dressed in his leather armour, his shield and sword buckled on. The red-headed warrior didn't look any the worse for wear from the previous evening; instead, he pulled open the shutters, allowing the sunlight to stream in.

'Ugh, it's too early for a battle,' Ardan said, pulling the blankets tighter. Mish agreed, emitting a sleepy meow.

'It's midmorning, now get up and meet me downstairs.'

Something in his voice made Ardan pause. He blinked, rubbing sleep out of his eyes. It was definitely too early for his liking, but he got out of bed. Fumbling with the straps on his leather armour, he equipped himself and donned his sword belt. He made his way downstairs to find Riordan in the open-aired garden, which was surprisingly empty of people. Mish followed him but set herself down under the table, immediately falling asleep.

Riordan stood in the centre of the clearing, proudly holding his new round shield. It had been painted green with a frayed sailor's knot. It was large enough that the man could hide behind it. He moved it back and forth easily, making it look light despite its size. *Looks like Raigel has finished the heartwood shield.*

'I didn't know you had a sigil,' Ardan said.

'I didn't—Marion did it. Blindsided me really, I thought we were just talkin' but next thing I know, the thing's on the shield.'

'A frayed knot?'

'Holds things together, despite being a bit battered.'

'That's ... actually really fitting.'

Riordan beamed. 'I was hoping we could test it out before the morning gets too late. Can you whistle up some of that green fire?'

Could I? Ardan wondered. He pulled his sword, found the Wild inside of him and let it flow towards the blade. A green flame licked across it, lighting up the sword. He looked at it in surprise. *I guess I can.*

'Just lightly now,' Riordan said, holding his shield out in front of him.

Ardan touched the sword to the shield, then pulled it away. The flame didn't jump onto the shield like last time, nor did the metal look marred. Over the next thirty minutes, they tried various ways of striking the shield, testing its strength. Ardan raised the intensity of the green flame to where eventually the sword was giving off the heat of a bonfire, but the shield simply absorbed it.

Ardan stared at the unmarred metal, wondering where the fire had gone. 'Surely the power has to go somewhere?'

'And the energy from your sword? Where does that come from?'

'Well, it comes from the Wild....' Ardan realized he didn't know where the Ancients' power came from.

'Best leave the thinking to those better suited for it.'

'Hey!'

'Well, it's good to know that the shield can absorb green fire. It'll give me some confidence if I have to face your brother—or something worse,' Riordan said. Then a moment passed, and his expression grew serious. 'There's something we need to talk about before it goes any further.'

'Is this about Koira?'

'What? No. I mean, well done and all that, but no, it's not about her. It's something that I know you won't be happy about,' Riordan said, looking down at his shield.

'Okay,' Ardan said slowly.

He opened his mouth several times but didn't get the words out. In the end he said, 'Wait here, it's better if I show you.'

He disappeared and Ardan wondered what in the heavens was happening. He didn't have to wait long before Riordan reappeared with a young man. Regan's lanky figure and sleek brown hair was unmistakable. He tried to stand tall, but there was something about his body language that screamed vulnerability.

'What is he doing here?'

'I'm mentoring him, same as you.'

Ardan stared at Regan, feeling the Wild rise up inside of him. He clamped down on it, hard. He would not let his primal emotions run rampant, even though he wanted to. In front of him was one of the people responsible for his father's murder.

'Why?' Ardan said, his voice sounding feral.

'Can you trust me to say that he's been hard done by too?'

The way Regan shuffled his feet, refusing to meet Ardan's eyes, and his slumped shoulders, almost made him believe it. Deep down he knew the only one really responsible for his father's death had been Verrick, but his emotions warned him off such logic.

'Why can't he join his father's guild?'

Regan visibly flinched.

Riordan put a hand on Regan's shoulder while looking over at Ardan. 'That's just it; his father rejected him. Set an impossible standard. There was nothing wrong with his form and he was perfectly able, yet he lost the last battle. Their side had no chance of winning anyway. Cillian wouldn't offer him a role and made it clear no one else was to either.'

'Not even the Wolves?'

'Plenty of applicants without the added trouble, and Cillian has a reputation.'

Ardan could picture Riordan seeing Regan as a lost puppy. Ardan felt pity for Regan too and cursed himself for it. He wondered if justice would ever find his father's murderers. Yet, as with Liam, he thought maybe it had hit Regan hard too. It just wasn't how he thought it would be.

'Flaming fine,' Ardan said. 'I don't like it, but by the nine hells I understand.'

Riordan beamed. Regan tentatively met Ardan's gaze, giving a shaky smile before looking away again.

'It's alright, I don't expect you to spend much time together, but for now let's get some food,' Riordan said, making his way towards the door, but a hulking figure was standing there.

It took a moment for Ardan to register that his brother was here, in his leather armour and with his axe strapped over his shoulder, standing in the centre of Marion's mansion.

His brother's usual confidence faltered for a bit. His feet shuffled, and he looked down, not really meeting anyone's gaze. 'The door guard is a friend, he let me in.'

'He *what?*' Riordan said. Ardan knew that tone. He almost felt sorry for the nameless guard.

'He knew what I was here for. I came here when I couldn't find you at the Trials to apologise. For ... you know.'

'Trying to kill me?' Riordan prompted.

'I wasn't—I mean I was, but I didn't intend to,' Davan said. He struggled for a moment, but then his voice hardened. 'I am not trying to make excuses, I just—I wasn't me. My emotions were running rampant, and you had to deal with it. I am glad none of you were seriously injured. For what it's worth, I am sorry and I'm here to make amends for the wrong I have done.'

The pronouncement settled across all of them. Ardan couldn't hide his surprise; his brother wasn't usually one to apologise.

'How long have you been practising that one?' Riordan asked.

'Since a day or two after you left.'

'It's a good one,' Riordan said.

Davan smiled, but it quickly faded as he turned his attention to Ardan. 'I know I was wrong in how I acted, but you still shouldn't have sold Liá to the Dark.'

That's more like Davan. 'Have you spoken to her?'

'No.'

'Maybe you should,' Ardan said. 'She hasn't grown horns or sprouted a tail. She's still our sister.'

Davan's mouth thinned, but he stayed silent.

An awkward silence filled the garden, broken when Marion came in, clutching a letter. She glanced at Davan and then at Regan. She frowned but otherwise ignored them. 'Riordan, Ardan—good. I need everyone who's available now.'

'What's happened?' Riordan said.

'I sent an envoy to the Dock Master.'

'Yes, I know,' Riordan said.

'He replied. Said to meet him at his warehouse within an hour.'

'So soon?'

'The note said now or never. I think he fears a trap, and the short notice is a safety measure.'

Riordan whistled. 'I'll see who's staying at the house, but there won't be many. We could take some of the Mansion guards—'

'No, just whoever else you can find,' Marion said.

'Marion.' Riordan looked at her levelly. 'Without them, we don't have enough.'

Marion cursed, paced around the garden, and cursed again. 'Damn it. I won't leave the house unprotected. But we can't miss this chance.'

'Maybe we should. We're going to be heading into the heart of his territory. If this is a trap, we won't have a chance,' Riordan said.

'If he wants to knock me off, then I have horribly misjudged who he is. If he kills me, then at least the succession will end, because my people won't follow the Fiddler. But I would like to make a show of force if we can.'

'He could hold us, extort us, demand anything from us once we're there,' Riordan said.

'I'll get you a bottle of Waterlord whisky.'

'Oh well, that's different,' Riordan said. He turned to Davan. 'You really want to make amends?'

Davan shrugged. 'Why not?'

'Well, that's four. I'll see if we can spare anyone around the house.' Riordan said.

'Koira has her own retinue of warriors,' Ardan said.

'I hadn't thought of that,' Marion said, looking thoughtful.

CHAPTER FORTY-EIGHT: THE
POWER OF THE PROSTITUTE

* * *

*W*hen word spread of Naberius' fall, the enemy soon
surrendered. Ballads will be sung of this victory. What they
will not say is that of our ten thousand warriors, fewer than five hundred
survived. Of the ten Templars present, eight have fallen and the ninth will
likely pass before morning. They will not sing of the fields of dead, the broken
walls or the burning standards of the Light.
— *Journals of Phillip, the twelfth Templar.*

* * *

ARDAN STOOD awkwardly out in front of the mansion while Marion
and Koira whispered. Their argument had been going back and forth
for almost ten minutes.

'If you want my warriors, then that is my price.'

'Something unique and exotic enough to satisfy you is not a price.
It is plain extortion. You don't even tell me whether it's a weapon or a
fruit. How am I supposed to know what I need?' Marion said.

Riordan came out of the mansion with Bree. Her silver hair had been done up, and she was wearing a dark blue dress with stockings underneath. She almost tripped over Mish, who had her paw extended through a crack in the stonework. She knelt down and began scratching the cat behind her ears. Though startled at the sudden attention, the lynx's eyes quickly closed in contentment.

'This is the cat you rescued from the forest?'

'That's Mish.'

'Short for Mishipeshu?' Bree asked with a laugh.

'You've heard of it?'

'Sure. Murieen used to refer to me as her Mishipeshu. I was wild and loved the water when I was young. Aren't Mishipeshu supposed to get pretty big?'

Ardan stared at Mish's black fur and tried to imagine. She was entering adolescence, which was clear in the sharp contrast of her kitten clumsiness and predatory grace, sometimes within a span of heartbeats. What would he do with her when she was fully grown? Could he keep her, or would he have to release her? He wanted her to stay. He shook his head, pushing the thoughts aside.

'This is all we have?' Regan asked, looking around. Riordan had only found a few guardsmen at such short notice.

'If the negotiations go well, it won't matter,' Riordan said.

Regan paused for a long time. 'And if they don't?'

'You don't have to come. No one will think less of you. I only want those who are willing.'

'And my place here?'

'You'll have a place here, as long as I'm alive.'

Regan stared at him accusingly. 'That's not a choice.'

'Guess you're coming, then,' Riordan said with a grin.

Marion threw up her hands. 'Fine; we're out of time. I'll find something exotic for you.'

Koira barely smiled, but Ardan could see how pleased she was. It didn't take long before she'd gone inside, quickly returning with six forest warriors. Talon was amongst them.

'Less than twenty,' Marion said. 'Six of us women.'

'The Dock Master isn't squeamish about that sort of thing,' Davan said.

'We're there to negotiate, not to fight.'

'Can they fight if needed?' Davan said.

'If needed,' Marion confirmed. The other women were dressed similarly to Bree, in stout boots, stockings and flowing dresses. 'We're here as a show of force. I trust the Dock Master, but that doesn't mean you can let your guard down. Any questions?'

'Who's in charge if a battle breaks out?' Ardan asked.

Marion looked pained. 'Riordan?'

'I'll command our troops—Talon, you command yours, but follow my lead?'

'Good, let us do this,' the forest warrior said, hand resting on one of his four belt hatchets.

'Anything else?' Marion asked. 'No? Alright, then let's go. I think we're still going to be late.'

Davan looked pained by their meandering, undisciplined group. As they got closer to the Docks, a sea breeze washed over them. Their party continued along the water's edge until Marion stopped outside a large warehouse. It was easily as large as the mansion, with six armed men standing at an entrance that was large enough to accommodate an entire wagon. One man waved them through, leading them inside.

There were crates, barrels and boxes stacked in even rows, creating a tiny city inside the warehouse. In the middle was a large empty area where over twenty men stood. They were silent as Marion's party approached. The man in the centre was tall and broad shouldered, with grey-streaked hair. Ardan remembered meeting the man with his father. His feet were bare and weathered as old rock. He wore a cutlass on his rope belt while the majority of the men around him were similarly armed. A man in brown looked shocked to see them, at least until Ardan realised he was missing his eyebrows. His clothes looked slightly singed at the edges and he carried a smouldering firebrand.

'That's Brody; he's a fire Shaper. I don't recognise anyone else,' Bree was whispering in Marion's ear.

As they got closer, he saw that there were people stationed amongst the crates who held crossbows and were aiming at their party.

'Marion, you old whore.'

Ardan felt a stab of outrage. He wasn't the only one, as Riordan's hand went to his sword while Bree raised her palm, the wind around her picking up.

'Crusty old sea crab,' Marion said back.

Quillen burst out laughing. The tension immediately eased. Their greeting had a ritual feel.

'Of all the people who have survived, I didn't expect you'd be one,' Quillen said.

'You too, old friend.'

'Enough blowing smoke up me arse. What's this meeting all about?'

'I understand, it's been an interesting time for us all. I recently had dinner with the Countess,' Marion paused as though hoping to see a reaction from the Dock Master, but he gave none. 'She wants the troubles to draw to a close.'

'She's finally pulling that spoon out to give a damn about us little folk?' Quillen said, spitting on the ground.

'It would be nice,' Marion said wryly. 'But not completely. She wants peace, something that could be beneficial for both of us. To return the city to normal after an agreement is reached.'

'You've been spending too much time with rich folk. You sound like 'em.'

'Peace good, war bad. That better?'

'Now we're talking. I want me harbour like it used to be.'

'Well,' Marion began, but just then one of the Dock Master's guards ran in.

'We're under attack!' he screamed as people burst into the warehouse behind him. He immediately fell with one of the intruders' axes in his back.

'Betrayal!' the Dock Master roared as he drew his cutlass.

'They're not mine,' Marion said. Then to her people: 'Join with the Dock Master's men. Prepare to fight.'

People were crashing through the door. They were wearing tattered rags, and only the odd person had anything resembling armour. Some carried swords or spears but most carried makeshift weapons, debris taken from fallen buildings. They poured in like a flood. They matched Marion's and Quillen's groups' size in less than a minute and it appeared it wouldn't take long for the party to be crushed under the weight of their ever-increasing numbers.

'Gather to me,' Riordan called. 'Those with a shield take the front. Crossbows, line up there and fire on my command. Fire mage,'—Riordan's barrage of orders had people pausing.

'Shaper,' Brody corrected.

'Get with the crossbowmen.'

They looked at the Dock Master, who bellowed, 'You heard him!'

The attackers' numbers continued to grow, and some of them advanced, though they looked apprehensively at the number of armed men in front of them.

'Crossbowmen take aim!' Riordan roared. The crossbows rose. 'Loose!'

Over forty men and woman charged towards them. Half a dozen crossbows twanged, and screams immediately followed as a few of the attackers went down from the quarrels. Their screams of pain were cut off, the victims trampled under the mob.

'Reload.' Riordan turned to Brody: 'Shaper, light them up.'

'Careful of the wood!' someone called.

'I know my business,' he said, and the torch he was holding suddenly flared as though someone had doused it in lamp oil. Ardan shied away from the heat as the fireball surged straight at the mob. It showered them with flame. The intense heat caused them to cower, with shouts of surprise and fear. Then the fire quickly dissipated. Little physical damage had been done, as the few rags or clothing that had caught were snuffed out, but it had stolen their momentum. The mob milled in confusion, some backing away while others pushed forward, but their numbers were continuing to grow.

'Loose!' Riordan ordered.

The bolts once again leapt forward, and another group of people went down screaming. This only increased the confusion.

Ardan saw movement out of the corner of his eye. He saw figures creeping among the crates. They wore the same rags but were armed with crossbows.

'Look out!' Ardan yelled. He saw them take aim at Marion, Koira, and Bree. He had his sword out and felt the familiar surge of the Wild. Without thinking, he channelled it, and his sword caught on fire, but he felt an odd tugging down another avenue. The need to protect fed the Wild within him and funnelled it down that second avenue. He could see the enemy crossbowmen taking aim. Without thinking, he funnelled the power through the connection and felt something inside him shift. He crouched and leapt, acting on instinct, and sailed through the air over what seemed like an impossible distance. At least a dozen bolts rained towards him, but their movements were bizarrely slow. Knowing where they were aimed, he tried to slice the bolts out of the air. His sword missed, and he felt two of the bolts hit him, penetrating his armour. One sunk deep into his shoulder, while the other glanced off his ribs. Both projected him back into Marion, knocking her over.

The barrage of bolts slammed down onto them. Some seemed to sprout out of Brody. He gurgled, the torch in his hand snuffing out, and he looked like an oversized pincushion. He fell to the ground. Ardan recognised the bald man amongst the crates. He was the one who had incited the riot that had ended in the massacre down Merchant Street.

'Fiddler,' Marion hissed.

'Bree, can you stop any more bolts from hitting us?' Riordan said.

'I can try.'

'Enough of this,' Davan said, raising his axe and charging.

'Wait!' Riordan yelled. 'Shit! Talon, go, go! Everyone with a shield stays here, the rest, help Talon!'

Davan's lone figure hit the centre of the mob. Ardan expected him to be cut down in moments, but his brother's first swing sent a shock wave through their lines. Four people were flung back into their comrades. Before they had any chance to recover, Davan was swinging again. Shouts of confusion and anguish raged through the mob as they shied away from the mercenary axeman.

Ardan's eyes scanned the crossbowmen amongst the crates. He could see clearly despite the darkness, though his mind felt clouded, and he had trouble counting. Mish came to stand protectively in front of him, her hackles raised as she hissed at the crossbowmen.

'I count fifteen,' Ardan said with some difficulty.

'Pick your targets. Alright then, lads, loose!' Riordan shouted. A small volley of bolts flew up at the surrounding crossbowmen. A couple of them fell screaming, but it didn't take long before they were returning fire. Bree shifted her hands furiously and air whipped up in front of them, blowing the bolts off course. Riordan stood in front, behind his heartwood shield. The other women were smashing crates, creating makeshift protections of their own.

The sound of smashing crates was drowned out by the melee as Talon and the others caught up to Davan. Ardan's brother was fighting like a hot knife through butter. His goal was obvious, as he cut and blasted his way to the entrance, effectively creating a bottle-neck in it. Talon broke off, with the rest of the forest warriors, his twin axes a blur as he led the clean-up crew in wiping out the two score enemies inside the warehouse.

Ardan tried to get up, but Koira was there, holding him down. She and the other women were holding up the smashed crates to act as improvised shields. Another wave of bolts descended on them. One woman went down, a bolt having penetrated her makeshift buckler and impaled her through the skull. Another man screamed as a bolt punctured through the wood and into his arm. Bree looked aghast that she had been unable to stop the bolts.

'Don't falter,' Riordan said. 'You're keeping us alive.'

Davan stood in the doorway. His axe kept any more reinforcements at bay while Talon led the rest of their fighters, cutting through the remnants of the assault. Their assailants weren't cut out to be fighters; they were only the poor and desperate.

The remaining crossbowmen had discarded their weapons after their last volley and were charging at them. They had swords and clubs. Ardan pushed Koira away and tried to rise. The remaining women took weapons from the fallen soldiers and stood beside Riordan. The mercenary's shield broke the enemy's charge, while the women fought on either side of him, using his bulk and armoured protection to strike out from behind in relative safety. They held them back long enough for the Dock Master's crossbowmen to turn the tide with a fresh shower of bolts.

The fighting was now clearly one-sided.

'Show yourself, Fiddler!' Marion called.

'Why?' came a crackling reply, echoing through the warehouse. 'I got what I wanted.'

As more of the Fiddler's men fell, Ardan yelled, 'Why aren't they giving up?'

'Surrender and you'll be spared,' Riordan called. The enemy faltered but didn't stop. Riordan roared with such ferocity that even Ardan was taken aback. 'Surrender, you dogs. We won't hurt you!'

What was left of the Fiddler's men backed away, throwing down their weapons.

'Find him,' Marion ordered.

Riordan took a few of the Dock Master's men and hunted through the warehouse.

While they were gone, Koira came to him, her brown eyes staring at the bolt sticking out of his shoulder.

He waved her off. 'I'm fine. Help the others that need saving.' He tried not to move his right arm. There was enough adrenaline running through him that he barely felt it, but he knew it would hurt like all the hells combined soon enough. He checked the other spot where the bolt had grazed over his ribs. That one stung. While he was looking at it, Mish came limping up to him on three legs. He examined her for injuries but couldn't seem to find any. She mewed in pain when he brushed his hand over her right shoulder.

Riordan and the other men returned shortly afterwards. 'He's gone. They smashed a hole in the wall. It's how they got behind us. We saw him running.'

'The Dock Master's dead,' Marion said.

It took a moment for Ardan to find Quillen's body. There were four bolts sticking out of him, and one had sliced his neck. There was a pool of dark blood staining the floor around him.

'The first volley,' Ardan said. 'They chose the leaders and the Shapers.'

The dead eyes of the Dock Master stared up at the ceiling.

'To the bowels of hell with that man,' Marion said. 'My plans have changed. I cannot let the Fiddler take control. He must be stopped.'

'If you promise to kill him, you'll have our support,' one of the Dock Master's men said.

'I'll find a way. For now, though, let us save whoever we can.'

Blood was spreading over the floor, a chorus of moans emanating from the wounded and dying.

PART III

CHAPTER FORTY-NINE: SOUL-MERGED

* * *

staroth has felled the Archangel Jophiel. Only Michael and Zadkiel remain to stand against us. If they fall, Darkness will consume this world.

— Titivillus, *Annals of Lucifer.*

* * *

ARDAN TRIED to keep his breathing slow and shallow, resting his hand against the wall. The bolt still stuck out of his shoulder, scraping and flaring with every breath he took, while Talon and Koira waited patiently for him. He'd wanted to go alone, but Koira had insisted on escorting him. He should have taken a litter. With a silent curse at his own pride, he pushed himself upright.

It was only another hundred feet. There were closer healers, but he wanted Eoin. The distance between the Docks and the Ancient Quarter hadn't seemed far. Yet here he was, sweat pouring off him as he struggled with each step. Mish limped after him. He resisted the urge to check her again for non-existent injuries.

'This is the place,' Ardan breathed, indicating the faded sign of Eoin's healing house. Koira knocked on the door. When there was no answer, she shot him a questioning look.

'It's fine, just head in.'

Tentatively, she pushed the door open and waited. Ardan entered first, making his way through the familiar room. No patients occupied the six neatly made cots. Eoin was asleep at his table with a jug of wine next to him on his otherwise meticulously clean work station. The herb jars lining the shelves above him were undisturbed.

'This is a plainsman herbalist?' Talon asked in a flat voice.

Ardan ignored him as he tried to wake Eoin. He shook gently at first and then with more vigour. Eventually, the man started awake.

'What in the hells?' Eoin said, his head snapping up as he looked around wildly. He took in the blood-stained shirt, the bolt sticking from his shoulder, and eventually Ardan's face. 'Oh, it's you.'

'I need healing and I need you sober,' Ardan said.

Eoin blinked a few times, his eyes coming into focus as he answered: 'Both are obvious, but I don't work without seeing money first.'

Talon growled, but they didn't pay him any heed.

Ardan placed some coins on the workbench. 'Coppers now, silver once the bolt is out of my shoulder.'

'Good enough; I'll need to sort myself out first,' he said, getting up. As he did so, he briefly took in Talon and Koira, assessing their foreign dress and weapons. His sobering process was starkly similar to Riordan's. He disappeared out back, and they could hear the splashing of water before he came back in, his hair dripping wet. He went to his workbench, pulling down several herbs, mixing them together and adding them to a cup, his motions methodical. When he was done, he gulped down his concoction. Koira watched the process curiously while Talon became less hostile.

'It'll be a few minutes before it kicks in. For now, let's see that wound you're bleeding from,' he said, pulling out a pair of scissors from his workbench. He made quick work of Ardan's shirt before properly examining the two wounds. While he was doing so, Ardan saw Koira's eyes running up and down his body. She realised she'd been caught, and she gave a shrug with a slight smile on her face.

Wounded as a stuck pig and she's admiring my body, Ardan thought with wonder.

'Not as bad as last time,' Eoin said, bringing his focus back.

'Painkillers?' Ardan asked.

'You'll need some more coin.'

Ardan grimaced and shook his head. Eoin shrugged, leading him to a stool, before retrieving an alcohol drenched cloth. The cloth stung like a lance of ice and fire. He clenched his fists so hard his nails were surely cutting into his own palms, as Eoin cleaned the blood from around the wound.

Mish hissed, falling onto her back, and furiously licked her ribs.

After the gash was clean, Eoin poured some alcohol over the bolt wound. Mish snarled, hopping back on three legs, her tail flashing like a whip. Talon's eyes flicked between Ardan and Mish, outrage and disbelief warring on his face.

'What?' Ardan said.

'It's nothing,' Koira said quickly.

'You know something about this?'

'Later,' she said forcefully.

Eoin braced the bolt sticking out of Ardan before taking out a small saw. Ardan clenched his jaw, ignoring the pain as the blade's tiny teeth cut the bolt to little more than a nub. Eoin then withdrew two odd-looking spoons. He rubbed them with alcohol before bringing them over and starting to work them into Ardan's wound. They slipped in and the pain spiked, but it was manageable.

Mish started licking her shoulder in response.

Eoin pushed, probed, prodded and wiggled the spoons closer to the bolt. Ardan grunted at the final flare of pain.

'Got it,' Eoin said. Then he slid the spoons out, grasping the tip of the bolt between them. Blood flowed from the wound, but Eoin was already pushing some clean cloth onto it. Ardan automatically took it from him and kept up the pressure.

'Remarkable,' Talon said. 'I have never seen such a tool.'

'I've got an old pair you can have,' Eoin said, picking up his needle and gut. He addressed Ardan as he was sewing him up. 'Keep it clean, and don't tear the stitches. So long as you avoid doing anything stupid, you should get full motion again.'

Ardan focused on his words, trying to block out the sting of the needle and the tugging of the gut. Eoin moved from his shoulder to the gash on his side, sticking him with more of the silver needle. Eoin had to wipe the sweat away from Ardan's wound several times before he could finish the stitches.

'Done. You'll want to avoid any motions that pull on it. You tear it, you'll be back here for me to sew it up again, and you'll be more coins short,' Eoin said, getting to his feet, still a little unsteady.

Talon gave a grunt of disapproval.

'What is it?' Eoin said.

'You should not drink when others are in your care.'

'Probably not,' Eoin agreed easily. He disappeared out the back before returning with two spoons. He held them out for Talon.

The warrior eyed them warily. 'How much?'

'Consider it a gift. To improve your judgemental disposition.'

'I will pay. I don't want to owe a drunkard any favours,' Talon said.

Eoin pushed them into the man's hands. His gaze held a steel that Ardan had never seen before. 'I drink to escape,' he said, and in that moment the man's careless mask cracked, showing a deep pain beneath. 'When you come across that one thing that breaks your spirit, I wonder how you will cope. Until then, kindly fuck off.'

Talon didn't answer as he took the spoons. Eoin gave Ardan a home spun shirt to wear and tied a sling for his shoulder.

'What happened to him?' Koira asked after they'd left.

'I don't know,' Ardan said. It was true; he didn't. The man never spoke about himself. He drank and he healed and Ardan hadn't pressed for more. Mish broke the silence by butting her head against him and stretching out, asking to be picked up. Ardan obliged, although not without some difficulty because of his wounds. Once she was nestled in the crook of his arm, they began walking again.

'What is happening between me and Mish?'

'No, it is not for you. Do not ask,' Talon said fiercely.

'Talon, hush. It has happened for a reason,' Koira said. 'Talon is one of my mother's most trusted men, and some of her... distrust for plainsmen has rubbed off on him. What is happening to you is what we thought was a lost art. I think you have soul-merged with Mish.'

'And that means what, exactly? She can feel what I feel?'

'That and more. Much more. Don't you find it strange that you could walk after being wounded as you have been? She has taken part of your pain and given part of her strength.'

'Are you sure it's not just because I'm incredibly tough and manly?'

Koira snorted. 'Sure, but I think it goes beyond that. My mother is one of the few people with the practical knowledge.'

'Your mother? Could she tell me more?'

'That would not be wise,' Koira said carefully. 'She distrusts plainsmen. Dangerously so.'

'Can you teach me?'

'She has taught you enough,' Talon growled.

'You forget yourself,' Koira said quietly.

'And you forget who you are,' Talon snapped back.

Koira stopped in the middle of the road, causing people behind them to move around their group. She glared at Talon. When she spoke, each word was cold and crisp. 'I have forgotten nothing. It is you who has forgotten. You have forgotten your oath and your responsibility. You blind yourself while trying to hold on to dying traditions.'

Talon stood a head taller than her, but he couldn't hold her gaze. He looked away, furious, as he muttered, 'My apologies, Mistress.'

'We will continue this in private.' Koira turned back to Ardan, and he saw her rage, the wildness of it. He hadn't seen it since she'd held the knife to the priest's throat.

Their journey back to the mansion was painfully slow. Neither Talon nor Koira made any attempt at conversation, and Ardan, still feeling weak from his injuries, focused on putting one foot in front of the other. The tension coming from them was enough to chill him.

They could hear the commotion from the mansion before they

saw it. Out front there was a hive of activity. Ardan didn't recognise half of the men and women crowding around the entrance. The resident ladies of the house created a human wall as they addressed the people surrounding them.

Riordan appeared from amongst the throng and immediately came over to them.

'Lady Koira,' Riordan said with a bow, 'Lady Marion requested you stay within the confines of the mansion for the next few days.'

'She did?'

'She wants nothing to damage future relations, and this is one of the safest places in the city.'

'Riordan, we are friends. Please speak plainly.'

Riordan smiled ruefully. 'The death of the Dock Master has changed everything. None of us expected it. Marion doesn't think you're in danger, but she would like you to be safe.'

Koira mused on that for a moment before she eventually inclined her head. 'I'll be guided by her, at least for now.'

'We appreciate it.'

'What do you need me to do?' Ardan asked after Koira, Talon and the rest of the forest warriors had disappeared inside the mansion.

'I don't think either of us expected you to be back already. You put your life on the line to save Marion. If not for you, we'd be bowing to the Fiddler—or dead. So take this time off. You need to rest and heal.'

'That's it?'

'If I'd been given the day to spend with Bree while sitting on my ass, I'd jump at it. If it's more fighting you're worried about, there will *always* be another battle.'

Ardan grunted.

'Marion wanted to see you, too. She's locked herself away in one of the back rooms.'

CHAPTER FIFTY: AUBURN HAIR
AND FAINT PERFUME

* * *

staroth has gone dark since her victory. My war with Michael holds me here, but my hound Naberius is cunning, intelligent and powerful. He will investigate as an extension of my will.
— Titivillus, *Annals of Lucifer.*

* * *

ARDAN never fully appreciated how big the mansion was until he couldn't find someone. *Who in the Light's name designed a house like this?* He'd thought it a simple, large house, but past the courtyard an extra floor was squeezed in, with a maze at the top and a labyrinth at the bottom. He ran into Aofie at a random corner of the place.

'What are you doing back here?' Aofie said. Behind her, rolls of cloth hung from the walls over a table with an impressive amount of sewing and knitting implements.

'Looking for Marion.'

'If it were anyone else...' she said. 'But I heard about what you did. Head downstairs, first left and the door at the end of the hall.'

Following her directions, Ardan found the open door. He knocked, but there was no answer. Glancing inside, he couldn't see anyone, so he entered. The room was littered with mismatched but comfortable-looking couches. The lone occupant was an elderly woman occupying one chair, knitting with some wool in her hands. She looked up, her face wrinkling into a frown.

'Another client? One of my girls will be with you shortly,' she said. The needles didn't stop as they moved.

'I'm, umm, looking for Marion.'

'What for?' The woman's eyes narrowed.

A moment later, Marion appeared. 'Ardan, what are you doing here?'

The woman's eyes widened in confusion. 'What are you doing in my room?'

'I was just straightening your bed.'

'Who are you?' the woman said, clutching her needles tightly. 'I warn you, I have guards ready to burst in here at any moment.'

'It's okay. Ardan, please wait outside,' Marion said as she knelt down in front of the older woman.

Ardan went outside to wait. After about ten minutes Marion reappeared, looking extremely worn. Ardan let her catch her breath and steady herself.

'She's getting worse,' Marion whispered.

'Who is she?'

Marion sighed heavily. 'My adopted mother—sort of. She was matron to at least half of the ladies, protecting us from the rougher customers, taking us in and giving us a safe place to eat and sleep. She...'

'Made you feel like family,' Ardan finished.

Marion smiled sadly. 'Exactly that. When we got to this place, we thought our lot in life was finally improving. Yet almost as soon as we'd moved in, she started losing her memory.'

'That can't be easy,' Ardan said, knowing how useless it sounded.

'Walk with me,' Marion said, her mask falling back into place.

Together, they walked through the halls.

'Who designed this place?' Ardan said after they'd gone up some stairs, across a hall, then down again.

'It has a unique design, but it's helped some girls escape a few of the more dangerous customers.'

'But you have so many guards.'

'That wasn't always the case, especially during the succession.'

Ardan had no answer for that. He looked about the place and considered how easily he'd gotten lost. He hoped intruders had been similarly baffled.

'You wanted to see me?'

'Yes, I wanted to confess something to you,' Marion said, pausing. She bowed her head, her slightly curled blond hair covering her face. 'If Riordan hadn't insisted, I wouldn't have taken you on. I thought you a firebrand, especially after the spat with your brother. I needed someone calm and experienced.'

'I'm sure there's a 'but' in here somewhere,' Ardan said.

'There is, after I finish talking about your lack of decorum,' she said, facing him with the ghost of a smile. 'You have proven far more valuable than I thought possible, and you also saved my life. I saw my death in those crossbow bolts, but you were there, saving me. For that, you have my thanks.'

Ardan didn't mention that Koira had been at the forefront of his mind when he leapt.

'Now I owe you two favours. If you ever need my help for anything, you will have it.'

'Anything?'

'Most things,' Marion conceded. 'Now rest up, heal and try to enjoy yourself. I'll make sure you're not bothered.'

Ardan felt his cheeks warm. He hadn't done it in the hopes of a reward.

'Here is one last thing,' Marion said. Ardan suddenly felt trepidation at her next words. 'Women, regardless of culture, like confidence. Be bold.'

'Umm—thanks?'

Marion waved him off as if it were nothing, leaving him lost in the centre of the mansion maze. *Be bold, I can do that,* Ardan thought, searching the mansion for Koira's rooms. After several dead ends, he found the open aired gardens. *The forest is easier to navigate.*

Outside of Koira's doors, he rapped his hand against the wood, suddenly wondering what he was doing. He put on his best jaunty smile, but the door swung open to reveal Talon. The man's face changed to naked hatred, but he stepped aside, letting him in.

Ardan unconsciously swallowed as he crossed the threshold. Koira didn't look any happier. *Maybe coming here now isn't the best idea.*

'Should I come back?'

'No, let us speak of the soul-merge. Maybe Talon will learn something,' Koira said, taking a seat and crossing her arms.

Before Talon could answer, Mish bolted forward, leaping for a couch. But she mistimed the jump and only hit the edge. Her claws dug into the cushions as she tried to scramble up, but she couldn't quite manage it.

Ardan snorted with laughter, but he was the only one. Koira smiled faintly, but her expression soon vanished. Ardan took the seat opposite her. 'She can feel what I feel?'

'And you her,' Koira said.

Mish lost her battle, landing on her back with an unceremonious thump. She then immediately sat up and started cleaning herself, as though it was what she had intended all along.

'I didn't feel that.'

'No, I don't think it works like that. Understand—it's been a long time since we've come across anyone who was soul-bonded. We weren't even sure it was possible anymore.'

'Who was the last one?'

Koira paused. 'It's not important.'

'Alright,' Ardan said, changing tack. 'So, what does it mean?'

Talon made a disgusted noise as he rested his hand on his axe.

'Ancients, save me from fools,' Koira said under her breath. 'You remember our conversation about how the Wild is a living thing?'

Ardan nodded.

'Your sword, the elements, these are all offshoots of the Wild. Its power is essentially limitless, provided you can direct it towards your goal.'

'Except for the backlash.'

'Exactly,' Koira said. 'The elements, the sword, these provide a buffer against the backlash. They allow you to use its power in a safer environment.'

'And Mish is different,' Ardan said.

'Mish is a living, breathing creature from the heart of the forest. To use the power through her would greatly increase its scope, while still keeping you safe from the recoil.'

'She's not going to catch on fire, is she?'

'This is not a joke,' Talon growled.

Ardan held up his hands in surrender.

Koira continued: 'Soul-merged, the power of the Wild is only limited by the two of you.'

'Could I control the air like Shapers do?' Ardan said, thinking of how useful Bree's ability was.

Koira mused on that. 'Yes and no.'

'Helpful,' Ardan said.

'Show some respect,' Talon snapped.

Ardan ignored him.

'The Shapers are a watered-down version of the Wild. They do not commune with the Wild directly; instead, they do it through the proxy of whichever element they draw upon. Like the metal, the elements are limited in what they can do. Everything that is unusual or powerful about the forest is fuelled by the Wild. It means that—'

'That's too much, he knows enough,' Talon interrupted her.

'Hold your tongue or get out and find another who can.'

'I will not allow you to tell the Children's secrets to this plainsman.'

'Aren't you in service to her?' Ardan interjected loudly. Then he saw Talon's face contort in rage. *Probably shouldn't have said that.*

Talon picked up one of the vases that decorated the table and threw it. Ardan tried to raise his arm to block it but remembered too late about the sling. The vase slammed into his forehead and shattered, the shards and flowers scattering over the floor. He stumbled back, dazed, not sure if he sat down or fell.

'I will teach you respect, even if I have to beat it into you.'

'Talon,' Koira said standing, 'You will stand trial in the vine court for this. Get out of my sight!'

'I won't leave you here alone with the plainsman,' he said.

'*Now*,' Koira said with absolute authority. Talon snarled something before turning on his heel and storming out. The door slammed behind him.

Koira knelt down next to Ardan.

'Here, let me have a look,' she said, touching his forehead. Her fingers were gentle as she inspected the injury. She went to the wash-basin and returned with a damp cloth, using it to gently clean away the blood. Despite the circumstances, he found her closeness warm and inviting. He met her eyes, getting lost in their soft depths. He noticed that, though brown, they were slightly green at the centre. Her touch felt warm and electric, and he glanced down at her lips.

There was a knock at the door as Talon's replacement arrived. Koira looked down and around, and her cheeks coloured slightly. She stood up as though they had been doing something they shouldn't have.

Mish was playing with the scattered flowers. She didn't seem perturbed by his head injury.

'I guess not everything is transferred.'

'I guess not,' she conceded. 'I think it will be like that with Mish. Without the guidance of her mother, she must still learn what she is capable of.'

'And I've got to do the same?'

Koira inclined her head with a gentle smile. She turned, moving to a window overlooking the Ancient Quarter. He got up, and as he did, he couldn't help but admire her figure. He came to stand next to her as they looked out over the city. This close, he could feel her warmth and smell her perfume of sage and sweetgrass.

'Plainsmen are not what I expected,' Koira said at last. 'I came here expecting to find a bunch of murdering savages.'

Ardan thought that that was rich coming from someone who had Talon as a bodyguard.

'Yet amongst them, there are surprises. Marion with her gentle rulership; Riordan and his warrior's mercy; a depth amongst plainsmen that has gone against all my expectations. Instead of disdain, I find I am the student, learning much.'

'Such as how amazing I am?'

'And how impressive your ego is.'

Ardan smiled, enjoying standing next to her at the window. The view of the city was beautiful, but all he could see was Koira. He took in the way her auburn hair shaped her face, the way her eyes twinkled as she stared up at him, and how her lips curved and came together.

His heart was pounding, having never felt such a pull. He leant down and her face turned upwards. Their lips met and a flash of heat sparked warmth through his entire body. He found his arms entangled around her as she leaned into him. The Wild was quiet as a still lake, not fuelling the passion this time. He was so lost in the moment; he didn't know how long they were locked together. But then there was an uncomfortable cough from the door.

One of Koira's guards, Ardan didn't know his name, was watching them with narrowed eyes.

Ardan could still feel her hand on his chest, the warmth of her lips on his, as she whispered to him. 'Come back tomorrow.'

He ignored the guard's glare as he left, his heart too light to care.

The rest of the day was a blur, his injuries forgotten. By the time he found his bed, his mind was full of auburn hair and the faint smell of perfume.

CHAPTER FIFTY-ONE: THE UNTAMED SHADOW

* * *

*N*aberius *believes Astaroth has harnessed the power of the Ancients. The initial elation I felt has quickly been replaced by apprehension. Why has she not informed me herself?*
— Titivillus, *Annals of Lucifer.*

* * *

The hatred Ardan felt for Riordan was intense. He'd said it was for his own good. Easy for him when he wasn't there, stretching every injured joint in his body, sweat pouring off him while he grunted through the pain. Every morning Ardan was amazed at how stiff his body had become, and each morning Riordan was there, insisting he limber up with an encouraging but evil smile. He swore the man was enjoying it.

Ardan almost collapsed with relief when Riordan said enough. He leaned against the stone pillars of the inner courtyard. It had been almost a week since the battle at the warehouse; every day when Riordan had gone out, Ardan had tried to join him.

'We're not desperate, and the fighting hasn't been bloody.'

The man forced him to stay inside as the summer days became longer. In the background, he could see Regan smirking.

Ardan resisted the urge to sit down, knowing it would encourage Riordan to start the next stage. He drew in a breath and took a sip of water. He wiped the sweat off his forehead and eyed his sword with trepidation. Using his left hand was worse than learning to fight all over again. He knew the techniques, but his left arm never moved correctly. He felt clumsy and stupid. It was why he didn't chase after Riordan. He knew he'd be a liability.

He ran his hands along his shoulder, flexing it and rotating his arm as much as he could.

'This power of yours,' Riordan said with a shake of his head. 'You shouldn't be able to do half these movements yet, but the wound looks like it's almost a month along, not a handful of days.'

Mish issued a loud meow from her resting spot. She was watching Koira descending the stairs. The forest woman gave the feline a quick scratch behind the ears, flashing a smile at Ardan.

'I wish to visit the Dark Temple today,' Koira announced.

'The streets are still a little wild,' Riordan said quickly.

'I am aware, but my task can no longer wait. The forest was attacked last night.'

'I'll have to run it by Marion,' Riordan said.

'Tell her, if you wish. I will leave in an hour.' Koira headed for the dining room.

If she's going, I'm going, Ardan thought as he ducked out, going to his rooms. He struggled to get his new armour on, the injuries making it difficult. By the time he was ready, he found Koira, surrounded by her warriors, speaking with Marion at the entrance.

'I appreciate your concern,' Koira said, holding up her hand. 'But I am your guest, and not your subordinate nor prisoner. Unless you wish to keep me here by force?'

A few of the forest warriors grinned, including Talon. Ardan wondered how the man made a smile look so terrifying.

Marion opened her mouth but hesitated, closing her eyes. She nodded. 'You are right, of course. I apologise. Please allow me to send some of my men with you to supplement your escort.'

Koira waved her hand. 'The Children here will be formidable enough.'

'Ardan can still act as your guide,' Marion said.

Trying to save face, Ardan thought.

'I have already secured passage. One of their priests, this Esalon, is expecting me.'

'Ardan has family there, it might help,' Marion said.

Koira glanced at Ardan, her eyes assessing him. He felt thoroughly undressed by the scrutiny. 'Are you able?'

'I am.'

Koira didn't look convinced. 'It's on you, then,' she said, gesturing for him to lead the way.

They left the mansion, filing out into the bright midmorning sun. The forest warriors with them spread out, causing many on the streets to find business elsewhere, while their retinue moved through the Ancient Quarter. They took the Merchant Road. It was much less stressful when they weren't being chased by a violent mob.

Ardan could sense Mish following along on the nearby rooftops. He was still trying to figure out their soul bond as the lynx made an impressive leap from one building over to the next. They turned down the fork towards the heart of the Dark Quarter.

'Ancients, that thing is intimidating,' Koira said.

The black pyramid rose up, towering above the buildings around it, its staircase wide and steep. It was a fortress, though wildly impractical.

As they got closer, one Black Guard charged up the stairs, moving quickly despite his bulky armour. The remaining soldiers moved into a line, hands on their uniform broadswords, ready to receive the forest warriors.

The forest warriors spread out in response.

The space between the two groups quickly emptied, the people gathering around them to watch the confrontation.

'We're here to talk. Stop thinking with your axes,' Koira said, exasperated.

Talon flicked with his hand and the warriors' posture eased, as though their hackles were lowering.

The Black Guards didn't move.

'State your business,' one guard said, his voice echoing oddly inside the helm.

'We wish to speak to one of your order. Priest Esalon is expecting us.'

The Black Guard tilted his helmet, looking at the group of warriors. 'A lot of men-at-arms for a planned meeting.'

Koira lifted her chin, her brown eyes going hard. 'Is that reason enough to keep me from my meeting with your priest?'

The guard eyed them through closed visor, taking his time before answering. 'Very well, you may proceed up, but only one may go with you.'

'Only one?'

'I am here to visit my sister,' Ardan said, interrupting. 'Is Liá inside?'

The Black Guard turned to him. It was difficult to read the man behind the visor. 'Is Liá really your sister?' his voice had a nasal quality.

'She is.'

'I like her. She's always nice to me,' he said. 'You can head up too.'

'Thanks. Good enough?' he said to Koira.

She nodded, walking up the stairs with Talon.

Ardan looked at Mish, perched on the nearby rooftop. 'You coming?'

The cat's tail swished in response, but she remained on the roof. Shrugging, Ardan followed the others up the stairs, but stopped half-way. The heavier his breathing became, the more the cut on his ribs hurt. He continued up to the top, where eight Black Guards stood near the entrance. Koira and Talon were near the murals that could double as battlements around the edge of the platform.

Ardan looked out, seeing the rise and fall of the city's hills. He observed the smaller figures moving through the different parts of the city, while the colour of the roofs varied from quarter to quarter, blending like a mosaic painting.

'My brave pup. You are still alive.'

Ardan turned to see Esalon standing at the entrance of the Temple. His dark robes were starkly black against the bright day.

Talon straightened, looking like a sword being unsheathed.

'Been lucky,' Ardan said. As the priest got closer, he realised they were the same height. He looked Esalon directly into his almost black eyes.

'You've grown.' Esalon's mouth quirked. 'Are you here to accept my offer? Do you want to become my apprentice?'

There was a sudden shock to Ardan's system. He'd forgotten about that. It had been a plea of desperation. He was in a good place now, but his injured shoulder reminded him how easily he could lose his usefulness. Should he join and try to improve his lot? He glanced at Koira.

'Not today. Today I am acting as a guide.'

Esalon raised an eyebrow in response. Then he looked over at Koira and Talon.

'Children of the Ancients,' Esalon said, his voice deep and penetrating. 'Welcome to the Temple of Lucifer. I am Esalon, second priest to Guillamere. I am at your service.' He finished with a slight bow of his head.

'I am Koira, daughter of the Queen of Autumn Leaves.'

Ardan rocked backwards. Koira was a princess? He'd known she was important, but a princess? Later, when he had time to think about it, he realised it made sense, but he always thought princesses wore puffy dresses and waited in towers, trapped there by demons. He hadn't expected the first one he'd met to throw a punch at him. He shook his head, turning back to the conversation.

'I came here today to meet you and explore the possibility of trade between our people,' Koira began.

'What can you offer us?'

Koira glanced at Ardan, eyebrows raised.

'I understand that the Children prefer direct speech,' Esalon continued clasping his hands together. 'We are here for the essence of what you offer, not the niceties.'

'That is refreshing,' Koira said.

'And a trap,' Ardan said.

Esalon glanced at him with a half-smile. 'Oh?'

'Be careful of your wording when you make a deal, the Priesthood is very crafty with their wording,' Ardan said. His hand didn't go for his sword, but he did watch the priest with wary eyes.

Esalon chuckled, 'The pup is right, but if you wish to make a deal then we must circle back to what you can offer us and more importantly, what are you after?'

Koira smiled, dipping her head. 'There are certain things we cannot make for ourselves and materials you can get nowhere else.'

'We are never closed to new deals,' Esalon said, clasping his hands together. 'It would depend on what you need and what you can provide us?'

'If you prefer directness, then I would prefer that you not act as a simpleton. You know very well what we can provide,' Koira said.

Tension filled the air as the Black Guards shifted, ready to move, while Talon shifted his weight. Ardan hoped it didn't come to blows. He'd be next to useless against the guards.

The corners of Esalon's mouth twitched. 'Very well. I was trying to figure out what you'd part with.'

'You're talking about Ancient steel and heartwood,' Koira said. 'Those would demand an exorbitant price.'

'Yet could you find other interested parties?'

'Those of the Merchant Guild and this Bishop Frederick were quite interested,' Koira said easily.

Esalon gave a broad smile. 'I think I will enjoy bargaining with you very much.'

'Ardan!' a voice rang out behind them.

Liá ran towards him in her grey robe. She crashed into him, immediately enveloping him in a hug. With the sudden onrush, Ardan barely kept his feet, wincing from the pain in his shoulder and ribs.

'You shouldn't be here, young one. Where is Orla?' Esalon said.

'Guillamere sent her out,'—Liá said and paused, glancing at those around her, and changed her words—'on duties.'

'Can you handle the consequences of being outside without her protection?' Esalon said.

Liá looked defiant as she nodded.

'Very well,' he said, returning his attention to Koira.

Liá led Ardan over to the end of the platform.

'I got your note,' Ardan said as they stood facing a gruesome mural depicting Naberius breathing fire down on a group of soldiers.

'Did you find her?' Liá asked, a tremor in her voice.

'She's alive,' Ardan said. His sister's face lit with hope as she pulled him into another hug. He held her, trying to pat her arm while ignoring his injuries. 'She's been a kind of prisoner of the Countess.'

When Liá pulled away, she left tear stains on his leather armour. 'She's ... what?'

Ardan relayed the story and Liá was an attentive audience, not interrupting until he was finished.

'She'd like you to visit when you can.'

'I want to, but I can't, not right now.' She looked around furtively, but whether she was looking at the guards, Esalon, or the Temple itself, Ardan couldn't tell. She focused back on Ardan. 'Is that true that you took a crossbow bolt to save Marion?'

'Sort of,' Ardan said, thinking about Koira.

'Does it hurt?'

'It's not pleasant.'

'I've been hugging you while you're wounded again, haven't I?' she asked, looking stricken.

Ardan rotated his right arm, trying to hide the pain. 'It's fine.'

'I can make it easier if you're willing?' Liá asked. Before he could answer, she hovered one hand over his shoulder while the other went to the symbol of Lucifer hanging around her neck. She focused for a moment and when she opened her eyes, he almost recoiled. Her eyes had gone completely black. Shadows gathered despite the sunlight and encased his shoulder. They came faster and stronger, ignoring the light, sinking through his clothing, as they formed a second skin around his arm. It was over in seconds, her eyes returning to normal.

Ardan kept his right arm completely still, pulling on his leather armour so he could look at his arm. It was now encased in cold, oily Darkness. 'What have you done?'

'Try moving it,' Liá said.

He tentatively moved his arm and he no longer felt pain as the muscles moved, only a slight twinge.

'Try to keep it out of light as it dissipates faster that way.'

'What exactly is this?'

'It encases your arm, lets you use it like normal.'

'It feels like—like cold liquid steel,' Ardan said at last. 'Does it heal faster?'

'Indirectly, yes, but it lets you keep motion and full function. At least it should. I am still learning how to control the Darkness.'

'You can do this to any injury?' Ardan said.

'Just about,' Liá said.

'How long does it last?'

'This one,' Liá mused, 'A few hours, maybe a couple of days. Longer if kept out of sunlight. The High Priest can make one last a lot longer, months, maybe even a full year.'

Ardan whistled. 'That's a big difference.'

She shrugged. 'He's the High Priest of Lucifer. He learnt his powers in the northern kingdoms and was one of the few survivors of the Dog War.'

Ardan started flexing his arm again. It felt great. *What will happen when I turn up to training tomorrow with this?* he wondered. He reached for his sword, wondering how the casing would deal with the extra weight, but as soon as he touched the hilt, he felt a surge of the Wild. The familiar power filled him, but try as he might, he couldn't make it flow to the sword. Instead, the stream went straight to the black-encased arm. Bits of darkness flaked off, floating up and disappearing.

Liá frowned.

'That's odd,' Liá said, reaching out, but just as her hands were about to touch it, green fire burst through, consuming the Darkness and making a hole in his clothing and armour.

Ardan wasn't sure what to do. His shoulder felt like it had been doused with a bucket of ice-cold water. He looked at Liá, but her eyes were wide, fear etched on her face.

Despite the light of the sun, shadows had coalesced around her like flotsam. They swirled like a tornado, multiplying as they went.

'What's happening? Liá? Liá!' Ardan said.

CHAPTER FIFTY-TWO: THE SOURCE

* * *

staroth has executed my envoys. At least I now know where she stands. My war with Michael traps me here, so I must send Naberius in my stead and trust he will rein Astaroth in.

— Titivillus, *Annals of Lucifer.*

* * *

THE SHADOWS COALESCED and dove towards Liá. Some struck her like physical blows, while others penetrated her skin, disappearing from sight. She screamed, crumpling to the ground and cowering, while the Darkness swooped like a flock of ravens.

Ardan ran forward but the shadows rebuffed him, sending him sprawling back. He heard the rasp of steel and Talon's unmistakable growl.

'Stop that, all of you,' Esalon commanded, his voice cracking like a whip.

It took a moment for Ardan to regain control. He was back on his feet, but Esalon was there, inside the vortex of shadows, kneeling by

Liá's side. She was writhing, curled into a ball as the Darkness continued to strike at her.

'Focus. You are better than this. You can control it,' Esalon said.

Deep within Liá's frantic movements and spasms, her dark eyes locked onto his. The surrounding shadows slowed, as though they were wading through thick mud. Then they stopped, suspended in mid-flight.

'Good, now take them as your own or disperse them,' Esalon said in a measured voice.

Liá lay there, her body straining. The surrounding shadows inched forward as beads of sweat appeared on her forehead. Her whole body shook as the coalescing shadows moved swiftly. She gasped as though surfacing for air.

'You need to help yourself. If you do not, you will die.'

The Wild inside of Ardan responded, rising like a torrent. For the first time, his emotions mirrored that of the Wild, and he drew his sword. He let the Wild flow into the weapon, green flame erupting along its edge. The shadows darted around the flame as he swung it forward, bringing the tip to Esalon's neck.

'If she dies, you die.'

Esalon scrambled back, but Ardan kept the blade close, knowing the heat of the flame would be painful in such proximity. The shadows kept coming as Liá's eyes lost focus, panic creeping in. The assault resumed, shadows diving and smashing into her as though they were stones.

'Help her,' Ardan said, bringing the sword closer, the green glow giving Esalon an eerie cast.

'What is happening here?' Orla said, coming up from the stairs of the Temple. She took one look at the Black Guards, their swords drawn, and Koira, Talon and Ardan. Then her eyes flung towards Liá and recognition flooded them.

She rushed forward, the shadows parting around her as she slid in front of Liá. One hand flew to the top of her robe, pulling out her necklace and the silver emblem of Lucifer. She clutched it hard, while her other hand took Liá's and grasped it tight. The Darkness that surrounded them dissipated, the shadows vanishing. Light drenched the area as though reappearing from behind a cloud.

Then Ardan could see it. Darkness, thick, oily and black, was flowing up out of Liá and into the emblem in Orla's hand. They all watched in mute fascination while the process went on. Esalon watched Orla, his expression unreadable.

Liá's laboured breathing became easier, her body sagging as the tension left her. The transition continued, but the flow eased until at last it dried up entirely.

Orla stood, her feet a little unsteady as she did so, sweat dampening the edges of her red hair. She glared at Esalon. 'You would just have let her die?'

Ardan took a step back, standing there, his weapon at Esalon's throat. He ignored it, looked at Orla. 'The choice and consequences were hers.'

'You could have helped her,' Orla said. The power in her eyes was blazing. 'I'm half tempted to order the Black Guards off, let her brother kill you.'

'You will not,' a powerful voice said. Ardan hadn't noticed the other newcomers. The man who spoke wore the traditional black robes. His hood was down, while his salt and pepper hair had been tied into five braids. He carried a staff with a small horned skull adorning the tip. 'Until I hear an explanation for what happened.'

'A minor disagreement, High Priest,' Esalon said.

The encounter had suddenly left Ardan feeling drained. The Wild inside of him had changed, as though recognising another predator. It had gone still, waiting for the other power to initiate first. He stepped back but kept the green flame alive.

'Shadows were threatening to overwhelm the initiate. He could have helped,' Orla said to Guillamere. She spun to Esalon. 'Why didn't you help her?'

'You will answer,' the High Priest said.

'We need strong priests and priestesses who can stand on their own without coddling. I warned her of the danger of coming out here, but her pride made her stay. It was an important lesson.'

Orla looked ready to lunge at Esalon, but Liá reached out a shaky hand, restraining her mentor. 'I can see why you are no longer welcome in the north,' Orla said scathingly.

Esalon's mouth thinned.

'Enough,' the High Priest said. His statement produced a profound silence and Ardan wondered if the man could lace his voice with power like Frederick or if it was natural. 'Orla, see to your apprentice. She is still exposed out here.'

'You, and you,' Orla said, pointing at two Black Guards. 'Take her to my quarters.'

The men stepped forward, lifting Liá to her feet and walking either side of her as they escorted her inside, with Orla a step behind.

'It doesn't explain why someone is wielding the fire of the Ancients on my Temple.'

All eyes turned towards Ardan. Tumultuous emotions were running rampant through him, being fed by the Wild. 'I think that is pretty obvious.'

The High Priest raised an eyebrow, then his eyes shifted to Esalon for an explanation.

'Liá is his sister.'

'Ah,' Guillamere said. 'And the Children of the Ancients?'

'Came here on a diplomatic mission.'

Ardan had almost forgotten about Koira and Talon. The forest warrior clutched both axes, his eyes constantly assessing the Black Guards and priests. Koira stood behind him, her face ashen.

'They were at the warehouse,' a new voice said. The speaker was medium height, with a clean-shaven head and beady dark eyes.

'Fiddler,' Ardan hissed.

The man smiled. 'Me.'

'He is the one responsible for the ambush?' Koira asked.

Ardan advanced on the Fiddler, ignoring the number of guards, feeling rage at all the deaths this man had caused.

'You were at the warehouse? Oh, my fierce pup, you have come a long way,' Esalon said, his eyes dancing with amusement. 'Before you attack him, know he is under our protection. If by Lucifer's luck you survive us, you'll have to contend with his men at the base of the Temple.'

Ardan hesitated, slowly gaining control over the Wild's need for vengeance.

'You are in allegiance with this man?' Koira demanded.

Esalon shrugged. 'We are open to bargains with anyone who can pay our prices.'

'I am also open to some negotiations,' the Fiddler said. 'I can provide many things for you,' he continued with a lecherous stare.

'If I thought your manhood could keep up, I might consider it,' Koira said.

Esalon barked a laugh, while Guillamere smiled.

'I'd be careful if I were you. The Prostitute's protection won't last forever,' the Fiddler said. 'Then we will see how amenable you are.'

Talon advanced, growling.

The Black Guards stepped forward, their armour clanking in unison, but Talon didn't back down. He held his two axes and looked ready to lunge forward, to take on the heavily armoured warriors. It was Koira who stepped up, putting her hand on his arm. He glanced back at her, his axes lowering.

'I think our negotiations are finished,' Koira said.

Esalon gave her a wry smile. 'They will remain open on our side. I think we could find something beneficial if you change your mind.'

'You're just letting her *go*?' the Fiddler practically screamed.

'Of course,' Esalon said. 'They came in peace, and they can leave as such.'

'What if I demanded you take them?'

Guillamere laughed, but Esalon answered: 'Despite our relationship, we know you could not match the price of that request. The Children offer things you cannot. They came in peace and unless they break it, they will leave the same way.'

The Fiddler looked outraged while Koira walked past, ignoring him. She reached the edge of the stairs, where two Black Guards blocked her. At a signal from Esalon, they parted. Ardan followed her and Talon, but he could feel the hairs on the back of his neck tingle, knowing the eyes of Esalon and Guillamere were on him.

A crowd of ragged people were waiting at the bottom. Just like those who had been at the warehouse, they were half starved, grubby, with barely a decent weapon amongst them.

The forest warriors drew their weapons, and it was enough to send half of them scattering. Some called for the Fiddler, but he didn't show himself. Instead, they were forced out of the way as the forest warriors carved a path. Ardan still felt a weight on him after they were through the throng of people. It was only once they were out of the Temple's shadow that he felt it lift. He was about to question Koira about it, but the woman was walking quickly towards the Ancient Quarter.

'What's the hurry?'

She glanced at him sideways but didn't slow down. 'Maybe your powers haven't progressed as far as I thought.'

A bit taken aback, Ardan caught up to her. 'Meaning?'

'Did you not feel it?'

'I have no flaming idea what you're talking about.'

'The power attacking my home is coming from that place. From one of those people.'

'Who?'

'I don't know, but the source was on that platform. I felt it once you wielded the fire of the Ancients.'

Thoughts jumbled in his head. Who had been up there? It could have been any of the priests or priestesses, or maybe a Black Guard, or the Fiddler. The only one he was sure it wasn't was his sister. They continued in silence all the way back to Marion's mansion.

Koira marched in, finding Marion sitting in the open aired garden. Riordan was lounging nearby with several guards.

'No, bring Delaney and his kids here until this blows over. You know how much the Fiddler hates him,' Marion was saying. She saw them coming and smiled despite how tired she looked. 'What is it?' Marion asked, her smiled fading.

'I found what I was looking for. The power is coming from the Temple, I could feel its residue,' Koira said, her voice stiff.

She could feel its residue? How the Hell does she know the difference?

Everyone went quiet. Koira was standing there, her eyes unfocused, as she clenched and unclenched her fists.

'Who is it?' Marion asked quietly.

'Could be one of many, but I will stop them.'

They waited for her to expand on that, but her eyes were unfocused again. Marion was the one who asked. 'How?'

'Kill all who are involved,' Talon said.

'That is not funny,' Marion said.

'It is not a joke,' Koira said. 'I will gather the armies of the Children, march on the Temple and raze it to the ground.'

CHAPTER FIFTY-THREE:
LOOMING SHADOW

* * *

I have been so focused on Astaroth that I've underestimated Zadkiel's Templars. They have shattered my eastern armies and half my Temples lie in ruin, all because of my arrogance.
— Titivillus, *Annals of Lucifer.*

* * *

SILENCE FILLED the garden at Koira's pronouncement. All conversation ceased, every eye turning to Marion. Ardan was holding his breath, waiting for her reaction, and from the surrounding stillness he didn't think he was the only one.

Marion's expression never changed. 'That is certainly one option.'

'You have been a gracious host. Make whatever preparations you need to,' Koira said, then turned to her warriors. 'Talon, gather everyone. We leave today.'

Talon nodded, turned to a few of the warriors and immediately began giving directions. The other warriors dashed off. He stayed, his hands resting on the axes in his belt.

'What you're proposing will cause the death of thousands,' Ardan said.

'My inaction will result in more.'

'There have to be other options,' Ardan said, but Koira ignored him, so he changed tact. 'Explain it to me, please.'

Koira paused, her face softening. 'The attacks are becoming more frequent. You have felt it, yes?'

Ardan had only been using the Wild consciously for a couple of weeks, but even he'd noticed the Wild becoming more feral. He nodded.

Koira pursed her lips and looked away for a moment. 'If the attacks are not stopped, I can see only two outcomes: either they succeed, subjugating the power of the forest and becoming unassailably powerful—'

'Can they actually do that?' Ardan whispered.

She nodded, and he felt horror creep into him.

'Lad, what does it mean?' Riordan said, looking alarmed.

Ardan looked at Koira, who didn't answer. 'I can only guess. The ancient fire we used against your shield, it's only a drop of water in the deep well of the forest. If someone could use all that power....'

'They could destroy Barleron?' Riordan asked.

'Without breaking a sweat,' Ardan said.

The garden grew so quiet you could have heard a leaf fall. Riordan looked horrified, his hand going for his weapon out of reflex. It was Marion who broke the silence. 'What happens if they can't subjugate the forest, what's the second outcome?'

Koira grimaced. 'The attacks would continue and the Wild will defend itself. It broke the world the last time it was unleashed. Our records spoke of skies filled with smoke and ash, rivers of fire and ground-shakes so fierce that buildings and trees fell to its strength.'

'Surely it's possible that neither of these things will happen,' Marion said.

'We cannot take that chance. The attacks must be stopped.'

Marion leaned back, folding her arms. 'The city will fight you if you do this. The mercenaries, church soldiers, the Merchant Guard, the priests of the Light and Dark, and the Shapers will all band together to stop you.'

Koira held Marion's eye for a long time before answering. 'I may have misjudged you. Are you too cowardly to do what is right?'

Marion's eyes narrowed and the air chilled. 'I would weigh your next words very carefully.'

It looked as though both women were personifying the Wild. For one reckless moment, Ardan wondered if the two might explode. *Focus, you idiot*, Ardan thought and racked his brain, trying to figure out how to defuse the situation. Riordan was struggling with the same problem. It was Mish who came to their rescue. She pranced into the courtyard, oblivious to the hostility in the air, and meowed loudly. A second later, she looked around at everyone and meowed again.

Through the bond, Ardan felt her confusion that her meowing hadn't resulted in any kind of attention.

He laughed. Everyone looked at him, then the cat, and some of them smiled.

There was a tightness to Koira's smile. 'You have only weeks to come up with an alternative.'

'Thank you,' Marion said.

Koira smiled grimly. 'It will take that long for our armies to assemble.'

The relief on Marion's face froze. She looked at Koira, then over her shoulder at Talon and the one other remaining forest warrior. 'And if I were to stop you from leaving?'

Talon's hand immediately went to his axes. Riordan leaned back, his hand twitching, ready to draw his own weapon.

'I have already sent runners, so the outcome would not change,' Koira said simply. The tension between them was growing again. 'For what it is worth, I wish it had not come to this.'

Marion said nothing, looking hopelessly at Koira. The forest woman's face was impassive as she left the room, her forest guard close behind. Once they left the room, Marion whispered, 'Me too.'

Nope, there's got to be something I can do, Ardan thought. He was wracking his brain. Maybe he could make her see reason—maybe.

'Where are you going?' Riordan said.

'To find another solution.'

He arrived at Koira's quarters to find them closed. The door looked like an unassailable wooden barrier. What was he going to say? He knew he needed to find a middle ground. He took a deep breath and knocked. The door opened to reveal Talon.

'The lady has requested a break from all visitors,' Talon said. When Ardan went to protest, he reiterated, '*All* visitors.'

'Surely,' Ardan tried, but Talon moved so swiftly, Ardan barely registered the man's open hand. The slap felt like a thunderclap. He stumbled, his ears ringing.

'Don't press your luck, boy.'

Still reeling, Ardan put his hand against the wall. It took him a moment to find his balance. Talon smirked as though daring him to try something, his hand twitching towards his axe.

The Wild was an almost open volcano inside of him. It welled up in response to his anger. He unconsciously reached towards his sword, but Talon was fast, locking his sword arm with one hand while the other moved to strike. Without contact with his sword, he internally fumbled to send the power into his connection with Mish, but the slap had made him sluggish. The Wild welled up and burst forth, exploding around them.

Ardan was flung back across the balcony, his back slamming hard into the banister. The railing stopped him from being thrown down into the courtyard as pain shot through his body. He fell to the ground, winded and gasping, unable to find his breath. The door had splintered inwards, while Talon was a dozen feet into the room. The forest warrior sprang to his feet, axe in hand and murder in his eyes.

'Talon,' Koira yelled.

Talon kept advancing. Ardan tried to get up, but his body was still too winded to respond. He could only watch as the man came forward, his eyes alight, like a lynx stalking its prey.

'Talon of the twin trees, you will stop,' Koira said, that distinct tone of command lacing her voice.

He never took his eyes off Ardan as he pointed with his axe. 'He attacked me.'

'We are guests here. Let us not make things worse.'

Thankfully, the axe lowered as he looked back at her, straightening up. 'So I should just accept someone attacking me?'

'He is the one on the floor, unable to defend himself. Are you attacking defenceless people now? Have you fallen that far?'

Talon glared for a moment longer before replacing his axes. A few people looked out to see what was happening, but after one look at Talon, they retreated.

'Go and wait outside. I'll be out shortly.'

Talon looked between Koira and Ardan, snarled something in their native tongue, and stalked out. After Talon had left, Koira came to stand before Ardan. 'Did you attack him?' she asked evenly.

Ardan coughed. He could do little more than shake his head. *I imagined this going differently than being sprawled on the floor battling to breathe.*

'I—came—to—talk.' He paid for the words in sharp stabs of pain as he slowly regained control of his breathing.

Her face softened, and then her brow furrowed. 'How did that lead to *this*?'

He gulped down some air before answering in a rush, 'He tried to... turn me... away. We argued.'

'And the Wild got the better of you,' Koira finished for him. 'Come inside, you big fool.'

Ardan got shakily to his feet and followed her inside. She went to her dresser, where she was filling her pack. She looked at the long dress she'd worn to the Countess' dinner, her hand clutching at the fabric for a moment before she let it fall.

'I wanted to find a compromise.'

'I will stop the attacks.'

'And I don't want the people of Barleron caught in the crossfire. They've suffered enough. If you march, it will cause the deaths of half the city. There has to be another way.'

'I know you want to protect your people, and that is admirable. I will do what I can to spare them.'

Ardan groped desperately for an argument. 'How many of your people will die?'

'Everyone who is needed to protect the Trees.'

'What if you're up against Naberius? Can your armies stop him? Can you even get past us? Marion is right. We will band together to stop invaders, you included.'

That, more than anything, gave Koira pause. She looked up, her eyes searching his. She went to the window that overlooked the Ancient Quarter.

'Out there I see what you plainsmen have accomplished. There is hope in your future, whereas ours, ours has been dwindling. Nothing will destroy our hope more than this threat.'

'Then let us work together. I will get the forces of the city together to fight against it. Once they know, I doubt anyone wouldn't be ready to stop what the Dark is doing.'

She turned to him, her auburn hair accentuating her face while her brown eyes searched his. He noticed again the way her lips came together. 'I never expected to find someone like you, someone who is often rash, quick to anger, and foolhardy but also wise and gentle in other moments. I never expected to have feelings for any plainsman.'

Before he knew what he was doing, he reached for her, and they were kissing again. It was hot, passionate and disappointingly brief. She pushed him away.

'But regardless of how I feel, I cannot let it impede the needs of my people. I will return with our armies, and we will defeat any who threaten our home.'

CHAPTER FIFTY-FOUR: THE SHOCK WOLF

* * *

I have sent agents to the heart of Zadkiel's power, where they will spread the word about Astaroth's rising strength. I do not know if they speak falsehoods, or if in truth Astaroth's power has grown, but regardless, I have achieved my desired outcome. Zadkiel has recalled his Templars.
— Titivillus, *Annals of Lucifer.*

* * *

ARDAN LEANED against a barrel in Mercenary Square. He knew he needed practice with his left hand, and Seamus was the best person to guide him. As he waited, he saw Riordan coming towards him with Regan in tow. The lanky man grimaced when he saw Ardan but said nothing.

'This business with the Children has been bad,' Riordan said.

Ardan murmured noncommittally, but when Riordan didn't respond, he looked up to see the man's blue eyes boring into him.

'If it comes down to it, can we count on you?' Riordan said.

'What?'

'If we stand across the killing fields from the Children of the Ancients, can we count on you?'

The thought struck him. He felt offended; anger at the choice, anger at the lack of trust. He hoped it would never come to actual blows, but if it did... 'I will fight,' Ardan said at last.

'I know, lad, but I wanted you to know it too.'

'But what about the Temple and the threat?' Ardan asked.

'We're not taking that lying down, either. Marion's in talks and we're coming up with a plan to attack the Temple if we need to. For now, though, we need more fighters,' Riordan said gravely. 'Speaking of—go to Seamus. He knows what's coming and will prepare you for it.'

'Wait, where are you going?' Ardan asked.

'I'll be making the rounds of the different mercenary groups. We need them ready to join us the instant we need it. I'll be walking around, looking for captains that don't have headquarters.'

'My father?' Regan said, his voice quavering.

'Will know about it, but we won't be hiring him.'

Regan gave a satisfied nod, standing taller.

'Best get to Seamus' class before you're late.'

'Is now the best time for classes?' Ardan asked.

'What else are you going to do than prepare for war?'

Feeling defeated, they made their way to the people waiting for class, Ardan's feet kicking up stones and dirt as he did so. He found an empty spot in one row, his mind elsewhere while Seamus made the rounds, eventually stopping in front of Ardan.

'First battle wounds? Good, you shouldn't fear getting hurt anymore,' Seamus said. 'And if you do, by all the demons of Hell, I will smack it out of you. Your left hand has never held a sword.' Ardan tried to reply but got smacked with the cane before he could answer. 'I wasn't asking. Maybe once we're done you won't be completely useless, but I doubt it.'

Seamus had them line up and go through the motions. His training with Riordan had made it easier, but the progress was still frustratingly slow, and his mind kept wandering. He had to keep correcting his form. Seamus passed him several times, but he never felt the sting of the man's cane. To his shock, Seamus said to rest himself and not overdo it. Despite this, by the time they hit midmorning, his left arm felt like iron. His right shoulder twinged from the bolt and his ribs pulled slightly. He could feel his forms getting sloppy.

'Don't thrust,' Seamus roared in his ear, and he jumped. He hadn't heard the man coming up behind him. 'It's too showy, leaves you far too open, and your sword isn't made for it. Slash and cut, slash and cut. How many times do I have to drill it into your head?'

'Eamon, get over here,' Seamus said. 'And you, Regan.'

Ardan immediately tensed as the tall boy came over, his sleek brown hair hanging past his ears. He had a broadsword that didn't look like it fit him.

'You two will fight as a team,' Seamus said to Regan and Ardan. 'I don't care what happened between your demon-fooled fathers. Regan is new to the forms and you're using your off-hand. Together you will fight against this useless idiot,' Seamus said, nodding towards Eamon.

Eamon grinned.

'With any luck, you'll force him to use his sword instead of just his shield.'

'But I'm so good with my shield,' Eamon said.

Seamus swung his cane, hitting Eamon on his thigh. It would sting, Ardan knew that from experience. He knew Eamon was quick and could have avoided the blow if he'd wanted to. It was probably wiser just to take it.

'First one to get past his shield gets excused from practice,' Seamus said.

'What do I get if I win?' Eamon asked.

'Only one lashing from my cane instead of two,' Seamus said. 'Use your sword, you demon-brained fool, or I will make you regret you were ever a twinkle in your father's eye. Get practising.'

Ardan's shoulders were tight, and he stayed as far from Regan as possible. The blond-haired man, grinning as his shield flashed, easily countered as the two came at him. Eamon forced their momentum and lack of coordination to work against them. He even used his practice sword a few times to get some hits in. They had been at it for almost thirty minutes, and neither he nor Regan had got past Eamon's guard.

'We need to work together,' Regan said.

Ardan felt a flash of rage.

'He's right, you know,' Eamon said.

'I know,' Ardan replied. It felt worse knowing. The Wild, so volatile at the moment, pushed and built. He tried to control it, stop the power from flowing into him, but it didn't help. To think he was standing next to one of his father's murderers. He'd thought he was past it, but the Wild had other ideas. He was quickly losing control. With no other outlet, he pushed the power into his connection with Mish. It was the first time he'd tried it since the warehouse. More aware, this time, he felt his senses change. His vision widened, and the colours and shapes became less distinct, but he could suddenly see every tiny movement, from the water dropping out of a gutter, to the scurrying mouse close to the nearby inn. His predatory instincts heightened as he looked at Regan. The lad was big, but he was weak and easy to exploit. Ardan felt his back hunch slightly as his feet began moving towards Regan.

Seamus appeared in front of him, as though he knew. 'That's enough. Can't have you tearing those wounds, and Regan is having trouble keeping up. His fitness needs work.'

The internal predator found the wizened weapon master too dangerous to be prey. He tried to think of a way to separate him from Regan. Seamus' cane swept up, snapping towards his head. With his heightened reflexes, he moved fast enough to take it on the shoulder. As the pain blossomed, his connection with Mish weakened.

'When I say enough,' Seamus growled, 'I mean it. I know of the bad blood between you two. If you want to stay in my class, you will master it.'

Ardan had regained enough of his senses to wrest control back, breaking the connection and forcing the Wild down. He nodded, his anger still bubbling just below the surface.

He stalked off to the weapon shed, exchanging his practice sword for his real one before heading to one of the recovery areas. He hated that his father's murderers still walked free, but he tried to calm himself, to keep himself distracted as he took off his shirt and washed at one of the nearby barrels, careful of his wounded shoulder and ribs.

Eamon came to join him in solidarity, standing there in silence. His presence was comforting. Ardan closed his eyes as he splashed water over his face.

'Are you the Shock Wolf?' Eamon asked.

Ardan, too busy in his own thoughts, hadn't noticed Davan joining them. He stood off to one side. Somehow the presence of his brother also helped Ardan get better control of his emotions. The rage inside him simmered down to where he didn't quite want to tear Regan's throat out with his bare hands.

'The what?' Davan said, his face genuinely confused.

'That's the axe that makes the ground shake, right?' Eamon said, pointing at it.

'Is that what they're calling me?' Davan said, but Ardan could see that he was secretly pleased.

'I heard you held off hundreds of men all by yourself,' Eamon said. 'I don't believe it, but I like the story.'

The screams of the wounded and dying rose in Ardan's memory, the crackle of the Fiddler's laughter as he threw away all those lives just to kill the Dock Master. He could feel his anger rising again. Ancients, what was wrong with him?

'It was a nasty business, that,' Davan said.

'It was,' Ardan replied quietly.

'I'm in the mood for a drink. How about you two?' Davan said.

It would get Ardan's mind off Koira, Regan, and the warehouse. Ardan nodded.

'Can't. My wife barely tolerates me training. If she knew we finished early and I didn't help in the fields—' Eamon said. 'Well, she'd castrate me at the very least.'

The comment brought a wan smile from Ardan.

After Eamon had left, Ardan and his brother wandered over to the corner of the Square where the Red Wolves made their home. It had once been several smaller buildings, but now they had ramshackle connections, making it one giant monstrosity. The arms store had bars on the windows and a heavy wooden door. The hammer of ringing steel on steel could be heard over the sounds in the stables.

'How big is this place?' Ardan said, not entirely sure where their quarters stopped.

Davan pointed up and down the buildings. 'That building over there, the big one, that's where I stay. It's the living quarters for those without families. The place is less crowded since the streets are open again. The family homes were the first vacated; they find this place too noisy.'

Ardan tried to act interested as his brother pointed out notables amongst the Red Wolves, but his mind was drifting to the Wild. Was it just the power changing, or was he changing with it? He wanted to ask Koira, but it reminded him of the impending invasion. He hadn't really been paying attention to what his brother was saying, but luckily, he needed little encouragement in his conversation.

He shook his head, trying to focus on the now as he followed his brother inside the tavern. Musicians were trying to play over the sound of the crowd, while over a hundred mercenaries sat and drank in the hall. Ardan tried to coax Mish inside, but a roar of laughter sent her scurrying down the wall. He could hear some banging as she scrambled up onto the rafters before a pair of emerald eyes peered at him from above. After one last fruitless attempt to get her inside, he shrugged and left her there.

A blond and curvy maid noticed Davan immediately and brought them two bowls of a meat and vegetable stew before they even sat down. Davan thanked her, having eyes only for the bowl. The maid's smile faltered, but someone else called for her attention. Ardan took the wooden spoon and ate a mouthful. It was warm and filling. Davan dug into his food like a man possessed. Ardan watched his brother in amazement as he finished his bowl, while Ardan had only taken a few mouthfuls. The maid returned in a heartbeat with a second bowl and two mugs of ale.

'Thanks, Cara,' Davan said, looking up at her.

She beamed, a blush creeping onto her cheeks.

Ardan focused on his drink, not wanting to embarrass her further. The ale was a dark amber, almost red.

'Red Wolf brew,' Davan said enthusiastically.

'You brew your own ale?' Ardan asked and took a sip. It had a sweet malt flavour with a tinge of roasted barley. 'This is good.'

'It has to be,' Davan said, 'Not much work for old disabled soldiers. If they don't brew well, they'll get replaced.'

Ardan took a longer sip, letting the stew settle.

Suddenly, Davan jumped to his feet. Captain Dásun had appeared with Lachlan at his side. They were both wearing their formal Red Wolf captain and deputy captain attire. Lachlan's long blond locks were a sharp contrast to Dásun's short cropped grey hair and beard, considering these were the two leaders of the Red Wolves.

'Enough of that,' Lachlan said as he and Dásun joined them. Cara quickly brought two more ales for them.

'Where's Riordan?' Dásun asked.

Ardan shrugged. 'Haven't seen him since this morning.'

'Ah, I assumed. He's meeting us here.'

'When are you joining the Wolves?' Lachlan said to Ardan.

Ardan shrugged again but was saved from answering by Dásun.

'Marion asked me not to poach him.'

'Still, it'd be nice to have both weapons,' Lachlan said.

'You and I will be the next ones with weapons of the Ancients. I put that forest stalker under contract about an hour ago. He said he'll get me some heartwood and forest metals soon.'

'He will?' Lachlan asked, surprised.

'With the amount of gold he wants, he'd better.'

Ardan thought about his weapon, his father's last gift. While his mind wandered, he could feel the turbulent Wild inside of him move. Ardan focused, barely containing it before he could burst the entire table apart. He got a handle on it and funnelled it into his connection with Mish. It was only a tiny amount, but it eased the pressure, letting him get it under control. He couldn't help but think Koira was right. The power was becoming more uncontrollable. Yet after a few minutes he could focus, feeling more himself as he steadily fed the overwhelming power into the connection.

'Good to see you up and moving, anyway,' Lachlan was saying. 'Davan said you handled yourself well at the Docks.'

Ardan raised his ale. 'To taking crossbow bolts with the best of them.'

The others smiled, raising their glasses in response. They all took a long draught. 'Some recruits aren't good for much else,' Dásun said.

'Including your son?' Lachlan asked.

Davan laughed, but caught Dásun glaring at him, and he hastily tried to turn it into a cough.

'How's your sister's training going?' Dásun asked. 'Those in the Black Clergy can still marry, can't they?'

Davan's face immediately clouded. Ardan smiled. When Davan didn't answer, Ardan supplied: 'She's good. Training can be a little tough.' There were murmurs of agreement. 'But she's still the same person.'

Lachlan looked between the two of them, focusing on Davan. 'You still haven't been to see her?'

Davan didn't answer.

'It's time you do. Visit her, I mean. Nothing will deflate your ego like meeting with people that have seen you eat your own shit. Something you need after that warehouse fight. Thinking you're a war hero. Yes, we've heard about your new nickname.'

Davan stayed silent.

'That's an order, by the way. I expect a full report in a few days' time,' Lachlan said, an evil grin on his face.

'Yes, sir.'

CHAPTER FIFTY-FIVE: GREEN
FLAME OF VENGEANCE

* * *

*Z*adkiel's Templars left some deep wounds in my armies, and we
continued to lose ground even after their departure. No longer
can I operate in the background. I have joined the armies of Darkness and for
the first time in a decade we push them back. Michael refuses to face me. I
believe he fears falling here and leaving Zadkiel to face the power of Astaroth
alone. He is right to be afraid.

— Titivillus, *Annals of Lucifer.*

DAVAN SAT IN SILENCE, while the two leaders of the Red Wolves
continued to drink, exchanging playful jibes. Mercenaries would
pass them, saluting as they went to the other long tables. The
surrounding area was sparsely occupied, as no one wanted to get too
close.

Eventually Riordan arrived, sitting down and passing out five
mugs of ale.

'How did you carry all that?' Ardan said.

'Experience, lad.'

'Free ale, always a good way to start a meeting,' Dásun said, taking his.

'He must want something,' Lachlan said.

'Shush, take a sip first, then talk business. Let him think he's buttering us up,' Dásun said in a stage whisper.

'Maybe I should order another round,' Riordan said.

'Must be serious,' Dásun murmured.

The smile slipped off Riordan's face. 'It is. Extremely so—'

'Before you start, I want you to know we won't be taking sides,' Dásun said. 'Against the Fiddler. Isn't that what this is about?'

'No, no, it's not that. It's much worse,' Riordan said. 'The Children may march on the city.'

'*What?*'

'Marion's trying to find a peaceful resolution but...'

Dásun exchanged a look with Lachlan. 'I think you better start at the beginning.'

Riordan sat back, taking a long draught of his ale, leaving some foam on his red beard as he began the tale. He was quick, telling them of the altercation at the Dark Temple.

'So, they're coming here to save their Tree?' Dásun asked, running a hand over the stubble on his head.

Ardan opened his mouth, but Riordan elbowed him before he could say anything. Pain flared, as the man had hit one of his wounds. He lost the next part of the conversation, trying to recover.

'When?' Dásun asked.

'Whenever they arrive. Maybe a week, maybe a month.'

'The Countess couldn't afford us for a month,' Dásun said. 'We're mercenaries. Like you. We don't work for free.'

'I'm not asking you to. Marion can pay enough for your entire force for maybe a week.'

Ardan whistled. How much would that be? A hundred silvers? Surely not a thousand.

'And you want us to keep our schedule free for that week of pay,' Dásun surmised. 'It's essentially the same thing, what you're asking.'

'I know.'

Dásun sighed and looked at Lachlan. The other captain shrugged. Dásun returned his attention to Riordan. 'When?'

It looked like Riordan was holding his breath. 'I think it will take them at least a week.'

'Alright. Starting one week from today, I will hold off taking any contracts. And you will owe us,' Dásun said. 'And Riordan, it won't be a small favour.'

Riordan's shoulders sagged with relief. 'Thank you. I know what this means.'

Dásun nodded.

Riordan drained his tankard and signalled Cara for some more drinks. 'Can't sit around drinking all night. Got more captains to ask to join our cause.'

Ardan got up to join him, but Riordan waved him to sit down. 'Stay, lad, enjoy these times when they come.'

The four of them sat in silence as Cara returned with more drinks. She gave Davan another bright smile, but his brother was too lost in thought to notice.

'I'll organise some group drills. The boys are out of practice,' Lachlan said.

'Aye, that's probably for the best. We'll let them have tonight, but get everyone not assigned out in the Square tomorrow. We need to prepare for the fight.'

Lachlan nodded, looking down at his mug. 'We may lose a lot of Wolves if it comes down to a fight.'

'They know the risks. The best we can do is to prepare them.'

Lachlan leaned back, staring at the ceiling, as though trying to find answers there. He returned his gaze to eye level. 'It's the forest stalker. If we're fighting the Children, a few magic weapons would be nice,' Lachlan said, standing.

The stalker's hands were no longer adorned with rings, and he had regained some of his lost weight, but the smug smile and weaselly features were unmistakable. Verrick stopped, his eyes widening slightly as he saw Ardan sitting there.

'What's wrong with you?' Davan said.

Ardan hadn't realised he'd been growling. The Wild had welled up inside of him, and he had unconsciously reached out and connected with Mish. His senses had increased and so had his predatory instincts. He wanted to tear this man apart, with or without his sword, it didn't matter. He forcibly pulled back from the connection and the need to growl didn't entirely vanish, but he got it under control.

'You,' Ardan said rising. 'You told me to find you in Mercenary Square.'

'What's this?' Lachlan said.

'This boy thinks I murdered his father,' Verrick said, taking a step back and looking defensive.

'I saw you do it.'

'Him? You? But we've shared drinks before,' Davan said accusingly. He turned to Ardan. 'Are you sure?'

Instead of replying, Ardan's hand went for his sword.

'Stop this right now,' Lachlan snapped. 'Nothing's happening until I know more.'

Dásun leaned back, his eyes assessing as he made a subtle gesture. Those nearby went quiet, while others started moving. Ardan ignored them, having eyes only for Verrick.

'Tristan was a thief and had failed to pay his tribute. The Magistrate had given me the coin to take his life. I executed him.'

Dásun spoke at the same time as Davan.

'That doesn't sound like Tristan.'

'You demonic bastard, step outside and let's settle this.'

'You will not,' Lachlan said. 'Not until we sort this out.'

'It's true,' Ardan said grudgingly, every eye turning towards him. 'But you lied to get the coin.'

'The coin is a mark of execution. I did nothing wrong,' Verrick said.

Davan looked like he was about to leap the table to get at him.

'You hit him, and you'll be cast out of the Wolves,' Lachlan said.

That made Davan stop. He blinked, realisation dawning on his face. He looked at Lachlan in disbelief.

'He is under contract and has done nothing to break it. You attack him under our banner, then you no longer have a place here, regardless of your reasoning.'

'Fine, then I'll kill him,' Ardan said.

It was at this point that Ardan noticed how quiet the tavern had gotten. Six men had surrounded them. Dásun made another gesture, and a couple stepped in front of Verrick.

'This is absolute demon shit,' Davan said.

'Enough,' Dásun said, his voice carrying over the hall, producing a sudden profound silence. 'Go to your bunk and don't come back until you've cooled off.' One mercenary put a comforting hand on Davan's shoulder.

'I've got a right to challenge him,' Ardan said.

'Not here, you don't. This is my house,' Dásun said. 'I decide what goes on here and in the Square. What he did may have been in bad taste...'

'My father never stole from anyone.'

'I don't care. He had the coin. You want to challenge him, you've got to get him to agree. Otherwise, you attack him, and you'll be the one I throw in irons.'

Verrick's smug smile taunted him.

Ardan spat at him.

'Get him out of here,' Dásun ordered.

Ardan was pulled away unceremoniously by two burly mercenaries. They tugged at his injured shoulder, so he didn't resist as they escorted him outside.

The man always hides behind other people. The more he thought about it, the more that smug smile played in his memory, the more his fury rose, his connection with Mish deepening. It was time he made good on his promise to avenge his father. Tonight was as good as any other. He stalked towards one exit to the Square, making sure whoever might be watching saw him leave.

His anger had risen high enough that he was unconsciously feeding his connection with Mish. He could feel his vision change, and he found he could see through the darkness. Shapes became less distinct and less vibrant, but a hairsbreadth of movement would catch his eye. A bird flying overhead. A drunken brawl and the uncoordinated punches, the shifting of a horse's hooves. He let his instincts take over, leaping higher than should have been possible, his feet finding purchase on a tiny ledge before taking another quick jump and landing softly on top of a building. He crouched and set in to wait.

Mish landed next to him a moment later. He reached out absently to pat her and could feel her hackles rising. He felt the same.

Time had no meaning as he waited. He barely moved as the moons passed overhead. Eventually Verrick appeared. The man was staggering from too much drink. He started towards the exit where Ardan was waiting. The anger still thrummed through him. He wouldn't let his father's murderer get away from him again. Deep inside of him, a voice was screaming at him that the anger wasn't entirely his own, but he ignored it.

He watched the man walk down the streets without a care in the world. Ardan followed him, keeping to the rooftops, his feet landing softly so as not to make a noise. He was waiting for his chance when Verrick's demeanour completely changed. He darted down an alley, quick as a rat.

With a growl, Ardan leapt down from the roof and was running. His steps evolved into an easy lope, the ground disappearing before him. He dashed down the alley, Mish close behind. He was caught up in the moment, his body following his prey. As he ran, he funnelled more of the Wild into his connection with Mish. His speed increased and so too did his sense of smell. The stench of stagnant water and rotting refuse assaulted his nostrils. He pushed those smells out of his mind as best he could.

He paused briefly at a junction of the alleys. Three options stood before him. His nose wrinkled, catching Verrick's odour, and he raced down that alley. He heard the man curse and the scuffle of footsteps. Ardan was getting close. A few corners later, he caught sight of the man's cloak. A grin crept onto his lips. He drew his sword in anticipation. Around the next corner, instinct took over. He saw the blade coming and his feet were already moving. Launching himself out of the way, his body curved around the sword. The blade swished past him, missing him by a hair, before clanging into the wall.

'Your family sent enough failed assassins that you came to do it yourself?' Verrick snarled as he swung his sword again. Mish leapt at him, her claws extended. She latched onto his leg. Verrick gave a howl as the cat's claws dug deep. He swung with his free hand, smashing Mish away. She landed on all fours with a hiss.

The rage Ardan felt was channelled into the sword, lighting it up. Its green fire illuminated the alley. Verrick's eyes went wide as he scrambled back, holding his sword in front of him.

Ardan went in, using the sword as an extension of himself. He swung viciously at the man. Verrick tried to block, but the green flames put him off and he held the blade awkwardly. Their blades connected and Verrick's weapon went flying. Ardan held the fiery sword in front of him.

'No, wait—please. Don't kill me.'

'Why?' Ardan said, barely recognising his own voice. He stepped forward, ready to end it.

Verrick fell to his knees. 'I have a family.'

Ardan stared incredulously at him. The audacity of the statement made him pause.

Verrick saw the hesitation and moved. A flash of metal appeared in the man's hand. Ardan slid to the side and the steel struck nothing but air. With a snarl, he thrust his sword forward, plunging the blade into the man's gut. Verrick stared down in disbelief, his eyes filling with fear. He feebly tried to pull it out, but the flames made it too hot for him to grasp.

'For your lies,' Ardan spat, funnelling more of the Wild into the sword. The flames rose to engulf the man. Ardan felt a grim satisfaction as Verrick screamed. With a grunt, he pulled the sword out and Verrick crumpled to the ground. His clothes melted away as the green flame immolated him.

The smell of burnt flesh hit him like a hammer, and he reeled back. Choking, he dropped his sword and forcibly broke the connection with Mish. The fire snuffed out, leaving Verrick as nothing more than a charred and sticky corpse.

The Wild swelled in jubilation, but it just made Ardan feel sick. *What have I done?* He panicked, grabbing his sword and bolting down the twisting alleys, not sure where he was going, trying to get away. His mad dash was stopped by a dead end. He threw up the contents of his stomach, heaving until there was nothing left but air. He stumbled back against one wall and slid to the ground. His thoughts rampaged inside of him.

He heard a meow behind him and looked over his shoulder. Mish's emerald eyes were staring up at him.

'What the Hell is happening to me?' he whispered to her.

CHAPTER FIFTY-SIX: NABERIUS' SHADOW

* * *

*T*he *threat of Astaroth keeps Michael cautious. I spread my power and strike at his strongholds, but never enough to make the Archangel commit, only to tip the balance in my favour.*
— Titivillus, *Annals of Lucifer.*

* * *

ARDAN STAGGERED, still in a daze. He was splattered with blood and bile, and the stench of smoke covered his clothes. The lateness of the hour allowed him to avoid anyone who might spot him, but morning was fast approaching. Mish followed him quietly, butting her head against him often, as though trying to wake him up. He wandered, not sure where to go. He feared the Tree of the Ancients, wondering if the power would exacerbate the Wild controlling him. Eventually he reverted to something infantile and stumbled his way across the city before ending up at the Countess' palace.

The man at the gate took in his dishevelled state, his nose wrinkling at the smell, but when he looked at Ardan his eyes widened in recognition. He sent someone to get Alaine. He wondered how the man knew him, but his mind remained mostly blank until his mother turned up.

'Ardan, are you okay?' Alaine exclaimed, rushing to his side, patting him down, looking for injuries. She lifted his chin and looked him in the eyes. 'Come with me.'

She led him through the gardens to the rear parlour. Her quarters were a clean, well lived-in collection of rooms. She spoke to some servants while he wandered over and collapsed on a sofa. Soon she had some sweet cakes and tea for him. She forced a cake into his mouth. He chewed automatically. The simple motion gave him something to do, while the taste of the cake helped pull him back from the feral edge.

His mother was sitting on a cushioned chair opposite him. There were floral patterns on the hem of her yellow dress. It gave him a target. He focused on it, the world slowly shifting back into focus.

'I killed him. Verrick. The man who killed...' Ardan's voice trailed off.

'Good, it's done then.'

Ardan stared at her, his words slow in coming. 'You approve?'

'The man needed to die,' Alaine said. 'Did anybody see you?'

'I don't think so.'

'What did you do with the body?'

He felt sick. 'Burned it.'

'Where?'

He told her about the general vicinity, unsure of its exact location.

She pursed her lips. 'Alright, I'll get things in motion,' she said as she picked up a small bell and gave it a soft jingle. 'Being a thief didn't always end glamorously; we occasionally had to get our hands dirty. I'll have it taken care of. It might take a few days, but suspicion will be thrown elsewhere.'

The door opened, and a red-haired woman entered. She gave a curtsey, her eyes looking down.

'Ma'am?'

'Roisin, could you be a dear and tell Sean to throw Verrick's shade?'

'Ma'am.' She curtseyed and left.

'I'll have to do some work too, but Sean knows his business.'

Ardan sat there in a stupor. He knew what she was doing, but it just didn't seem important. She looked at him in concern, taking the seat across from him.

'There's something else.' Ardan let out a long breath. He couldn't meet her eyes. 'It's just that I don't know what's happening to me.'

She frowned in concern, waiting for him to speak.

His words came out in a rush. He told her everything: his flaming sword, the connection with Mish, how he could channel the Wild to strengthen their connection and the emotions the power brought and how it was changing him. Finally, in halting breaths, he told her about his overwhelming rage and how he had lost himself.

'Look at me,' she commanded, and he reluctantly looked up at her. 'I don't know what sort of power is playing with you, but you are my son. You are a reasonable, strong, and loving person. You didn't lose yourself then, and you won't in future.'

The words comforted him. He could feel Mish butting her head against his hand. He briefly considered whether he should blame her for it, but those thoughts disappeared in the depths of her green eyes. They were in this together. He pulled her in close, clutching her tightly.

They were interrupted by another knock at the door and his mother answered. She spoke quietly with the person there before closing the door, not immediately turning around.

'It may be more work than I originally thought. The Red Wolves have already started asking questions. It will take time to sort this out, but you're welcome to stay.'

He looked at the room's opulence, the guards patrolling outside the windows, the stone walls. It would be a gilded cage. He shook his head.

She looked at him sadly.

'I'll come back and visit, it's just—I just can't stay here.'

She nodded in understanding. 'You could visit your father's grave.'

His head whipped around to stare at her.

'It will allow you to leave the city for a while. You can tell him he's been avenged, even if he'd never approve. He never knew what was best for him.'

Ardan felt guilty that he hadn't gotten away to visit at least once. The purpose sparked something in him. He stood, ready to leave.

'First, you need to clean yourself up. If you get rid of your armour and wear a guard's cloak, you should be mostly invisible, at least until you can find something more suitable. I'm guessing you have some money, but—' she said, going to the dressers and pulling out a small golden pendant. 'It's from my dear cousin. Ever since your last visit, she's given me a lot more freedom, but no allowance or money. She's worried I might do something nefarious with it, as if there isn't a fortune lying around. Take this to one of the more savvy merchants. They'll trade well for it.'

Ardan was still a little numb and accepted her orders without question. He used the cloth at the washbasin and cleaned off the worst of the grime, donned a simple white shirt, brown trousers, and the blue cloak of a Merchant Guard. Before he was out the door, she was already at her writing desk. He left the palace and entered to the streets, feeling people watching him, but their eyes would quickly slide past. The blue cloak really made him invisible.

The road to the Ancient Quarter felt long, the trip dragging out past the limit of his patience, until he eventually found himself outside Raigel's door. He didn't know if anyone else would take the pendant. He avoided looking at the dark stain on the cobblestones as he entered the shop. The aroma of the dried herbs assaulted him, but underlying it was the faint smell of sulphur. The demon was there. His bright red skin looked like glowing coals, his wings tucked close to his body and his head bowed as he worked the mortar and pestle with his spindly red fingers. He looked up, his red horns narrowly missing the herbs hanging from the ceiling.

'Ardan,' Raigel's rough voice greeted him. 'It pleases me to see you.'

'Hello,' Ardan said, feeling awkward.

'I was worried some mishap may have befallen you. You are one of the few whose company I enjoy. I wonder if you would share in my amusement about the mortal that burnt a hole through their tongue by using too much frog venom.'

Ardan gave a dutiful chuckle. Still feeling awkward, he placed the pendent on the counter. 'What can I get for this?'

Raigel picked up the pendant and scrutinized it. 'It is real,' he said at last. Then he looked up and gave a huff that carried the smell of sulphur. 'Where did you get it?'

'The Countess' palace.'

The demon's wings shook as it growled. Ardan stepped back, arms raised defensively. Had he miscalculated? The growls came in short and sharp. It took Ardan a long time to realise the demon was laughing. He still wasn't used to it.

'You humans. I wonder how I got through the first few centuries on Eden without you. You certainly keep life interesting.' He showed a glint of his fangs. The thing was trying to smile, or at least Ardan hoped it was a smile.

Being here, in this shop next to a fully-fledged demon, felt surreal. He wondered if he would know anything about it. With the impending invasion of the Children, it couldn't hurt to know more. Could it?

'Do you know anything about the powers at the Temple?'

This time the 'smile' vanished and Raigel's red and green eyes narrowed in the first human-like expression Ardan had seen. 'Why do you ask?'

'Curiosity,' Ardan said quickly. 'A Child of the Ancients mentioned how they are attacking the forest.'

'I will take this information off the price I offer you for the pendant.'

Ardan didn't think it was a question but nodded anyway.

'The Children are right to be worried.'

'Oh?'

'It takes immense power to attack the forest. Once you know what could do it, then you will know the peril they are in,' Raigel said. The demon's speech was halting, as though trying to navigate through the right words.

'Who could do such a thing?' Ardan asked. 'The High Priest?'

The demon shook his head. 'I cannot say.'

'Why?'

'They serve Hell. If Lucifer or Naberius discovered my treachery, well. At one point or another, I will return to Hell. They would take time to extract vengeance.'

'You have no say of your own?'

'It is our lot,' Raigel said, his wings shifting.

'But why here? Why now?'

'How much do you know about the war between Heaven and Hell?'

It took Ardan a moment to follow the change in topic. 'Little,' he admitted.

Raigel paused, using one of its long fingers to scratch one of its horns. The nail made a screeching noise.

'I will try to keep it brief, but know the war is vast and has stretched over aeons. Control of this world offers power beyond that of most worlds. It interests the Archangels and High Demons to control it. The Wild offers a weapon neither side has possessed before. It may permanently tip the balance.'

'Why here, though?'

'The forest, mortal,' Raigel said, as though it were obvious. 'The power there is immense, and if anyone could bend it to their will, well, they would be a power difficult to stop.'

'Surely there are other places of power,' Ardan said with a sinking feeling.

'There are,' Raigel conceded, 'but few are as weakly defended. What is there to stop them? One Templar and his pitiful army, a handful of Shapers and a bunch of mercenaries that have few magic weapons among them?'

'Then why haven't they done it already?'

Raigel let out a sigh, filling the air with the smell of sulphur. 'I cannot say.'

'What of you?'

'If I had warning, I would flee.'

Ardan mused on this information. He asked some minor questions, but it was clear the demon wouldn't elaborate. Eventually Ardan relented and bartered for new clothes, armour and added a special bottle of liquor to his price. As he was trying on his armour, Raigel spoke.

'If I had known you two were to be ambushed, I would have.... No matter, it is done,' Raigel said. 'I give you this advice because I was fond of your father. Do not get in their way. Their leader is not cruel, for a servant of Darkness, but if you intentionally cross or hinder him, well, I can tell you he will find unique ways to make you regret it,' Raigel finished, and its wings gave a small quiver as though it were cold.

Ardan nodded, a deep, sinking feeling in his chest as he thought about it. After leaving the store, he realized how little he had gotten for the pendant. He wondered if the demon had been telling him stories, but he doubted it. Raigel had used the truth to put him off balance and to barter him down without him suspecting it. He'd been tired and out of sorts, which didn't help, but regardless he'd been thoroughly outmanoeuvred.

'Blasted demon,' he said, but his voice lacked conviction.

CHAPTER FIFTY-SEVEN:
FAREWELL AT LAST

* * *

he Ancients are now dead. A group of mortals and the last of the Ancients recognised Astaroth's growing threat. Details are scarce and survivors are few, but I have gleaned that they confronted and the Ancients sacrificed themselves to bind the High Demon with chains stretching into Eden, binding her here.

— Titivillus, *Annals of Lucifer.*

ARDAN ENTERED the forest alone for the first time in many months. A streak of black raced past him and crashed into a nearby shrub. A moment later, Mish's head popped out, covered in leaves. *Well, not completely alone,* he thought. Mish was ecstatic to be back in the forest, racing into the distance before rushing back, then running off again. She made so much noise that Ardan was constantly on edge. After a few hours, he suspected she didn't attract the forest's attention the same way he did. He was grateful, despite how unfair he found it.

They continued on and passed familiar trail markers, taking the steady incline that led up. Verrick's death had left him feeling numb and detached, but the green surroundings were a balm to his mind. Yet beneath it, there was still a lingering fear. He thought of Raigel and what the demon couldn't say. There was a hidden message there.

The trail was barely visible beneath the overgrowth, and Ardan had to concentrate to see it. Ahead, he heard a soft meow. Mish had been climbing a tree and slipped off a branch. She hung there, paws outstretched, unable to pull herself up. Before Ardan could rescue her, she fell, tumbling and disappearing into the forest floor. Instantly back on her feet, Mish was already bounding away in a very kittenish manner.

'I can't believe you are the same lynx that attacked Verrick.'

Mish ignored him, dashing ahead and waiting for him to catch up. Sometimes he had to shake himself, forcing Raigel's words from his mind, and focus on the path. His concentration broke when he felt a faint warmth coming from within, like the heat from a fire. He thought he was imagining it, but the closer he got to the glade, the warmer it got. Feeling uneasy, he gripped his sword and stepped even softer than usual. Once he made it to the small clearing, he inspected it with a wary eye. He scanned the place several times before realising the warmth was coming from the idol at the top of the stone altar. He looked at its swirling and shifting form. The more he focused on it, the more he couldn't determine its shape or colour. Before he fell into the trap, he looked away, knowing it would give him a headache. He didn't understand the idols, but he was glad that they protected the glades from the dangers of the forest.

He looked over the clearing for what felt like the first time. A crystal-clear stream trickled over some rocks, creating a small waterfall, and fed a pool deep enough to drink from. The sun shone through the break in the trees, bathing the glade in light. A pile of stones adorned the centre of green grass, a large rock acting as a headstone behind it.

Here lies Tristan. Beloved Father and Husband.

He walked the forest like one of the Children themselves.

Images flashed of holding his father's blood covered body. Then to Verrick's charred corpse. With some effort, he quashed both memories, focusing on happier thoughts. He remembered how his father

PURGATORY OF THE ANCIENTS

had always tried to bring back a special treat from the markets. How he had helped Ardan string his first bow. How he had always encouraged him, been there to support him, and his never-ending stream of advice. Ardan felt a tear roll down his cheek. He replayed all the fond memories of his father, knowing there would never be any new ones.

He knelt in front of the grave, his tears now coming more freely.

'Verrick's dead. You wouldn't approve of how it happened, but I hope it makes you rest easier.'

Mish butted her head against him. He sat down on the soft green grass, pulling her into his lap. She put up with it patiently as his tears gently pattered onto her black fur. He didn't know if the tears were for his father or for himself. They sat there until the sun dipped towards the horizon. Reluctantly he got up. Feeling stiff, he stretched before collecting some firewood.

Once the fire was crackling, Ardan got lost in the flame. The pettiness of the Magistrate had killed his father. The Wild rose at the injustice of it. He forcibly quashed it, feeling a hatred of the Wild and what it was doing to him. Yet its anger persisted. People should be free from oppression and the whims of men, angels or demons. No one should suffer the same fate as his father.

He pulled out the bottle of liquor, and the cork made a loud pop as it was released. He smiled in remembrance as he looked at the brown liquid. It was the first strong drink he'd ever had. When he'd first been curious about wine and beer, his father had wasted no time in getting this particular drink for him. He took a swig in remembrance. He coughed and spluttered as it burned unpleasantly all the way down. It had effectively turned him off having a drink for years.

'Here's to all the lessons you taught me, Father,' he said and took another swig. It burned as much as the first.

When he lay down on his bedroll, he didn't feel better exactly, but he felt something. Killing Verrick had left him empty. Near to his father, he found some semblance of peace. He hoped he could emulate some of his father's measured patience in the future.

CHAPTER FIFTY-EIGHT: A DEEP TERROR

* * *

As the threat of Astaroth has been halted, Michael is free to join the front lines, and Zadkiel's Templars have returned. I have recalled Naberius. Without him, I am outmatched, and my armies are in constant retreat.

— Titivillus, *Annals of Lucifer.*

* * *

THE SUN WAS high in the sky by the time Ardan roused himself from his bedroll. He felt more himself than he had in days. A nausea was seated in his stomach, which hadn't come from the alcohol, but he hoped it would fade. He stood, disturbing Mish, who gave a meow of protest before settling down again. Ardan casually pulled out some rations.

He was sitting there, chewing on a trail biscuit and debating how many days he should stay in the glade, when a thunderous crack erupted deep within the forest. He stood, his hand unconsciously going for his sword. A sudden pain exploded inside him. He dropped to his knees, clutching his chest before falling to the ground and writhing. His blood was like fire, and his muscles felt laced with venom. Time and thought became immaterial as he shuddered in the dirt. As suddenly as it began, it was over. Sweat beaded his forehead while he lay gasping. He pushed himself to his feet at the same time as Mish. There were claw marks on his bedroll.

Deep within the pain he had felt something shatter. An image flashed in his mind. A winged demon loomed over an idol. An urgency to get to the other clearing pushed at him. The same need for brash action that had led to the killing of Verrick was fuelling him. More aware of it this time, he kept some control over his actions. He paused long enough to don his armour and take a skin of water, leaving his bedroll and pack behind, and set off.

It took him almost an hour to make it to the main road. Without the heavy jungle in his way, he fell into an easy run while Mish effortlessly kept pace. He briefly wondered if he could use his connection with the lynx to run faster, but the pressure of the Wild was growing like a red fury. He withdrew from it and didn't let it fill him like he usually did. Running naturally would have to suffice.

Ardan could hear the battle cries from the clearing before he arrived. At the clash of metal on metal, he drew his sword, but without his connection to Mish he felt clumsy. *No choice*, he thought, and funnelled just a tiny amount of the Wild into their connection. It burst forth, and suddenly he was trying to hold back a flood. The connection felt incredibly powerful while his vision widened, and his muscles changed. He came round the bend of trees to see the battle unfolding.

A score of mercenaries, four Black Guards and a single black priest were engaged in combat with a cohort of forest warriors. At the centre, next to the pillar that normally held the shifting idol, Raigel was slumped against the poll. The shards of the idol lay on the ground, unmoving.

Talon was leading the charge against the four Black Guards. Armoured giants wielding large broadswords, they moved with speed and precision, but Talon was something else. He was agile and his hatchets were extensions of himself. He blocked and dodged past their line, using the blunt end of his hatchet like a hammer to smash a guard off balance. The man stumbled awkwardly enough to expose a gap in his armour. Talon's other axe found the knee joint, and the guard fell, screaming.

Ardan started forward. He could see Koira amongst their number. She appeared unarmed, in her forest warrior garb of tight-fitting clothing, her hair tied back. She darted past Talon to a second Black Guard and touched his armour before dancing nimbly back. The guard dropped his sword, scratching at his armour, desperately trying to pull it off. Before his hands could find the buckles, he screamed as green flame poured out of him. He fell, and it was enough to draw the attention of the lone priest. His hand held fast to his symbol of Lucifer. A slender stream of Darkness wove out from it and pooled into a black blob above his head.

Talon threw one of his hatchets. It spun towards the priest, spinning end over end. But the pool of Darkness shot out a tendril, knocking the axe aside.

Ardan jumped over the circle of stones and sprinted towards them. The mercenaries and the main body of forest warriors were in his path. War cries and the screams of the wounded filled the air. Ardan was acting purely on instinct; he saw it all as if from a distance. One of the forest warriors struck, forcing a mercenary back. It created a gap. He channelled the Wild into his sword, causing it to flare up, and the mercenaries hesitated long enough for him to slip through.

The pool of Darkness above the priest was the size of a boulder. It broke into two, shooting forth and knocking both Talon and Koira off their feet. It wrapped them in tendrils of Darkness as effectively as if they were tied with rope. Koira was trying to reach the tendrils with her hands, but she couldn't quite curve her wrist enough.

Forest warriors charged the priest. The two remaining Black Guards got in their way, effectively blocking them. The forest warriors were skilled, but the guards used their armour to absorb their blows so they could strike at the relatively unarmoured opponents. Two forest warriors fell before the others pulled back.

Ardan remembered how the green flame had cut Davan's shock-wave, and he hoped it would work on the tendrils. He got to Koira first. The black tendrils resisted as he cut, the Darkness fighting against the green flame. He poured more of the Wild into it and the flame sliced through. The green fire consumed the Darkness in a fiery flash and was gone.

Koira sprang to her feet and was over by Talon's side. As she went, one Black Guard came for Ardan. He jumped away from the first blow and tried to block the second, but he was holding his sword awkwardly in his left hand. The sword snapped out of his hand and went flying. The flame winked out as it flew. Panicked, he looked up at the looming black figure. He felt the Wild in his chest build up without the sword as an outlet. Not wanting an explosion to happen, he fed it into the connection with Mish. His strength and power grew. It allowed him to move nimbly away from the next sword strike and jump backwards, neatly picking his sword up. He didn't need to block the man's strikes; his superior agility was enough. But the second guard moved towards him and Ardan could see the Priest building up his pool again.

Talon appeared beside him.

'Go,' he yelled, grabbing the attention of both the Black Guards. 'Help Koira.'

Ardan didn't hesitate. He made for the Priest. Before he got there, the newly formed black pool sacrificed some of its mass to form a spear. The spear turned and flew straight towards Koira. She held out a palm and a shot a green line of flame to meet it. The two combined and resulted in a green and black explosion. It sent Koira flying backwards, but she twisted enough to break and roll when she hit the ground.

Suddenly Ardan was facing the Priest alone. The pool shot a tendril towards him. He slashed at it, feeling as though he were pushing his sword through tar, the tendril erupting in green flame. The Priest frowned and suddenly the sphere separated into four spears. Two were aimed at him and two aimed at Koira. He raced for the Priest, trying to catch him before the spears were released.

Talon threw an axe. One spear disintegrated and shot out to meet it, leaving three spears. One shot towards Koira, who again used the green flame to meet it. The resulting explosion was much larger, and she tumbled across the clearing.

The two spears spread out, lining up like a marksman's quarrels. They were too far apart to block, and Ardan wouldn't reach the Priest in time.

There was a sudden streak of Darkness as Mish leapt from behind the Priest. Her claws tore into him. He reflexively let go of the talisman and the black spears disintegrated. The Priest flung Mish away, but she had bought Ardan enough time to close the distance. The Priest raised his arms in a futile attempt to block the weapon. He could hear Seamus yelling at him not to thrust, but he ignored it, stabbing forward, the metal piercing the Priest's chest. Pushing more of the Wild into the sword, he saw the green flame grow, overwhelming and engulfing the Priest. Screams similar to Verrick's filled his ears. It weakened the Wild in him and the primal instincts abated.

There was a roar from a Black Guard. The man was charging, his sword swinging in a broad arc. His connection with Mish was still strong enough that he could leap out of the way. He continued to use his superior dexterity to avoid the man's blows, but he didn't have the precision with his left arm to find the gaps in the man's armour. They repeated the dance a few times, but Ardan could see the guard tiring. Realising his advantage, Ardan knew he'd only have to keep this up for a short while longer.

Suddenly Talon was there, slamming a foot into the man's back, sending him sprawling onto the ground.

'You were taking too long,' Talon said, grinning at him as he brought the axe down at an opening at the guard's neck.

With the Priest and Black Guards down, Raigel attempted to stand, using the pillar to get to his feet. Both Talon and Ardan were immediately on guard, but made no move to attack or fight. His wings were drooping, and his usually vibrant red skin had transformed to a forlorn grey. He tried to take a step forward, but without the support of the pillar he fell to his knees. Even that soon proved too much, and he dropped to a sitting position.

Upon seeing the fall of the demon and the death of the Black Clergy, the remaining mercenaries were quick to throw down their weapons. The forest warriors herded them into a circle and bound their hands.

Ardan's eyes scanned the battlefield, his eyes going past the score of wounded and dead until he found Koira. She was sitting up, and he and Talon went to her side. Besides a few bumps and bruises, she seemed okay.

'You felt it too,' Koira said, looking a little dazed.

'It hurt like the nine Hells,' Ardan said. 'What happened?'

'They attacked an idol. Destroyed it,' Koira said. Her voice was faint, but she had steel in her eyes. 'They destroyed a gift from the Ancients.'

'Can it be repaired?'

'No. But I will make them pay for this treachery.'

Ardan fell into silence, feeling conflicting emotions about the Children coming to Barleron.

'The Priests and Black Guard almost proved too much. If you hadn't shown up when you did, we may not have won.'

'You move well, but your sword work is awful,' Talon said.

'Still healing,' Ardan said, pointing at his right shoulder.

'Not an excuse for your other arm. Get better.'

Despite the words, Ardan felt a grudging respect from the man.

'So that is one of the legendary demons,' Talon said, retrieving one of his fallen axes, putting it in the belt with the others.

'I know him,' Ardan said.

Koira's eyes narrowed, while Talon paused, re-sheathing another axe.

'He was a trading merchant back in the city,' Ardan said quickly. 'Let me speak to him.'

'Fine,' Koira said, 'But we will be ready and watching.'

Talon signalled the remaining forest warriors. Some watched the mercenaries, but the rest joined them, approaching the demon in a semicircle. Four warriors surrounded Koira. The demon again reached for the pillar, and it was almost painful to watch as it pushed himself to its feet.

'It seems you have me at a disadvantage,' Raigel said.

'You destroyed it,' Ardan said, looking at the shattered remains of the idol.

'I did.'

Talon strode forward and swung his axe at one of the demon's arms. It sliced straight through, hitting the stone with a clang. The demon stumbled backwards, losing its balance as it fell onto the ground. He bared his fangs in pain as he clutched onto the stump. Talon looked a little surprised at how effortless it had been.

'Talon, easy, we need information,' Koira said.

Small black tendrils of Darkness were creeping along the demon's arm. It slowly started covering the wound, stemming the black ichor that was seeping out onto the grass.

'Why did you do it?'

Raigel looked up at him, its red and green eye penetrating. 'I cannot tell you.'

Talon growled. The demon looked at the axe without fear. 'I do not hide it by choice. I am bound by my Master's leash.'

Ardan looked at the downed demon. The grey scales tickled at his memory, and their previous conversation flooded his mind. He knew what the demon had been hinting at.

'No human has the power to attack the forest, do they?' Ardan said, realisation filling his voice.

Raigel shook his head.

'You're working for Naberius.'

Raigel held Ardan's gaze but stayed silent.

'We need answers,' Ardan said, understanding.

'Ask. I will lead you to the right answers if I can.'

'Why would you do that?' Talon growled.

'Because I dislike being a slave.'

'Is Naberius in Barleron?' Ardan asked.

'I cannot say.'

'Is he planning on assaulting Barleron?'

'Do you remember our discussion yesterday?' Raigel asked as the Darkness covered the wound, and the ichor stopped dripping.

'That there were several places of power, but Barleron is the most weakly defended.'

Raigel nodded and continued in its gravelly voice, 'If I were my Master, I would pick the weakest.'

'Then he will attack Barleron,' Ardan concluded.

'I cannot say.'

'When?'

At this point, Raigel looked around. He opened his mouth several times but closed it again. 'Tomorrow evening, the Black Temple is holding a ritual to initiate new Priests. Your brood sister will be among them.'

The pieces kept coming together. 'Was this attack to isolate the city?'

Raigel opened his mouth several times, grimacing in pain. He answered in a halting voice, as though trying to navigate through a maze. 'I can only speculate. If I had the power to subdue the Wild, I know it would weaken me tremendously. I would make myself as protected as I could, give myself time to recover.'

'Then when?'

Raigel's green and red eyes focused on Koira. 'He knows of your coming and is making haste to be ready.'

'How soon will your armies arrive?' Ardan demanded of Koira, but her eyes were widening in horror. 'How soon?'

Talon was the one who answered. 'In three days, half the tribes could be gathered.'

'By which time it will be too late,' Raigel said, his whole body shuddering as he coughed.

'How can we stop him?' Ardan said.

'He is powerful and has many allies. The forces of the Light at Dentwall, or the armies of the Children would challenge him, but they will not make it in time. I do not believe you can stop him. There are too few powers nearby; even combined, it is unlikely that you could fight him. However, subduing the Wild takes time and energy. If it were me, I would want no one to attack me while I was subduing the Wild.'

'How long will it take to subdue the Tree? How will we know when to attack?'

'I cannot say.'

They lapsed into silence, unsure of what to ask next.

'This information will not save you,' Talon said.

'No, I did not expect it would. This form will return to Hell soon. If I had a choice, I would have liked to remain on this plane, but you have killed my escort home. Without them, I trust the forest will finish me,' Raigel said, remarkably calm.

'Can you really not save yourself?'

'Before attacking the idol, yes. Now...' Raigel shook his horned head.

'Why did you do it?' Ardan asked.

Raigel stared at the ground while he answered. 'You humans take your free will for granted. The hierarchy in Hell is everything. Naberius is so far above me as to be a distant star. I cannot deny him.'

'Why didn't he do it?'

'The forest is a dangerous place, especially for my kind. I don't expect anyone to come off well if they encounter the shadow colossus. In addition, time is short,' Raigel said. 'And I am viewed as expendable.'

'You said this ritual is tomorrow night?' Koira said.

'No,' Talon snapped, 'Absolutely not.'

'We're going, Talon. Mother will not get here in time, you know this. Only we can make a difference.'

'Let the plainsmen weaken it, and if they cannot destroy it, she can use her powers to finish it off.'

Koira's eyes bored into him as she responded: 'You know that isn't an option. Mother cannot face it in direct combat. If it gains control of the city, we do not have the strength to remove it. How long will we survive if it takes over the forest? We must take this chance now.'

Talon looked mutinous before throwing up his hands. 'By the

Ancients, fine. Fine! Are you happy? I am going to get myself killed to save plainsmen!' He stormed off. 'At least I can interrogate these ones, maybe kill some of them.'

Raigel sat down with his back against the pillar, gazing at the sun shining through the forest canopy.

Ardan left him there and walked over to see the six kneeling, disarmed mercenaries. He recognised Cillian's thinning hair and sharp features. The man stared defiantly up at them. This man had yet to atone for his father's murder.

'Of course, you've gone to those barbarians,' Cillian muttered. 'Going to kill me while I'm defenceless, are you? How about you fight me like a real man?'

'Like the four of you did when you ambushed my father?'

Cillian spat at him. The man expected to die. Ardan had dreamed of the day when his father's killers saw justice. Liam had shown remorse, Verrick was dead and Regan, well, that was a tough one. He stared at Cillian, weighing what he should do. He remembered how it felt to have killed Verrick, how empty it had felt.

'No one would blame you if you were to kill him. We cannot burden ourselves with prisoners,' Talon said.

Ardan didn't answer.

'If we leave them tied up here, they will die. Do you wish to set them free?' Koira said.

'Where would they go? It is unlikely they could make it to the next clearing in time,' Ardan said. 'The Legions of Light are coming through the forest. They must be warned. If we set them free, they could do it.'

'They might make it,' Talon said.

'It is appropriate,' Koira said. 'They fought against us and must earn redemption.'

'Can you send word in case they don't make it?'

Koira looked at Talon, who nodded.

'You people are animals,' Cillian yelled at them as the ropes were being untied. 'You don't even have the balls to kill us yourselves.'

'The boy gave you a chance. If you are tired of life, I can assist you,' Talon said, his hand resting on an axe.

Cillian continued to glare at Ardan but said nothing further. His ropes had been untied first. He took one slashing glance at them before he removed his armour and took off towards the second clearing.

After the mercenaries had been freed, the injured warriors disappeared into the trees, the ones with minor injuries assisting those with heavier injuries, while the rest of them made their way towards Barleron.

Ardan knew that their chances of winning against one of the High Demons were slim, but he would die trying to kill it before he would bow down before it or anything else.

CHAPTER FIFTY-NINE: THE CALM
BEFORE THE STORM

* * *

ichael and his armies have cut us off from the sea, surrounding us from the south, east and west. The frozen tundra to the north bars our retreat. We are trapped and must fight. I will make them pay so dearly for their victory that my name will inspire dread for a thousand years.

— Titivillus, *Annals of Lucifer.*

* * *

ARDAN FOLLOWED the group of forest warriors. They left behind the still-breathing Raigel, and he felt a pang of regret. The demon didn't have any choice in his masters. He wasn't exactly innocent, but he was another unwilling casualty in Naberius' war. He wondered how much of the civil war had resulted from Naberius' machinations. It had been easier to stay hidden in the chaos.

Talon hissed. Broken from his reverie, Ardan saw the warriors had peeled off and disappeared into the brush. He fell in behind them. They went into the thick of the forest and each member pulled out his pack, complete with bedroll, from their hidden spots in the brush. Ardan suddenly felt self-conscious. He had no pack, a nearly empty skin of water and no food. He fell into single file behind a warrior who had shaved his head to reveal tribal tattoos going up from his neck and across his scalp.

There was no talking amongst the Children as they walked. They moved as his father had, treading quietly while maintaining their speed. Even Mish picked up on the mood, silently following in his footsteps. Ardan had to concentrate to move quickly while remaining silent. The still-healing wounds on his shoulder and ribs were protesting their poor treatment. He used the Wild to create a small connection with Mish in order to keep up.

They kept moving through the brush, with only the sound of insects and the songs of birds to keep them company. The sun slowly set. None of the other warriors seemed worried and Ardan tried to emulate their lack of concern, but images of the shadow colossus kept intruding on his thoughts.

He was so focused on his footing that Ardan almost ran into the back of a warrior. Before them, a small clearing opened up with an idol in its centre. It was only now that Ardan felt the inner warmth that the shifting, turning object projected.

The others had already gathered wood. Ardan hastened to help. They picked up wood in a manner that was unfamiliar to Ardan. A couple glared at him for picking up the wrong wood.

It all burns, doesn't it? Ardan thought.

'You don't pick up wood that is clearly visible in the open. It shows too much of humans passing,' Koira explained. 'You need to get the less noticeable ones.'

'And the path we trampled getting here?'

'We can't leave no trace of our passing, but we can make it as difficult to follow as possible. It's why Talon went last. He will close our passing as best he can, make it challenging to track.'

As she spoke, Ardan noticed that two of the warriors were digging a fire pit and a third was piling stones around it. Before long the fire was going, the stones effectively blocking the light. It took time, but eventually the heat soaked through the stones, radiating warmth. Ardan realized how little he understood about living in the forest.

'You travel light,' Koira said as she sat down next to him, going through her own small pack.

'When the idol shattered, I felt I had to get to the clearing quickly. I left my pack and bedroll behind.'

Talon gave a snort of derision.

Koira pulled out some strips of dried meat and handed them to him.

Ardan thanked her for the meat and took a bite. It was soft, almost tender. A moment later, a wave of flavour washed over him. The venison tasted like it had just come off the fire, smoked and succulent, with a small fiery spice. He quickly swallowed before taking a much larger bite the next time.

'Plainsmen don't spice things properly,' Koira said as she sat down next to him.

Ardan ripped off another mouthful.

Her eyes focused on the ground as her foot moved over the grass. He knew her well enough to realise that she was trying to work through something in her mind. The other warriors had laid out their own bedrolls and were gathering around the fire pit, having their evening meal while they talked quietly amongst each other.

'Can you explain something to me?' Koira asked at last.

Ardan's mouth was too full of jerky to speak, so he gestured for her to continue.

'We fight this demon because it will destroy our home, likely our way of life. But why do you fight? Would it be so terrible to let this Naberius take control? Barleron has not had a powerful ruler in some time. Would this demon not bring stability?'

Startled, Ardan chewed and swallowed while he considered it. Naberius had devout followers in the north, and that meant he couldn't be all bad, could he? Raigel had said he wasn't cruel, only vengeful if wronged. Would his father have been murdered if Naberius had ruled the city?

Ardan took time to weigh the question. It didn't take him long to find his answer. 'The cost would be too high. Our freedom would vanish. If Naberius took control, I fear we would be nothing more than pawns. Then, if he succeeded, what then? I doubt he has any love for humans. Would he still rule us when he no longer needed us? Or would he kill us, or make us continue our servitude in his wars? As bad as things have been, there is still hope and the belief that things will get better. It may not, but our hope remains. I believe hope would die under Naberius.'

Koira stared into the fire for a long time before she answered: 'There is a lot to be said for being free.'

Ardan felt the pain behind that admission, but he didn't press it. 'Is your mother really so powerful?' he asked, thinking about her comment that she couldn't face Naberius directly.

Her brown eyes regarded him as she spoke. 'She doesn't use any tools like your sword, and doesn't think I should, either. Her ability with the Wild far exceeds my own,' she finished with a rueful smile. Ardan had a flashback of her sailing through the air when she blocked one of the Dark Priest's attacks, imagining that the fall wouldn't have been pleasant.

'Why no buffer?'

'Mother is firmly against it. She says the Wild was different once. The Ancients would wield it for life, and it would respond. But after the angels and demons arrived, they twisted its purpose. It became something feral, striking any who touch it. Mother says using a buffer just further bastardises it.' Her voice took on a hard edge as she went on, 'I fear the longer this war between Heaven and Hell continues, the more unstable the Wild will become.'

Silence fell, with only the crackling of the fire to break it. Eventually most of the forest warriors sought their bedrolls. Ardan had drawn the first watch and Koira the second. Forest royalty she might be, but it didn't exempt her from watch duty. Without saying anything, she stayed up with him.

'What was it like growing up here?' Ardan asked in a low voice. 'I mean, it would be extremely dangerous for children, wouldn't it?'

'Our homeland is deep in the forest, but we have some idols to shield us, and my mother has enough power to create her own special brand of protection. It is dangerous, but the adults diligently watch over the children. I had a great time growing up, though I'm not sure my mother would always agree. One time, as a child, I found a forest viper and carried it to my mother. I don't know how I didn't get bitten; just lucky, I guess,' she said with a shrug. 'My mother was so startled that she let loose the Wild. The explosion sent us all flying across our home. The poor viper was burned to a crisp, and I was a mess, crying and distraught. I thought I had brought her the best gift in the world while she berated me for doing something so dangerous.'

Ardan was trying desperately to stifle his laugher as the story continued. He eventually earned a glare from one of the forest warriors who pointedly turned over in his bedroll, so his back was facing them.

Their conversation stayed on lighter topics as they spoke late into the night. Ardan could feel her closeness. His eyes were constantly drawn to her lips, and he thought about kissing her again. But something about their last meeting made him hesitate. He tried to focus on her headband instead, the way it held back her auburn hair. Then he caught her eyes and his thoughts ceased.

'I don't know what the future holds for us, or if anything between us is possible, but I am glad I met you.'

She smiled, her hand reaching out to pull him close. Their lips met. The looming battle added a desperate passion. He wasn't sure how long their kiss lasted, but they eventually split apart, realising that it was difficult to keep a lookout while they were that focused on each other.

When their watch was over and without considering the consequences, he followed her to her bedroll. It had been placed a significant distance from the others. As she lay down, he took a position behind her, his arms wrapping around her body. He could feel the warmth of her, his hands running up and down the soft skin of her arms. He could smell her perfume of sage and sweetgrass. *How does she still smell so good?* His hands trailed circles, brushing across the leather jerkin. She leaned back into him. Her hand reaching down for the strings of his breeches.

'What about the others?' Ardan whispered.

'Foolish plainsman, what we do is nothing to be ashamed of, nor will they watch,' Koira said.

Ardan made no other protests as they continued to kiss, slowly undressing each other, using the light of the stars to illuminate them. They proceeded to make love under the night sky, their bodies entwined like the vines of the trees. The Wild rose up between them, celebrating their union, the power complimenting and matching their passion in a crescendo of emotions and tenderness.

He had no idea how much time has passed, but when they were done, there was a light sheen of sweat covering their bodies. Ardan pulled Koira close, wrapping his arms around her. They didn't speak; there was no need. Eventually, Koira fell asleep in his arms. Ardan felt like he never knew what to expect from her, but she kept life exciting.

CHAPTER SIXTY: CITY AFLAME

* * *

*M*ichael has grown overconfident. He has charged blindly into my domain. My armies strike from the shadows, destroying supply lines and food stores. Communications are intercepted and misdirected. We fight at his weak points, inflicting cuts to his underbelly. Only time will dictate if the confrontation between us is finally forced.

— Titivillus, *Annals of Lucifer.*

* * *

ARDAN OPENED his eyes to the predawn light. Koira's hair was tickling his nose, his back felt stiff, the arm that cradled her head was numb and the wound on his ribs was itching irritably. Despite the discomforts, he didn't want the moment to end.

An acrid smell of smoke intruded on them; it was more than just their campfire. He reluctantly looked up. Talon was standing at the edge of the clearing, his cloak discarded, showing off the whipcord muscles beneath his tattooed back. The warrior was looking above the trees. Ardan followed the man's gaze. He could see an orange glow but realised it wasn't from the sun.

Ardan disturbed Koira in his haste to get up. He ignored the pain that ran through his arm as blood rushed back into it. He arrived next to Talon. The man held out an arm, stopping him from going past the invisible line of safety.

'What is it?' Ardan demanded.

'Your city is on fire.'

'Why didn't you wake me?'

'What good would it have done? We cannot leave the clearing.'

Ardan cursed, frustrated.

Talon remained silent.

'Has it begun already?' Koira said, coming up behind them.

'So it would seem,' Talon said. 'I will go to the city, but I suggest you stay behind. It will be dangerous.'

Koira said nothing, but there was a set to her jaw that made her answer clear.

'I didn't think so,' Talon said, his eyes never leaving the orange glow and column of smoke.

Ardan stood there, practically dancing in his impatience. He knew rushing would help no one, but it still pushed him to do something, anything. Yet Talon stood there, his presence enough to stop Ardan from doing anything rash.

At some unseen signal, Talon gave a shrill whistle. The entire camp responded, the soldiers moving, gathering up their bedrolls, cooking utensils and anything that wasn't weapons, armour and water skins and placing it at the edge of the clearing.

Whatever they were doing, they were not doing it fast enough, in Ardan's opinion. They should move now. He tried to step forward, but Talon slapped him back as though he were an unruly toddler. Koira laid a hand on his arm, and it settled him enough to stop him from trying. Mish watched the entire exchange with patient green eyes.

Talon finally gave the signal to enter the forest but pointedly took the lead, keeping an agonisingly slow pace. Ardan wanted to push past him and run towards the city, but the dense jungle made it virtually impossible. Grumbling, he kept his place until they reached the main road.

Once they were out of the dense brush, their speed increased, but it wasn't enough to sate Ardan. The roadway stretched out with more turns than he remembered. After an eternity, they finally made it to the edge. Judging by the sun, it was only an hour or two past midday. *I could have sworn it was later*, he thought, and he forcibly calmed himself. Their party broke through the barrier that marked the border between the forest and the fields. The fields were empty; not a single soul moved between the rows of crops. No one walked the roads. Ardan looked at the moss-covered walls. He could see Barleron was on fire, but he couldn't tell which parts. Only the Tree of the Ancients, the Cathedral of Light, and the Dark Temple rose above the skyline. None of them appeared touched by the flame.

'Impatience and agitation help no one. Take a second now to save two later.'

Ardan felt his father's advice float into his mind and was embarrassed over his frustrations.

Talon whistled and their party spread out, covering the road to the city in a staggered line. Now that they were in the open, Talon urged their group into an easy jog.

The smoke rose, black and red, as it strove to blot out the sky. When they reached the unmanned gates, Talon gave another whistle, and everyone drew their weapons. Two checked the immediate interior of the gates. Their pace was slow, but Talon treated every intersection as an ambush site and each open window as a potential hiding spot for an enemy.

Ardan tried to stop his imagination from growing out of hand. *Had Naberius already attacked the city? What had happened to all the people?* He tried to focus on the task before them, but with each street his dread grew, and every corner devoid of people made his fear rise.

After dozens of blocks, they came across a group of men, covered in ash and with rags tied over their mouths, pushing a wagon laden with water barrels. Behind them were several women and children trying to fill buckets at a nearby well.

Talon didn't pause; he whistled, and they continued past them. The closer to the plume of smoke they got, the more common these bands of people became. Ardan coughed, having difficulty breathing in the heavy smoke.

Eventually the streets opened up into a clear view of the harbour.

It was what Ardan imagined the fires of Hell would look like. The entire Dock area was ablaze. Wharves that had once reached deep into the harbour were now smouldering ruins. Ships had been reduced to little more than floating, burning debris. The fire had spread to all the waterfront buildings, most of them burnt down to their charred foundations, while bucket brigades desperately tried to stop the fire from spreading further. Ardan lifted his shirt over his mouth to give relief from the heavy smoke in the air.

'It seems no help will come from the sea,' Talon said as he too tied a rag over his mouth.

The ships had effectively been sunk across the harbour mouth, making entrance into the city difficult, if not impossible.

'And no one can escape either,' Koira said, muffled by the rag over her lower face.

It felt like a game of Kings. Naberius was making his move, trying to block all actions against him.

Ardan tried to suppress a shiver and failed.

Groups of church soldiers, mercenaries and even some of the Fiddler's men were working together to fight the fires. There were four funnels of water rising from the harbour. They curved over the Docks and showered water onto the nearby burning buildings. Ardan found the group of Shapers, using Bree's distinctive silver hair as a beacon. Next to her, in a myriad of greens, blues and greys, was a figure who could only be her mentor Murieen, the water Shaper. The others Ardan didn't recognise.

Murieen raised her hands in the air, as though calling out to the ocean. Then Ardan saw it: a mound of water approaching rapidly from the other side of the harbour. It grew as it got closer, rising higher than the Docks. A few people ran in panic, but most watched calmly as the wall of water made a distinct route for the area burning most brightly. The wave crashed against the Docks, its water rushing down the streets, extinguishing every fire in its path. The flames around that area of the Docks immediately subsided. Murieen staggered once it was done. Ardan had never seen a water Shaper unleashing their power fully before. Despite the woman's efforts, the wave of water quickly receded. The fires were growing again, but it had given a space for the bucket brigades.

Ardan shook himself. He needed to find Riordan or Marion.

Numerous people were going in and out of an untouched dockside Inn. Ardan moved towards it, suspecting it was a makeshift headquarters, and if he didn't find either of them there, he'd at likely find their whereabouts.

Inside the Inn, the assault of the smoke immediately lessened. The common room was filled with people. Men and woman shouted, talked and gave orders. Lachlan and Dásun were off in one corner, both covered in soot, as they directed different mercenaries with a roughly drawn map hung up on the wall. Thinking of Verrick, Ardan knew he didn't want to talk to the two of them.

'Where in the blazes of Hell have you been?' Ardan spun to see Riordan coming towards him. His red hair was almost black with ash. His outburst barely halted the cacophony of conversation between the other groups inside the Inn.

Behind him at another table was Marion. Soot covered her once fine dress and dark smudges covered her fair skin.

'Riordan, I need to speak to you and Marion in private,' Ardan said.

'Not until you—' Riordan began.

'You'd best listen to him,' Talon said, coming to his defence. 'It is important.'

'You're back. Of course you are, just as the Docks are ablaze.'

'Riordan,' Marion said, a warning in her tone. 'There is a private room out the back.'

They followed Riordan to an intimate room adorned with a round table and half a dozen chairs. A banister held some small casks. It had the feel of a private drinking parlour.

Marion and Riordan walked around the table but didn't sit. Koira and Talon came in behind Ardan.

'Naberius is here, in the city,' Ardan said without preamble.

His statement was met with stunned silence.

'It can't be,' Riordan said. Beneath his soot covered face, his skin seemed to grow paler. He was the only one who had seen the demon in battle.

'The merchant demon Raigel, under the command of Naberius, destroyed the idol in the first clearing. The forest road is a death trap. He all but confirmed Naberius is about to make his move. I think that this,' Ardan waved a hand at the Docks, 'is part of it.'

'Sweet angels,' Marion said. 'There's no way out. We're stuck in the city with a High Demon.'

'He is seeking to control the power of the forest,' Ardan said. 'The Tree of the Ancients is the key.'

'How do you know this?' Marion said, then shook her head. 'It doesn't matter. I believe you. What matters is the people. We need to save as many as we can.'

'Where can we send them?' Riordan asked.

Marion looked at Koira.

'No. We will not take any plainsmen.'

Marion and Riordan stared at Koira in disbelief.

'There are thousands of lives you could save.'

'If Naberius takes control of this city, my home will soon fall to his power. If you are forced to stay, you will fight,' Koira said.

Riordan started forward angrily. Talon immediately stepped in front of him, towering over the mercenary, but Riordan had the greater bulk. They stared at each other, each waiting for the other man to draw his weapon.

'And what of your armies? Are they still marching here?' Marion demanded.

'They will be too late. It is only the advance force and I.'

'If escape is out of the question, perhaps we should surrender,' Marion said.

'No,' it was Riordan who spoke, his eyes never leaving Talon's. 'The survivors from Naberius' legions were half starved, ragged and disease-ridden. They spoke of how their children were abandoned because they served no purpose in the hound's army. Those that resisted were killed, those that were slow were flogged.'

'So we must fight,' Ardan said.

'We will die,' Riordan said.

'Raigel said we might have a chance. If we attack while Naberius is focused on the Tree, he will be weakened and distracted.'

'Fighting a High Demon,' Marion said slowly, turning to Riordan. 'Would fighting it be possible? Could we win?'

'We might have a chance if what the lad says is true. He has little more than his Black Guards and Priests. If subduing the Tree weakens him enough, and we hit him with every soldier, mercenary, Shaper, Priest of the Light and washerwoman who can hold a weapon—then maybe, maybe we have a chance,' Riordan said, but they all heard the undercurrent in his tone.

'We will fight with you,' Koira said.

The statement drained some of tension from the room. Riordan took a step back, and Talon's hand moved away from his axes.

Marion looked at Koira. 'If we fight and lose, will you consider getting some of the people out?'

'If we try and fail, I will do my best to get your people out,' Koira conceded.

'Then we must make plans,' Marion said, her hands resting on the table. 'The first question is: when will Naberius make his move?'

'The Dark Temple is holding a ritual tonight. I think Naberius is using it to bolster his position before he strikes,' Ardan said. 'Considering the Docks, either tonight or tomorrow. It wouldn't make any sense to wait longer.'

'Luckily we have gathered most of the mercenaries, ready to meet the Children,' Marion said.

'It won't be enough. We'll need the Cathedral and anyone else we can find.'

'Whoever fought against this fire is not in the demon's confidence, and would be potential allies to our cause,' Talon said.

'I can do my best to bring the merchants around. Can your mother help?' Marion asked, her green eyes on Ardan.

'If anyone could, it would be her,' Ardan said. Though he knew how the merchants liked to stay clear of conflicts.

'How many can you muster?' Talon asked.

Ardan did the calculations in his head, counting the rough numbers of mercenaries, and guessing the amount of church soldiers. 'Maybe a thousand soldiers, one Templar, several Priests of the Light and however many Shapers that join us.'

'I saw the hound absorb a hundred arrows without slowing. It took ten Templars and scores of Priests to take him down,' Riordan said.

'A fool's gambit, then,' Talon said. 'At least I will fall fighting something worthy.'

A grim silence followed that statement.

'Do we know who Naberius is?' Marion asked. 'The form he has taken? Or she?'

'I never saw his human form,' Riordan said.

'It is likely one of the three Priests at the Temple. Guillamere the High Priest, Esalon, or Orla,' Ardan said, though he desperately hoped it wasn't Orla. 'Either that or—'

'Or?'

'The Fiddler.'

'Him?' Marion asked, shocked.

'He was there,' Koira confirmed.

Ardan nodded, adding: 'Where did he come from, before the battle of Jophiel's Pass? He's been trying to take control of the city. People have seen him with the Dark Priests.'

'It's possible,' Riordan said. 'He has the same callous disregard for his followers.'

'Does it matter?' Talon asked. They looked at him. 'Does it matter if we know who this demon is hiding as? We will find out soon enough.'

'I guess not,' Ardan said.

'We need to split up to gather everyone in time. The lad has given us a time frame. Let's use it,' Riordan said.

CHAPTER SIXTY-ONE:
RESERVATIONS OF THE LIGHT

* * *

Michael has taken the bait. He believes me weak, that I have expended myself in his recent defeats. He has stormed the centre of my power and challenges me to single combat, something we have not done for aeons.

— Titivillus, *Annals of Lucifer.*

* * *

ARDAN STARED up at the bell tower rising high into the sky, supported by the tall grey Cathedral walls. Mish sat at his heels. Most of the church soldiers milling about the entrance were covered in black soot. They grinned at each other while indulging in mutual, overenthusiastic back slapping. There didn't seem to be a single grizzly-haired, bad-tempered veteran amongst them.

Two large oak doors guarded the Cathedral entrance and Ardan wondered if he was the right person to be here. They were short on time and options. Marion was the obvious choice to deal with the Countess. Only Riordan knew the intricacies and different deals among the mercenaries. Bree was finding what Shapers she could, and that left him to deal with the Cathedral.

The seven Archangels had been carved intricately above the entrance, their eyes looking down on him judgementally. Ardan suppressed a shiver, knowing he didn't want to walk through those doors. Nor did he want to encounter Frederick. Had the Bishop forgiven him? He sighed; he needed to finish here and get to the Temple. There was still time to turn Liá. What he needed was an easier path. The only person he knew who might help him was Donnacha, the Cathedral cook. Ardan walked towards the side entrance. A few church soldiers gave him cautious glances. He was armed, and he held no obvious allegiance to the Light, but none bothered him.

Ardan could smell the aroma of the stew before he got there. The place had been practically barren when he was cast out. Now there were hunks of meat hanging from racks, and cheeses lining the shelves. There were loaves of bread cooling on one bench and Donnacha was sprinkling some spices into the large pot. The contents were thick enough that he was having trouble stirring it. Mish immediately jumped onto the bench to sniff at the pot. Donnacha smiled, but when he looked up, the smile vanished.

'You,' he said coldly.

'I need to see the Templar. Please trust me, it's important.'

'You're not welcome,' he said, holding the stirring spoon in front of him like a club. *Great,* Ardan thought, *what now?*

'Back again?'

Ardan turned to see a man shuffling as he carried in an enormous cauldron. Liam's small eyes shifted between Donnacha and Ardan.

'He's had dealings with the devil.'

'We've all done things we're not proud of,' Liam said.

'I need to see the Templar,' Ardan said.

Liam closed his eyes for a moment. 'Am I going to regret taking you there?'

'No.'

'He's a heathen,' Donnacha hissed.

Instead of answering, Liam put the cauldron down and gestured for Ardan to follow him to the cloisters. They could hear Donnacha spluttering in the background. Ardan and Liá had stayed in the same cloisters when they'd first arrived.

Liam knocked on one of the cloister doors. The Templar Phillip opened it almost immediately. He was in the middle of donning his breastplate. Several books lay open on his bed, while an assortment of weapons was lined neatly up against his wall.

'Liam and,' he looked at Ardan curiously for a moment, 'Ardan isn't it? Why do I get a sinking feeling seeing you here?' he asked, but his smile was warm.

Ardan shifted uncomfortably, not sure how to begin.

'What brings you to my doorstep?' Phillip prompted.

'Naberius is in the city.'

Liam, who had been scratching Mish under the chin, stopped and stared at him.

'I suspected as much. I'm guessing the fire was his work?'

'We think so,' Ardan said. 'We also think he is going to attack the Tree of the Ancients.'

'And through it, control the Wild of the forest,' Phillip concluded. Ardan's surprise must have been clear because the man explained, 'I've been dealing with the demons and their schemes for years. What about you?'

'Raigel told me.'

'A demon told you this,' Phillip said, his eyes narrowing.

'He told me when he was on the verge of death. After he destroyed the idol in the forest.'

'So the only trail east is now closed,' Phillip said slowly. 'Naberius knew. I thought I had kept it quiet—that help was coming from the Empire and the Citadel,' Phillip said, pacing. Ardan felt a stirring in his chest as Phillip continued, 'But he's stopped both. Damn that beast,' Phillip said, and slammed a fist into the wall. The entire room shook, with dust shifting out from the walls. The blow would have broken a normal person's hand, but Phillip gave it a quick shake and appeared fine.

'Marion is gathering all the forces in the city.'

'Admirable.'

'Raigel said that during the assault on the Tree, Naberius will be vulnerable. If we strike then...'

'He might be weak enough to slay,' Phillip mused. 'Do you trust this demon?'

Ardan hesitated for only a moment. 'Yes.'

Phillip picked up his spear, staring at the point before he answered: 'These hallowed walls would not hold out against a concentrated attack from a High Demon. We have no other options. We must operate as though this is true. At Jophiel's Pass, we had ten Templars, half the Priests from the Citadel, and ten thousand warriors. We won by the barest of threads. We only have a tiny fraction of that now,' he said, putting the spear back against the wall. 'Still, we are with you.'

'I can get the men ready. When will they be needed?' Liam asked.

'Ardan?' Phillip asked.

'There is a ritual tonight, one that could strengthen Naberius. My sister is involved but I think I can turn her,' Ardan said, a half-formed plan already playing out in his mind.

Phillip paused. 'You have family with the Black?'

Before he could even think about answering, Phillip moved impossibly fast. The man had his hands around his throat, lifting him into the air. A sudden surge of Light flowed through him. There was a hot flash, as though fire was being poured through his veins. Mish started yowling as she fell to the floor. Calloused hands choked off any scream he tried to make. The longer it continued, the more his anger and panic built up. The Wild responded and met the Light coursing through his body.

An explosion of white and green flung the two of them against opposite walls. Ardan hit hard. He fumbled, dazed and gasping, but he drew his sword, the blade instantly alight with green fire.

Phillip looked unfazed. Liam stared at them, looking like he wanted to be anywhere else.

'You channel the Wild,' Phillip said at last. 'When you mentioned your family in the Darkness, I thought you had slipped, and this was an elaborate trap. Despite knowing you are not one of their agents, I am no longer sure I can trust you.'

'You're not sure you can trust me?' Ardan said incredulously as he massaged his throat.

'I am aware of the irony. However, I am less certain about committing our forces.'

'Without you, we won't have a chance.'

'I cannot make any promises.'

'We will die without you. If you do not back us, then we will throw our lot in with Naberius,' Ardan said, his mouth getting away from him. It was a wild bluff, but he kept his face still, willing the Templar to believe it.

Phillip paused, his eyes searching.

'You play a dangerous game,' Phillip said at last. 'You show me I have a slight chance in trusting you, or no chance at all.'

Ardan breathed a sigh of relief. He'd done it.

'If you have lied to us, you had best hope I do not survive.'

The tone sent a shiver through Ardan's body. He looked Phillip squarely in the eyes. 'We're going to fight a High Demon. I don't think either of us will survive.'

The Templar eyed him for a long time before answering: 'I will prepare. What are the details?'

Ardan relayed everything he knew before leaving. He closed the door, walking down the long hallway to the courtyard. It was still possible to reach the Temple. He patted the coin purse on his belt to reassure him of its weight. It might work.

Ardan faced a dozen spears as he entered the courtyard. A squad of soldiers was lined up shoulder to shoulder, their weapons and shields blocking him in. Behind them were Donnacha and the Bishop. The cook pointed enthusiastically.

'See, I told you he came for the Templar.'

Ardan sighed. This was the last thing he needed. They were running out of time. Mish was between his legs, her hackles raised as she let out a warning yowl.

'This is the second time you have broken your banishment,' Frederick said. The Bishop had a fresh purple sash of office. 'Explain yourself.'

The Wild rose in annoyance. Ardan quashed it as best he could. Time was running out. He needed to make it to the Temple of Darkness soon, and he couldn't let them search him. He opened his mouth to respond.

'Let him go,' a voice boomed. Ardan jumped, the Wild inside him scattering at the same time. The Templar was there, a light glow emanating from his features. 'Bishop, we have much to discuss. The rest of you, who's in command?'

One soldier, with a wispy mismatched beard, raised a spear. 'I am.'

'Good, find commander Oisin. Tell him to mobilise everyone, and I mean everyone. We are going to war.'

The soldiers looked to the Bishop.

'You heard him, go.'

The Templar leaned down and whispered to Ardan. 'You'd best go. I will be at your rendezvous. We will be ready.'

CHAPTER SIXTY-TWO: THE RITUAL OF SHADOW

* * *

*B*oth Lucifer and Titivillus are dead. I arrived too late. Michael was too weak after the fight to oppose me; I tore off his wings, one chunk at a time. After I'd removed his wings, he became mortal. I gored him and left his entrails across the stone, slaying any who were foolish enough to approach. Michael's dying screams were some comfort as I mourned the fall of my Master.

— Naberius, *Annals of Lucifer.*

* * *

ARDAN'S FEET pounded on the cobbles as he raced through the streets. The acrid smell of smoke lingered in the air, sometimes making breathing difficult. Ardan let the connection between him and Mish flow, reducing his fatigue and helping him to run lightly and quickly. The Dock fires were a smouldering glow in the darkness.

The Temple dominated the southern part of the city, its very presence sending a wave of trepidation through him. The Wild inside of Ardan rose defiantly in spite of it. A sizeable crowd filled the bottom of the stairs. Mish stayed on Ardan's heels despite the number of people, as he pushed his way through the crowd to find some Black Guards blocking his way.

'You made it.'

Ardan turned to see his brother's hulking figure turn towards him. Davan was in chainmail, the axe strapped across his back. Ardan's connection with Mish made his thoughts sluggish.

'I sent messages everywhere. Where have you been? It doesn't matter; come on, it's bound to start at any moment.' Davan grabbed him by the shoulder and half led, half dragged him towards the Temple steps.

THE BLACK GUARDS let them pass.

Halfway up to the Temple, a glow of red and black cascaded down the steps. Ardan thought it was a trick of the light but then he realised the Temple was getting darker. At the top was a flame made of pure darkness, sucking in the surrounding light.

'Best guess, that's hellfire,' Davan said.

'You know it?'

'Some Wolves tell stories about it and how Naberius breathes the stuff.'

That's comforting, Ardan thought as they ascended the stairs. The two moons shone their light on the steps despite the fire.

They reached the top of the stairs, and at the centre was a huge bonfire of black and red flame, twisting and turning like seaweed in a turbulent ocean. It cast an eerie light over the onlookers, most of whom were pressed up against the battlements with a line of Black Guards creating a wall between the onlookers and the flame.

Ardan followed Davan as his brother pushed people aside. A few turned to curse him but stayed silent after seeing his size. The dark, hooded Priests created an inner ring around the fire. Interspersed between them were a half dozen acolytes in their grey robes.

One of the grey robes stepped forward, directly before the flame. It rose like a wild beast, twisting and writhing. The acolyte plunged their hand into the heart of the blaze and dark fire leapt out in response. The flames raced up their arm as though it were kindling. They tried to beat out the flames, but the fire kept spreading. Their movements became more frantic and within moments they were fully engulfed like a human torch. Then the screams started. The figure dropped and rolled around, trying to douse the flames, but they continued to spread.

Ardan stared in horror as it immolated him. He had vivid flash-backs of Verrick's death, and the screams echoed in his mind. The smell of charred flesh wafted over to them. Davan's hand uncon-sciously reached for his axe. The screaming died down quickly, but the smouldering figure lay there as the fire consumed his robes, body, and his bones before it finally puttered out.

What kind of messed up ritual is this? Ardan thought.

A second figure stepped up. Their motions were hesitant as they reached for the flame. They fared little better. The flames caught on the edge of their robes and stayed there, neither advancing nor reced-ing. Though the figure stood there calmly at first, their motions were becoming more frantic until the fire spread, consuming them too.

'Is this just a sacrifice?' Ardan asked, feeling sick.

'I will not let Liá die.'

'I'm behind you,' Ardan said, then reached out and grabbed his brother's arm. 'That's her now.'

'Are you sure?' Davan said, drawing his axe.

'Definitely.' Ardan wasn't sure how he knew. It might have been her movements, her frame, or something else, but he knew. His hand reached for his sword. It was suicide going up against so many Black Guards.

'Liá, no!' Ardan shouted just as she put her hands in the fire. Her head turned in surprise as the flame raced up her arm. She spun back to the flame. The spreading fire slowed, then stopped. It started retreating, going back down her arm until it became a small flame of Darkness that hovered above her hand. Her other hand held the silver symbol of Lucifer. She raised it to the flame, and it was funnelled into Lucifer's eyes. As she finished, the symbol had a silvery black sheen.

He and his brother hadn't even taken a step, too entranced by their sister controlling the blaze. There were four Black Guards in front of them, their hands on their weapons, ready to draw on them in a moment.

Besides some singing on her robe, Liá appeared fine. A black-robed figure came up behind Liá. Their sister turned and hugged the person. After their embrace, the figure looked towards Davan and Ardan, gesturing them forward.

'That sort of distraction could have gotten her killed,' Orla whispered, lowering her hood.

'I don't think they knew any better,' Liá said. 'What? I was going to explain, but they were late. You were meant to be here hours ago.'

'His fault,' Davan said, hiking a thumb at Ardan.

'What were you doing?' Ardan asked.

'My final test. I had to control the Darkness without help and take it as my own.'

'It's beyond stupid,' Orla said.

'She thinks we're pushing people through too early.'

'You were the only one who should be here. It'll be Lucifer's luck if even one more survives.'

'Have some faith,' Liá said. 'They're stronger than you think.'

Ardan felt eyes on him. He looked for the source, and through a flicker of the hellfire he saw light shining on Esalon's features. He smiled.

Next to him stood the High Priest. His hood was down, and he wore an elaborate headdress covering his braided hair. He held the same staff with the horned skull adorning the end. It reminded Ardan of why they were here. Who was Naberius? Was it him? Was it Orla?

The next poor acolyte had already lost control of the flames. Her screaming drew Ardan's attention.

'You must watch,' Orla snapped at Liá, who looked as sick as Ardan felt.

'But it's Trisha.'

'Watch and remember her sacrifice, so that it gives you strength to make things better.'

Thankfully, she was the last to fall. The next candidate gained control of the Darkness. His attempt wasn't as smooth as Liá's had been. He had to focus, and the flame kept threatening to spill out and onto his arms, but eventually, he controlled it and forced it into the symbol on his chest. His face flushed with success as he took his place by his mentor's side.

The High Priest stood before the flames, holding the symbol of Lucifer and his staff. The flame leapt towards him, but unlike the others, the Darkness split, being absorbed by the symbol at his neck and the horned skull at the end of the staff.

Ardan could feel the Wild build up inside him. An undercurrent of fear eroded its defiance. The need to flee, run, and hide was becoming overwhelming. Mish crouched low, almost making him stumble as she lay against his ankle.

When the flame was gone, the natural light of the stars and moons returned. The High Priest turned towards them, a smile etched in his features as he spoke.

'Congratulations to Lucifer's newest children. You have called the Darkness, and the Darkness has obeyed. You are now members of our order,' Guillaume said. Next to him stood Esalon, the man's dark eyes scanning the crowd.

Guillaume's speech continued in a monotone, about the glories of the Darkness and the wonders of Lucifer. It allowed Ardan to get his emotions under control. After it was done, everybody applauded and the High Priest bowed, before leading a small retinue inside the Temple. The remaining crowd dispersed, some heading inside the Temple, others heading down the stairs.

'It's done,' Liá said.

'We will mourn,' Orla said. 'Three souls died tonight—and that could have been avoided.'

'Then why did they push them through?' Ardan asked.

It was only a pent breath of hesitation, and Ardan almost missed it. 'The High Priest is worried about the legions of the Light. He thinks they may make a move soon.'

'But you made it, little one,' Davan said, and just like they had when they were children, he quickly had her in a headlock, ruffling her hair with his hand. She gasped in shock, her dark hair quickly spilling out in all directions. 'I would love to stay and help celebrate, but I have duties tonight,' he said, letting her go while she spluttered with indignation.

'I'll see you at Marion's mansion,' Ardan said.

'I'll be at the park of the Ancients,' Davan said, puzzled. 'Lachlan is giving me my first command.'

'Aren't you meeting with Marion to discuss strategy?' Ardan said, confused.

It was Davan's turn to look confused. 'Marion? Why would she be involved? The rest of the ritual is at the park. The major mercenary companies will be there to stop the Light interfering.'

'You're working for the Dark Priesthood?' Ardan felt a dread creep over him.

'Yeah, they hired us a few days ago. We'll still be ready for when the Children arrive. Sorry, but I've already stayed too late. I've got to go.'

Ardan watched him go, people parting around him as he went down the steps. Ardan turned back to see Liá and Orla studying him.

'Ardan,' Liá said slowly, 'How much do you know?'

Ardan was inwardly cursing himself for forgetting his mother's lessons. His face became a mask. He was playing Kings. This was another tactic, another move he had to make.

'About the impending attack on the Tree or Naberius' overall plan?'

'Shh,' Orla said, her eyes wide with shock. She glanced around, but no one seemed to have taken notice. Most of the crowd had already dispersed. She gestured them over to a corner of the battlements.

Ardan followed without speaking. There was a depiction on the wall of Lucifer holding Naberius' leash while the three-headed hound breathed fire.

'Should I even bother asking you to stay out of it?' Liá asked.

Ardan thought about the question. Did they have a chance without the mercenaries? Ardan didn't think so. Should he stay out of it? He could get out, could survive. It wouldn't be the first time. Yet he thought about what he'd be leaving behind. His cowardice would cause the people to be enslaved. His father had taught him morals, Riordan had taught him to make things better, and his mother had helped show him how. Could he really make a difference? He knew it in his bones. He would try, regardless.

'I can't.'

'You'll be killed,' Liá said.

'If I die, it will be doing what's right.' Ardan said, reaching for his coin pouch. He had to shuffle through the different coins until he found it. The coin was cold and heavy as he pulled it out and held it towards Liá. 'I am calling the bargain due.'

'You can't be serious,' Liá said, staring at the coin imprinted with the impression of Lucifer.

'I want you to join me against Naberius.'

'Even with the coin, no price you offer would ever be enough,' Orla said.

'Think this through, Ardan,' Liá said. 'Naberius is acting on orders from Lucifer. This is his Temple, and we are part of his Clergy.'

'Naberius means to kill Astaroth,' Ardan said, his mouth running things before his mind could catch up.

'He does,' Orla said slowly.

'The attack on the Tree is not killing Astaroth.'

Orla's eyes narrowed as she glanced at the coin.

'I will make any bargain that will get your help against Naberius.'

'Impossible,' Orla said.

'Do you know what happens if the bargain is unfulfilled?' Liá asked.

'It doesn't matter.'

'It does. Orla, show him,' Liá said, then looked at Orla's raised eyebrow. 'Please.'

Orla nodded and stepped forward. Her blue eyes had gone glacial as they bore into his. He wanted to look away, but something about her gaze transfixed him.

Ardan found himself on the battlefield. The clash of weapons surrounded him. An Angel with a golden sword came for him. He dodged the first attack and struck back instinctively. His blade caught the Angel on the wing, tearing off a slice. The Angel snarled in response, attacking again. In a few exchanges, Ardan had bested him. The Angel was kneeling on the ground, exhaustion and injuries keeping him down. Ardan wanted to give clemency, the thing was beaten. Yet his arm moved instinctively. He drew the sword back and plunged it into the Angel's chest. It crumpled and fell, its golden lifeblood spilling out onto the ground.

Ardan went for the next being in front of him.

This continued until the battle was over. Then he was transported to the next war. He killed, and sometimes he was killed. The reincarnation was torturous as his body was burned into being. He could never rest, never given a moment of respite. Always marching towards the next fight. He wasn't being tortured or burned like the Light scriptures claimed. No, this was much worse. He was condemned to a body he couldn't control. Not really. He would be a pawn in Hell's war machine. He could never rebel, never run away, never hope for freedom because free will would be a distant memory.

As quickly as it began, it was over.

Ardan fell to his knees, gasping for breath. Fear coursed through him. He couldn't be that thing, not now.

'Will the bargain hold if I fall in battle?'

'Depends on the bargain,' Liá said.

'What would it cost for you to side with me?'

Liá looked at Orla, who looked frustrated but remained silent. 'You would need to slay Astaroth in Naberius' place.'

Ardan stared at the ground. Then he looked out of the city. The thoughts of his family surfaced and of his time living on the streets, starved and half beaten. How he had sworn to Riordan he would stop this from happening to others. Were they empty words, when he faced damnation?

'I will slay Astaroth.'

'You are a fool,' Orla said.

'You're committed to doing this?'

'I am,' Ardan said, conviction giving his voice strength.

'He has the coin,' Liá said quickly.

'It's not him I'm worried about. If you accept this, you'll be going up against a High Demon. If you pull off a miracle and defeat him, how will you explain yourself in the afterlife?'

'If Naberius falls here, then he is not worthy.'

Orla's mouth opened, but no words were forthcoming. She closed it again, looking furious.

'We have already been requisitioned. I will accept this bargain on two conditions. The bargain will not be bound until you have a clear advantage.'

'If we had a clear advantage, I wouldn't be here.'

She considered it. 'Fine. We will join in if it looks like you have a chance, but I will be the judge of when and how. Good enough?'

It wasn't what he was hoping for, but Ardan nodded anyway.

'The second is if it is clear that you will fail, I will use my power to bind you. I don't want you to die if I can help it.'

'What? No.'

'I won't be moved on this,' Liá said firmly.

'Only if there is absolutely no chance and I am in imminent peril.'

'Agreed. Anything else?' Liá asked. Ardan shook his head and Liá continued, 'The bargain is sealed.'

Ardan felt a shiver run through him.

'That is your first bargain,' Orla said stiffly.

'I was hoping to make my second bargain with you. For your assistance.'

'You're out of your mind. The both of you.' Orla said.

'It will be a reasonable bargain,' she said, but her voice wavered as she spoke. 'A gift for my graduation.'

Orla drew in a breath and visibly calmed herself. 'Please excuse us,' she said to Ardan.

The two of them walked a short distance away. Ardan watched them, knowing that having Orla on their side, one of the leading Priestesses, would be a great boon. Their exchange was heated, though Ardan couldn't hear what they were saying. It was clear how angry Orla was with her sharp controlled motions. Whenever Liá spoke, she kept her hands demurely in front of her. In the end, Orla gave a furious nod.

They came back to him.

'We'll join you,' Liá said.

'In a way we see fit.'

'Any help is good help,' Ardan said. 'Do you think you can get anyone else?'

Liá looked at Orla.

'Time is short. We will do what we can,' Orla said. 'Going against Lucifer's hound is—unwise. Let me iterate that you have no chance and must not expect our help. We will protect you if we can, but no aid will be forthcoming until it looks like you might actually stop him.'

Ardan wanted more, but he knew when to count his blessings. 'Do you know when Naberius will act?'

'The last thing before we begin was this ritual. I believe you have an hour, maybe two, before it starts.'

CHAPTER SIXTY-THREE:
EMERGENCY MEETING

* * *

I have returned for the sake of my Master's last will and testament. Yet Astaroth is more powerful than I could have imagined. Thrice I have failed. I thank the Darkness she is chained, as her power would overwhelm any who opposed her.
— Naberius, *Annals of Lucifer.*

* * *

ARDAN RAN down the steps of the Black Temple. He could feel the Wild bubbling within him in response to the encounter. He funnelled it to Mish. Their connection changed him; his muscles adjusted, his vision shifted. The sensation was familiar enough that it gave him no pause in his dash. Mish, a loping black shadow, easily kept pace with him.

The streets were virtually empty. Ardan could feel it without the Wild: the primal powers in the city were rising, ready to contest each other. Every door and window Ardan ran past was shut to wait out the storm. Even the beggars, alley cats and street dogs were nowhere to be seen.

As the newer but smaller buildings of the Dark Quarter were replaced by the older stone construction of the Ancient Quarter, Ardan saw the first signs of life since leaving the Temple. There were soldiers out. He passed a contingent of church soldiers, their tabards showing the holy flame insignia. They carried shields and spears, talking amongst each other in hushed whispers. When they saw Ardan, a couple of them lowered their spears. His heightened predatory instincts made him aware of them, their stances and postures. They'd be easy to scare and scatter, then he would be able to pick them off as they separated from the herd.

'Stop jumping at every person who comes by,' one of them growled, a nasty gash on his jaw that broke his beard line. 'When we're needed, we'll be told.'

'They are right to be wary of outsiders,' Father Walter said, wearing the white robes of the Priesthood. 'We must be wary of the Darkness and infidels alike.'

Ardan kept moving, ignoring them as he came across the next group of soldiers, from the Merchant Guard. Like the church soldiers, most were armed with spears and shields. Ardan remembered them during the riot amid the civil war and how they had held the line against the mob while their bowmen shot into the crowd. The men and women were joking around. His predatory instincts made him give them a wide berth.

Ardan visibly shook himself and forced his connection with Mish to break. The feline instincts subsided as vibrant colour flooded his vision. The ancient vines and twisting leaves that decorated Marion's mansion commanded his attention. Reverting to normal was always jarring.

He was himself again after a moment. His muscles were less feline, his mind less predatory. He looked at everyone milling around. There were enough people with officer insignias standing around.

'Ardan,' a familiar voice called. He turned to see Eamon coming towards him. The man was in leather armour, sword at his belt and shield strapped to his arm. The mercenary had painted black beneath his eyes.

'Eamon,' Ardan said, surprised, 'What are you doing here?'

'Finding work out of my depth as usual,' Eamon said with a grin, 'Riordan hired every sword and spear he could find.'

'Did he tell you what for?'

'Said there'd be blood and to sit out if we weren't up for it,' Eamon said, his grin fading.

'He wasn't lying,' Ardan said. 'How many came?'

'Everyone in residence. Over a hundred.'

Ardan blinked. 'That many?'

'He's giving an entire gold temple for one night of work. Everyone signed up.'

Over a hundred gold pieces. Did Riordan even have that much? He probably wouldn't need it by the end, Ardan thought, a shiver running down his spine.

'Where is Riordan?'

'Said he'd join us here,' Eamon said. 'Something about needing to finish something.'

'Hell of a time to take off.'

'Probably went to see a woman.'

Ardan spotted Bree off in a corner. Her shoulder-length silver hair was smudged with soot from the fires, and she spoke casually with Murieen. The older woman was draped in bright blues, greens and greys, still looking like a turbulent ocean despite sitting in a chair.

'Can't be, she's over there,' Ardan said, nodding at Bree.

'Her?' Eamon exclaimed. 'Man's fighting out of his class.'

'Plainsmen,' Talon called. He stood at the double door entrance to the mansion, flanked by two forest warriors. He stood tall, tattoos twined around his bare chest and arms clearly visible. His large belt held his four hatchets. 'Gather your commanders and join us in the war room.'

Ardan glanced at Eamon, who shrugged. They followed Captain Callum in. He was wearing a polished breastplate and carried a long sword at his side. He held his helmet under his arm, careful not to ruffle the officer plumes adorning it.

'I'll be out here, dear,' Murieen said to Bree. The young silver haired Shaper grimaced.

Ardan paused, letting Bree head in first, but Walter stormed past, barging into Ardan with enough force that he stumbled. A few other church soldiers followed the man inside. One glanced at him apologetically.

Ardan rolled his eyes and followed their procession the dining room, where all the chairs and the table were pushed away from the centre. A map of Barleron hung on the wall. Ardan walked past the contingent of the Light's representatives.

Templar Phillip stood there in his white cloak, wearing a dented breastplate, and carrying a long spear. He nodded to Ardan while Frederick's expression remained flat. He wore simple white robes with the purple stole of the Bishop over his shoulders. Walter had his back to Ardan.

Off in one corner, Marion was talking to Koira, wearing a simple but elegant blue dress. The forest woman wore close-fitting leathers, a large dagger at her belt. Once it was clear everyone had arrived, Marion stepped forward, addressing the leaders and officers of the armies waiting out in the streets.

'Ladies and Gentlemen, Shapers and men of the cloth. You know why I have called you here,' Marion said. 'Barleron is under attack. We have little time before we begin. Naberius has a large army of mercenaries and will soon assault the Tree of the Ancients. If successful, he will turn his attention on the rest of us. Our best chance is to strike him while he is occupied. Is that a correct assessment, Templar Phillip?'

All eyes turned to the Templar.

Phillip cleared his throat. 'It is. The harbour is destroyed, and the forest path is cut off. We must stop him on our own.'

'How many soldiers do we have?' Ardan asked.

All turned to him, and he suddenly felt self-conscious.

'The plainsman is right to ask,' Talon said, resting his hands on his axes. 'Before we can proceed, we need to know our strengths and weaknesses. I will begin. We number twenty-one, each battle proven, though we are not accustomed to fighting in this stone jungle.'

His statement fell over the room, creating a silence that stretched.

'There are over sixty fighting men and women with me,' Marion said. 'My commander is absent, but I am confident he will return soon. My people have fought in many battles, both large and small. I have hired mercenaries to bolster our numbers. Eamon can give a better evaluation of the freelancers.'

'Uh, yeah, so—we're a little over a hundred. Not much good for formations, but we know how to scrap.'

'One second,' Phillip said and went over to the map. He started pulling pins and putting them on the wall to represent their forces. One green pin for the forest warriors, two grey for the mercenaries, one yellow for Marion's forces.

'Captain Callum?' Phillip asked.

'Eighty-eight soldiers, armed with spears and short swords. Fifty-three archers. Experience varies, but we are solid.'

Three blue pins went on the map.

'Bree, how many Shapers do we have?' Marion asked.

The silver-haired woman stood up, her voice clear. 'Five water Shapers and an air Shaper, me.'

'Which leaves us,' Phillip said and began putting pins on the wall. He stopped at seven pins. 'We have a little over three hundred church soldiers.'

'How will they fight?' Talon asked.

'How will they ... fight?' Phillip asked.

'I saw them. Most are warriors in training. Will they break in battle?'

'They are soldiers of the Light,' Walter said stiffly.

'Do not take offence,' Talon said. 'Men are men, no matter what cult they belong to. If they have not seen battle, they do not know the horror it holds. Will they break?'

A flash of anger spread across Walter's face. He raised his hand, but

Frederick put a hand on his shoulder and whispered to him. The Priest closed his mouth, though he looked furious.

'Perhaps fifty have been in battle,' Phillip conceded.

Talon nodded, showing no disapproval. 'I know what your kind can do. You will need to be with them to strengthen their spines.'

'You do not tell a chosen of Zadkiel himself what to do!' Walter yelled, shrugging off Frederick's restraining hand.

'Leave your ego behind. He is right,' Phillip said. 'If I do so, I may not have the strength to face Naberius at the end.'

'The Darkness will fall by the Light's hand,' Walter declared.

'If they break, we will lose. What of your Light wielders? Can they not also battle against this creature?' Talon asked.

'They are Priests of the Light,' Walter bellowed.

'We will hold ourselves back as best we can,' Frederick said, ignoring Walter. 'Save our strength for Naberius if possible.'

'It will have to do. Master Talon is right, I am needed on the front lines,' Phillip said.

Phillip put in another pin representing himself, and one to represent the Priests.

'Near seven hundred soldiers,' Marion said.

'We should break their lines, but that leaves the creature itself. We need more than blind courage to deal with it.'

'Beyond the Light wielders, we have five water Shapers, one air Shaper and the archers to inflict damage against Naberius,' Marion said. 'Riordan's shield and Ardan's sword may help.'

'I have seen what your Shapers can do, but they are tired. They should remain with the Light wielders until the right time.'

Talon's fingers traced the park of the Ancients. He pointed at the Tree that stuck out in the centre. 'This is the Demon's goal. A hundred mercenaries with a complement of Dark Priests and Black Guards are stationed at each entrance,' he said, pointing to three places on the map. 'I recognise Lachlan at this entrance, the Shock Wolf at this one and the third commander we could not name. We couldn't get an accurate gauge of their numbers inside the park. If fortune favours us, then their strength is only at the entrances, but if it does not, we must expect a large number in the centre guarding the creature Naberius.'

'You paint a bleak picture, Master Talon,' Callum said. 'We may not even have the advantage of numbers. Besides that, their soldiers are better trained and more experienced and their Priests alone would cut a swathe through our forces.'

'That is why we must plan. Fight with intelligence,' Talon said.

'Why must we fight at all?' Callum asked. 'In all my dealings with the Dark, they have always honoured their word.'

'You would side with the Dark?' Walter said, glaring at the Captain.

'I will not throw away our lives if it can be avoided,' Callum replied calmly.

'Your soul is stained with cowardice,' Walter said, his voice rising as though it were delivering a sermon. He took purposeful steps towards the Captain of the Merchant Guard.

Ardan felt the Wild stirring in response to the Light now emanating from Walter.

'Take another step and you will die,' Callum said. Behind him, several of his guards had drawn their bows, their arrows aimed directly at Walter. The Priest looked as though he might charge forward anyway.

'I know of your power. If you try to fight me, they will riddle you with arrows. I may die, but you certainly will.'

Phillip stepped in front of Walter. Though Ardan couldn't tell if it was to protect him or stop him.

'We don't have time for this,' Ardan said, the Wild driving him. He could feel its recklessness, but he didn't bother trying to constrain it. 'You want to bargain with the Dark, yet all you offer is your throat.'

Silence followed his words, the effect spreading. People around the room were nodding while others remained silent.

'With such forces arrayed against us, going against them is suicide.' Callum said.

'The Light will always prevail against the Darkness,' Walter snapped.

'Unless you have some battle angels with you, it won't this time,' Callum said.

'Enough. If you wish to be a coward, then leave.' Talon said and turned his back on Callum and his coterie.

'One moment please,' Marion said. She went over to Merchant Guard Captain and silently handed him a letter. The entire room watched the exchange in mute curiosity.

Callum read the letter, his face going progressively more red. 'The command of the Merchant Guard is mine,' he said through clenched teeth.

'No one is disputing that. But do you really want to go against the Countess?'

'The Merchant Guard is under the control of the Merchant Guild,' Callum said, heat colouring his voice.

'Of course they are,' Marion said in a patronising tone.

'I have a duty to the lives of my soldiers.'

'And a duty to protect the city.'

Callum opened his mouth to reply but closed it again, looking troubled.

'It is a no-win scenario for you, Captain,' Marion said.

'How so?' Callum said coldly.

'If you do not fight now, you will fight soon. Either the High Demon will win and come after you, or we will.'

'Do not threaten me.'

Marion looked completely unruffled, her voice carrying over everyone in the room. In that moment, Ardan understood why she was a leader of Barleron. 'I will threaten you and anyone else that I need to.'

'Unless you two destroy each other.'

'The legions of Light will arrive with no opposition. The aftermath would likely herald an inquisition.'

Callum swallowed. Emotions warred over his face, his eyes searching. He glanced at his guards, who offered no suggestions. He looked up at those surrounding him. 'This is low, even for you. Fine, we will fight. Maybe I won't get all of my men killed.'

'Excellent,' Marion said.

'But,' Callum said firmly, 'my soldiers will not be part of the vanguard. We will be part of the reserve, with the Priests and the Shapers.'

No one objected, though muttering filled the room.

'We are many, from many places. We must keep our tactics simple,' Talon said.

'We will also need a single commander,' Phillip said. 'I will fight in the front lines. It cannot be me,' Phillip said, looking at Talon.

'Plainsmen will not respect my command.'

A few looked at Callum.

'No,' Talon said. 'I will not follow him.'

'I will lead,' Walter said.

'You will not,' Marion said at the same time as Frederick.

'What about Riordan?' Ardan called.

'If he ever gets here,' Marion said.

'On his way,' Eamon said.

There were nods from around the room.

'He is a good choice—but for now, let us form our battle plan,' Phillip said. 'Our advantage here is our archers, as the Red Wolves have few of them. They employ no Shapers. Their strengths are the Black Guards and their Priests. Can we get the archers onto the rooftops?'

'Onto the roofs?' Callum considered. 'It won't be quick, and we may lose the element of surprise while doing it.'

Sudden inspiration struck Ardan. 'Which entrance is guarded by my brother?' Every face turned towards Ardan, but he looked at Talon. 'The Shock Wolf.'

'The southern entrance.'

Ardan swallowed, feeling every eye on him. 'He may turn to our side.'

A few people raised eyebrows at that.

'If it doesn't work, I'll have created a distraction,' Ardan said. He felt his heart sinking, hoping he could turn Davan, but he didn't know which side his brother would take.

The commanders of the platoons were divided up, the order of approach decided. Ardan wasn't paying much attention, his focus on how his conversation with his brother might go. As they were discussing how to use the Shapers, Riordan burst into the room. The man wore a chain-mail shirt, broadsword at his side, with spear and shield in his hand. He was sporting a bruise on his cheek and a split lip.

'Where have you been?' Marion demanded.

'Trying to secure more forces,' Riordan said.

Marion spread her arms as though to say, *where are they?*

'We'll know if they join us soon enough. We're out of time. We need to move,' Riordan said.

'Our forces are ready,' Phillip said, 'Though you should know that you are the overall commander here, my friend.'

'Me?' Riordan looked bewildered, glancing around at the gathered people. 'Surely, there are others?' But his voice faded. 'It had better be a good reason. Is there a battle plan, or am I expected to come up with that too?'

'There is a plan,' Talon said.

'Good. Eamon, you'll fill me in on the way. Also, you're second.'

'Me?' Eamon exclaimed. 'We are desperate, aren't we?'

'Yep. Now let's go.'

'May the Light guide our path,' Phillip said.

CHAPTER SIXTY-FOUR: FOOL'S GAMBIT

* * *

There aren't any usable sources of the Ancients' power here. I must travel south of the great divide to learn how to wield the Wild.
— Naberius, *Annuals of Lucifer.*

* * *

ARDAN WALKED ALONE down the deserted street. Every building had its doors barred shut and its shutters closed. In the distance, he could see the Tree of the Ancients. Its great branches, illuminated by moonlight, stood over the city. The road stretched out, each step taking an age. Up ahead, he could see the southern entrance to the park of the Ancients. The way was barred by makeshift fortifications, manned by mercenaries, Black Guards and members of the Dark Clergy.

Ardan swallowed as each step caused more of the mercenaries' attention to shift towards him. When the first guard noticed him, he was grateful he had cajoled Aoife to take care of Mish and keep her safe in the mansion.

The fortifications were portable frames that were covered in wooden spikes and could be easily moved to block a charge. As Ardan got closer to them, talk amongst the mercenaries ceased.

Davan's hulking form was easily recognisable as he looked up to see the cause of the silence. His expression darkened as he spotted Ardan. He strode out from behind the fortifications, making a placating gesture to the others.

'What are you doing here?'

'Trying to get you to change sides.' Davan's brow furrowed in confusion. 'I know what you're here for. It's not too late to change sides. Join us, help to save the city.'

Davan looked incredulous. He shook his head and glanced behind Ardan. 'What side? All I see is you.'

'You're working for one of the High Demons.'

'Yes, I know.'

'You know?'

'Dásun told us who we'd be working for. No one had to join the contract if they were uncomfortable. It was you that convinced me it was fine when I went to see Liá. Maybe the Dark isn't so bad.'

Ardan spluttered, 'There's a difference between family and a High Demon that wants to rule the city.'

'How is it different from your Prostitute? She wants to rule too.'

Ardan felt incredulity creep through his mask. He could see Davan's smug expression, as though he had just struck the winning blow. Trying to compare the two was absurd. Marion wasn't perfect, but he knew she was trying.

'She cares for people in a way that a Demon never will,' Ardan said at last.

'If she cared about—'

But his words were cut off. Pain shot through Ardan, hitting every fibre of his being as though it were being pressed against burning coal. He collapsed, gasping in agony. The Tree of the Ancients flared up, every branch, every leaf, every vine erupting in green flames. The mercenaries glanced at it, but their eyes returned to the road as though they had been expecting it. Davan's face scrunched in pain but seemed to get it under control faster than Ardan.

'Davan, join us. It is not too late,' Ardan whispered, the pain lessening.

'The Wolves are under contract. They are my sword- and shield-brothers. I wouldn't turn on them for all the gold in the Countess' palace.'

'Then do it for your family,' Ardan said, getting to his feet. 'Join us.'

Davan laughed. 'Mother doesn't fight, and Liá is with us.' Then his laughter cut off. 'Is she? No, of course she would be,' he said, as though trying to convince himself.

'Please, Davan.'

'There is no force in the city that can challenge us,' Davan said dismissively. 'Why don't you join us? We could use that sword of yours.'

'I will not serve him,' Ardan said. 'You failed us once. This is your chance to make amends. Join us.'

Davan's expression hardened. 'Go. We are done here.'

Ardan tried to say something else, but Davan interrupted him.

'My decision is made.'

'You stubborn ass,' Ardan said, frustration getting the better of him as he drew his sword. 'Do one thing for me.'

'What?' Davan said, stepping backwards as he drew his axe. The mercenaries and Black Guards tensed, drawing their own weapons.

'Don't get your stubborn mule ass killed,' Ardan said and channelled the Wild into the sword. The green flame spread along the sword like kindling, the flame matching that of the Tree.

Davan leaned back in a defensive posture, gripping his axe tightly.

Ardan held the sword aloft and waited. The seconds stretched out. Nothing happened. He resisted the urge to look behind him. Davan's eyes scanned the surrounding streets.

'Loose,' a voice shouted.

The twang of bowstrings could be heard, heralding the arrows that flew overhead. Shouts of alarm were quickly replaced by screams of pain as arrows found their mark. The arrows bounced off the Black Guards' armour, but the Dark Clergy were the primary targets. One fell with an arrow in her throat. The other stumbled around, sprouting so many arrows he resembled a pincushion.

A battle cry came from the side streets as forest warriors poured out, led by Riordan and Talon.

'Hold the entrance,' Davan shouted, holding his axe aloft. He could have attacked. Ardan had no illusions about who would win, but his brother backed up. 'Get word to the Captain, we're under attack!' he yelled as he swung his axe and sent a shock wave at the approaching force.

Riordan was there, his new heartwood shield absorbing the blow, but it sent the man stumbling.

'It worked,' Ardan said.

'Aye. Still getting used to it,' Riordan said, regaining his balance as he held up his sword. The forest warriors stopped at his side, waiting. Behind them, the church soldiers were marching in line down the street.

The archers on the rooftops kept up a steady barrage. It forced the Black Guards to keep their face masks down in case an arrow found a slit in their visors. Davan yelled at the mercenaries to get their shields up.

Riordan glanced behind him, checking the church soldiers were close enough. He waited for the next volley of arrows before he yelled the order to charge.

Ardan ran towards the bulwarks. The archers rained death on the enemy while Ardan faced down a Black Guard. Ardan had learnt his lesson the previous time and dodged rather than parried. Through his visor, Ardan could see the man's wide eyes as they followed the movement of his flaming sword. He struck the guard, the green flame scattering across the black armour before vanishing. Without Mish, he knew he wasn't a match for this man.

The church soldiers joined them, their numbers pushing back the mercenaries and Black Guards.

'Pull back, stay together,' Davan called. His brother was continually sending shock waves at their lines. Ardan left the Black Guard to the church soldiers and took his position next to Riordan. Together, they blocked most of the shock waves, allowing their force to move past the fortifications and push the enemy back.

The green bonfire that was pouring out of the Tree of the Ancients illuminated the entire park. Near the Tree, a pool of hovering Darkness, thick and oily, continually tried to penetrate the wall of green flames. At the base Esalon, leading a contingent of six Priests, was controlling the attack.

A second contingent of Priests stood between them and the Tree. The High Priest Guillaume, Orla and Liá were among their number. They were surrounded by at least forty Black Guards. Directly in front of them, Captain Dásun was ordering the mercenary companies into lines to meet them. There had to be at least three hundred mercenaries in Dásun's force.

'Light have mercy,' a church soldier said.

'Your Light has no sway here,' Talon said grimly. 'Only the swing of your axe.'

With that, he and the forest warriors led the charge.

'Zadkiel will shield you,' Phillip shouted from the front line of his soldiers. He was glowing with Light as he joined the charge. Ardan yelled his own war cry, joining in with a chorus of others as their line surged forward.

The Templar quickly outpaced them, the Light granting him speed.

Davan stood as a rear-guard, sending shock waves to give his men time to retreat. A shock wave hit Phillip and made the Light surrounding him flicker, but his momentum never faltered. He smashed into their lines like a boulder. The Templar was a blur of Light, carving a path through the enemy. Then the forest warriors were at his side. Talon used his two axes to block and attack in equal measure. They carved a breach into the lines, and just as the mercenaries were recovering, the church soldiers joined them, and the melee descended into chaos.

Ardan found himself fighting a mercenary. He struck and the man barely parried, his eyes too focused on the flaming sword. Ardan used the distraction to sweep the man's leg. It wasn't graceful, but by a stroke of luck, he caught the man's foot and he tumbled. One of the church warriors stabbed the fallen man.

Ardan tried to open up a connection with Mish. He would need the extra agility. With a curse, he realised the distance was too great and he couldn't quite connect to her.

'Eamon!' Riordan called.

Despite the Templar's efforts, the more experienced enemy mercenaries hadn't broken. They were holding the line, causing the church soldiers to lose momentum. Near the Tree, Guillaume was building his own pool of Darkness, his eyes fixed on the battle.

Eamon led the combined force of freelance mercenaries and Marion's own soldiers. They weren't in formation; instead, they filled the gaps that were forming. The battle line was now stretching from wall to wall across the park.

Ardan found a wall of spears in front of him. He tried to cut at them, but his flame wouldn't catch. The jostling from behind and to his sides soon squeezed him out. He cut off the flow to his sword, trying not to let it harm the mercenaries or church soldiers around him. The screams of the dying and the grunts of fighting filled the air. Ardan was eventually pushed to the back, his foot finding the body of one of the wounded. He slipped, falling to one knee.

Further down, their forces were breaking. Seeing the opening, he joined with some of the freelance mercenaries running towards it.

The cause of the break in their lines was Seamus. The old weapon master was jumping and spinning. His injured leg was encased in darkness. *He must have made a deal with the Dark*, Ardan thought. The augmentation gave him strength, and he was cutting through their lines like a scythe through wheat.

Ardan slowed, along with at least half a dozen others. Seamus had taught them how to fight. Ardan grimaced, realising the few who still fought the man had quickly fallen. Then Eamon stepped forward with grim determination. His shield flashed as it caught their instructor's sword. Again and again, the shield was a wall as Seamus' sword struck like a serpent. Eamon, never great with his sword, didn't attack; he was content with just blocking. The instructor was getting frustrated.

He leapt into the air, but as he did, a sudden rush of wind sent him tumbling back.

Bree appeared, her silver hair flailing, while Murieen and the other water Shapers charged in.

Eamon struck at their fallen instructor. Even on his back, Seamus blocked the sword and then used his foot to kick at his attacker. Without hesitation, Eamon jumped forward and slammed the shield into Seamus' head. Their instructor fell limp.

A collective gasp washed through the surrounding fighters.

The spell of the duel had vanished, and the clanging of metal resumed.

Small globes of water raced around, smashing into enemy mercenaries, the water dissipating on impact but knocking them off balance before the globes reformed and were moving again. Gusts of wind struck gatherings of soldiers, breaking their lines. The sudden change was enough, and the enemy mercenaries faltered.

'Back, back to the Priests,' Captain Dásun called.

Davan kept up a steady stream of shock waves, giving their forces time to withdraw. A group of enthusiastic church soldiers gave chase, but Guillaume was waiting. The High Priest held his staff in front of him, raising it towards the charging soldiers. An orb of oily blackness as large as a wagon hovered above his head, being fed by the Dark Priests around him. The globe of darkness shot out a dozen spear-like tendrils. They impaled the church soldiers before snapping back. To a man, the soldiers of the Light collapsed.

Phillip roared a challenge for his fallen comrades. The light around him became blinding. He stepped in front of his soldiers, taking on the spiking tendrils of darkness. Each strike caused the light to flicker like a candle in the breeze.

Ardan looked for Liá. She stood amongst the other Dark Clergy around the High Priest. They were surrounded by forty Black Guards. Despite the chaos between them, she caught his eye and shook her head. Ardan cursed. *What is holding them back?* Ardan thought furiously. *We're flaming winning!*

A horn sounded from behind the Tree. Close to two hundred

soldiers were coming from the northern entrance. Lachlan was in front, beating his sword against his shield in a steady rhythm. He'd gathered the soldiers from the other entrances. They were lined up and in formation. Behind them were another four Priests. Ardan suppressed a shiver. They had only held the advantage by a sliver. He wasn't given long to despair as he dodged a spear thrust from an enemy mercenary. He struck forward, his blazing sword hitting the man's shield, the fire racing along the wood. The thing caught fire, as had happened with Riordan's shield in the forest. The mercenary panicked. Ardan thrust again, hearing Seamus' voice in his head shouting at him not to thrust. The blade cut through the man's leather armour with frightening ease, plunging into his chest. He stared at Ardan, then down at the flaming sword, terror and disbelief in his eyes.

'Callum!' Riordan roared, his voice carrying above the melee.

Ardan looked up to see Lachlan's troop marching closer. Phillip was trying to break through the lines, but the continuous strikes from Guillaume kept him at bay. There was no answering call. *Where are they?* Ardan thought, between strikes at the nearest enemy.

'Merchant Guard,' Riordan boomed. There was no answering call. 'Eamon, go get them.'

Eamon took off at a run. He was graceful as he ran over the blood-coated grass, dodging around the wounded and dead.

'It's no use,' one of the church soldiers shouted, taking a step back. His movements were panicked as he slipped, falling to the ground and dropping his spear.

'Strengthen your spine,' Murieen yelled as several globes of water smashed into mercenaries in front of her. 'We fight or we die.'

A black spear shot at Murieen. She moved to the side with surprising deftness, but the spear still pierced her shoulder. The older woman kept her feet without screaming, her face paling.

'No,' Bree shouted, coming forward.

'You,' Riordan said to the panicking church soldier, 'get her out.'

The terrified church soldier looked happy to obey.

'No, I'm fine,' Murieen said, though she swayed. She directed three more globes of water forward, smashing into mercenaries. Then the swaying became more pronounced, and she collapsed.

'Now, soldier,' Riordan said.

He nodded, helping the older woman to her feet.

'We stay,' she said, her voice as cold as iron.

Ardan was already engaged with another soldier by the time they were moving. He dodged a spear thrust and swung his flaming weapon forward; the mercenary stepped back to avoid the blow.

A howling roar could be heard in the distance. Startled, Ardan was almost speared by his opponent.

The howling grew louder and the fighting around them slowed. Hundreds of feet could be heard thudding on cobblestones. At the western entrance, a wave of unwashed, ragged and starving people charged in. The battle appeared to pause.

'Be ready. Let's see if my gamble paid off,' Riordan said.

'What?' Ardan yelled as he parried another strike from the spearman.

'I asked the Fiddler for help.'

Ardan dodged around one spear. Moving in close, he sliced the soldier across the bicep. The spearman dropped his weapon, jumping back and clutching at his wound.

'You what?'

'We were dead anyway,' Riordan said with a shrug.

'Attack the Darkness, my people. Don't let them destroy our city, don't let them take us!' The Fiddler's familiar voice could be heard above the raging battle.

'You did this?' Ardan said, his voice clouded with disbelief.

Lachlan's men were still too far from the main mercenary force. He directed his soldiers into lines to meet the influx of men and woman.

'Can't let the whore have all the fun,' the Fiddler shouted at them as his soldiers crashed over the approaching mercenaries like water over rock. He kept six men around him who were well fed and armoured, unlike the rest of his soldiers.

The mercenaries quickly pushed back the Fiddler's men, but they were assaulted again and again, numbers making up for their lack of battle prowess.

'This is our chance. Phillip, break their lines, destroy the Priests!' Riordan called. The Templar raised his spear in acknowledgement. 'Everyone, forward,' Riordan screamed.

Their lines pushed inwards towards the Tree as the chaotic melee raged on. Ardan got between their forces and Davan. Bree and the few water Shapers with her were keeping the mercenaries and Black Guards off balance sufficiently to bridge the gap between their inexperienced soldiers and the enemy mercenaries.

Ardan stood across from his brother. He used his blade to strike at any shock wave Davan sent his way, destroying it in a display of green flame. They were reluctant to engage each other.

The Tree's light was dimming as it was slowly being smothered by the surrounding darkness.

'Go, lad, help the Templar with the Priests,' Riordan said as he squared off against Davan. His brother had no hesitation in engaging Riordan and charged forward, his axe pulsating as he went. Riordan moved to meet him, his shield ready. Davan leapt into the fray in an awesome display of strength and agility. He swung the axe down hard on Riordan's shield. The shield responded, sending a pulse in response, and both of them went flying backwards. Davan's axe went spinning out of his grasp while Riordan crashed into a group of church soldiers. Davan immediately pounced for his axe, but Bree was there first, picking the axe up with the wind and flinging it out of his range. Without Davan's powers, their line surged forward, and the Shock Wolf and the remaining mercenaries were forced back.

A horn sounded behind them. The Merchant Guard were coming at last, their soldiers heading for the Fiddler's men, going to reinforce them.

Without Davan's axe, the remaining line of mercenaries was thinning, and they broke, running for the Priests and the Black Guard.

Guillaume smiled grimly. He directed the orb to send spears at anyone who got too close.

Phillip charged forth, his blazing light blocking the blows, but each time he was struck, his light became a little dimmer. Any church soldiers that tried to join him were struck down. Phillip was making a valiant attempt, but his pace was slowing. One strike sent him stumbling.

Ardan stared at the black orb, an idea forming.

'Bree!' Ardan shouted, 'I think I can take down that black thing if you can launch me at it.'

Bree stared at him, taking in the sword and then at the orb. 'You're insane.'

'Can you do it?'

She pursed her lips, gauging the distance. 'Maybe. I don't know if I can catch you.' Ardan waved that off as unimportant. 'Fine, then run towards it, and leap when you feel the wind at your back.'

Ardan didn't hesitate, breaking free from their battle line and charging the formation of Priests and Black Guards. Immediately, the orb sent a dark spear at him. One slash and his sword engulfed it in green flame. The High Priest frowned, the braids of his head twisting as he moved his arms, causing the orb to send another spear. Ardan blocked that one too. The next attack comprised three spears, hurtling towards him. In a panic, he leapt, hoping Bree was ready.

He spun as the air caught him and he felt the spears whistle past him. It was then, as his momentum picked up and he was hurtling through the air, he realised how absurd the situation was. Guillaume's expression was all astonishment, a hand raised almost in disbelief.

The orb was fast approaching. He channelled more of the Wild into the sword. The sword burned a brighter, more brilliant green flame. He held onto the sword with both hands as he awkwardly twisted in the air, his blade catching the orb. It was like trying to drag a knife through honey. The push from Bree carried him through, causing the orb burst in a magnificent display of green and black.

It sent him spinning off in a different direction. He no longer felt the air supporting him and the fast approaching ground spiked his fear. It lent him the extra emotional spike he needed to connect with Mish. He pumped everything he had into their connection. He felt the change in his muscles, his vision blurred, and his hearing intensified.

499

Instinct took over. He twisted in the air, putting his feet first. As he hit the ground, he felt himself collapse and roll. He tumbled, innately glad that his blade only had one edge. He sprang to his feet, standing in front of the contingent of Priests attacking the Tree. They looked at him in shock. The savagery of the Wild and of Mish had taken over. He let loose a primal snarl. His sword claimed two of them before they could even try to organise a defence. A third crumpled with a spray of blood. Ardan leapt at the fourth, his sword sinking into the man's chest and slamming him into the ground. He pulled it out, seeing the flame around the Tree had almost been extinguished. It fuelled his rage and the sword's fire exploded. He made two quick slashes at the two remaining Priests, and they fell as the green flame engulfed them.

There was only Esalon left. But the Black Guard had moved into position around him. Behind him, Guillaume was channelling again, trying to replace the dark orb.

The whole time the battled raged on behind Ardan.

'Now,' Orla called.

Suddenly six Black Guards backed away, creating an opening in the lines. Guillaume looked shocked and spun on them. Liá and Orla channelled their power. Four Priests fell, twined in darkness. Alive but disabled.

Orla and Liá squared off against the High Priest.

'Men of the Light, forward!' Phillip yelled as he charged into the newly created gap.

Without the constant barrage of darkness, he smashed through their lines.

Guillaume looked about at his flagging line. He gave a roar of frustration and thrust his staff out in front of him. Darkness erupted from the demon skull in waves, spears shooting out wildly, hitting the church soldiers and remaining Black Guards alike. Liá and Orla joined their power together but were completely on the defensive. Phillip's glow was so diminished by this point that each strike he absorbed was a visible blow. He staggered back.

Frederick stepped in front of Phillip, blazing like the sun. Koira and the last of their forces were behind him.

The Bishop had drawn the High Priest's attention. Every spear and tendril shot at Frederick, but the light absorbed the blows as though they were nothing more than raindrops. The High Priest paused in his attacks, building up his darkness and then let it loose all at once. Like a dam breaking, darkness poured out of him, building up into a wave that crashed over Frederick. It collided with his Light, cascading and completely engulfing him.

The battle paused, awestruck at the display of power.

Like the sun behind the clouds, beams of light shone through, and the darkness eventually broke to reveal the Bishop in a much smaller globe of light, down on one knee, panting from the effort. Guillaume's teeth glinted as he gathered more power.

Off to the side, Ardan could see Koira sprinting towards the High Priest. The man turned at the last second and sent a stray lance of darkness at her. She reached her hand out and unleashed the Wild. The green shot out to meet the black and the explosion hit them both. She had braced for it, and as she went flying back, her descent slowed. Bree was behind her, her hands moving deftly, using the air to catch her.

Guillaume was not prepared and hit the ground hard. He lay there dazed. Talon was the one who broke through their lines. One of his axes flew towards the High Priest as he got to his feet. It struck him in the chest. Guillaume stared down at the protruding axe in disbelief and collapsed.

Black Guards held the line after the last mercenary forces collapsed. Lachlan's forces were locked in combat with the Fiddler's and the Merchant Guard, their victory far from certain. Their own forces had barely fifty able bodies among them. Ardan glanced over at the Tree. The green flame was almost completely extinguished. It was Esalon, alone, focusing on the Tree.

It had to be Naberius. It snapped him out of the primal fury. If the High Demon subdued the Tree, then it was all over. Lucifer's hound would have its own substantial power, coupled with that of the Tree. All their efforts would be for nothing, and hope would be lost.

'That's him, that's Naberius!' Ardan shouted, pointing at the final Priest. He had several Black Guards around him but was otherwise unprotected.

'Men of the Light!' Phillip roared. 'Forward, finish this!'

Talon appeared with the two remaining forest warriors as they charged the Black Guards.

Ardan waited until they were fully engaged before he went straight at Esalon. A tiny green font of flame, barely larger than a candle, was still a light at the base of the Tree. He funnelled as much energy as he could into the sword. The fire on his sword almost blinded him as he ran. He felt no compunction as he plunged the sword into Esalon's back. Like Verrick, the green flame encompassed him, consuming his fading robes as the Priest fell to his knees screaming under the intense green flame.

Esalon fell and as he did, the Tree of the Ancients' fire grew, burning the slick oily darkness. In less than a minute, it resembled a Tree inside a huge green bonfire. The heat was so intense that Ardan had to turn away, shielding his exposed skin.

Ardan looked down at the smouldering body and wondered if he had been wrong. Maybe Esalon hadn't been Naberius.

CHAPTER SIXTY-FIVE: NABERIUS

***

The mortals and Zadkiel's pets have repelled me from Jophiel's Pass. My impatience ruled when guile and cunning would have better suited. I have retreated into the mountains. My recovery will be slow, but my goal has not wavered. I will bend the Ancients' power to my will and present Eden to my master on a platter.

— Naberius, *Annals of Lucifer.*

***

THE MERCHANT GUARD and the Fiddler's men were still engaged with the remnants of the forces of Darkness and the Red Wolves. The Priests were giving them an edge. It wouldn't be long before they cut through. Riordan ordered the water Shapers and their freelance mercenaries to engage.

'All that planning wasted.'

Esalon rose from the ground, the green flame still smouldering on his skin. As he stood, darkness began cascading over his naked body, cutting away the flame like a knife. Ardan watched, feeling dread rise at the Priest's casual use of power. The sound of the distant fighting faded into the background. 'All my preparations have been for naught. I never, not in a millennium, would have suspected you of banding together, let alone having the strength to challenge me,' Esalon said, his voice carrying over them all. The man laughed—a feral, manic sound.

He continued to stand there, his physique rivalling that of the angelic statues. His laughter subsided, and he observed them all. To Ardan's surprise, he clapped. The others approached tentatively. 'I applaud you. This is the second time that humans have thwarted me in a single century. It seems you have brought every available warrior that I did not control. An effort in itself. You have even turned some of mine. Fiddler, did we not have a deal?'

The Fiddler, to his credit, did not cower. 'We never made a bargain.'

'Ah,' Esalon said, 'Yet you turned on me when I helped you keep your position?'

'Do you think I was blind? I had almost outlived my usefulness.'

The human form of Naberius smiled mirthlessly. 'There is some truth in that.' The smile vanished as he took in Liá and her mentor. 'And you, Priestess Orla, I did not expect betrayal from Lucifer's own.'

'We made a bargain, but I must stress, we didn't attack you. No bargain could be struck on that accord,' Orla said.

'And you think that will save you?' Esalon said, his voice as biting as an arctic wind. 'It must have been an exceptional bargain.'

Orla's eyes flicked to Liá for a moment. 'It was.'

'I should never have turned you away,' Esalon said, turning his attention to Ardan. 'With the forest warriors here, I trust Raigel is dead?'

'I think so.'

'Ah,' Esalon said. 'Yet you survived despite the idol being destroyed?'

'We found a way,' Ardan said, then added cautiously: 'You don't seem angry.'

'Oh, I am,' Esalon said without inflection, looking at the Tree, still alight with green flame. 'Frustration, rage and shame war within me. I am well beyond angry. I had questions, and you were the ones with the answers. Now that I am sated, none of you will leave here alive. I will bathe the entire city in blood before I am done.' Esalon said it so matter-of-factly that Ardan wasn't sure if it were some sort of poor joke. Then his dark eyes glowed red, the shadow behind him growing before his form began to change. He fell forward onto all fours as his body bulged, his hands morphing into paws. He shook his head, gently at first, but then with more vigour. Each shake left shadows, and they solidified, until his single head became three. The creature rose larger than a horse, muscles rippling under the sleek black coat. The large hound turned to face them, its six red eyes blinking into focus. As Ardan took it in, he realised the coat was made of moving, slick, oily darkness. All three heads growled.

They had only a second to appreciate Naberius' true form before he lunged at Talon. The man narrowly avoided the jaws of the lead head, but the second head snatched him up. Talon screamed as the fangs pierced his flesh, his body shaken like a rag doll. He had held on to one of his axes and flailed it wildly. He got lucky, and the blade caught the dog in the eye. The head yelped and flung him away. Talon rolled as he hit the ground before coming to a stop. He groaned. His body was a latticework of gored flesh, with one arm completely severed.

'No!' Koira screamed, running forward, forest warriors trailing behind her, as she got to Talon's side.

Ardan felt a flash of fear. Talon had been their best warrior, and he'd been struck down in an instant. The rest of them stared in shock at the sudden attack. It was Phillip who acted first, charging forward in his heavy armour, blazing with light. He used his spear as he had on the shadow monster in the forest. Naberius' centre head drew a deep breath and breathed black fire down on him. The Templar stood firm; the light blocked the fire as it washed over him, obscuring him from view. When the hellfire subsided, Phillip's spear shot upwards into the Demon's chest, causing it to rear back. Dark red blood started oozing from the wound.

Naberius leapt back, growling, his eyes locked on Phillip.

'I remember you, little Templar,' the lead head growled. 'No brothers to shield you this time.'

The left head laughed. The sound was rough, like a waterfall of gravel.

'The Light shields me,' Phillip said, the light around him burning brighter.

Naberius' three heads grinned. 'But does it shield others?' he said and made an impossibly high leap to land directly in front of the now-exposed church soldiers. They had been the ones brave enough to come close. They stood stock still at the creature's sudden movements.

Ardan's connection with Mish enabled his recognition of another predator, to know its intent. He ran for the soldiers, fearing he'd be too slow. He leapt, putting himself between the Demon and the men. His sword was his only defence as the lead head rained black fire down on them.

His sword cut through the black flame, but he could feel the heat wash on either side of him. The sounds of screams pierced his ears while the smell of sizzled flesh and burnt hair filled his nostrils. The flames slowly and painfully abated. He looked behind him. He had saved three church soldiers. Over twenty had fallen from the Demon's wrath.

Phillip and Frederick rushed Naberius, both glowing with Light, but the creature easily leapt over them and went for Bree and the few remaining soldiers that hadn't run.

Her hands were moving, her silvery hair twirling like a tornado as she sent blast after blast at Naberius. He bore down on her with terrible speed, shrugging off her blasts of air as though they were loose hay.

Ardan strengthened his connection with Mish and felt himself able to move faster as he tried to catch up to the demonic hound, but he wouldn't make it in time. Behind her, he could see Riordan running to throw himself in between them.

Bree's hair settled back down as she stopped her constant blasts of air. She concentrated, despite the black hound charging her down, and made a slicing motion with her hand. At Naberius' next lope, the air struck his left foreleg, and he missed a step. He was going too fast to recover. The heads yelped as they fell forward into the dirt. The momentum caused Naberius to cartwheel, slamming him onto the ground. In an instant, the dog was back on his feet, but it had given Riordan time to get between them. Naberius roared, spitting fire down on them.

'The Tree!' he could hear Koira scream. 'Get Naberius into the Tree!' He looked for her, using it as an excuse not to see his friends burnt alive. She was struggling as two of the forest warriors dragged her away. Suddenly, they were knocked down by a small green explosion. Koira quickly regained her feet and raced towards him.

Ahead of him, the flame abated. Bree and Riordan were still standing. There were lines of smoke coming off his heartwood shield, but they had survived.

Ardan channelled the Wild as fast as he could, straight into his sword and the connection with Mish. His inhibitions and fear vanishing, he charged Naberius, getting close enough to slash at the creature. The green fire caught the black oily skin like kindling and the fire spread quickly at first, but as with the spear wound the darkness congealed and smothered the flame.

With a snarl, Naberius leapt away from Ardan, straight onto Phillip's waiting spear. The Templar had expected the move and braced the butt of the spear against the ground, the blazing steel sinking deep into the creature's ribcage. All three heads howled in union as light poured from the Templar through the spear and into the creature. The howling turned into yelps of pain. Phillip pushed the spear deeper, his light now barely visible as he poured everything into the attack. The Demon's paw rose, and Phillip realised his mistake.

He was too close.

The strike slammed into him faster than a charging bull. Phillip hit the ground with bone crunching force. As he lay dazed, one of Naberius' heads reached down, its giant maw engulfing the top half of

Phillip while another head tried to reach around and pull out the spear.

Ardan ran forward to distract him. As Naberius shook Phillip's body, his teeth gnawed through the armour and into the man's flesh. Phillip's scream was cut short as the jaws crunched closed. Ardan's green sword flashed, causing a small yelp from Naberius as he leapt away, dropping Phillip's severed body. One of the hound's heads snapped at Ardan to keep his distance while the middle head sucked in a breath to unleash more black flame. Ardan felt the rage in his chest and channelled more of the Wild into his sword.

The green and black flames met, fighting against each other. It quickly became apparent to Ardan that the black flame would over-whelm his own. He felt terror hit him as he stared at the black fire that was working like the incoming tide, encroaching on his green-glowing sword.

Riordan came to save him. He stood with his shield in front of the black Demon. The wood from the forest shone like a beacon. Together, they withstood the dark fire. The flames stopped as the Demon pulled out the spear. It had mangled the wound in doing so, but the Darkness was already sealing it, albeit slower than before.

It was weakening, Ardan thought with hope, but then he looked around him. Most of their soldiers were down or already engaged. The Templar was dead, and none of them were a match for the demonic hound. What was left of their forces had fled or were keeping their distance.

'We need to get him near the Tree!' Ardan shouted at Riordan.

'Yeah, no problem lad,' Riordan said, but charged anyway. He distracted Naberius as he did so. The hound leapt, but a gust of wind caught it in mid-air, sending it tumbling back. Bree had used the distraction to stand with them. He could see the last of the church soldiers that hadn't run coming to join them, along with Father Walter and Koira.

'Bree, push him into the Tree!' Ardan yelled. Naberius heard him, one head whipping around to stare at the Tree. The other heads looked at them. At instant later, the hound was charging them. It was buffeted by the wind, but its momentum was too great. It came down on Riordan and smashed him to the ground. Riordan screamed as one of his legs was bent the wrong way and snapped.

Ardan barely avoided getting snatched up like Talon. He felt the stink of its breath and a strand of the dog's saliva hit him in the face. The middle head drew in a breath, its eyes fixed on Bree. Ardan tried to attack it, to distract it from breathing fire on Bree, but he couldn't get past the right head snapping at him, its feral face lined with dagger-shaped teeth.

Terror was painted on Bree's face as she raised her arms reflexively. The fire rained on her for a moment, catching her hair on fire and scorching her skin. It was interrupted by a huge church soldier running solidly into the beast from the side.

It was Liam. The giant barely lost momentum when he hit the creature, pushing it towards the Tree. Naberius was unbalanced enough that it couldn't quite get its feet underneath to resist or stop itself. One head managed to reach around and bite into the man's arm. With a roar, Liam kept pushing.

Ardan chased after the pair. The man glowed faintly with the power of the Light and Ardan was having trouble gaining on them. Blood poured from Liam's shoulder as the head continued to bite, tear and gnaw at him.

Nothing could stop Liam as he slammed Naberius into the trunk of the Tree of the Ancients. The green flame from the Tree immediately leapt onto the Demon, the fire rushing over its body. Liam held Naberius there, but he was weakening. Ardan was a dozen feet away, but the Demon struggled and squirmed, continuing to attack his assailant. Before Ardan could close the distance, Liam collapsed, blood pouring from his severed shoulder.

The vines hanging from the Tree suddenly whipped towards the creature, as though commanded.

Koira was nearby, her hands glowing green.

Ardan caught up to the Demon and slashed wildly, trying to distract it from fighting off the vines. His sword added bits of flame to the onslaught. Naberius snapped at Ardan while the other two tore at the vines. The vines stretched, and a couple broke. Then an immense surge of wind hit Ardan from behind and he went flying, barely missing the Tree as he flew forward. He used the same technique as before to break and roll.

Bree was standing there, her hands outstretched, her expression furious, with half of her silver hair burnt down to her scalp and burns marring the left side of her face. The wind held the Demon against the Tree. The green flames continued to rush over his skin, while the darkness continually tried to smother it. But the green fire was getting the upper hand.

But then the wind died, and Bree stumbled and fell, succumbing to her injuries and to exhaustion.

Naberius' three heads howled. The Demon was twisting and turning, tearing all the vines that were holding it to the Tree while the darkness on its body tried to fight the flames. *It was losing*, Ardan thought. They just had to hold it there. He ran forward, wanting to add the green flame from his sword to the fray. Before Ardan could close the distance, the Demon had broken enough vines to tear itself free. He leapt out of range of the vines and rolled, quenching the fire. After the last flame went out, he rose to his paws. Naberius looked at them and Ardan wondered if anything could stop it.

The hound took a step forward, gingerly. His movements were slow and tired. He glanced wearily at the remaining mercenaries and Black Guards who were still trying to fight their way through to him and hobbled on three legs towards them.

'We need to stop it now,' Ardan yelled. 'With me!'

Ardan looked around. Frederick was on the ground, unmoving. Those not engaged with Lachlan's forces were staying by the entrance, making no move to join them. Walter tried to stand but stumbled, retching, onto the ground. Bree was on her hands and knees. Riordan had somehow got to Bree's side despite the bone sticking out of his leg. Liá looked at him helplessly. Neither she nor Orla could help.

'Just us,' Koira said.

'We get all the glory then.'

Naberius wearily turned towards him, the middle head inhaling. Ardan funnelled more power into his connection with Mish and he felt himself land lightly on his feet as he ran, his sword in his left hand, as he charged the beast.

It breathed its black fire at him, but the blaze didn't carry the ferocity it had before. The green flame of Ardan's sword met Naberius' black fire, and this time they negated each other in mid-air. He used his agility through the connection and leapt at the dog.

Naberius spun, the three heads snapping, but the Demon had lost much of his speed. Ardan darted in and out, his sword slicing. Each cut sent a flicker of flame along its black skin. Each time the green flame lasted a little longer. Yet the dog was just keeping him at bay while it hobbled towards the mercenaries. Koira hung back, waiting for an opening as she didn't have his increased speed.

They danced around each other for dozens of steps, but they were nearly in range of their forces. If the hound breathed fire on their lines, Lachlan's forces could save the Demon.

Ardan ran and leapt like he had at the ball of black liquid. He flew over the demon dog, barely avoiding a snapping jaw. On the other side, he misjudged the landing and stumbled. The three heads loomed and Ardan wondered if this was the end. But the Demon yelped, green flame appearing on its hindquarters. Koira had touched it from behind, but the backlash sent her flying backwards. It gave Ardan enough time to recover.

Ardan used the last of his rage, hate and anger at what Naberius represented and funnelled it into his sword. In the back of his mind, he could imagine Seamus berating him for thrusting as his sword pierced the Demon's chest. The weapon flared up, the green flame pouring over it. The blackness surged, but this time it couldn't stop the flame. It began to encompass its entire body. Naberius gave an exhausted wuff as he slumped to his haunches, flames engulfing him.

The demon dog barely had the strength left to keep his heads off the ground. He started speaking in that gravelly voice, each of the heads talking in turn.

'I was your best hope for killing Astaroth,' the left head said before it collapsed.

'Zadkiel will be no match for her,' the right said, amidst flames engulfing its skull.

'When Astaroth breaks her chains, she will do far worse than I ever could,' the lead head said.

A smile appeared on all three of its heads as green flame poured out of its eyes. 'At last, I return to my master,' they said in unison.

The Demon burned like dry leaves. His body flared up in the green fire before disintegrating like ash in the wind. In its wake was left a black, oily ooze.

The mercenaries, unaware of the Demon's fall, continued to fight.

'Naberius is dead!' Ardan shouted, his sword still held a green flame as he held it aloft. 'There is no need to fight.'

The mercenaries slowed, Lachlan looking around for guidance.

Orla stepped forward. 'I am the highest ranking member of the Black Clergy left alive. I command you to stop fighting.'

There was little resistance to the order, as both sides had suffered heavy casualties.

Ardan surveyed the battlefield. Over a thousand dead and dying littered the battlefield.

It was over.

CHAPTER SIXTY-SIX: AFTERMATH

* * *

he Children of the Ancients appeared from the forest, their numbers spanning our fields. I walked out with Lady Koira to meet their advance party. They had come ready for war, not realising they had already won. We had earned a grudging respect amongst their leaders, though I never got to meet their Queen. Lady Koira insisted it was for the best.

— Marion, *The Rise of Barleron.*

* * *

ARDAN STOOD beneath the stone vaults of the Cathedral hall. The place was filled to bursting with both young and old, dressed in their best clothes. They had come to honour and mourn the fallen. Despite the crowd, the press of bodies, and the encroaching smell of body odour, Ardan felt alone. He tried to focus on the procession.

Behind the podium, on the white stone altar, stood Father Walter. He wore a white robe with a golden shawl. His voice carried through the halls, echoing off the stone vaults. He spoke about the Light standing alone against the Darkness, and having only won through sacrifice and devout faith.

That and an incredible amount of luck, Ardan thought. He tried to school his thoughts, ignoring Walter's words as he focused on why he was here. He too had come to honour the fallen. Three of the deceased lay on tables at the front of the Cathedral, their bodies surrounded by candles.

The first table was occupied by Liam. His wounds had been cleaned and his plain funeral robe enhanced the rapidly growing legend of a layman who had tackled Naberius into the Tree of the Ancients. The second bore Frederick, wearing robes similar to Liam's but with the purple sash of the Bishop. He had died from exhaustion, gifting all his power to enable Liam to perform his inhuman feat. The final table bore Templar Phillip. He was hidden mostly by a white cloth, but his head was uncovered, and he looked peaceful. The broken spear that had pierced Naberius had been placed at his side.

The sunlight shone through the stained-glass windows, illuminating the three bodies in a full spectrum of colours.

Ardan gave a silent prayer to the Light for their souls. It felt right. Once he had finished, he felt suffocated, worse than before. It was the people, Walter's insufferable voice, and the closed-in walls. He needed to get out. He couldn't wait for the end of the mass; he just started pushing through the crowd to the exit.

As the people parted around him, several times he heard 'demonslayer' whispered.

Even out in the free air, he felt uneasy. The Wild pulsed and stirred within him. It was reacting to being this close to a stronghold of the Light. He had endured it for the three men and their selflessness.

Ardan's feet moved of their own accord. He soon found himself on the familiar path towards the Tree of the Ancients. Everything felt more subdued; the people were quieter and even the street animals looked forlorn. The battle had touched every corner of the city, with everyone losing someone they knew.

Ahead of him, the Tree's branches sprawled over the Ancient Quarter, but for the first time Ardan could remember, some leaves had turned brown and others even black. He wandered through the western entrance and surveyed the field. Some of the grass had been scorched and other sections stained with blood. Here Ardan felt a deeper sense of loss and wondered if this place would ever be the sanctuary it had been. The people here looked as Ardan felt, plagued with a bone-deep weariness.

If this was what battles between Light and Darkness normally involved, he didn't want any part in it. So many had fallen. It felt odd that this part of the city looked so untouched outside the park. He found himself on his way towards Eoin's healing house. He needed to see some familiar faces. The road seemed long, but eventually his feet dragged him to his door.

He entered without knocking. All six beds were full.

Bree, the burned half of her face wrapped in bandages, lay in one bed. Riordan sat on a stool next to her, his leg in splints.

Murieen had a corner bed, with seashells and a toy ship set up in the corner. She held a mug of steaming caudle in one hand and her shoulder had been heavily bandaged.

Talon lay unconscious in another. Koira hovered over him like a mother hen. The man's many puncture wounds had been painstakingly stitched. His right arm had been further amputated.

Eamon and Seamus occupied the other beds. Their wounds were less serious, and they would likely recover in a few days.

'He never would have gotten me if not for that wind witch,' Seamus said, pointing at the opposite corner.

'Bree,' Riordan corrected.

'Bree, whatever,'

'No,' Murieen said sternly. 'Not whatever. You will address her with respect. She was my apprentice, a master of the wind and she helped take down a High Demon.'

'Are you still harping on about that?' Ardan asked. Seamus grumbled and Ardan felt a lot of satisfaction at seeing the weapon master humbled for a change.

'Admit it, you couldn't get past my shield,' Eamon said. 'Ardan, you were there, you saw it. I knocked the legendary Seamus on his ass, and it was glorious.'

Ardan felt the corners of his lips turn up into a reluctant smile.

'I told you he had help from...' Seamus said, his words cutting off as he looked at Murieen and Riordan, 'Mistress Bree.'

Murieen nodded, taking a sip of her caudle.

'You had your leg enchanted,' Ardan said.

'Yeah, fat lot of good that did. Had it for one day, then the High Priest gets himself killed and I'm back to being a cripple. Useless gutter shite.'

'You or the Priest?' Eamon said.

'Him obviously. And you still can't use a sword worth a damn.'

Eamon grinned.

Ardan went over to Talon's bedside. Koira had a small gash on one cheek. Her eyes were red, and she looked on the verge of tears. She gave him a weak smile as he sat on a stool next to her.

'How is he?' Ardan asked.

'It's hard to know,' Koira said softly, 'Eoin said if he hasn't died yet he probably won't.'

Ardan inwardly groaned at Eoin's bedside manner. 'And the dreams?' Ardan said, meaning the warrior's fever dreams. It was only Koira's touch that softened them.

She grimaced.

They sat there in silence, watching the steady rise and fall of Talon's chest. Koira's hand eventually reached out and found his. He squeezed it. They sat there for some time, while Koira watched over Talon.

Bree stirred in her bed, shifting over. Riordan looked at her anxiously until he was sure she looked relaxed.

'She seems better,' Ardan said.

Riordan looked down at her. She looked peaceful, despite the burns on her face.

'Eoin's still not sure she'll pull through. He's given her something that makes her sleep, but when it wears off, I can see it. The pain.'

'She'll pull through,' Ardan said, remembering the way her eyes had blazed as she'd used the wind to smash Naberius against the Tree. 'She's got a strong will.'

'She'd better.'

'She will. She's got a wedding to attend,' Murieen said.

Riordan looked puzzled.

'You and her, you oaf.'

Riordan's eyes went wide, not knowing where to look, and he even blushed.

'Be good to settle her down. I've seen how you look at her,' Murieen continued.

None of them had anything to say to that.

'Ardan, how's your family doing?' Eamon asked, breaking the silence.

Everyone turned to look at Eamon.

'What? I'm bored, and it's good gossip. His family's caught on opposite sides,' Eamon said.

Ardan sighed. 'Prisoners in one sense or another. My siblings are holed up in the Temple. The people aren't too fond of the Dark or the Red Wolves at the moment.'

'Least they're safe. Not enough warriors left to take the place,' Seamus said.

Ardan silently agreed.

'What about your mother? Isn't she related to the Countess?' Eamon pressed.

'Marion's still trying to organise her release.'

'The Countess didn't like her forging her signature again?' Riordan asked with a half-hearted smile.

'Not when it led to a quarter of the Merchant Guard getting killed or injured,' Ardan said, leaning back against the chair.

'Rich bastards. Everyone else suffered much worse, but because of their wealth, it makes the loss harder,' Seamus said.

Ardan shrugged.

'I'm just glad we won,' Eamon said.

Ardan thought about their losses and wondered if they truly had.

'Though Seamus didn't,' Eamon finished with a grin.

Seamus picked up a nearby wooden water cup and flung it at him. It hit him hard enough to make him wince, but his smile returned wider than before.

Eoin appeared in the doorway. His eyes appeared to be clear. He saw Eamon holding his own cup, ready to throw at Seamus. Eamon looked mildly guilty before throwing it anyway.

The healer gave a long-suffering sigh before going to see to each patient individually.

Ardan remained there for hours, making small talk and offering minor comforts before he eventually said his farewells and promised he'd be back the next day. He left the healing house and took the road that led to Marion's mansion. The sun was setting across the ocean, illuminating the sky in a brilliant orange.

He'd barely made it through the large stone entrance of Marion's place before he was accosted by Aoife.

'There you are,' the woman screeched. It was the first time he had seen her look genuinely angry. She held Mish at arm's length. 'I won't take this little hell-spawn again. When you took off to that battle, she tore up a dozen of my dresses and today she pissed all over my fabrics.'

Ardan looked at Mish, who looked completely innocent. He took the lynx in his arms.

'I don't think I ever properly thanked you, Aoife, but you literally saved her life, and most likely mine. I promise to pay you back,' Ardan said.

'Damn right you will,' Aoife said, but looked mollified.

Ardan took Mish upstairs to his small room. When they were inside, she jumped up onto his cot and made herself comfortable. Ardan opened the window that looked out over the city and watched the sun slowly dip across the harbour.

He didn't know when he fell asleep, but he woke up to a quiet knocking on his door. Mish was already there, her tail swishing. He'd barely opened it a crack before Mish was through it and into the house. Koira stood there. She wore her usual sleeveless tunic, showing off her tattoos on her tanned arms. Her eyes were red, she was crying and immediately pulled him into an embrace.

'What happened? Is Talon okay?' Ardan asked, fearing the worst.

'He woke up and was semi-coherent for the first time,' she breathed as she hugged him tighter. 'Eoin gave him some tonic and broth. Said he should sleep soundly. Provided there are no complications, he'll be fine.'

'That's fantastic news,' Ardan said, and meant it.

She suddenly pulled him closer and kissed him. It was hot and desperate. He was stunned, but after a moment, he surrendered to it. They stood there in the door, their lips locked, and Ardan didn't know how long it was until they eventually broke apart.

'Are you sure you want to do this now?' Ardan asked as she closed the door behind them.

'Ardan,' she drawled, 'shut up.'

He smiled as she pushed him back onto the cot.

Afterwards, they lay next to each other, enjoying the warm afterglow of their lovemaking. Koira's hands traced idly over his chest. Ardan felt drunk with the closeness of her. His arms were wrapped around her slender shoulders. They didn't speak; they didn't need to. Her company was enough. They drifted off to sleep, lost in each other.

* * *

A SHARP RAP on wood startled Ardan awake. He saw a slip of paper slide underneath his door. Careful not to wake Koira, Ardan got to his feet and picked up the sheet of paper. It read:

* * *

'WE FULFILLED *our side of the bargain*
 — Liádan.'

* * *

ARDAN CRUNCHED THE NOTE. *Oh Light and Darkness,* he thought as realisation crashed down on him. He'd been desperate when he'd made that bargain. It had been rash and foolhardy; he hadn't really expected to survive. But he had. Now he had to fulfil the bargain—he would have to kill Astaroth. It had been hard enough to kill Naberius in his weakened state. Now he had to figure out a way to kill a Demon far more powerful. If he didn't...

'I'll be damned,' Ardan said.

AFTERWORD

Want to join me behind the scenes and receive bonus content, early access or discount on my books?

Then join my newsletter or to pick up the sequel, join me at:

StewAdamsAuthor.com

ACKNOWLEDGMENTS

Holy shit. It's finished. Like it's finally done. The first book is published. And you the reader are continuing to read on. Like any novel, it is no where near a one person show. So I want to pass on particular thanks to a large number of people.

First to my folks, who were supportive in the way only parents can be when I said I wanted to be a writer. Even all the way back when I first read Harry Potter when I was twelve or thirteen.

To Dad, who along with my sister helped introduce me the magical world of fiction and giving me my introduction to fantasy with Pawn of Prophecy.

To Mum, who never wavered in her support and over the years said something along the lines, 'I would like to read this book before I die you know.' It helped more than you know.

To my writing group, Christine, Matt, David and all the others. I appreciate your patience in listening to my work, despite hearing random excerpts and giving great advice despite having little contextual knowledge.

To the beta readers, the bread and butter of any decent novel. Those who helped both before and after I changed the book to adhere to my former agents' recommendations.

My sister, Natalie for your boundless enthusiasm and managing to give constructive criticism while still boosting my fragile ego. Plus I can't forget the countless hours you put into each line with amazing advice.

To Ben, for your no nonsense review of the book. The example that pops to mind is, 'I'm sick of Ardan being poor.' These sort of straight shooting advice is, at times, definitely what I needed.

To Tom, for your advice on how to properly pace the book, what worked and what didn't. It helped in far more ways than you know.

To Rachel, for your meticulous line by line advice and (I'm paraphrasing here but) 'You can tell which scenes you like to write, you need to spend just as much time on the scenes you don't like to write.' It helped me recognise weakness in my work.

To Matt, for your in-depth review and how to help me recover the novel from the culling it endured before I decided against a traditional published deal. In the end, your advice helped make this a much stronger novel with better characters and character arcs.

To my editor Tarryn Thomas who has great line edits to make every word flow better, smoother and stronger. Your vocabulary is incredible. Your ability to edit some of my more atrocious lines and still make it sound like my voice is a gift.

To the proof reader Fibenne, amazing work is catching what I thought was a mostly grammatically flawless novel.

To the cover artist Dragan Paunovic your work is better than I could have imagined.

To my dog, Zara, who would listen patiently while I read out the novel to try and discover mistakes and bad flows, often tilting her head in confusion.

Finally to my beautiful wife Mary. I couldn't have done this without you. Your endless patience with reading the novel, prose, story and character advice were invaluable in helping me get the story to the point where I was confident to show it to other people. This one's for you!

The absolute last thanks I want to say is to you, the reader, for getting this far, reading the novel and even going so far as to read the author's note. You're a legend!

www.ingramcontent.com/pod-product-compliance
Lightning Source LLC
Chambersburg PA
CBHW031730180726
48283CB00005B/1441